THE LUCK OF ROARING CAMP AND OTHER SKETCHES

BRET HARTE

CONTENTS

ALSO AVAILABLE

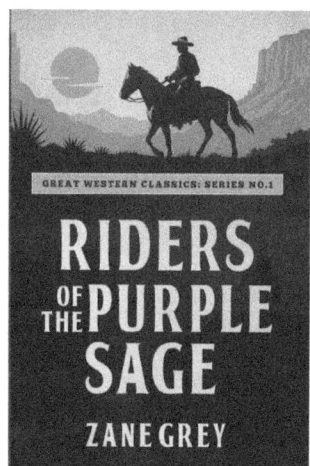

GREAT WESTERN CLASSICS: SERIES NO.1

RIDERS OF THE PURPLE SAGE

ZANE GREY

GREAT WESTERN CLASSICS: SERIES NO.2

THE LONE STAR RANGER

ZANE GREY

GREAT WESTERN CLASSICS: SERIES NO.3

THE LOG OF A COWBOY

ANDY ADAMS

GREAT WESTERN CLASSICS: SERIES NO.5

THE RAINBOW TRAIL

ZANE GREY

PUBLISHERS' NOTE

In 1882, it was felt to be desirable that Mr. Harte's scattered work should be brought together in convenient form, and the result was a compact edition of five volumes. After that date, as before, he continued to produce poems, tales, sketches, and romances in steady succession, and in 1897 his publishers undertook a uniform and orderly presentation of the results of more than thirty years of his literary activity. The fourteen volumes that embodied those results were enriched by Introductions and a Glossary prepared by Mr. Harte himself.

The present Riverside Edition is based on the collection made in 1897, but is enlarged by the inclusion of later work.

Boston, 4 Park Street, Autumn, 1902.

GENERAL INTRODUCTION

The opportunity here offered [Footnote: By the appearance in England several years ago of an edition of the author's writings as then collected.] to give some account of the genesis of these Californian sketches, and the conditions under which they were conceived, is peculiarly tempting to an author who has been obliged to retain a decent professional reticence under a cloud of ingenious surmise, theory, and misinterpretation. He very gladly seizes this opportunity to establish the chronology of the sketches, and incidentally to show that what are considered the "happy accidents" of literature are very apt to be the results of quite logical and often prosaic processes.

The author's *first* volume was published in 1865 in a thin book of verse, containing, besides the titular poem, "The Lost Galleon," various patriotic contributions to the lyrics of the Civil War, then raging, and certain better known humorous pieces, which have been hitherto interspersed with his later poems in separate volumes, but are now restored to their former companionship. This was followed in 1867 by "The Condensed Novels," originally contributed to the "San Francisco Californian," a journal then edited by the author, and a number of local sketches entitled "Bohemian Papers," making a single not very plethoric volume, the author›s first book of prose. But he deems it worthy of consideration that during this period, i.e. from 1862 to 1866, he produced "The Society upon the Stanislaus" and "The Story of M›liss,"—the first a dialectical poem, the second a Californian romance,—his first efforts toward indicating a peculiarly characteristic Western American literature. He would like to offer these facts as evidence of his very early, half-boyish but very enthusiastic belief in such a possibility,—a belief which never deserted him, and which, a few years later, from the better-known pages of "The Overland Monthly," he was able to demonstrate to a larger and more cosmopolitan audience in the story of "The Luck of Roaring Camp" and the poem of the "Heathen Chinee." But it was one of the anomalies of the very condition of life that he worked amidst, and endeavored to portray, that these first efforts were rewarded by very little success; and, as he will presently show, even "The Luck of Roaring Camp" depended for its recognition in California upon its success elsewhere. Hence the critical reader will observe that the bulk of these earlier efforts, as shown in the first two volumes, were marked by very little flavor of the soil, but were addressed to an audience half foreign in their sympathies, and still imbued with Eastern or New England habits and literary traditions. "Home" was still potent with these voluntary exiles in their moments of relaxation. Eastern magazines and current Eastern literature formed their literary recreation, and the sale of the better class of periodicals was singularly great. Nor was the taste confined to American literature. The illustrated and satirical English journals were as frequently seen in California as in Massachusetts; and the author records that he has experienced more difficulty in procuring a copy of "Punch" in an English provincial town than was his fortune at "Red Dog" or "One-Horse Gulch." An audience thus liberally equipped and familiar with the best modern writers was naturally critical and exacting, and no one appreciates more than he does the salutary effects of this severe discipline upon his earlier efforts.

When the first number of "The Overland Monthly" appeared, the author, then its editor, called the publisher's attention to the lack of any distinctive Californian romance in its pages, and averred that, should no other contribution come in, he himself would supply the omission in the next number. No other contribution was offered, and the author, having the plot and general idea already in his mind, in a few days sent the manuscript of "The Luck of Roaring Camp" to the printer. He had not yet received the proof-sheets when he was suddenly summoned to the office of the publisher, whom he found standing the picture of dismay and anxiety with the proof before him. The indignation and stupefaction of the author can be well understood when he was told that the printer, instead of returning the proofs to him, submitted them to the publisher, with the emphatic declaration that the matter thereof was so indecent, irreligious, and improper that his proof-reader—a young lady—had with difficulty been induced to continue its perusal, and that he, as a friend of the publisher and a well-wisher of the magazine, was impelled to present to him personally this shameless evidence of the manner in which the editor was imperilling the future of that enterprise. It should be premised that the critic was a man of character and standing, the head of a large printing establishment, a church member, and, the author thinks, a deacon. In which circumstances the publisher frankly admitted to the author that, while he could not agree with all of the printer's criticisms, he thought the story open to grave objection, and its publication of doubtful expediency.

Believing only that he was the victim of some extraordinary typographical blunder, the author at once sat down and read the proof. In its new dress, with the metamorphosis of type,—that metamorphosis which every writer so well knows changes his relations to it and makes it no longer seem a part of himself,—he was able to read it with something of the freshness of an untold tale. As he read on he found himself affected, even as he had been affected in the conception and writing of it—a feeling so incompatible with the charges against it, that he could only lay it down and declare emphatically, albeit hopelessly, that he could really see nothing objectionable in it. Other opinions were sought and given. To the author's surprise, he found himself in the minority. Finally, the story was submitted to three gentlemen of culture and experience, friends of publisher and author,—who were unable, however, to come to any clear decision. It was, however, suggested to the author that, assuming the natural hypothesis that his editorial reasoning might be warped by his literary predilections in a consideration of one of his own productions, a personal sacrifice would at this juncture be in the last degree heroic. This last suggestion had the effect of ending all further discussion, for he at once informed the publisher that the question of the propriety of the story was no longer at issue: the only question was of his capacity to exercise the proper editorial judgment; and that unless he was permitted to test that capacity by the publication of the story, and abide squarely by the result, he must resign his editorial position. The publisher, possibly struck with the author's confidence, possibly from kindliness of disposition to a younger man, yielded, and "The Luck of Roaring Camp" was published in the current number of the magazine for which it was written, as it was written, without emendation, omission, alteration, or apology. A not inconsiderable part of the grotesqueness of the situation was the feeling, which the author retained throughout the whole affair, of the perfect sincerity, good faith, and seriousness of his friend's—the printer's—objection, and for many days thereafter he was haunted by a consideration of the sufferings of this conscientious man, obliged to assist materially in disseminating the dangerous and subversive doctrines contained in this baleful fiction. What solemn protests must have been laid with the ink on the rollers and impressed upon those wicked sheets! what pious warnings must have been secretly folded and stitched in that number of "The Overland Monthly"! Across the chasm of years and distance the author stretches forth the hand of sympathy and forgiveness, not forgetting the gentle proof-reader, that chaste and unknown nymph, whose mantling cheeks and downcast eyes gave the first indications of warning.

But the troubles of the "Luck" were far from ended. It had secured an entrance into the world, but, like its own hero, it was born with an evil reputation, and to a community that had yet to learn to love it. The secular press, with one or two exceptions, received it coolly, and referred to its "singularity;" the religious press frantically excommunicated it, and anathematized it as the offspring of evil; the high promise of "The Overland Monthly" was said to have been ruined by its birth; Christians were cautioned against pollution by its contact; practical business men were gravely urged to condemn and frown upon this picture of Californian society that was not conducive to Eastern immigration; its hapless author was held up to obloquy as a man who had abused a sacred trust. If its life and reputation had depended on its reception in

California, this edition and explanation would alike have been needless. But, fortunately, the young "Overland Monthly" had in its first number secured a hearing and position throughout the American Union, and the author waited the larger verdict. The publisher, albeit his worst fears were confirmed, was not a man to weakly regret a position he had once taken, and waited also. The return mail from the East brought a letter addressed to the "Editor of the 'Overland Monthly,'" enclosing a letter from Fields, Osgood & Co., the publishers of "The Atlantic Monthly," addressed to the—to them—unknown "Author of 'The Luck of Roaring Camp.'" This the author opened, and found to be a request, upon the most flattering terms, for a story for the "Atlantic" similar to the "Luck." The same mail brought newspapers and reviews welcoming the little foundling of Californian literature with an enthusiasm that half frightened its author; but with the placing of that letter in the hands of the publisher, who chanced to be standing by his side, and who during those dark days had, without the author's faith, sustained the author's position, he felt that his compensation was full and complete.

Thus encouraged, "The Luck of Roaring Camp" was followed by "The Outcasts of Poker Flat," "Miggles," "Tennessee's Partner," and those various other characters who had impressed the author when, a mere truant schoolboy, he had lived among them. It is hardly necessary to say to any observer of human nature that at this time he was advised by kind and well-meaning friends to content himself with the success of the "Luck," and not tempt criticism again; or that from that moment ever after he was in receipt of that equally sincere contemporaneous criticism which assured him gravely that each successive story was a falling off from the last. Howbeit, by reinvigorated confidence in himself and some conscientious industry, he managed to get together in a year six or eight of these sketches, which, in a volume called "The Luck of Roaring Camp and Other Sketches," gave him that encouragement in America and England that has since seemed to justify him in swelling these records of a picturesque passing civilization into the compass of the present edition.

A few words regarding the peculiar conditions of life and society that are here rudely sketched, and often but barely outlined. The author is aware that, partly from a habit of thought and expression, partly from the exigencies of brevity in his narratives, and partly from the habit of addressing an audience familar with the local scenery, he often assumes, as premises already granted by the reader, the existence of a peculiar and romantic state of civilization, the like of which few English readers are inclined to accept without corroborative facts and figures. These he could only give by referring to the ephemeral records of Californian journals of that date, and the testimony of far-scattered witnesses, survivors of the exodus of 1849. He must beg the reader to bear in mind that this emigration was either across a continent almost unexplored, or by the way of a long and dangerous voyage around Cape Horn, and that the promised land itself presented the singular spectacle of a patriarchal Latin race who had been left to themselves, forgotten by the world, for nearly three hundred years. The faith, courage, vigor, youth, and capacity for adventure necessary to this emigration produced a body of men as strongly distinctive as the companions of Jason. Unlike most pioneers, the majority were men of profession and education; all were young, and all had staked their future in the enterprise. Critics who have taken large and exhaustive views of mankind and society from club windows in Pall Mall or the Fifth Avenue can only accept for granted the turbulent chivalry that thronged the streets of San Francisco in the gala days of her youth, and must read the blazon of their deeds like the doubtful quarterings of the shield of Amadis de Gaul. The author has been frequently asked if such and such incidents were real,—if he had ever met such and such characters. To this he must return the one answer, that in only a single instance was he conscious of drawing purely from his imagination and fancy for a character and a logical succession of incidents drawn therefrom. A few weeks after his story was published, he received a letter, authentically signed, *correcting some of the minor details of his facts* (!), and enclosing as corroborative evidence a slip from an old newspaper, wherein the main incident of his supposed fanciful creation was recorded with a largeness of statement that far transcended his powers of imagination.

He has been repeatedly cautioned, kindly and unkindly, intelligently and unintelligently, against his alleged tendency to confuse recognized standards of morality by extenuating lives of recklessness, and often criminality, with a single solitary virtue. He might easily show that he has never written a sermon, that he has never moralized or commented upon the actions of his heroes, that he has never voiced a creed or obtrusively demonstrated an ethical opinion. He might easily allege that this merciful effect of his art arose from the reader's weak human sympathies, and hold himself irresponsible. But he would be conscious of a more miserable weakness in thus divorcing himself from his fellow-men who in the domain of art must ever walk hand in hand with him. So he prefers to say that, of all the various forms in which Cant presents itself to suffering humanity, he knows of none so outrageous, so illogical, so undemonstrable, so marvelously absurd, as the Cant of "Too Much Mercy." When it shall be proven to him that communities are degraded and brought to guilt and crime, suffering or destitution, from a predominance of this quality; when he shall see pardoned ticket-of-leave men elbowing men of austere lives out of situation and position, and the repentant Magdalen supplanting the blameless virgin in society,—then he will lay aside his pen and extend his hand to the new Draconian discipline in fiction. But until then he will, without claiming to be a religious man or a moralist, but simply as an artist, reverently and humbly conform to the rules laid down by a Great Poet who created the parable of the "Prodigal Son" and the "Good Samaritan," whose works have lasted eighteen hundred years, and will remain when the present writer and his generation are forgotten. And he is conscious of uttering no original doctrine in this, but of only voicing the beliefs of a few of his literary brethren happily living, and one gloriously dead, who never made proclamation of this "from the housetops."

THE LUCH OF ROARING CAMP

There was commotion in Roaring Camp. It could not have been a fight, for in 1850 that was not novel enough to have called together the entire settlement. The ditches and claims were not only deserted, but "Tuttle's grocery" had contributed its gamblers, who, it will be remembered, calmly continued their game the day that French Pete and Kanaka Joe shot each other to death over the bar in the front room. The whole camp was collected before a rude cabin on the outer edge of the clearing. Conversation was carried on in a low tone, but the name of a woman was frequently repeated. It was a name familiar enough in the camp,—"Cherokee Sal."

Perhaps the less said of her the better. She was a coarse and, it is to be feared, a very sinful woman. But at that time she was the only woman in Roaring Camp, and was just then lying in sore extremity, when she most needed the ministration of her own sex. Dissolute, abandoned, and irreclaimable, she was yet suffering a martyrdom hard enough to bear even when veiled by sympathizing womanhood, but now terrible in her loneliness. The primal curse had come to her in that original isolation which must have made the punishment of the first transgression so dreadful. It was, perhaps, part of the expiation of her sin that, at a moment when she most lacked her sex's intuitive tenderness and care, she met only the half-contemptuous faces of her masculine associates. Yet a few of the spectators were, I think, touched by her sufferings. Sandy Tipton thought it was "rough on Sal," and, in the contemplation of her condition, for a moment rose superior to the fact that he had an ace and two bowers in his sleeve.

It will be seen also that the situation was novel. Deaths were by no means uncommon in Roaring Camp, but a birth was a new thing. People had been dismissed the camp effectively, finally, and with no possibility of return; but this was the first time that anybody had been introduced *ab initio*. Hence the excitement.

"You go in there, Stumpy," said a prominent citizen known as "Kentuck," addressing one of the loungers. "Go in there, and see what you kin do. You've had experience in them things."

Perhaps there was a fitness in the selection. Stumpy, in other climes, had been the putative head of two families; in fact, it was owing to some legal informality in these proceedings that Roaring Camp—a city of refuge—was indebted to his company. The crowd approved the choice, and Stumpy was wise enough to bow to the majority. The door closed on the extempore surgeon and midwife, and Roaring Camp sat down outside, smoked its pipe, and awaited the issue.

The assemblage numbered about a hundred men. One or two of these were actual fugitives from justice, some were criminal, and all were reckless. Physically they exhibited no indication of their past lives and character. The greatest scamp had a Raphael face, with a profusion of blonde hair; Oakhurst, a gambler, had the melancholy air and intellectual abstraction of a Hamlet; the coolest and most courageous man was scarcely over five feet in height, with a soft voice and an embarrassed, timid manner. The term "roughs" applied to them was a distinction rather than a definition. Perhaps in the minor details of fingers, toes, ears, etc., the camp may have been deficient, but these slight omissions did not detract from their aggregate force. The strongest man had but three fingers on his right hand; the best shot had but one eye.

Such was the physical aspect of the men that were dispersed around the cabin. The camp lay in a triangular valley between two hills and a river. The only outlet was a steep trail over the summit of a hill that faced the cabin, now illuminated by the rising moon. The suffering woman might have seen it from the rude bunk whereon she lay,—seen it winding like a silver thread until it was lost in the stars above.

A fire of withered pine boughs added sociability to the gathering. By degrees the natural levity of Roaring Camp returned. Bets were freely offered and taken regarding the result. Three to five that "Sal would get through with it;" even that the child would survive; side bets as to the sex and complexion of the coming stranger. In the midst of an excited discussion an exclamation came from those nearest the door, and the camp stopped to listen. Above the swaying and moaning of the pines, the swift rush of the river, and the crackling of the fire rose a sharp, querulous cry,—a cry unlike anything heard before in the camp. The pines stopped moaning, the river ceased to rush, and the fire to crackle. It seemed as if Nature had stopped to listen too.

The camp rose to its feet as one man! It was proposed to explode a barrel of gunpowder; but in consideration of the situation of the mother, better counsels prevailed, and only a few revolvers were discharged; for whether owing to the rude surgery of the camp, or some other reason, Cherokee Sal was sinking fast. Within an hour she had climbed, as it were, that rugged road that led to the stars, and so passed out of Roaring Camp, its sin and shame, forever. I do not think that the announcement disturbed them much, except in speculation as to the fate of the child. "Can he live now?" was asked of Stumpy. The answer was doubtful. The only other being of Cherokee Sal's sex and maternal condition in the settlement was an ass. There was some conjecture as to fitness, but the experiment was tried. It was less problematical than the ancient treatment of Romulus and Remus, and apparently as successful.

When these details were completed, which exhausted another hour, the door was opened, and the anxious crowd of men, who had already formed themselves into a queue, entered in single file. Beside the low bunk or shelf, on which the figure of the mother was starkly outlined below the blankets, stood a pine table. On this a candle-box was placed, and within it, swathed in staring red flannel, lay the last arrival at Roaring Camp. Beside the candle-box was placed a hat. Its use was soon indicated. "Gentlemen," said Stumpy, with a singular mixture of authority and *ex officio* complacency,—"gentlemen will please pass in at the front door, round the table, and out at the back door. Them as wishes to contribute anything toward the orphan will find a hat handy." The first man entered with his hat on; he uncovered, however, as he looked about him, and so unconsciously set an example to the next. In such communities good and bad actions are catching. As the procession filed in comments were audible,—criticisms addressed perhaps rather to Stumpy in the character of showman: "Is that him?" "Mighty small specimen;" "Hasn't more'n got the color;" "Ain't bigger nor a derringer." The contributions were as characteristic: A silver tobacco box; a doubloon; a navy revolver, silver mounted; a gold specimen; a very beautifully embroidered lady's handkerchief (from Oakhurst the gambler); a diamond breastpin; a diamond ring (suggested by the pin, with the remark from the giver that he "saw that pin and went two diamonds better"); a slung-shot; a Bible (contributor not detected); a golden spur; a silver teaspoon (the initials, I regret to say, were not the giver's); a pair of surgeon's shears; a lancet; a Bank of England note for L5; and about $200 in loose gold and silver coin. During these proceedings Stumpy maintained a silence as impassive as the dead on his left, a gravity as inscrutable as that of the newly born on his right. Only one incident occurred to break the monotony of the curious procession. As Kentuck bent over the candle-box half curiously, the child turned, and, in a spasm of pain, caught at his groping finger, and held it fast for a moment. Kentuck looked foolish and embarrassed. Something like a blush tried to assert itself in his weather-beaten cheek. "The d—d little cuss!" he said, as he extricated his finger, with perhaps more tenderness and care than he might have been deemed capable of showing. He held that finger a little apart from its fellows as he went out, and examined it curiously. The examination provoked the same original remark in regard to the child. In fact, he seemed to enjoy repeating it. "He rastled with my finger," he remarked to Tipton, holding up the member, "the d—d little cuss!"

It was four o'clock before the camp sought repose. A light burnt in the cabin where the watchers sat, for Stumpy did not go to bed that night. Nor did Kentuck. He drank quite freely, and related with great gusto his experience, invariably ending with his characteristic condemnation of the newcomer. It seemed to relieve him of any unjust implication of sentiment, and Kentuck had the weaknesses of the nobler sex. When everybody else had gone to bed, he walked down to the river and whistled reflectingly. Then he walked up the gulch past the cabin, still whistling with demonstrative unconcern. At a large redwood-tree he paused and retraced his steps, and again passed the cabin. Halfway down to the river's bank he again paused, and then returned and knocked at the door. It was opened by Stumpy. "How goes it?" said Kentuck, looking past Stumpy toward the candle-box. "All serene!" replied Stumpy. "Anything up?" "Nothing." There was a pause—an embarrassing one—Stumpy still holding the door. Then Kentuck had recourse to his finger, which he held up to Stumpy. "Rastled with it,— the d—d little cuss," he said, and retired.

The next day Cherokee Sal had such rude sepulture as Roaring Camp afforded. After her body had been committed to the hillside, there was a formal meeting of the camp to discuss what should be done with her infant. A resolution to adopt it was unanimous and enthusiastic. But an animated discussion in regard to the manner and feasibility of providing for its wants at once sprang up. It was remarkable that the argument partook of none of those fierce personalities with which discussions were usually conducted at Roaring Camp. Tipton proposed that they should send the child to Red Dog,—a distance of forty miles,—where female attention could be procured. But the unlucky suggestion met with fierce and unanimous opposition. It was evident that no plan which entailed parting from their new acquisition would for a moment be entertained. "Besides," said Tom Ryder, "them fellows at Red Dog would swap it, and ring in somebody else on us." A disbelief in the honesty of other camps prevailed at Roaring Camp, as in other places.

The introduction of a female nurse in the camp also met with objection. It was argued that no decent woman could be prevailed to accept Roaring Camp as her home, and the speaker urged that "they didn't want any more of the other kind." This unkind allusion to the defunct mother, harsh as it may seem, was the first spasm of propriety,—the first symptom of the camp's regeneration. Stumpy advanced nothing. Perhaps he felt a certain delicacy in interfering with the selection of a possible successor in office. But when questioned, he averred stoutly that he and "Jinny"—the mammal before alluded to—could manage to rear the child. There was something original, independent, and heroic about the plan that pleased the camp. Stumpy was retained. Certain articles were sent for to Sacramento. "Mind," said the treasurer, as he pressed a bag of gold-dust into the expressman's hand, "the best that can be got,—lace, you know, and filigree-work and frills,—d—n the cost!" Strange to say, the child thrived. Perhaps the invigorating climate of the mountain camp was compensation for material deficiencies. Nature took the foundling to her broader breast. In that rare atmosphere of the Sierra foothills,—that air pungent with balsamic odor, that ethereal cordial at once bracing and exhilarating,— he may have found food and nourishment, or a subtle chemistry that transmuted ass's milk to lime and phosphorus. Stumpy inclined to the belief that it was the latter and good nursing. "Me and that ass," he would say, "has been father and mother to him! Don't you," he would add, apostrophizing the helpless bundle before him, "never go back on us."

By the time he was a month old the necessity of giving him a name became apparent. He had generally been known as "The Kid," "Stumpy's Boy," "The Coyote" (an allusion to his vocal powers), and even by Kentuck's endearing diminutive of "The d—d little cuss." But these were felt to be vague and unsatisfactory, and were at last dismissed under another influence. Gamblers and adventurers are generally superstitious, and Oakhurst one day declared that the baby had brought "the luck" to Roaring Camp. It was certain that of late they had been successful. "Luck" was the name agreed upon, with the prefix of Tommy for greater convenience. No allusion was made to the mother, and the father was unknown. "It's better," said the philosophical Oakhurst, "to take a fresh deal all round. Call him Luck, and start him fair." A day was accordingly set apart for the christening. What was meant by this ceremony the reader may imagine who has already gathered some idea of the reckless irreverence of Roaring Camp. The master of ceremonies was one "Boston," a noted wag, and the occasion seemed to promise the greatest facetiousness. This ingenious satirist had spent two days in preparing a burlesque of the Church service, with pointed local allusions. The choir was properly trained, and Sandy Tipton was to stand godfather. But after the procession had marched to the grove with music and banners, and the child had been deposited before a mock altar, Stumpy stepped before the expectant crowd. "It ain't my style to spoil fun, boys," said the little man, stoutly eying the faces around him, "but it strikes me that this thing ain't exactly on the squar. It's playing it pretty low down on this yer baby to ring in fun on him that he ain't goin' to understand. And ef there's goin' to be any godfathers round, I'd like to see who's got any better rights than me." A silence followed Stumpy's speech. To the credit of all humorists be it said that the first man to acknowledge its justice was the satirist thus stopped of his fun. "But," said Stumpy, quickly following up his advantage, "we're here for a christening, and we'll have it. I proclaim you Thomas Luck, according to the laws of the United States and the State of California, so help me God." It was the first time that the name of the Deity had been otherwise uttered than profanely in the camp. The form of christening was perhaps even more ludicrous than the satirist had conceived; but strangely enough, nobody saw it and nobody laughed. "Tommy" was christened as seriously as he would have been under a Christian roof, and cried and was comforted in as orthodox fashion.

And so the work of regeneration began in Roaring Camp. Almost imperceptibly a change came over the settlement. The cabin assigned to "Tommy Luck"—or "The Luck," as he was more frequently called—first showed signs of improvement. It was kept scrupulously clean and whitewashed. Then it was boarded, clothed, and papered. The rosewood, cradle, packed eighty miles by mule, had, in Stumpy's way of putting it, "sorter killed the rest of the furniture." So the rehabilitation of the cabin became a necessity. The men who were in the habit of lounging in at Stumpy's to see "how 'The Luck' got on" seemed to appreciate the change, and in self-defense the rival establishment of "Tuttle's grocery" bestirred itself and imported a carpet and mirrors. The reflections of the latter on the appearance of Roaring Camp tended to produce stricter habits of personal cleanliness. Again Stumpy imposed a kind of quarantine upon those who aspired to the honor and privilege of holding The Luck. It was a cruel mortification to Kentuck—who, in the carelessness of a large nature and the habits of frontier life, had begun to regard all garments as a second cuticle, which, like a snake's, only sloughed off through decay—to be debarred this privilege from certain prudential reasons. Yet such was the subtle influence of innovation that he thereafter appeared regularly every afternoon in a clean shirt and face still shining from his ablutions. Nor were moral and social sanitary laws neglected. "Tommy," who was supposed to spend his whole existence in a persistent attempt to repose, must not be disturbed by noise. The shouting and yelling, which had gained the camp its infelicitous title, were not permitted within hearing distance of Stumpy's. The men conversed in whispers or smoked with Indian gravity. Profanity was tacitly given up in these sacred precincts, and throughout the camp a popular form of expletive, known as "D—n the luck!" and "Curse the luck!" was abandoned, as having a new personal bearing. Vocal music was not interdicted, being supposed to have a soothing, tranquilizing quality; and one song, sung by "Man-o'-War Jack," an English sailor from her Majesty's Australian colonies, was quite popular as a lullaby. It was a lugubrious recital of the exploits of "the Arethusa, Seventy-four," in a muffled minor, ending with a prolonged dying fall at the burden of each verse, "On b-oo-o-ard of the Arethusa." It was a fine sight to see Jack holding The Luck, rocking from side to side as if with the motion of a ship, and crooning forth this naval ditty. Either through the peculiar rocking of Jack or the length of his song,—it contained ninety stanzas, and was continued with conscientious deliberation to the bitter end,— the lullaby generally had the desired effect. At such times the men would lie at full length under the trees in the soft summer twilight, smoking their pipes and drinking in the melodious utterances. An indistinct idea that this was pastoral happiness pervaded the camp. "This 'ere kind o' think," said the Cockney Simmons, meditatively reclining on his elbow, "is 'evingly." It reminded him of Greenwich.

On the long summer days The Luck was usually carried to the gulch from whence the golden store of Roaring Camp was taken. There, on a blanket spread over pine boughs, he would lie while the men were working in the ditches below. Latterly there was a rude attempt to decorate this bower with flowers and sweet-smelling shrubs, and generally some one would bring him a cluster of wild honeysuckles, azaleas, or the painted blossoms of Las Mariposas. The men had suddenly awakened to the fact that there were beauty and significance in these trifles, which they had so long trodden carelessly beneath their feet. A flake of glittering mica, a fragment of variegated quartz, a bright pebble from the bed of the creek, became beautiful to eyes thus cleared and strengthened, and were invariably put aside for The Luck. It was wonderful how many treasures the woods and hillsides yielded that "would do for Tommy." Surrounded by playthings such as never child out of fairyland had before, it is to be hoped that Tommy was content. He appeared to be serenely happy, albeit there was an infantine gravity about him, a contemplative light in his round gray eyes, that sometimes worried Stumpy. He was always tractable and quiet, and it is recorded that once, having crept beyond his "corral,"—a hedge of tessellated pine boughs, which surrounded his bed,—he dropped over the bank on his head in the soft earth, and remained with his mottled legs in the air in that position for at least five minutes with unflinching gravity. He was extricated without a murmur. I hesitate to record the many other instances of his sagacity, which rest, unfortunately, upon the statements of prejudiced friends. Some of them were not without a tinge of superstition. "I crep' up the bank just now," said Kentuck one day, in a breathless state of excitement, "and dern my skin if he wasn't a-talking to a jaybird as was a-sittin' on his lap. There they was, just as free and sociable as anything you please, a-jawin' at each other just like two cherrybums." Howbeit, whether creeping over the pine boughs or lying lazily on his back blinking at the leaves above him, to him the birds sang, the squirrels chattered, and the flowers bloomed. Nature was his nurse and playfellow. For him she would let slip between the leaves golden shafts of sunlight that fell just within his grasp; she would send wandering breezes to visit him with the balm of bay and resinous gum; to him the tall redwoods nodded familiarly and sleepily, the bumblebees buzzed, and the rooks cawed a slumberous accompaniment.

Such was the golden summer of Roaring Camp. They were "flush times," and the luck was with them. The claims had yielded enormously. The camp was jealous of its privileges and looked suspiciously on strangers. No encouragement was given to immigration, and, to make their seclusion more perfect, the land on either side of the mountain wall that surrounded the camp they duly preempted. This, and a reputation for singular proficiency with the revolver, kept the reserve of Roaring Camp inviolate. The expressman—their only connecting link with the surrounding world—sometimes told wonderful stories of the camp. He would say, "They've a street up there in 'Roaring' that would lay over any street in Red Dog. They've got vines and flowers round their houses, and they wash themselves twice a day. But they're mighty rough on strangers, and they worship an Ingin baby."

With the prosperity of the camp came a desire for further improvement. It was proposed to build a hotel in the following spring, and to invite one or two decent families to reside there for the sake of The Luck, who might perhaps profit by female companionship. The sacrifice that this concession to the sex cost these men, who were fiercely skeptical in regard to its general virtue and usefulness, can only be accounted for by their affection for Tommy. A few still held out. But the resolve could not be carried into effect for three months, and the minority meekly yielded in the hope that something might turn up to prevent it. And it did.

The winter of 1851 will long be remembered in the foothills. The snow lay deep on the Sierras, and every mountain creek became a river, and every river a lake. Each gorge and gulch was transformed into a tumultuous watercourse that descended the hillsides, tearing down giant trees and scattering its drift and debris along the plain. Red Dog had been twice under water, and Roaring Camp had been forewarned.

"Water put the gold into them gulches," said Stumpy. "It's been here once and will be here again!" And that night the North Fork suddenly leaped over its banks and swept up the triangular valley of Roaring Camp.

In the confusion of rushing water, crashing trees, and crackling timber, and the darkness which seemed to flow with the water and blot out the fair valley, but little could be done to collect the scattered camp. When the morning broke, the cabin of Stumpy, nearest the river-bank, was gone. Higher up the gulch they found the body of its unlucky owner; but the pride, the hope, the joy, The Luck, of Roaring Camp had disappeared. They were returning with sad hearts when a shout from the bank recalled them.

It was a relief-boat from down the river. They had picked up, they said, a man and an infant, nearly exhausted, about two miles below. Did anybody know them, and did they belong here?

It needed but a glance to show them Kentuck lying there, cruelly crushed and bruised, but still holding The Luck of Roaring Camp in his arms. As they bent over the strangely assorted pair, they saw that the child was cold and pulseless. "He is dead," said one. Kentuck opened his eyes. "Dead?" he repeated feebly. "Yes, my man, and you are dying too." A smile lit the eyes of the expiring Kentuck. "Dying!" he repeated; "he's a-taking me with him. Tell the boys I've got The Luck with me now;" and the strong man, clinging to the frail babe as a drowning man is said to cling to a straw, drifted away into the shadowy river that flows forever to the unknown sea.

THE OUTCASTS OF POKER FLAT

As Mr. John Oakhurst, gambler, stepped into the main street of Poker Flat on the morning of the 23d of November, 1850, he was conscious of a change in its moral atmosphere since the preceding night. Two or three men, conversing earnestly together, ceased as he approached, and exchanged significant glances. There was a Sabbath lull in the air, which, in a settlement unused to Sabbath influences, looked ominous.

Mr. Oakhurst's calm, handsome face betrayed small concern in these indications. Whether he was conscious of any predisposing cause was another question. "I reckon they're after somebody," he reflected; "likely it's me." He returned to his pocket the handkerchief with which he had been whipping away the red dust of Poker Flat from his neat boots, and quietly discharged his mind of any further conjecture.

In point of fact, Poker Flat was "after somebody." It had lately suffered the loss of several thousand dollars, two valuable horses, and a prominent citizen. It was experiencing a spasm of virtuous reaction, quite as lawless and ungovernable as any of the acts that had provoked it. A secret committee had determined to rid the town of all improper persons. This was done permanently in regard of two men who were then hanging from the boughs of a sycamore in the gulch, and temporarily in the banishment of certain other objectionable characters. I regret to say that some of these were ladies. It is but due to the sex, however, to state that their impropriety was professional, and it was only in such easily established standards of evil that Poker Flat ventured to sit in judgment.

Mr. Oakhurst was right in supposing that he was included in this category. A few of the committee had urged hanging him as a possible example and a sure method of reimbursing themselves from his pockets of the sums he had won from them. "It's agin justice," said Jim Wheeler, "to let this yer young man from Roaring Camp—an entire stranger—carry away our money." But a crude sentiment of equity residing in the breasts of those who had been fortunate enough to win from Mr. Oakhurst overruled this narrower local prejudice.

Mr. Oakhurst received his sentence with philosophic calmness, none the less coolly that he was aware of the hesitation of his judges. He was too much of a gambler not to accept fate. With him life was at best an uncertain game, and he recognized the usual percentage in favor of the dealer.

A body of armed men accompanied the deported wickedness of Poker Flat to the outskirts of the settlement. Besides Mr. Oakhurst, who was known to be a coolly desperate man, and for whose intimidation the armed escort was intended, the expatriated party consisted of a young woman familiarly known as "The Duchess;" another who had won the title of "Mother Shipton;" and "Uncle Billy," a suspected, sluice-robber and confirmed drunkard. The cavalcade provoked no comments from the spectators, nor was any word uttered by the escort. Only when the gulch which marked the uttermost limit of Poker Flat was reached, the leader spoke briefly and to the point. The exiles were forbidden to return at the peril of their lives.

As the escort disappeared, their pent-up feelings found vent in a few hysterical tears from the Duchess, some bad language from Mother Shipton, and a Parthian volley of expletives from Uncle Billy. The philosophic Oakhurst alone remained silent. He listened calmly to Mother Shipton's desire to cut somebody's heart out, to the repeated statements of the Duchess that she would die in the road, and to the alarming oaths that seemed to be bumped out of Uncle Billy as he rode forward. With the easy good humor characteristic of his class, he insisted upon exchanging his own riding-horse, "Five-Spot," for the sorry mule which the Duchess rode. But even this act did not draw the party into any closer sympathy. The young woman readjusted her somewhat draggled plumes with a feeble, faded coquetry; Mother Shipton eyed the possessor of "Five-Spot" with malevolence, and Uncle Billy included the whole party in one sweeping anathema.

The road to Sandy Bar—a camp that, not having as yet experienced the regenerating influences of Poker Flat, consequently seemed to offer some invitation to the emigrants—lay over a steep mountain range. It was distant a day's severe travel. In that advanced season the party soon passed out of the moist, temperate regions of the foothills into the dry, cold, bracing air of the Sierras. The trail was narrow and difficult. At noon the Duchess, rolling out of her saddle upon the ground, declared her intention of going no farther, and the party halted.

The spot was singularly wild and impressive. A wooded amphitheatre, surrounded on three sides by precipitous cliffs of naked granite, sloped gently toward the crest of another precipice that overlooked the valley. It was, undoubtedly, the most suitable spot for a camp, had camping been advisable. But Mr. Oakhurst knew that scarcely half the journey to Sandy Bar was accomplished, and the party were not equipped or provisioned for delay. This fact he pointed out to his companions curtly, with a philosophic commentary on the folly of "throwing up their hand before the game was played out." But they were furnished with liquor, which in this emergency stood them in place of food, fuel, rest, and prescience. In spite of his remonstrances, it was not long before they were more or less under its influence. Uncle Billy passed rapidly from a bellicose state into one of stupor, the Duchess became maudlin, and Mother Shipton snored. Mr. Oakhurst alone remained erect, leaning against a rock, calmly surveying them.

Mr. Oakhurst did not drink. It interfered with a profession which required coolness, impassiveness, and presence of mind, and, in his own language, he "couldn't afford it." As he gazed at his recumbent fellow exiles, the loneliness begotten of his pariah trade, his habits of life, his very vices, for the first time seriously oppressed him. He bestirred himself in dusting his black clothes, washing his hands and face, and other acts characteristic of his studiously neat habits, and for a moment forgot his annoyance. The thought of deserting his weaker and more pitiable companions never perhaps occurred to him. Yet he could not help feeling the want of that excitement which, singularly enough, was most conducive to that calm equanimity for which he was notorious. He looked at the gloomy walls that rose a thousand feet sheer above the circling pines around him, at the sky ominously clouded, at the valley below, already deepening into shadow; and, doing so, suddenly he heard his own name called.

A horseman slowly ascended the trail. In the fresh, open face of the newcomer Mr. Oakhurst recognized Tom Simson, otherwise known as "The Innocent," of Sandy Bar. He had met him some months before over a "little game," and had, with perfect equanimity, won the entire fortune—amounting to some forty dollars—of that guileless youth. After the game was finished, Mr. Oakhurst drew the youthful speculator behind the door and thus addressed him: "Tommy, you're a good little man, but you can't gamble worth a cent. Don't try it over again." He then handed him his money hack, pushed him gently from the room, and so made a devoted slave of Tom Simson.

There was a remembrance of this in his boyish and enthusiastic greeting of Mr. Oakhurst. He had started, he said, to go to Poker Flat to seek his fortune. "Alone?" No, not exactly alone; in fact (a giggle), he had run away with Piney Woods. Didn't Mr. Oakhurst remember Piney? She that used to wait on the table at the Temperance House? They had been engaged a long time, but old Jake Woods had objected, and so they had run away, and were going to Poker Flat to be married, and here they were. And they were tired out, and how lucky it was they had found a place to camp, and company. All this the Innocent delivered rapidly, while Piney, a stout, comely damsel of fifteen, emerged from behind the pine-tree, where she had been blushing unseen, and rode to the side of her lover.

Mr. Oakhurst seldom troubled himself with sentiment, still less with propriety; but he had a vague idea that the situation was not fortunate. He retained, however, his presence of mind sufficiently to kick Uncle Billy, who was about to say something, and Uncle Billy was sober enough to recognize in Mr. Oakhurst's kick a superior power that would not bear trifling. He then endeavored to dissuade Tom Simson from delaying further, but in vain. He even pointed out the fact that there was no provision, nor means of making a camp. But, unluckily, the Innocent met this objection by assuring the party that he was provided with an extra mule loaded with provisions, and by the discovery of a rude attempt at a log house near the trail. "Piney can stay with Mrs. Oakhurst," said the Innocent, pointing to the Duchess, "and I can shift for myself."

Nothing but Mr. Oakhurst's admonishing foot saved Uncle Billy from bursting into a roar of laughter. As it was, he felt compelled to retire up the canon until he could recover his gravity. There he confided the joke to the tall pine-trees, with many slaps of his leg, contortions of his face, and the usual profanity. But when he returned to the party, he found them seated by a fire—for the air had grown strangely chill and the sky overcast—in apparently amicable conversation. Piney was actually talking in an impulsive girlish fashion to the Duchess, who was listening with an interest and animation she had not shown for many days. The Innocent was holding forth, apparently with equal effect, to Mr. Oakhurst and Mother Shipton, who was actually relaxing into amiability. "Is this yer a d—d picnic?" said Uncle Billy, with inward scorn, as he surveyed the sylvan group, the glancing firelight, and the tethered animals in the foreground. Suddenly an idea mingled with the alcoholic fumes that disturbed his brain. It was apparently of a jocular nature, for he felt impelled to slap his leg again and cram his fist into his mouth.

As the shadows crept slowly up the mountain, a slight breeze rocked the tops of the pine-trees and moaned through their long and gloomy aisles. The ruined cabin, patched and covered with pine boughs, was set apart for the ladies. As the lovers parted, they unaffectedly exchanged a kiss, so honest and sincere that it might have been heard above the swaying pines. The frail Duchess and the malevolent Mother Shipton were probably too stunned to remark upon this last evidence of simplicity, and so turned without a word to the hut. The fire was replenished, the men lay down before the door, and in a few minutes were asleep.

Mr. Oakhurst was a light sleeper. Toward morning he awoke benumbed and cold. As he stirred the dying fire, the wind, which was now blowing strongly, brought to his cheek that which caused the blood to leave it,—snow!

He started to his feet with the intention of awakening the sleepers, for there was no time to lose. But turning to where Uncle Billy had been lying, he found him gone. A suspicion leaped to his brain, and a curse to his lips. He ran to the spot where the mules had been tethered—they were no longer there. The tracks were already rapidly disappearing in the snow.

The momentary excitement brought Mr. Oakhurst back to the fire with his usual calm. He did not waken the sleepers. The Innocent slumbered peacefully, with a smile on his good-humored, freckled face; the virgin Piney slept beside her frailer sisters as sweetly as though attended by celestial guardians; and Mr. Oakhurst, drawing his blanket over his shoulders, stroked his mustaches and waited for the dawn. It came slowly in a whirling mist of snowflakes that dazzled and confused the eye. What could be seen of the landscape appeared magically changed. He looked over the valley, and summed up the present and future in two words, "Snowed in!"

A careful inventory of the provisions, which, fortunately for the party, had been stored within the hut, and so escaped the felonious fingers of Uncle Billy, disclosed the fact that with care and prudence they might last ten days longer. "That is," said Mr. Oakhurst *sotto voce* to the Innocent, "if you›re willing to board us. If you ain›t—and perhaps you›d better not—you can wait till Uncle Billy gets back with provisions." For some occult reason, Mr. Oakhurst could not bring himself to disclose Uncle Billy›s rascality, and so offered the hypothesis that he had wandered from the camp and had accidentally stampeded the animals. He dropped a warning to the Duchess and Mother Shipton, who of course knew the facts of their associate›s defection. "They›ll find out the truth about us *all* when they find out anything," he added significantly, "and there's no good frightening them now."

Tom Simson not only put all his worldly store at the disposal of Mr. Oakhurst, but seemed to enjoy the prospect of their enforced seclusion. "We'll have a good camp for a week, and then the snow'll melt, and we'll all go back together." The cheerful gayety of the young man and Mr. Oakhurst's calm infected the others. The Innocent, with the aid of pine boughs, extemporized a thatch for the roofless cabin, and the Duchess directed Piney in the rearrangement of the interior with a taste and tact that opened the blue eyes of that provincial maiden to their fullest extent. "I reckon now you're used to fine things at Poker Flat," said Piney. The Duchess turned away sharply to conceal something that reddened her cheeks through their professional tint, and Mother Shipton requested Piney not to "chatter." But when Mr. Oakhurst returned from a weary search for the trail, he heard the sound of happy laughter echoed from the rocks. He stopped in some alarm, and his thoughts first naturally reverted to the whiskey, which he had prudently cached. "And yet it don't somehow sound like whiskey," said the gambler. It was not until he caught sight of the blazing fire through the still blinding storm, and the group around it, that he settled to the conviction that it was "square fun."

Whether Mr. Oakhurst had cached his cards with the whiskey as something debarred the free access of the community, I cannot say. It was certain that, in Mother Shipton's words, he "didn't say 'cards' once" during that evening. Haply the time was beguiled by an accordion, produced somewhat ostentatiously by Tom Simson from his pack. Notwithstanding some difficulties attending the manipulation of this instrument, Piney Woods managed to pluck several reluctant melodies from its keys, to an accompaniment by the Innocent on a pair of bone castanets. But the crowning festivity of the evening was reached in a rude camp-meeting hymn, which the lovers, joining hands, sang with great earnestness and vociferation. I fear that a certain defiant tone and Covenanter's swing to its chorus, rather than any devotional quality, caused it speedily to infect the others, who at last joined in the refrain:—

25

"I'm proud to live in the service of the Lord, And I'm bound to die in His army."

The pines rocked, the storm eddied and whirled above the miserable group, and the flames of their altar leaped heavenward, as if in token of the vow.

At midnight the storm abated, the rolling clouds parted, and the stars glittered keenly above the sleeping camp. Mr. Oakhurst, whose professional habits had enabled him to live on the smallest possible amount of sleep, in dividing the watch with Tom Simson somehow managed to take upon himself the greater part of that duty. He excused himself to the Innocent by saying that he had "often been a week without sleep." "Doing what?" asked Tom. "Poker!" replied Oakhurst sententiously. "When a man gets a streak of luck,—nigger-luck,—he don't get tired. The luck gives in first. Luck," continued the gambler reflectively, "is a mighty queer thing. All you know about it for certain is that it's bound to change. And it's finding out when it's going to change that makes you. We've had a streak of bad luck since we left Poker Flat,—you come along, and slap you get into it, too. If you can hold your cards right along you're all right. For," added the gambler, with cheerful irrelevance—

"'I'm proud to live in the service of the Lord, And I'm bound to die in His army.'"

The third day came, and the sun, looking through the white-curtained valley, saw the outcasts divide their slowly decreasing store of provisions for the morning meal. It was one of the peculiarities of that mountain climate that its rays diffused a kindly warmth over the wintry landscape, as if in regretful commiseration of the past. But it revealed drift on drift of snow piled high around the hut,—a hopeless, uncharted, trackless sea of white lying below the rocky shores to which the castaways still clung. Through the marvelously clear air the smoke of the pastoral village of Poker Flat rose miles away. Mother Shipton saw it, and from a remote pinnacle of her rocky fastness hurled in that direction a final malediction. It was her last vituperative attempt, and perhaps for that reason was invested with a certain degree of sublimity. It did her good, she privately informed the Duchess. "Just you go out there and cuss, and see." She then set herself to the task of amusing "the child," as she and the Duchess were pleased to call Piney. Piney was no chicken, but it was a soothing and original theory of the pair thus to account for the fact that she didn't swear and wasn't improper.

When night crept up again through the gorges, the reedy notes of the accordion rose and fell in fitful spasms and long-drawn gasps by the flickering campfire. But music failed to fill entirely the aching void left by insufficient food, and a new diversion was proposed by Piney,—story-telling. Neither Mr. Oakhurst nor his female companions caring to relate their personal experiences, this plan would have failed too, but for the Innocent. Some months before he had chanced upon a stray copy of Mr. Pope's ingenious translation of the Iliad. He now proposed to narrate the principal incidents of that poem—having thoroughly mastered the argument and fairly forgotten the words—in the current vernacular of Sandy Bar. And so for the rest of that night the Homeric demigods again walked the earth. Trojan bully and wily Greek wrestled in the winds, and the great pines in the canon seemed to bow to the wrath of the son of Peleus. Mr. Oakhurst listened with quiet satisfaction. Most especially was he interested in the fate of "Ash-heels," as the Innocent persisted in denominating the "swift-footed Achilles."

So, with small food and much of Homer and the accordion, a week passed over the heads of the outcasts. The sun again forsook them, and again from leaden skies the snowflakes were sifted over the land. Day by day closer around them drew the snowy circle, until at last they looked from their prison over drifted walls of dazzling white, that towered twenty feet above their heads. It became more and more difficult to replenish their fires, even from the fallen trees beside them, now half hidden in the drifts. And yet no one complained. The lovers turned from the dreary prospect and looked into each other's eyes, and were happy. Mr. Oakhurst settled himself coolly to the losing game before him. The Duchess, more cheerful than she had been, assumed the care of Piney. Only Mother Shipton—once the strongest of the party—seemed to sicken and fade. At midnight on the tenth day she called Oakhurst to her side. "I'm going," she said, in a voice of querulous weakness, "but don't say anything about it. Don't waken the kids. Take the bundle from under my head, and open it." Mr. Oakhurst did so. It contained Mother Shipton's rations for the last week, untouched. "Give 'em to the child," she said, pointing to the sleeping Piney. "You've starved yourself," said the gambler. "That's what they call it," said the woman querulously, as she lay down again, and, turning her face to the wall, passed quietly away.

The accordion and the bones were put aside that day, and Homer was forgotten. When the body of Mother Shipton had been committed to the snow, Mr. Oakhurst took the Innocent aside, and showed him a pair of snow-shoes, which he had fashioned from the old pack-saddle.

"There's one chance in a hundred to save her yet," he said, pointing to Piney; "but it's there," he added, pointing toward Poker Flat. "If you can reach there in two days she's safe."

"And you?" asked Tom Simson. "I'll stay here," was the curt reply. The lovers parted with a long embrace.

"You are not going, too?" said the Duchess, as she saw Mr. Oakhurst apparently waiting to accompany him. "As far as the canon," he replied. He turned suddenly and kissed the Duchess, leaving her pallid face aflame, and her trembling limbs rigid with amazement.

Night came, but not Mr. Oakhurst. It brought the storm again and the whirling snow. Then the Duchess, feeding the fire, found that some one had quietly piled beside the hut enough fuel to last a few days longer. The tears rose to her eyes, but she hid them from Piney.

The women slept but little. In the morning, looking into each other's faces, they read their fate. Neither spoke, but Piney, accepting the position of the stronger, drew near and placed her arm around the Duchess's waist. They kept this attitude for the rest of the day. That night the storm reached its greatest fury, and, rending asunder the protecting vines, invaded the very hut.

Toward morning they found themselves unable to feed the fire, which gradually died away. As the embers slowly blackened, the Duchess crept closer to Piney, and broke the silence of many hours: "Piney, can you pray?" "No, dear," said Piney simply. The Duchess, without knowing exactly why, felt relieved, and, putting her head upon Piney's shoulder, spoke no more. And so reclining, the younger and purer pillowing the head of her soiled sister upon her virgin breast, they fell asleep.

The wind lulled as if it feared to waken them. Feathery drifts of snow, shaken from the long pine boughs, flew like white winged birds, and settled about them as they slept. The moon through the rifted clouds looked down upon what had been the camp. But all human stain, all trace of earthly travail, was hidden beneath the spotless mantle mercifully flung from above.

They slept all that day and the next, nor did they waken when voices and footsteps broke the silence of the camp. And when pitying fingers brushed the snow from their wan faces, you could scarcely have told from the equal peace that dwelt upon them which was she that had sinned. Even the law of Poker Flat recognized this, and turned away, leaving them still locked in each other's arms.

But at the head of the gulch, on one of the largest pine-trees, they found the deuce of clubs pinned to the bark with a bowie-knife. It bore the following, written in pencil in a firm hand:—

BENEATH THIS TREE LIES THE BODY OF JOHN OAKHURST, WHO STRUCK A STREAK OF BAD LUCK ON THE 23D OF NOVEMBER 1850. AND HANDED IN HIS CHECKS ON THE 7TH DECEMBER, 1850.

And pulseless and cold, with a Derringer by his side and a bullet in his heart, though still calm as in life, beneath the snow lay he who was at once the strongest and yet the weakest of the outcasts of Poker Flat.

MIGGLES

We were eight including the driver. We had not spoken during the passage of the last six miles, since the jolting of the heavy vehicle over the roughening road had spoiled the Judge's last poetical quotation. The tall man beside the Judge was asleep, his arm passed through the swaying strap and his head resting upon it,—altogether a limp, helpless looking object, as if he had hanged himself and been cut down too late. The French lady on the back seat was asleep too, yet in a half-conscious propriety of attitude, shown even in the disposition of the handkerchief which she held to her forehead and which partially veiled her face. The lady from Virginia City, traveling with her husband, had long since lost all individuality in a wild confusion of ribbons, veils, furs, and shawls. There was no sound but the rattling of wheels and the dash of rain upon the roof. Suddenly the stage stopped and we became dimly aware of voices. The driver was evidently in the midst of an exciting colloquy with some one in the road,—a colloquy of which such fragments as "bridge gone," "twenty feet of water," "can't pass," were occasionally distinguishable above the storm. Then came a lull, and a mysterious voice from the road shouted the parting adjuration—

"Try Miggles's."

We caught a glimpse of our leaders as the vehicle slowly turned, of a horseman vanishing through the rain, and we were evidently on our way to Miggles's.

Who and where was Miggles? The Judge, our authority, did not remember the name, and he knew the country thoroughly. The Washoe traveler thought Miggles must keep a hotel. We only knew that we were stopped by high water in front and rear, and that Miggles was our rock of refuge. A ten minutes' splashing through a tangled byroad, scarcely wide enough for the stage, and we drew up before a barred and boarded gate in a wide stone wall or fence about eight feet high. Evidently Miggles's, and evidently Miggles did not keep a hotel.

The driver got down and tried the gate. It was securely locked.

"Miggles! O Miggles!"

No answer.

"Migg-ells! You Miggles!" continued the driver, with rising wrath.

"Migglesy!" joined in the expressman persuasively. "O Miggy! Mig!"

But no reply came from the apparently insensate Miggles. The Judge, who had finally got the window down, put his head out and propounded a series of questions, which if answered categorically would have undoubtedly elucidated the whole mystery, but which the driver evaded by replying that "if we didn't want to sit in the coach all night we had better rise up and sing out for Miggles."

So we rose up and called on Miggles in chorus, then separately. And when we had finished, a Hibernian fellow passenger from the roof called for "Maygells!" whereat we all laughed. While we were laughing the driver cried, "Shoo!"

We listened. To our infinite amazement the chorus of "Miggles" was repeated from the other side of the wall, even to the final and supplemental "Maygells."

"Extraordinary echo!" said the Judge.

"Extraordinary d—d skunk!" roared the driver contemptuously. "Come out of that, Miggles, and show yourself! Be a man, Miggles! Don't hide in the dark; I wouldn't if I were you, Miggles," continued Yuba Bill, now dancing about in an excess of fury.

"Miggles!" continued the voice, "O Miggles!"

"My good man! Mr. Myghail!" said the Judge, softening the asperities of the name as much as possible. "Consider the inhospitality of refusing shelter from the inclemency of the weather to helpless females. Really, my dear sir"—But a succession of "Miggles," ending in a burst of laughter, drowned his voice.

Yuba Bill hesitated no longer. Taking a heavy stone from the road, he battered down the gate, and with the expressman entered the inclosure. We followed. Nobody was to be seen. In the gathering darkness all that we could distinguish was that we were in a garden—from the rose bushes that scattered over us a minute spray from their dripping leaves—and before a long, rambling wooden building.

"Do you know this Miggles?" asked the Judge of Yuba Bill.

"No, nor don't want to," said Bill shortly, who felt the Pioneer Stage Company insulted in his person by the contumacious Miggles.

"But, my dear sir," expostulated the Judge, as he thought of the barred gate.

"Lookee here," said Yuba Bill, with fine irony, "hadn't you better go back and sit in the coach till yer introduced? I'm going in," and he pushed open the door of the building.

A long room, lighted only by the embers of a fire that was dying on the large hearth at its farther extremity; the walls curiously papered, and the flickering firelight bringing out its grotesque pattern; someone sitting in a large armchair by the fireplace. All this we saw as we crowded together into the room after the driver and expressman. "Hello! be you Miggles?" said Yuba Bill to the solitary occupant.

The figure neither spoke nor stirred. Yuba Bill walked wrathfully toward it and turned the eye of his coach-lantern upon its face. It was a man's face, prematurely old and wrinkled, with very large eyes, in which there was that expression of perfectly gratuitous solemnity which I had sometimes seen in an owl's. The large eyes wandered from Bill's face to the lantern, and finally fixed their gaze on that luminous object without further recognition.

Bill restrained himself with an effort.

"Miggles! be you deaf? You ain't dumb anyhow, you know," and Yuba Bill shook the insensate figure by the shoulder.

To our great dismay, as Bill removed his hand, the venerable stranger apparently collapsed, sinking into half his size and an undistinguishable heap of clothing.

"Well, dern my skin," said Bill, looking appealingly at us, and hopelessly retiring from the contest.

The Judge now stepped forward, and we lifted the mysterious invertebrate back into his original position. Bill was dismissed with the lantern to reconnoitre outside, for it was evident that, from the helplessness of this solitary man? there must be attendants near at hand, and we all drew around the fire. The Judge, who had regained his authority, and had never lost his conversational amiability,—standing before us with his back to the hearth,—charged us, as an imaginary jury, as follows:—

"It is evident that either our distinguished friend here has reached that condition described by Shakespeare as 'the sere and yellow leaf,' or has suffered some premature abatement of his mental and physical faculties. Whether he is really the Miggles"—

Here he was interrupted by "Miggles! O Miggles! Migglesy! Mig!" and, in fact, the whole chorus of Miggles in very much the same key as it had once before been delivered unto us.

We gazed at each other for a moment in some alarm. The Judge, in particular, vacated his position quickly, as the voice seemed to come directly over his shoulder. The cause, however, was soon discovered in a large magpie who was perched upon a shelf over the fireplace, and who immediately relapsed into a sepulchral silence, which contrasted singularly with his previous volubility. It was, undoubtedly, his voice which we had heard in the road, and our friend in the chair was not responsible for the discourtesy. Yuba Bill, who reentered the room after an unsuccessful search, was both to accept the explanation, and still eyed the helpless sitter with suspicion. He had found a shed in which he had put up his horses, but he came back dripping and skeptical. "Thar ain't nobody but him within ten mile of the shanty, and that ar d—d old skeesicks knows it."

But the faith of the majority proved to be securely based. Bill had scarcely ceased growling before we heard a quick step upon the porch, the trailing of a wet skirt, the door was flung open, and with a flash of white teeth, a sparkle of dark eyes, and an utter absence of ceremony or diffidence, a young woman entered, shut the door, and, panting, leaned back against it.

"Oh, if you please, I'm Miggles!"

And this was Miggles! this bright-eyed, full-throated young woman, whose wet gown of coarse blue stuff could not hide the beauty of the feminine curves to which it clung; from the chestnut crown of whose head, topped by a man's oil-skin sou'wester, to the little feet and ankles, hidden somewhere in the recesses of her boy's brogans, all was grace,—this was Miggles, laughing at us, too, in the most airy, frank, off-hand manner imaginable.

"You see, boys," said she, quite out of breath, and holding one little hand against her side, quite unheeding the speechless discomfiture of our party or the complete demoralization of Yuba Bill, whose features had relaxed into an expression of gratuitous and imbecile cheerfulness,—"you see, boys, I was mor'n two miles away when you passed down the road. I thought you might pull up here, and so I ran the whole way, knowing nobody was home but Jim,—and—and—I'm out of breath—and—that lets me out." And here Miggles caught her dripping oilskin hat from her head, with a mischievous swirl that scattered a shower of raindrops over us; attempted to put back her hair; dropped two hairpins in the attempt; laughed, and sat down beside Yuba Bill, with her hands crossed lightly on her lap.

The Judge recovered himself first and essayed an extravagant compliment.

"I'll trouble you for that ha'rpin," said Miggles gravely. Half a dozen hands were eagerly stretched forward; the missing hairpin was restored to its fair owner; and Miggles, crossing the room, looked keenly in the face of the invalid. The solemn eyes looked back at hers with an expression we had never seen before. Life and intelligence seemed to struggle back into the rugged face. Miggles laughed again,—it was a singularly eloquent laugh,—and turned her black eyes and white teeth once more towards us.

"This afflicted person is"—hesitated the Judge.

"Jim!" said Miggles.

34

"Your father?"

"No!"

"Brother?"

"No?"

"Husband?"

Miggles darted a quick, half-defiant glance at the two lady passengers, who I had noticed did not participate in the general masculine admiration of Miggles, and said gravely, "No; it's Jim!" There was an awkward pause. The lady passengers moved closer to each other; the Washoe husband looked abstractedly at the fire, and the tall man apparently turned his eyes inward for self-support at this emergency. But Miggles's laugh, which was very infectious, broke the silence.

"Come," she said briskly, "you must be hungry. Who'll bear a hand to help me get tea?"

She had no lack of volunteers. In a few moments Yuba Bill was engaged like Caliban in bearing logs for this Miranda; the expressman was grinding coffee on the veranda; to myself the arduous duty of slicing bacon was assigned; and the Judge lent each man his good-humored and voluble counsel. And when Miggles, assisted by the Judge and our Hibernian "deck-passenger," set the table with all the available crockery, we had become quite joyous, in spite of the rain that beat against the windows, the wind that whirled down the chimney, the two ladies who whispered together in the corner, or the magpie, who uttered a satirical and croaking commentary on their conversation from his perch above. In the now bright, blazing fire we could see that the walls were papered with illustrated journals, arranged with feminine taste and discrimination. The furniture was extemporized and adapted from candle-boxes and packing-cases, and covered with gay calico or the skin of some animal. The armchair of the helpless Jim was an ingenious variation of a flour-barrel. There was neatness, and even a taste for the picturesque, to be seen in the few details of the long, low room.

The meal was a culinary success. But more, it was a social triumph,— chiefly, I think, owing to the rare tact of Miggles in guiding the conversation, asking all the questions herself, yet bearing throughout a frankness that rejected the idea of any concealment on her own part, so that we talked of ourselves, of our prospects, of the journey, of the weather, of each other,—of everything but our host and hostess. It must be confessed that Miggles's conversation was never elegant, rarely grammatical, and that at times she employed expletives the use of which had generally been yielded to our sex. But they were delivered with such a lighting up of teeth and eyes, and were usually followed by a laugh—a laugh peculiar to Miggles—so frank and honest that it seemed to clear the moral atmosphere.

Once during the meal we heard a noise like the rubbing of a heavy body against the outer walls of the house. This was shortly followed by a scratching and sniffling at the door. "That's Joaquin," said Miggles, in reply to our questioning glances; "would you like to see him?" Before we could answer she had opened the door, and disclosed a half-grown grizzly, who instantly raised himself on his haunches, with his fore paws hanging down in the popular attitude of mendicancy, and looked admiringly at Miggles, with a very singular resemblance in his manner to Yuba Bill. "That's my watch-dog," said Miggles, in explanation. "Oh, he don't bite," she added, as the two lady passengers fluttered into a corner. "Does he, old Toppy?" (the latter remark being addressed directly to the sagacious Joaquin). "I tell you what, boys," continued Miggles, after she had fed and closed the door on Ursa Minor, "you were in big luck that Joaquin wasn't hanging round when you dropped in to-night."

"Where was he?" asked the Judge.

"With me," said Miggles. "Lord love you! he trots round with me nights like as if he was a man."

We were silent for a few moments, and listened to the wind. Perhaps we all had the same picture before us,—of Miggles walking through the rainy woods with her savage guardian at her side. The Judge, I remember, said something about Una and her lion; but Miggles received it, as she did other compliments, with quiet gravity. Whether she was altogether unconscious of the admiration she excited,—she could hardly have been oblivious of Yuba Bill's adoration,—I know not; but her very frankness suggested a perfect sexual equality that was cruelly humiliating to the younger members of our party.

The incident of the bear did not add anything in Miggles's favor to the opinions of those of her own sex who were present. In fact, the repast over, a chillness radiated from the two lady passengers that no pine boughs brought in by Yuba Bill and cast as a sacrifice upon the hearth could wholly overcome. Miggles felt it; and suddenly declaring that it was time to "turn in," offered to show the ladies to their bed in an adjoining room. "You, boys, will have to camp out here by the fire as well as you can," she added, "for thar ain't but the one room."

Our sex—by which, my dear sir, I allude of course to the stronger portion of humanity—has been generally relieved from the imputation of curiosity or a fondness for gossip. Yet I am constrained to say, that hardly had the door closed on Miggles than we crowded together, whispering, snickering, smiling, and exchanging suspicions, surmises, and a thousand speculations in regard to our pretty hostess and her singular companion. I fear that we even hustled that imbecile paralytic, who sat like a voiceless Memnon in our midst, gazing with the serene indifference of the Past in his passionless eyes upon our wordy counsels. In the midst of an exciting discussion the door opened again and Miggles reentered.

But not, apparently, the same Miggles who a few hours before had flashed upon us. Her eyes were downcast, and as she hesitated for a moment on the threshold, with a blanket on her arm, she seemed to have left behind her the frank fearlessness which had charmed us a moment before. Coming into the room, she drew a low stool beside the paralytic's chair, sat down, drew the blanket over her shoulders, and saying, "If it's all the same to you, boys, as we're rather crowded, I'll stop here to-night," took the invalid's withered hand in her own, and turned her eyes upon the dying fire. An instinctive feeling that this was only premonitory to more confidential relations, and perhaps some shame at our previous curiosity, kept us silent. The rain still heat upon the roof, wandering gusts of wind stirred the embers into momentary brightness, until, in a lull of the elements, Miggles suddenly lifted up her head, and, throwing her hair over her shoulder, turned her face upon the group and asked,—

"Is there any of you that knows me?"

There was no reply.

"Think again! I lived at Marysville in '53. Everybody knew me there, and everybody had the right to know me. I kept the Polka Saloon until I came to live with Jim. That's six years ago. Perhaps I've changed some."

The absence of recognition may have disconcerted her. She turned her head to the fire again, and it was some seconds before she again spoke, and then more rapidly—

"Well, you see I thought some of you must have known me. There's no great harm done anyway. What I was going to say was this: Jim here"—she took his hand in both of hers as she spoke—"used to know me, if you didn't, and spent a heap of money upon me. I reckon he spent all he had. And one day—it's six years ago this winter—Jim came into my back room, sat down on my sofy, like as you see him in that chair, and never moved again without help. He was struck all of a heap, and never seemed to know what ailed him. The doctors came and said as how it was caused all along of his way of life,—for Jim was mighty free and wild-like,—and that he would never get better, and couldn't last long anyway. They advised me to send him to Frisco to the hospital, for he was no good to any one and would be a baby all his life. Perhaps it was something in Jim's eye, perhaps it was that I never had a baby, but I said 'No.' I was rich then, for I was popular with everybody,—gentlemen like yourself, sir, came to see me,—and I sold out my business and bought this yer place, because it was sort of out of the way of travel, you see, and I brought my baby here."

With a woman's intuitive tact and poetry, she had, as she spoke, slowly shifted her position so as to bring the mute figure of the ruined man between her and her audience, hiding in the shadow behind it, as if she offered it as a tacit apology for her actions. Silent and expressionless, it yet spoke for her; helpless, crushed, and smitten with the Divine thunderbolt, it still stretched an invisible arm around her.

Hidden in the darkness, but still holding his hand, she went on:—

"It was a long time before I could get the hang of things about yer, for I was used to company and excitement. I couldn't get any woman to help me, and a man I dursn't trust; but what with the Indians hereabout, who'd do odd jobs for me, and having everything sent from the North Fork, Jim and I managed to worry through. The Doctor would run up from Sacramento once in a while. He'd ask to see 'Miggles's baby' as he called Jim, and when he'd go away, he'd say, 'Miggles, you're a trump,—God bless you,' and it didn't seem so lonely after that. But the last time he was here he said, as he opened the door to go, 'Do you know, Miggles, your baby will grow up to be a man yet and an honor to his mother; but not here, Miggles, not here!' And I thought he went away sad,—and—and"—and here Miggles's voice and head were somehow both lost completely in the shadow.

"The folks about here are very kind," said Miggles, after a pause, coming a little into the light again. "The men from the Fork used to hang around here, until they found they wasn't wanted, and the women are kind, and don't call. I was pretty lonely until I picked up Joaquin in the woods yonder one day, when he wasn't so high, and taught him to beg for his dinner; and then thar's Polly—that's the magpie—she knows no end of tricks, and makes it quite sociable of evenings with her talk, and so I don't feel like as I was the only living being about the ranch. And Jim here," said Miggles, with her old laugh again, and coming out quite into the firelight,—"Jim—Why, boys, you would admire to see how much he knows for a man like him. Sometimes I bring him flowers, and he looks at 'em just as natural as if he knew 'em; and times, when we're sitting alone, I read him those things on the wall. Why, Lord!" said Miggles, with her frank laugh, "I've read him that whole side of the house this winter. There never was such a man for reading as Jim."

"Why," asked the Judge, "do you not marry this man to whom you have devoted your youthful life?"

"Well, you see," said Miggles, "it would be playing it rather low down on Jim to take advantage of his being so helpless. And then, too, if we were man and wife, now, we'd both know that I was *bound* to do what I do now of my own accord."

"But you are young yet and attractive"—

"It's getting late," said Miggles gravely, "and you'd better all turn in. Good-night, boys;" and throwing the blanket over her head, Miggles laid herself down beside Jim's chair, her head pillowed on the low stool that held his feet, and spoke no more. The fire slowly faded from the hearth; we each sought our blankets in silence; and presently there was no sound in the long room but the pattering of the rain upon the roof and the heavy breathing of the sleepers.

It was nearly morning when I awoke from a troubled dream. The storm had passed, the stars were shining, and through the shutterless window the full moon, lifting itself over the solemn pines without, looked into the room. It touched the lonely figure in the chair with an infinite compassion, and seemed to baptize with a shining flood the lowly head of the woman whose hair, as in the sweet old story, bathed the feet of him she loved. It even lent a kindly poetry to the rugged outline of Yuba Bill, half reclining on his elbow between them and his passengers, with savagely patient eyes keeping watch and ward. And then I fell asleep and only woke at broad day, with Yuba Bill standing over me, and "All aboard" ringing in my ears.

Coffee was waiting for us on the table, but Miggles was gone. We wandered about the house and lingered long after the horses were harnessed, but she did not return. It was evident that she wished to avoid a formal leave-taking, and had so left us to depart as we had come. After we had helped the ladies into the coach, we returned to the house and solemnly shook hands with the paralytic Jim, as solemnly setting him back into position after each handshake. Then we looked for the last time around the long low room, at the stool where Miggles had sat, and slowly took our seats in the waiting coach. The whip cracked, and we were off!

But as we reached the highroad, Bill's dexterous hand laid the six horses back on their haunches, and the stage stopped with a jerk. For there, on a little eminence beside the road, stood Miggles, her hair flying, her eyes sparkling, her white handkerchief waving, and her white teeth flashing a last "good-by." We waved our hats in return. And then Yuba Bill, as if fearful of further fascination, madly lashed his horses forward, and we sank back in our seats.

We exchanged not a word until we reached the North Fork and the stage drew up at the Independence House. Then, the Judge leading, we walked into the bar-room and took our places gravely at the bar.

"Are your glasses charged, gentlemen?" said the Judge, solemnly taking off his white hat.

They were.

"Well, then, here's to *Miggles*—GOD BLESS HER!"

Perhaps He had. Who knows?

TENNESSEE'S PARTNER

I do not think that we ever knew his real name. Our ignorance of it certainly never gave us any social inconvenience, for at Sandy Bar in 1854 most men were christened anew. Sometimes these appellatives were derived from some distinctiveness of dress, as in the case of "Dungaree Jack;" or from some peculiarity of habit, as shown in "Saleratus Bill," so called from an undue proportion of that chemical in his daily bread; or from some unlucky slip, as exhibited in "The Iron Pirate," a mild, inoffensive man, who earned that baleful title by his unfortunate mispronunciation of the term "iron pyrites." Perhaps this may have been the beginning of a rude heraldry; but I am constrained to think that it was because a man's real name in that day rested solely upon his own unsupported statement. "Call yourself Clifford, do you?" said Boston, addressing a timid newcomer with infinite scorn; "hell is full of such Cliffords!" He then introduced the unfortunate man, whose name happened to be really Clifford, as "Jaybird Charley,"—an unhallowed inspiration of the moment that clung to him ever after.

But to return to Tennessee's Partner, whom we never knew by any other than this relative title. That he had ever existed as a separate and distinct individuality we only learned later. It seems that in 1853 he left Poker Flat to go to San Francisco, ostensibly to procure a wife. He never got any farther than Stockton. At that place he was attracted by a young person who waited upon the table at the hotel where he took his meals. One morning he said something to her which caused her to smile not unkindly, to somewhat coquettishly break a plate of toast over his upturned, serious, simple face, and to retreat to the kitchen.

He followed her, and emerged a few moments later, covered with more toast and victory. That day week they were married by a justice of the peace, and returned to Poker Flat. I am aware that something more might be made of this episode, but I prefer to tell it as it was current at Sandy Bar,—in the gulches and bar-rooms,—where all sentiment was modified by a strong sense of humor.

Of their married felicity but little is known, perhaps for the reason that Tennessee, then living with his partner, one day took occasion to say something to the bride on his own account, at which, it is said, she smiled not unkindly and chastely retreated,—this time as far as Marysville, where Tennessee followed her, and where they went to housekeeping without the aid of a justice of the peace. Tennessee's Partner took the loss of his wife simply and seriously, as was his fashion. But to everybody's surprise, when Tennessee one day returned from Marysville, without his partner's wife,—she having smiled and retreated with somebody else,—Tennessee's Partner was the first man to shake his hand and greet him with affection. The boys who had gathered in the canon to see the shooting were naturally indignant. Their indignation might have found vent in sarcasm but for a certain look in Tennessee's Partner's eye that indicated a lack of humorous appreciation. In fact, he was a grave man, with a steady application to practical detail which was unpleasant in a difficulty.

Meanwhile a popular feeling against Tennessee had grown up on the Bar. He was known to be a gambler; he was suspected to be a thief. In these suspicions Tennessee's Partner was equally compromised; his continued intimacy with Tennessee after the affair above quoted could only be accounted for on the hypothesis of a copartnership of crime. At last Tennessee's guilt became flagrant. One day he overtook a stranger on his way to Red Dog. The stranger afterward related that Tennessee beguiled the time with interesting anecdote and reminiscence, but illogically concluded the interview in the following words: "And now, young man, I'll trouble you for your knife, your pistols, and your money. You see your weppings might get you into trouble at Red Dog, and your money's a temptation to the evilly disposed. I think you said your address was San Francisco. I shall endeavor to call." It may be stated here that Tennessee had a fine flow of humor, which no business preoccupation could wholly subdue.

This exploit was his last. Red Dog and Sandy Bar made common cause against the highwayman. Tennessee was hunted in very much the same fashion as his prototype, the grizzly. As the toils closed around him, he made a desperate dash through the Bar, emptying his revolver at the crowd before the Arcade Saloon, and so on up Grizzly Canon; but at its farther extremity he was stopped by a small man on a gray horse. The men looked at each other a moment in silence. Both were fearless, both self-possessed and independent, and both types of a civilization that in the seventeenth century would have been called heroic, but in the nineteenth simply "reckless."

"What have you got there?—I call," said Tennessee quietly.

"Two bowers and an ace," said the stranger as quietly, showing two revolvers and a bowie-knife.

"That takes me," returned Tennessee; and, with this gambler's epigram, he threw away his useless pistol and rode back with his captor.

It was a warm night. The cool breeze which usually sprang up with the going down of the sun behind the chaparral-crested mountain was that evening withheld from Sandy Bar. The little canon was stifling with heated resinous odors, and the decaying driftwood on the Bar sent forth faint sickening exhalations. The feverishness of day and its fierce passions still filled the camp. Lights moved restlessly along the bank of the river, striking no answering reflection from its tawny current. Against the blackness of the pines the windows of the old loft above the express-office stood out staringly bright; and through their curtainless panes the loungers below could see the forms of those who were even then deciding the fate of Tennessee. And above all this, etched on the dark firmament, rose the Sierra, remote and passionless, crowned with remoter passionless stars.

The trial of Tennessee was conducted as fairly as was consistent with a judge and jury who felt themselves to some extent obliged to justify, in their verdict, the previous irregularities of arrest and indictment. The law of Sandy Bar was implacable, but not vengeful. The excitement and personal feeling of the chase were over; with Tennessee safe in their hands, they were ready to listen patiently to any defense, which they were already satisfied was insufficient. There being no doubt in their own minds, they were willing to give the prisoner the benefit of any that might exist. Secure in the hypothesis that he ought to be hanged on general principles, they indulged him with more latitude of defense than his reckless hardihood seemed to ask. The Judge appeared to be more anxious than the prisoner, who, otherwise unconcerned, evidently took a grim pleasure in the responsibility he had created. "I don't take any hand in this yer game," had been his invariable but good-humored reply to all questions. The Judge—who was also his captor—for a moment vaguely regretted that he had not shot him "on sight" that morning, but presently dismissed this human weakness as unworthy of the judicial mind. Nevertheless, when there was a tap at the door, and it was said that Tennessee's Partner was there on behalf of the prisoner, he was admitted at once without question. Perhaps the younger members of the jury, to whom the proceedings were becoming irksomely thoughtful, hailed him as a relief.

For he was not, certainly, an imposing figure. Short and stout, with a square face, sunburned into a preternatural redness, clad in a loose duck "jumper" and trousers streaked and splashed with red soil, his aspect under any circumstances would have been quaint, and was now even ridiculous. As he stooped to deposit at his feet a heavy carpetbag he was carrying, it became obvious, from partially developed legends and inscriptions, that the material with which his trousers had been patched had been originally intended for a less ambitious covering. Yet he advanced with great gravity, and after shaking the hand of each person in the room with labored cordiality, he wiped his serious perplexed face on a red bandana handkerchief, a shade lighter than his complexion, laid his powerful hand upon the table to steady himself, and thus addressed the Judge:—

"I was passin' by," he began, by way of apology, "and I thought I'd just step in and see how things was gittin' on with Tennessee thar,—my pardner. It's a hot night. I disremember any sich weather before on the Bar."

He paused a moment, but nobody volunteering any other meteorological recollection, he again had recourse to his pocket-handkerchief, and for some moments mopped his face diligently.

"Have you anything to say on behalf of the prisoner?" said the Judge finally.

"Thet's it," said Tennessee's Partner, in a tone of relief. "I come yar as Tennessee's pardner,—knowing him nigh on four year, off and on, wet and dry, in luck and out o' luck. His ways ain't aller my ways, but thar ain't any p'ints in that young man, thar ain't any liveliness as he's been up to, as I don't know. And you sez to me, sez you,—confidential-like, and between man and man,—sez you, 'Do you know anything in his behalf?' and I sez to you, sez I,—confidential-like, as between man and man,—'What should a man know of his pardner?'"

"Is this all you have to say?" asked the Judge impatiently, feeling, perhaps, that a dangerous sympathy of humor was beginning to humanize the court.

"Thet's so," continued Tennessee's Partner. "It ain't for me to say anything agin' him. And now, what's the case? Here's Tennessee wants money, wants it bad, and doesn't like to ask it of his old pardner. Well, what does Tennessee do? He lays for a stranger, and he fetches that stranger; and you lays for *him*, and you fetches *him*; and the honors is easy. And I put it to you, bein' a fa'r-minded man, and to you, gentlemen all, as fa'r-minded men, ef this isn't so."

"Prisoner," said the Judge, interrupting, "have you any questions to ask this man?"

"No! no!" continued Tennessee's Partner hastily. "I play this yer hand alone. To come down to the bed-rock, it's just this: Tennessee, thar, has played it pretty rough and expensive-like on a stranger, and on this yer camp. And now, what's the fair thing? Some would say more, some would say less. Here's seventeen hundred dollars in coarse gold and a watch,—it's about all my pile,—and call it square!" And before a hand could be raised to prevent him, he had emptied the contents of the carpetbag upon the table.

For a moment his life was in jeopardy. One or two men sprang to their feet, several hands groped for hidden weapons, and a suggestion to "throw him from the window" was only overridden by a gesture from the Judge. Tennessee laughed. And apparently oblivious of the excitement, Tennessee's Partner improved the opportunity to mop his face again with his handkerchief. When order was restored, and the man was made to understand, by the use of forcible figures and rhetoric, that Tennessee's offense could not be condoned by money, his face took a more serious and sanguinary hue, and those who were nearest to him noticed that his rough hand trembled slightly on the table. He hesitated a moment as he slowly returned the gold to the carpetbag, as if he had not yet entirely caught the elevated sense of justice which swayed the tribunal, and was perplexed with the belief that he had not offered enough. Then he turned to the Judge, and saying, "This yer is a lone hand, played alone, and without my pardner," he bowed to the jury and was about to withdraw, when the Judge called him back:—

"If you have anything to say to Tennessee, you had better say it now."

For the first time that evening the eyes of the prisoner and his strange advocate met. Tennessee smiled, showed his white teeth, and saying, "Euchred, old man!" held out his hand. Tennessee's Partner took it in his own, and saying, "I just dropped in as I was passin' to see how things was gettin' on," let the hand passively fall, and adding that "it was a warm night," again mopped his face with his handkerchief, and without another word withdrew.

The two men never again met each other alive. For the unparalleled insult of a bribe offered to Judge Lynch—who, whether bigoted, weak, or narrow, was at least incorruptible—firmly fixed in the mind of that mythical personage any wavering determination of Tennessee's fate; and at the break of day he was marched, closely guarded, to meet it at the top of Marley's Hill.

How he met it, how cool he was, how he refused to say anything, how perfect were the arrangements of the committee, were all duly reported, with the addition of a warning moral and example to all future evil-doers, in the "Red Dog Clarion," by its editor, who was present, and to whose vigorous English I cheerfully refer the reader. But the beauty of that midsummer morning, the blessed amity of earth and air and sky, the awakened life of the free woods and hills, the joyous renewal and promise of Nature, and above all, the infinite serenity that thrilled through each, was not reported, as not being a part of the social lesson. And yet, when the weak and foolish deed was done, and a life, with its possibilities and responsibilities, had passed out of the misshapen thing that dangled between earth and sky, the birds sang, the flowers bloomed, the sun shone, as cheerily as before; and possibly the "Red Dog Clarion" was right.

Tennessee's Partner was not in the group that surrounded the ominous tree. But as they turned to disperse, attention was drawn to the singular appearance of a motionless donkey-cart halted at the side of the road. As they approached, they at once recognized the venerable "Jenny" and the two-wheeled cart as the property of Tennessee's Partner, used by him in carrying dirt from his claim; and a few paces distant the owner of the equipage himself, sitting under a buckeye-tree, wiping the perspiration from his glowing face. In answer to an inquiry, he said he had come for the body of the "diseased," "if it was all the same to the committee." He didn't wish to "hurry anything;" he could "wait." He was not working that day; and when the gentlemen were done with the "diseased," he would take him. "Ef thar is any present," he added, in his simple, serious way, "as would care to jine in the fun'l, they kin come." Perhaps it was from a sense of humor, which I have already intimated was a feature of Sandy Bar,—perhaps it was from something even better than that, but two thirds of the loungers accepted the invitation at once.

It was noon when the body of Tennessee was delivered into the hands of his partner. As the cart drew up to the fatal tree, we noticed that it contained a rough oblong box,—apparently made from a section of sluicing,—and half filled with bark and the tassels of pine. The cart was further decorated with slips of willow and made fragrant with buckeye-blossoms. When the body was deposited in the box, Tennessee's Partner drew over it a piece of tarred canvas, and gravely mounting the narrow seat in front, with his feet upon the shafts, urged the little donkey forward. The equipage moved slowly on, at that decorous pace which was habitual with Jenny even under less solemn circumstances. The men—half curiously, half jestingly, but all good-humoredly—strolled along beside the cart, some in advance, some a little in the rear of the homely catafalque. But whether from the narrowing of the road or some present sense of decorum, as the cart passed on, the company fell to the rear in couples, keeping step, and otherwise assuming the external show of a formal procession. Jack Folinsbee, who had at the outset played a funeral march in dumb show upon an imaginary trombone, desisted from a lack of sympathy and appreciation,—not having, perhaps, your true humorist's capacity to be content with the enjoyment of his own fun.

The way led through Grizzly Canon, by this time clothed in funereal drapery and shadows. The redwoods, burying their moccasined feet in the red soil, stood in Indian file along the track, trailing an uncouth benediction from their bending boughs upon the passing bier. A hare, surprised into helpless inactivity, sat upright and pulsating in the ferns by the roadside as the cortege went by. Squirrels hastened to gain a secure outlook from higher boughs; and the blue-jays, spreading their wings, fluttered before them like outriders, until the outskirts of Sandy Bar were reached, and the solitary cabin of Tennessee's Partner.

Viewed under more favorable circumstances, it would not have been a cheerful place. The unpicturesque site, the rude and unlovely outlines, the unsavory details, which distinguish the nest-building of the California miner, were all here with the dreariness of decay superadded. A few paces from the cabin there was a rough inclosure, which, in the brief days of Tennessee's Partner's matrimonial felicity, had been used as a garden, but was now overgrown with fern. As we approached it, we were surprised to find that what we had taken for a recent attempt at cultivation was the broken soil about an open grave.

The cart was halted before the inclosure, and rejecting the offers of assistance with the same air of simple self-reliance he had displayed throughout, Tennessee's Partner lifted the rough coffin on his back, and deposited it unaided within the shallow grave. He then nailed down the board which served as a lid, and mounting the little mound of earth beside it, took off his hat and slowly mopped his face with his handkerchief. This the crowd felt was a preliminary to speech, and they disposed themselves variously on stumps and boulders, and sat expectant.

"When a man," began Tennessee's Partner slowly, "has been running free all day, what's the natural thing for him to do? Why, to come home. And if he ain't in a condition to go home, what can his best friend do? Why, bring him home. And here's Tennessee has been running free, and we brings him home from his wandering." He paused and picked up a fragment of quartz, rubbed it thoughtfully on his sleeve, and went on: "It ain't the first time that I've packed him on my back, as you see'd me now. It ain't the first time that I brought him to this yer cabin when he couldn't help himself; it ain't the first time that I and Jinny have waited for him on yon hill, and picked him up and so fetched him home, when he couldn't speak and didn't know me. And now that it's the last time, why"—he paused and rubbed the quartz gently on his sleeve—"you see it's sort of rough on his pardner. And now, gentlemen" he added abruptly, picking up his long-handled shovel, "the fun'l's over; and my thanks, and Tennessee's thanks, to you for your trouble."

Resisting any proffers of assistance, he began to fill in the grave, turning his back upon the crowd, that after a few moments' hesitation gradually withdrew. As they crossed the little ridge that hid Sandy Bar from view, some, looking back, thought they could see Tennessee's Partner, his work done, sitting upon the grave, his shovel between his knees, and his face buried in his red bandana handkerchief. But it was argued by others that you couldn't tell his face from his handkerchief at that distance, and this point remained undecided.

In the reaction that followed the feverish excitement of that day, Tennessee's Partner was not forgotten. A secret investigation had cleared him of any complicity in Tennessee's guilt, and left only a suspicion of his general sanity. Sandy Bar made a point of calling on him, and proffering various uncouth but well-meant kindnesses. But from that day his rude health and great strength seemed visibly to decline; and when the rainy season fairly set in, and the tiny grass-blades were beginning to peep from the rocky mound above Tennessee's grave, he took to his bed.

One night, when the pines beside the cabin were swaying in the storm and trailing their slender fingers over the roof, and the roar and rush of the swollen river were heard below, Tennessee's Partner lifted his head from the pillow, saying, "It is time to go for Tennessee; I must put Jinny in the cart;" and would have risen from his bed but for the restraint of his attendant. Struggling, he still pursued his singular fancy: "There, now, steady, Jinny,—steady, old girl. How dark it is! Look out for the ruts,—and look out for him, too, old gal. Sometimes, you know, when he's blind drunk, he drops down right in the trail. Keep on straight up to the pine on the top of the hill. Thar! I told you so!—thar he is,—coming this way, too,—all by himself, sober, and his face a-shining. Tennessee! Pardner!"

And so they met.

THE IDYL OF BED GULCH

andy was very drunk. He was lying under an azalea-bush, in pretty much the same attitude in which he had fallen some hours before. How long he had been lying there he could not tell, and didn't care; how long he should lie there was a matter equally indefinite and unconsidered. A tranquil philosophy, born of his physical condition, suffused and saturated his moral being.

The spectacle of a drunken man, and of this drunken man in particular, was not, I grieve to say, of sufficient novelty in Red Gulch to attract attention. Earlier in the day some local satirist had erected a temporary tombstone at Sandy's head, bearing the inscription, "Effects of McCorkle's whiskey—kills at forty rods," with a hand pointing to McCorkle's saloon. But this, I imagine, was, like most local satire, personal; and was a reflection upon the unfairness of the process rather than a commentary upon the impropriety of the result. With this facetious exception, Sandy had been undisturbed. A wandering mule, released from his pack, had cropped the scant herbage beside him, and sniffed curiously at the prostrate man; a vagabond dog, with that deep sympathy which the species have for drunken men, had licked his dusty boots and curled himself up at his feet, and lay there, blinking one eye in the sunlight, with a simulation of dissipation that was ingenious and dog-like in its implied flattery of the unconscious man beside him.

Meanwhile the shadows of the pine-trees had slowly swung around until they crossed the road, and their trunks barred the open meadow with gigantic parallels of black and yellow. Little puffs of red dust, lifted by the plunging hoofs of passing teams, dispersed in a grimy shower upon the recumbent man. The sun sank lower and lower, and still Sandy stirred not. And then the repose of this philosopher was disturbed, as other philosophers have been, by the intrusion of an unphilosophical sex.

"Miss Mary," as she was known to the little flock that she had just dismissed from the log schoolhouse beyond the pines, was taking her afternoon walk. Observing an unusually fine cluster of blossoms on the azalea-bush opposite, she crossed the road to pluck it, picking her way through the red dust, not without certain fierce little shivers of disgust and some feline circumlocution. And then she came suddenly upon Sandy!

Of course she uttered the little staccato cry of her sex. But when she had paid that tribute to her physical weakness she became overbold and halted for a moment,—at least six feet from this prostrate monster,—with her white skirts gathered in her hand, ready for flight. But neither sound nor motion came from the bush. With one little foot she then overturned the satirical headboard, and muttered "Beasts!"—an epithet which probably, at that moment, conveniently classified in her mind the entire male population of Red Gulch. For Miss Mary, being possessed of certain rigid notions of her own, had not, perhaps, properly appreciated the demonstrative gallantry for which the Californian has been so justly celebrated by his brother Californians, and had, as a newcomer, perhaps fairly earned the reputation of being "stuck up."

As she stood there she noticed, also, that the slant sunbeams were heating Sandy's head to what she judged to be an unhealthy temperature, and that his hat was lying uselessly at his side. To pick it up and to place it over his face was a work requiring some courage, particularly as his eyes were open. Yet she did it and made good her retreat. But she was somewhat concerned, on looking back, to see that the hat was removed, and that Sandy was sitting up and saying something.

The truth was, that in the calm depths of Sandy's mind he was satisfied that the rays of the sun were beneficial and healthful; that from childhood he had objected to lying down in a hat; that no people but condemned fools, past redemption, ever wore hats; and that his right to dispense, with them when he pleased was inalienable. This was the statement of his inner consciousness. Unfortunately, its outward expression was vague, being limited to a repetition of the following formula: "Su'shine all ri'! Wasser maar, eh? Wass up, su'shine?"

Miss Mary stopped, and, taking fresh courage from her vantage of distance, asked him if there was anything that he wanted.

"Wass up? Wasser maar?" continued Sandy, in a very high key.

"Get up, you horrid man!" said Miss Mary, now thoroughly incensed; "get up and go home."

Sandy staggered to his feet. He was six feet high, and Miss Mary trembled. He started forward a few paces and then stopped.

"Wass I go home for?" he suddenly asked, with great gravity.

"Go and take a bath," replied Miss Mary, eying his grimy person with great disfavor.

To her infinite dismay, Sandy suddenly pulled off his coat and vest, threw them on the ground, kicked off his boots, and, plunging wildly forward, darted headlong over the hill in the direction of the river.

"Goodness heavens! the man will be drowned!" said Miss Mary; and then, with feminine inconsistency, she ran back to the schoolhouse and locked herself in. That night, while seated at supper with her hostess, the blacksmith's wife, it came to Miss Mary to ask, demurely, if her husband ever got drunk. "Abner," responded Mrs. Stidger reflectively,—"let's see! Abner hasn't been tight since last 'lection." Miss Mary would have liked to ask if he preferred lying in the sun on these occasions, and if a cold bath would have hurt him; but this would have involved an explanation, which she did not then care to give. So she contented herself with opening her gray eyes widely at the red-cheeked Mrs. Stidger,—a fine specimen of Southwestern efflorescence,—and then dismissed the subject altogether. The next day she wrote to her dearest friend in Boston: "I think I find the intoxicated portion of this community the least objectionable, I refer, my dear, to the men, of course. I do not know anything that could make the women tolerable."

In less than a week Miss Mary had forgotten this episode, except that her afternoon walks took thereafter, almost unconsciously, another direction. She noticed, however, that every morning a fresh cluster of azalea blossoms appeared among the flowers on her desk. This was not strange, as her little flock were aware of her fondness for flowers, and invariably kept her desk bright with anemones, syringas, and lupines; but, on questioning them, they one and all professed ignorance of the azaleas. A few days later, Master Johnny Stidger, whose desk was nearest to the window, was suddenly taken with spasms of apparently gratuitous laughter, that threatened the discipline of the school. All that Miss Mary could get from him was, that some one had been "looking in the winder." Irate and indignant, she sallied from her hive to do battle with the intruder. As she turned the corner of the schoolhouse she came plump upon the quondam drunkard, now perfectly sober, and inexpressibly sheepish and guilty-looking.

These facts Miss Mary was not slow to take a feminine advantage of, in her present humor. But it was somewhat confusing to observe, also, that the beast, despite some faint signs of past dissipation, was amiable-looking,—in fact, a kind of blond Samson, whose corn-colored silken beard apparently had never yet known the touch of barber's razor or Delilah's shears. So that the cutting speech which quivered on her ready tongue died upon her lips, and she contented herself with receiving his stammering apology with supercilious eyelids and the gathered skirts of uncontamination. When she reentered the schoolroom, her eyes fell upon the azaleas with a new sense of revelation; and then she laughed, and the little people all laughed, and they were all unconsciously very happy.

It was a hot day, and not long after this, that two short-legged boys came to grief on the threshold of the school with a pail of water, which they had laboriously brought from the spring, and that Miss Mary compassionately seized the pail and started for the spring herself. At the foot of the hill a shadow crossed her path, and a blue-shirted arm dexterously but gently relieved her of her burden. Miss Mary was both embarrassed and angry. "If you carried more of that for yourself," she said spitefully to the blue arm, without deigning to raise her lashes to its owner, "you'd do better." In the submissive silence that followed she regretted the speech, and thanked him so sweetly at the door that he stumbled. Which caused the children to laugh again,—a laugh in which Miss Mary joined, until the color came faintly into her pale cheek. The next day a barrel was mysteriously placed beside the door, and as mysteriously filled with fresh spring-water every morning.

Nor was this superior young person without other quiet attentions. "Profane Bill," driver of the Slumgullion Stage, widely known in the newspapers for his "gallantry" in invariably offering the box-seat to the fair sex, had excepted Miss Mary from this attention, on the ground that he had a habit of "cussin' on up grades," and gave her half the coach to herself. Jack Hamlin, a gambler, having once silently ridden with her in the same coach, afterward threw a decanter at the head of a confederate for mentioning her name in a bar-room. The over-dressed mother of a pupil whose paternity was doubtful had often lingered near this astute Vestal's temple, never daring to enter its sacred precincts, but content to worship the priestess from afar.

With such unconscious intervals the monotonous procession of blue skies, glittering sunshine, brief twilights, and starlit nights passed over Red Gulch. Miss Mary grew fond of walking in the sedate and proper woods. Perhaps she believed, with Mrs. Stidger, that the balsamic odors of the firs "did her chest good," for certainly her slight cough was less frequent and her step was firmer; perhaps she had learned the unending lesson which the patient pines are never weary of repeating to heedful or listless ears. And so one day she planned a picnic on Buckeye Hill, and took the children with her. Away from the dusty road, the straggling shanties, the yellow ditches, the clamor of restless engines, the cheap finery of shop-windows, the deeper glitter of paint and colored glass, and the thin veneering which barbarism takes upon itself in such localities, what infinite relief was theirs! The last heap of ragged rock and clay passed, the last unsightly chasm crossed,—how the waiting woods opened their long files to receive them! How the children—perhaps because they had not yet grown quite away from the breast of the bounteous Mother—threw themselves face downward on her brown bosom with uncouth caresses, filling the air with their laughter; and how Miss Mary herself—felinely fastidious and intrenched as she was in the purity of spotless skirts, collar, and cuffs—forgot all, and ran like a crested quail at the head of her brood, until, romping, laughing, and panting, with a loosened braid of brown hair, a hat hanging by a knotted ribbon from her throat, she came suddenly and violently, in the heart of the forest, upon the luckless Sandy!

The explanations, apologies, and not overwise conversation that ensued need not be indicated here. It would seem, however, that Miss Mary had already established some acquaintance with this ex-drunkard. Enough that he was soon accepted as one of the party; that the children, with that quick intelligence which Providence gives the helpless, recognized a friend, and played with his blond beard and long silken mustache, and took other liberties,—as the helpless are apt to do. And when he had built a fire against a tree, and had shown them other mysteries of woodcraft, their admiration knew no bounds. At the close of two such foolish, idle, happy hours he found himself lying at the feet of the schoolmistress, gazing dreamily in her face as she sat upon the sloping hillside weaving wreaths of laurel and syringa, in very much the same attitude as he had lain when first they met. Nor was the similitude greatly forced. The weakness of an easy, sensuous nature, that had found a dreamy exaltation in liquor, it is to be feared was now finding an equal intoxication in love.

I think that Sandy was dimly conscious of this himself. I know that he longed to be doing something,—slaying a grizzly, scalping a savage, or sacrificing himself in some way for the sake of this sallow-faced, gray-eyed schoolmistress. As I should like to present him in an heroic attitude, I stay my hand with great difficulty at this moment, being only withheld from introducing such an episode by a strong conviction that it does not usually occur at such times. And I trust that my fairest reader, who remembers that, in a real crisis, it is always some uninteresting stranger or unromantic policeman, and not Adolphus, who rescues, will forgive the omission.

So they sat there undisturbed,—the woodpeckers chattering overhead and the voices of the children coming pleasantly from the hollow below. What they said matters little. What they thought—which might have been interesting—did not transpire. The woodpeckers only learned how Miss Mary was an orphan; how she left her uncle's house to come to California for the sake of health and independence; how Sandy was an orphan too; how he came to California for excitement; how he had lived a wild life, and how he was trying to reform; and other details, which, from a woodpecker's view-point, undoubtedly must have seemed stupid and a waste of time. But even in such trifles was the afternoon spent; and when the children were again gathered, and Sandy, with a delicacy which the schoolmistress well understood, took leave of them quietly at the outskirts of the settlement, it had seemed the shortest day of her weary life.

As the long, dry summer withered to its roots, the school term of Red Gulch—to use a local euphuism—"dried up" also. In another day Miss Mary would be free, and for a season, at least, Red Gulch would know her no more. She was seated alone in the schoolhouse, her cheek resting on her hand, her eyes half closed in one of those daydreams in which Miss Mary, I fear, to the danger of school discipline, was lately in the habit of indulging. Her lap was full of mosses, ferns, and other woodland memories. She was so preoccupied with these and her own thoughts that a gentle tapping at the door passed unheard, or translated itself into the remembrance of far-off woodpeckers. When at last it asserted itself more distinctly, she started up with a flushed cheek and opened the door. On the threshold stood a woman, the self-assertion and audacity of whose dress were in singular contrast to her timid, irresolute bearing. Miss Mary recognized at a glance the dubious mother of her anonymous pupil. Perhaps she was disappointed, perhaps she was only fastidious; but as she coldly invited her to enter, she half unconsciously settled her white cuffs and collar, and gathered closer her own chaste skirts. It was, perhaps, for this reason that the embarrassed stranger, after a moment's hesitation, left her gorgeous parasol open and sticking in the dust beside the door, and then sat down at the farther end of a long bench. Her voice was husky as she began,—

"I heerd tell that you were goin' down to the Bay tomorrow, and I couldn't let you go until I came to thank you for your kindness to my

Tommy." Tommy, Miss Mary said, was a good boy, and deserved more than the poor attention she could give him.

"Thank you, miss; thank ye!" cried the stranger, brightening even through the color which Red Gulch knew facetiously as her "war paint," and striving, in her embarrassment, to drag the long bench nearer the schoolmistress. "I thank you, miss, for that; and if I am his mother, there ain't a sweeter, dearer, better boy lives than him. And if I ain't much as says it, thar ain't a sweeter, dearer, angeler teacher lives than he's got."

Miss Mary, sitting primly behind her desk, with a ruler over her shoulder, opened her gray eyes widely at this, but said nothing.

"It ain't for you to be complimented by the like of me, I know," she went on hurriedly. "It ain't for me to be comin' here, in broad day, to do it, either; but I come to ask a favor,—not for me, miss,—not for me, but for the darling boy."

Encouraged by a look in the young schoolmistress's eye, and putting her lilac-gloved hands together, the fingers downward, between her knees, she went on, in a low voice:—

"You see, miss, there's no one the boy has any claim on but me, and I ain't the proper person to bring him up. I thought some, last year, of sending him away to Frisco to school, but when they talked of bringing a schoolma'am here, I waited till I saw you, and then I knew it was all right, and I could keep my boy a little longer. And, oh! miss, he loves you so much; and if you could hear him talk about you in his pretty way, and if he could ask you what I ask you now, you couldn't refuse him.

"It is natural," she went on rapidly, in a voice that trembled strangely between pride and humility,—"it's natural that he should take to you, miss, for his father, when I first knew him, was a gentleman,—and the boy must forget me, sooner or later,—and so I ain't a-goin' to cry about that. For I come to ask you to take my Tommy,—God bless him for the bestest, sweetest boy that lives,—to—to—take him with you."

She had risen and caught the young girl's hand in her own, and had fallen on her knees beside her.

"I've money plenty, and it's all yours and his. Put him in some

59

good school, where you can go and see him, and help him to—to—to forget his mother. Do with him what you like. The worst you can do will be kindness to what he will learn with me. Only take him out of this wicked life, this cruel place, this home of shame and sorrow. You will! I know you will,—won't you? You will,—you must not, you cannot say no! You will make him as pure, as gentle as yourself; and when he has grown-up, you will tell him his father's name,—the name that hasn't passed my lips for years,—the name of Alexander Morton, whom they call here Sandy! Miss Mary!—do not take your hand away! Miss Mary, speak to me! You will take my boy? Do not put your face from me. I know it ought not to look on such as me. Miss Mary!—my God, be merciful!—she is leaving me!" Miss Mary had risen, and, in the gathering twilight, had felt her way to the open window. She stood there, leaning against the casement, her eyes fixed on the last rosy tints that were fading from the western sky. There was still some of its light on her pure young forehead, on her white collar, on her clasped white hands, but all fading slowly away. The suppliant had dragged herself, still on her knees, beside her.

"I know it takes time to consider. I will wait here all night; but I cannot go until you speak. Do not deny me now. You will!—I see it in your sweet face,—such a face as I have seen in my dreams. I see it in your eyes, Miss Mary!—you will take my boy!"

The last red beam crept higher, suffused Miss Mary's eyes with something of its glory, flickered, and faded, and went out. The sun had set on Red Gulch. In the twilight and silence Miss Mary's voice sounded pleasantly.

"I will take the boy. Send him to me to-night."

The happy mother raised the hem of Miss Mary's skirts to her lips. She would have buried her hot face in its virgin folds, but she dared not. She rose to her feet.

"Does—this man—know of your intention?" asked Miss Mary suddenly.

"No, nor cares. He has never even seen the child to know it."

"Go to him at once—to-night—now! Tell him what you have done.

Tell him I have taken his child, and tell him—he must never see—see—the child again. Wherever it may be, he must not come; wherever I may take it, he must not follow! There, go now, please,—I'm weary, and—have much yet to do!"

They walked together to the door. On the threshold the woman turned.

"Good-night!"

She would have fallen at Miss Mary's feet. But at the same moment the young girl reached out her arms, caught the sinful woman to her own pure breast for one brief moment, and then closed and locked the door.

It was with a sudden sense of great responsibility that Profane Bill took the reins of the Slumgullion stage the next morning, for the schoolmistress was one of his passengers. As he entered the highroad, in obedience to a pleasant voice from the "inside," he suddenly reined up his horses and respectfully waited, as Tommy hopped out at the command of Miss Mary.

"Not that bush, Tommy,—the next."

Tommy whipped out his new pocket-knife, and cutting a branch from a tall azalea-bush, returned with it to Miss Mary. "All right now?"

"All right!"

And the stage-door closed on the Idyl of Red Gulch.

BROWN OF CALAVERAS

A subdued tone of conversation, and the absence of cigar-smoke and boot-heels at the windows of the Wingdam stagecoach, made it evident that one of the inside passengers was a woman. A disposition on the part of loungers at the stations to congregate before the window, and some concern in regard to the appearance of coats, hats, and collars, further indicated that she was lovely. All of which Mr. Jack Hamlin, on the box-seat, noted with the smile of cynical philosophy. Not that he depreciated the sex, but that he recognized therein a deceitful element, the pursuit of which sometimes drew mankind away from the equally uncertain blandishments of poker,—of which it may be remarked that Mr. Hamlin was a professional exponent.

So that, when he placed his narrow boot on the wheel and leaped down, he did not even glance at the window from which a green veil was fluttering, but lounged up and down with that listless and grave indifference of his class, which was, perhaps, the next thing to good-breeding. With his closely buttoned figure and self-contained air he was a marked contrast to the other passengers, with their feverish restlessness and boisterous emotion; and even Bill Masters, a graduate of Harvard, with his slovenly dress, his over-flowing vitality, his intense appreciation of lawlessness and barbarism, and his mouth filled with crackers and cheese, I fear cut but an unromantic figure beside this lonely calculator of chances, with his pale Greek face and Homeric gravity.

The driver called "All aboard!" and Mr. Hamlin returned to the coach. His foot was upon the wheel, and his face raised to the level of the open window, when, at the same moment, what appeared to him to be the finest eyes in the world suddenly met his. He quietly dropped down again, addressed a few words to one of the inside passengers, effected an exchange of seats, and as quietly took his place inside. Mr. Hamlin never allowed his philosophy to interfere with decisive and prompt action.

I fear that this irruption of Jack cast some restraint upon the other passengers, particularly those who were making themselves most agreeable to the lady. One of them leaned forward, and apparently conveyed to her information regarding Mr. Hamlin's profession in a single epithet. Whether Mr. Hamlin heard it, or whether he recognized in the informant a distinguished jurist, from whom, but a few evenings before, he had won several thousand dollars, I cannot say. His colorless face betrayed no sign; his black eyes, quietly observant, glanced indifferently past the legal gentleman, and rested on the much more pleasing features of his neighbor. An Indian stoicism—said to be an inheritance from his maternal ancestor—stood him in good service, until the rolling wheels rattled upon the river gravel at Scott's Ferry, and the stage drew up at the International Hotel for dinner. The legal gentleman and a member of Congress leaped out, and stood ready to assist the descending goddess, while Colonel Starbottle of Siskiyou took charge of her parasol and shawl. In this multiplicity of attention there was a momentary confusion and delay. Jack Hamlin quietly opened the *opposite* door of the coach, took the lady›s hand, with that decision and positiveness which a hesitating and undecided sex know how to admire, and in an instant had dexterously and gracefully swung her to the ground and again lifted her to the platform. An audible chuckle on the box, I fear, came from that other cynic, Yuba Bill, the driver. "Look keerfully arter that baggage, Kernel," said the expressman, with affected concern, as he looked after Colonel Starbottle, gloomily bringing up the rear of the triumphant procession to the waiting-room.

Mr. Hamlin did not stay for dinner. His horse was already saddled and awaiting him. He dashed over the ford, up the gravelly hill, and out into the dusty perspective of the Wingdam road, like one leaving an unpleasant fancy behind him. The inmates uf dusty cabins by the roadside shaded their eyes with their hands and looked after him, recognizing the man by his horse, and speculating what "was up with Comanche Jack." Yet much of this interest centred in the horse, in a community where the time made by "French Pete's" mare, in his run from the Sheriff of Calaveras, eclipsed all concern in the ultimate fate of that worthy.

The sweating flanks of his gray at length recalled him to himself. He checked his speed, and turning into a byroad, sometimes used as a cut-off, trotted leisurely along, the reins hanging listlessly from his fingers. As he rode on, the character of the landscape changed and became more pastoral. Openings in groves of pine and sycamore disclosed some rude attempts at cultivation,—a flowering vine trailed over the porch of one cabin, and a woman rocked her cradled babe under the roses of another. A little farther on, Mr. Hamlin came upon some bare-legged children wading in the willowy creek, and so wrought upon them with a badinage peculiar to himself, that they were emboldened to climb up his horse's legs and over his saddle, until he was fain to develop an exaggerated ferocity of demeanor, and to escape, leaving behind some kisses and coin. And then, advancing deeper into the woods, where all signs of habitation failed, he began to sing, uplifting a tenor so singularly sweet, and shaded by a pathos so subdued and tender, that I wot the robins and linnets stopped to listen. Mr. Hamlin's voice was not cultivated; the subject of his song was some sentimental lunacy, borrowed from the negro minstrels; but there thrilled through all some occult quality of tone and expression that was unspeakably touching. Indeed, it was a wonderful sight to see this sentimental blackleg, with a pack of cards in his pocket and a revolver at his back, sending his voice before him through the dim woods with a plaint about his "Nelly's grave," in a way that overflowed the eyes of the listener. A sparrow-hawk, fresh from his sixth victim, possibly recognizing in Mr. Hamlin a kindred spirit, stared at him in surprise, and was fain to confess the superiority of man. With a superior predatory capacity *he* couldn't sing.

But Mr. Hamlin presently found himself again on the highroad and at his former pace. Ditches and banks of gravel, denuded hillsides, stumps, and decayed trunks of trees, took the place of woodland and ravine, and indicated his approach to civilization. Then a church-steeple came in sight, and he knew that he had reached home. In a few moments he was clattering down the single narrow street that lost itself in a chaotic ruin of races, ditches, and tailings at the foot of the hill, and dismounted before the gilded windows of the Magnolia saloon. Passing through the long bar-room, he pushed open a green-baize door, entered a dark passage, opened another door with a passkey, and found himself in a dimly lighted room, whose furniture, though elegant and costly for the locality, showed signs of abuse. The inlaid centre-table was overlaid with stained disks that were not contemplated in the original design, the embroidered armchairs were discolored, and the green velvet lounge, on which Mr. Hamlin threw himself, was soiled at the foot with the red soil of Wingdam.

Mr. Hamlin did not sing in his cage. He lay still, looking at a highly colored painting above him, representing a young creature of opulent charms. It occurred to him then, for the first time, that he had never seen exactly that kind of a woman, and that, if he should, he would not, probably, fall in love with her. Perhaps he was thinking of another style of beauty. But just then some one knocked at the door. Without rising, he pulled a cord that apparently shot back a bolt, for the door swung open, and a man entered.

The new-comer was broad-shouldered and robust,—a vigor not borne out in the face, which, though handsome, was singularly weak and disfigured by dissipation. He appeared to be, also, under the influence of liquor, for he started on seeing Mr. Hamlin, and said, "I thought Kate was here;" stammered, and seemed confused and embarrassed.

Mr. Hamlin smiled the smile which he had before worn on the Wingdam coach, and sat up, quite refreshed and ready for business.

"You didn't come up on the stage," continued the newcomer, "did you?"

"No," replied Hamlin; "I left it at Scott's Ferry. It isn't due for half an hour yet. But how's luck, Brown?"

"D—d bad," said Brown, his face suddenly assuming an expression of weak despair. "I'm cleaned out again, Jack," he continued, in a whining tone, that formed a pitiable contrast to his bulky figure; "can't you help me with a hundred till to-morrow's clean-up? You see I've got to send money home to the old woman, and—you've won twenty times that amount from me."

The conclusion was, perhaps, not entirely logical, but Jack overlooked it, and handed the sum to his visitor. "The old-woman business is about played out, Brown," he added, by way of commentary; "why don't you say you want to buck ag'in' faro? You know you ain't married!"

"Fact, sir," said Brown, with a sudden gravity, as if the mere contact of the gold with the palm of the hand had imparted some dignity to his frame. "I've got a wife—a d—d good one, too, if I do say it—in the States. It's three years since I've seen her, and a year since I've writ to her. When things is about straight, and we get down to the lead, I'm going to send for her."

"And Kate?" queried Mr. Hamlin, with his previous smile.

Mr. Brown of Calaveras essayed an archness of glance to cover his confusion, which his weak face and whiskey-muddled intellect but poorly carried out, and said,—

"D—n it, Jack, a man must have a little liberty, you know. But come, what do you say to a little game? Give us a show to double this hundred."

Jack Hamlin looked curiously at his fatuous friend. Perhaps he knew that the man was predestined to lose the money, and preferred that it should flow back into his own coffers rather than any other. He nodded his head, and drew his chair toward the table. At the same moment there came a rap upon the door.

"It's Kate," said Mr. Brown.

Mr. Hamlin shot back the bolt and the door opened. But, for the first time in his life, he staggered to his feet utterly unnerved and abashed, and for the first time in his life the hot blood crimsoned his colorless cheeks to his forehead. For before him stood the lady he had lifted from the Wingdam coach, whom Brown, dropping his cards with a hysterical laugh, greeted as,—

"My old woman, by thunder!"

They say that Mrs. Brown burst into tears and reproaches of her husband. I saw her in 1857 at Marysville, and disbelieve the story. And the "Wingdam Chronicle" of the next week, under the head of "Touching Reunion," said: "One of those beautiful and touching incidents, peculiar to California life, occurred last week in our city. The wife of one of Wingdam's eminent pioneers, tired of the effete civilization of the East and its inhospitable climate, resolved to join her noble husband upon these golden shores. Without informing him of her intention, she undertook the long journey, and arrived last week. The joy of the husband may be easier imagined than described. The meeting is said to have been indescribably affecting. We trust her example may be followed."

Whether owing to Mrs. Brown's influence, or to some more successful speculations, Mr. Brown's financial fortune from that day steadily improved. He bought out his partners in the "Nip and Tuck" lead, with money which was said to have been won at poker a week or two after his wife's arrival, but which rumor, adopting Mrs. Brown's theory that Brown had forsworn the gaming-table, declared to have been furnished by Mr. Jack Hamlin. He built and furnished the Wingdam House, which pretty Mrs. Brown's great popularity kept overflowing with guests. He was elected to the Assembly, and gave largess to churches. A street in Wingdam was named in his honor.

Yet it was noted that in proportion as he waxed wealthy and fortunate, he grew pale, thin, and anxious. As his wife's popularity increased, he became fretful and impatient. The most uxorious of husbands, he was absurdly jealous. If he did not interfere with his wife's social liberty, it was because it was maliciously whispered that his first and only attempt was met by an outburst from Mrs. Brown that terrified him into silence. Much of this kind of gossip came from those of her own sex whom she had supplanted in the chivalrous attentions of Wingdam, which, like most popular chivalry, was devoted to an admiration of power, whether of masculine force or feminine beauty. It should be remembered, too, in her extenuation, that, since her arrival, she had been the unconscious priestess of a mythological worship, perhaps not more ennobling to her womanhood than that which distinguished an older Greek democracy. I think that Brown was dimly conscious of this. But his only confidant was Jack Hamlin, whose infelix reputation naturally precluded any open intimacy with the family, and whose visits were infrequent.

It was midsummer and a moonlit night, and Mrs. Brown, very rosy, large-eyed, and pretty, sat upon the piazza, enjoying the fresh incense of the mountain breeze, and, it is to be feared, another incense which was not so fresh nor quite as innocent. Beside her sat Colonel Starbottle and Judge Boompointer, and a later addition to her court in the shape of a foreign tourist. She was in good spirits.

"What do you see down the road?" inquired the gallant Colonel, who had been conscious, for the last few minutes, that Mrs. Brown's attention was diverted.

"Dust," said Mrs. Brown, with a sigh. "Only Sister Anne's 'flock of sheep.'"

The Colonel, whose literary recollections did not extend farther back than last week's paper, took a more practical view. "It ain't sheep," he continued; "it's a horseman. Judge, ain't that Jack Hamlin's gray?"

But the Judge didn't know; and, as Mrs. Brown suggested the air was growing too cold for further investigations, they retired to the parlor.

Mr. Brown was in the stable, where he generally retired after dinner. Perhaps it was to show his contempt for his wife's companions; perhaps, like other weak natures, he found pleasure in the exercise of absolute power over inferior animals. He had a certain gratification in the training of a chestnut mare, whom he could beat or caress as pleased him, which he couldn't do with Mrs. Brown. It was here that he recognized a certain gray horse which had just come in, and, looking a little farther on, found his rider. Brown's greeting was cordial and hearty; Mr. Hamlin's somewhat restrained. But, at Brown's urgent request, he followed him up the back stairs to a narrow corridor, and thence to a small room looking out upon the stable-yard. It was plainly furnished with a bed, a table, a few chairs, and a rack for guns and whips.

"This yer's my home, Jack," said Brown with a sigh, as he threw himself upon the bed and motioned his companion to a chair. "Her room's t' other end of the hall. It's more'n six months since we've lived together, or met, except at meals. It's mighty rough papers on the head of the house, ain't it?" he said with a forced laugh. "But I'm glad to see you, Jack, d—d glad," and he reached from the bed, and again shook the unresponsive hand of Jack Hamlin.

"I brought ye up here, for I didn't want to talk in the stable; though, for the matter of that, it's all round town. Don't strike a light. We can talk here in the moonshine. Put up your feet on that winder and sit here beside me. Thar's whiskey in that jug."

Mr. Hamlin did not avail himself of the information. Brown of Calaveras turned his face to the wall, and continued,—

"If I didn't love the woman, Jack, I wouldn't mind. But it's loving her, and seeing her day arter day goin' on at this rate, and no one to put down the brake; that's what gits me! But I'm glad to see ye, Jack, d—d glad."

In the darkness he groped about until he had found and wrung his companion's hand again. He would have detained it, but Jack slipped it into the buttoned breast of his coat, and asked listlessly, "How long has this been going on?"

"Ever since she came here; ever since the day she walked into the Magnolia. I was a fool then; Jack, I'm a fool now; but I didn't know how much I loved her till then. And she hasn't been the same woman since.

"But that ain't all, Jack; and it's what I wanted to see you about, and I'm glad you've come. It ain't that she doesn't love me any more; it ain't that she fools with every chap that comes along; for perhaps I staked her love and lost it, as I did everything else at the Magnolia; and perhaps foolin' is natral to some women, and thar ain't no great harm done, 'cept to the fools. But, Jack, I think,—I think she loves somebody else. Don't move, Jack! don't move; if your pistol hurts ye, take it off.

"It's been more'n six months now that she's seemed unhappy and lonesome, and kinder nervous and scared-like. And sometimes I've ketched her lookin' at me sort of timid and pitying. And she writes to somebody. And for the last week she's been gathering her own things,—trinkets, and furbelows, and jew'lry,—and, Jack, I think she's goin' off. I could stand all but that. To have her steal away like a thief!" He put his face downward to the pillow, and for a few moments there was no sound but the ticking of a clock on the mantel. Mr. Hamlin lit a cigar, and moved to the open window. The moon no longer shone into the room, and the bed and its occupant were in shadow. "What shall I do, Jack?" said the voice from the darkness.

The answer came promptly and clearly from the window-side, "Spot the man, and kill him on sight."

"But, Jack"—

"He's took the risk!"

"But will that bring her back?"

Jack did not reply, but moved from the window towards the door.

"Don't go yet, Jack; light the candle and sit by the table. It's a comfort to see ye, if nothin' else."

Jack hesitated and then complied. He drew a pack of cards from his pocket and shuffled them, glancing at the bed. But Brown's face was turned to the wall. When Mr. Hamlin had shuffled the cards, he cut them, and dealt one card on the opposite side of the table towards the bed, and another on his side of the table for himself. The first was a deuce; his own card a king. He then shuffled and cut again. This time "dummy" had a queen and himself a four-spot. Jack brightened up for the third deal. It brought his adversary a deuce and himself a king again. "Two out of three," said Jack audibly.

"What's that, Jack?" said Brown.

"Nothing."

Then Jack tried his hand with dice; but he always threw sixes and his imaginary opponent aces. The force of habit is sometimes confusing.

Meanwhile some magnetic influence in Mr. Hamlin's presence, or the anodyne of liquor, or both, brought surcease of sorrow, and Brown slept. Mr. Hamlin moved his chair to the window and looked out on the town of Wingdam, now sleeping peacefully, its harsh outlines softened and subdued, its glaring colors mellowed and sobered in the moonlight that flowed over all. In the hush he could hear the gurgling of water in the ditches and the sighing of the pines beyond the hill. Then he looked up at the firmament, and as he did so a star shot across the twinkling field. Presently another, and then another. The phenomenon suggested to Mr. Hamlin a fresh augury. If in another fifteen minutes another star should fall—He sat there, watch in hand, for twice that time, but the phenomenon was not repeated.

The clock struck two, and Brown still slept. Mr. Hamlin approached the table and took from his pocket a letter, which he read by the flickering candlelight. It contained only a single line, written in pencil, in a woman's hand,—

"Be at the corral with the buggy at three."

The sleeper moved uneasily and then awoke. "Are you there, Jack?"

"Yes."

"Don't go yet. I dreamed just now, Jack,—dreamed of old times. I thought that Sue and me was being married agin, and that the parson, Jack, was—who do you think?—you!"

The gambler laughed, and seated himself on the bed, the paper still in his hand.

"It's a good sign, ain't it?" queried Brown.

"I reckon! Say, old man, hadn't you better get up?"

The "old man," thus affectionately appealed to, rose, with the assistance of Hamlin's outstretched hand.

"Smoke?"

Brown mechanically took the proffered cigar.

"Light?"

Jack had twisted the letter into a spiral, lit it, and held it for his companion. He continued to hold it until it was consumed, and dropped the fragment—a fiery star—from the open window. He watched it as it fell, and then returned to his friend.

"Old man," he said, placing his hands upon Brown's shoulders, "in ten minutes I'll be on the road, and gone like that spark. We won't see each other agin; but, before I go, take a fool's advice: sell out all you've got, take your wife with you, and quit the country. It ain't no place for you nor her. Tell her she must go; make her go if she won't. Don't whine because you can't be a saint and she ain't an angel. Be a man, and treat her like a woman. Don't be a d-d fool. Good-by."

He tore himself from Brown's grasp and leaped down the stairs like a deer. At the stable-door he collared the half-sleeping hostler, and backed him against the wall. "Saddle my horse in two minutes, or I'll"—The ellipsis was frightfully suggestive.

"The missis said you was to have the buggy," stammered the man.

"D—n the buggy!" The horse was saddled as fast as the nervous hands of the astounded hostler could manipulate buckle and strap.

"Is anything up, Mr. Hamlin?" said the man, who, like all his class, admired the elan of his fiery patron, and was really concerned in his welfare.

"Stand aside!"

The man fell back. With an oath, a bound, and clatter, Jack was into the road. In another moment, to the man's half-awakened eyes, he was but a moving cloud of dust in the distance, towards which a star just loosed from its brethren was trailing a stream of fire.

But early that morning the dwellers by the Wingdam turnpike, miles aways, heard a voice, pure as a sky-lark's, singing afield. They who were asleep turned over on their rude couches to dream of youth, and love, and olden days. Hard-faced men and anxious gold-seekers, already at work, ceased their labors and leaned upon their picks to listen to a romantic vagabond ambling away against the rosy sunrise.

CONDENSED NOVELS

MUCK-A-MUCK

A MODERN INDIAN NOVEL
AFTER COOPER

CHAPTER I

It was toward the close of a bright October day. The last rays of the setting sun were reflected from on*e of those sylvan lakes peculiar to the Sierras of California. On the right the curling smoke of an Indian village rose between the columns of the lofty pines, while to the left the log cottage of Judge Tompkins, embowered in buckeyes, completed the enchanting picture.

Although the exterior of the cottage was humble and unpretentious, and in keeping with the wildness of the landscape, its interior gave evidence of the cultivation and refinement of its inmates. An aquarium, containing goldfishes, stood on a marble centre-table at one end of the apartment, while a magnificent grand piano occupied the other. The floor was covered with a yielding tapestry carpet, and the walls were adorned with paintings from the pencils of Van Dyke, Rubens, Tintoretto, Michael Angelo, and the productions of the more modern Turner, Kensett, Church, and Bierstadt. Although Judge Tompkins had chosen the frontiers of civilization as his home, it was impossible for him to entirely forego the habits and tastes of his former life. He was seated in a luxurious armchair, writing at a mahogany escritoire, while his daughter, a lovely young girl of seventeen summers, plied her crotchet-needle on an ottoman beside him. A bright fire of pine logs flickered and flamed on the ample hearth.

Genevra Octavia Tompkins was Judge Tompkins's only child. Her mother had long since died on the Plains. Reared in affluence, no pains had been spared with the daughter's education. She was a graduate of one of the principal seminaries, and spoke French with a perfect Benicia accent. Peerlessly beautiful, she was dressed in a white moire antique robe trimmed with tulle. That simple rosebud, with which most heroines exclusively decorate their hair, was all she wore in her raven locks.

The Judge was the first to break the silence.

"Genevra, the logs which compose yonder fire seem to have been incautiously chosen. The sibilation produced by the sap, which exudes copiously therefrom, is not conducive to composition."

"True, father, but I thought it would be preferable to the constant crepitation which is apt to attend the combustion of more seasoned ligneous fragments."

The Judge looked admiringly at the intellectual features of the graceful girl, and half forgot the slight annoyances of the green wood in the musical accents of his daughter. He was smoothing her hair tenderly, when the shadow of a tall figure, which suddenly darkened the doorway, caused him to look up.

CHAPTER II

It needed but a glance at the new-comer to detect at once the form and features of the haughty aborigine,—the untaught and untrammeled son of the forest. Over one shoulder a blanket, negligently but gracefully thrown, disclosed a bare and powerful breast, decorated with a quantity of three-cent postage-stamps which he had despoiled from an Overland Mail stage a few weeks previous. A cast-off beaver of Judge Tompkins's, adorned by a simple feather, covered his erect head, from beneath which his straight locks descended. His right hand hung lightly by his side, while his left was engaged in holding on a pair of pantaloons, which the lawless grace and freedom of his lower limbs evidently could not brook.

"Why," said the Indian, in a low sweet tone,—"why does the Pale Face still follow the track of the Red Man? Why does he pursue him, even as O-kee chow, the wild cat, chases Ka-ka, the skunk? Why are the feet of Sorrel-top, the white chief, among the acorns of Muck-a-Muck, the mountain forest? Why," he repeated, quietly but firmly abstracting a silver spoon from the table,—"why do you seek to drive him from the wigwams of his fathers? His brothers are already gone to the happy hunting-grounds. Will the Pale Face seek him there?" And, averting his face from the Judge, he hastily slipped a silver cake-basket beneath his blanket, to conceal his emotion.

"Muck-a-Muck has spoken," said Genevra softly. "Let him now listen. Are the acorns of the mountain sweeter than the esculent and nutritious bean of the Pale Face miner? Does my brother prize the edible qualities of the snail above that of the crisp and oleaginous bacon? Delicious are the grasshoppers that sport on the hillside,—are they better than the dried apples of the Pale Faces? Pleasant is the gurgle of the torrent, Kish-Kish, but is it better than the cluck-cluck of old Bourbon from the old stone bottle?"

"Ugh!" said the Indian,—"ugh! good. The White Rabbit is wise. Her words fall as the snow on Tootoonolo, and the rocky heart of Muck-a-Muck is hidden. What says my brother the Gray Gopher of Dutch Flat?"

"She has spoken, Muck-a-Muck," said the Judge, gazing fondly on his daughter. "It is well. Our treaty is concluded. No, thank you,—you need *not* dance the Dance of Snow-shoes, or the Moccasin Dance, the Dance of Green Corn, or the Treaty Dance. I would be alone. A strange sadness overpowers me."

"I go," said the Indian. "Tell your great chief in Washington, the Sachem Andy, that the Red Man is retiring before the footsteps of the adventurous pioneer. Inform him, if you please, that westward the star of empire takes its way, that the chiefs of the Pi-Ute nation are for Reconstruction to a man, and that Klamath will poll a heavy Republican vote in the fall."

And folding his blanket more tightly around him, Muck-a-Muck withdrew.

CHAPTER III

Genevra Tompkins stood at the door of the log-cabin, looking after the retreating Overland Mail stage which conveyed her father to Virginia City. "He may never return again," sighed the young girl, as she glanced at the frightfully rolling vehicle and wildly careering horses,—"at least, with unbroken bones. Should he meet with an accident! I mind me now a fearful legend, familiar to my childhood. Can it be that the drivers on this line are privately instructed to dispatch all passengers maimed by accident, to prevent tedious litigation? No, no. But why this weight upon my heart?"

She seated herself at the piano and lightly passed her hand over the keys. Then, in a clear mezzo-soprano voice, she sang the first verse of one of the most popular Irish ballads:—

> "O Arrah ma dheelish, the distant dudheen
> Lies soft in the moonlight, ma bouchal vourneen:
> The springing gossoons on the heather are still,
> And the caubeens and colleens are heard on the hill."

But as the ravishing notes of her sweet voice died upon the air, her hands sank listlessly to her side. Music could not chase away the mysterious shadow from her heart. Again she rose. Putting on a white crape bonnet, and carefully drawing a pair of lemon-colored gloves over her taper fingers, she seized her parasol and plunged into the depths of the pine forest.

CHAPTER IV

Genevra had not proceeded many miles before a weariness seized upon her fragile limbs, and she would fain seat herself upon the trunk of a prostrate pine, which she previously dusted with her handkerchief. The sun was just sinking below the horizon, and the scene was one of gorgeous and sylvan beauty. "How beautiful is nature!" murmured the innocent girl, as, reclining gracefully against the root of the tree, she gathered up her skirts and tied a handkerchief around her throat. But a low growl interrupted her meditation. Starting to her feet, her eyes met a sight which froze her blood with terror.

The only outlet to the forest was the narrow path, barely wide enough for a single person, hemmed in by trees and rocks, which she had just traversed. Down this path, in Indian file, came a monstrous grizzly, closely followed by a California lion, a wild cat, and a buffalo, the rear being brought up by a wild Spanish bull. The mouths of the three first animals were distended with frightful significance, the horns of the last were lowered as ominously. As Genevra was preparing to faint, she heard a low voice behind her.

"Eternally dog-gone my skin ef this ain't the puttiest chance yet!" At the same moment, a long, shining barrel dropped lightly from behind her, and rested over her shoulder.

Genevra shuddered.

"Dern ye—don't move!"

Genevra became motionless.

The crack of a rifle rang through the woods. Three frightful yells were heard, and two sullen roars. Five animals bounded into the air and five lifeless bodies lay upon the plain. The well-aimed bullet had done its work. Entering the open throat of the grizzly it had traversed his body only to enter the throat of the California lion, and in like manner the catamount, until it passed through into the respective foreheads of the bull and the buffalo, and finally fell flattened from the rocky hillside.

Genevra turned quickly. "My preserver!" she shrieked, and fell into the arms of Natty Bumpo, the celebrated Pike Ranger of Donner Lake.

CHAPTER V

The moon rose cheerfully above Donner Lake. On its placid bosom a dug-out canoe glided rapidly, containing Natty Bumpo and Genevra Tompkins.

Both were silent. The same thought possessed each, and perhaps there was sweet companionship even in the unbroken quiet. Genevra bit the handle of her parasol, and blushed. Natty Bumpo took a fresh chew of tobacco. At length Genevra said, as if in half-spoken reverie:—

"The soft shining of the moon and the peaceful ripple of the waves seem to say to us various things of an instructive and moral tendency."

"You may bet yer pile on that, miss," said her companion gravely. "It's all the preachin' and psalm-singin' I've heern since I was a boy." "Noble being!" said Miss Tompkins to herself, glancing at the stately Pike as he bent over his paddle to conceal his emotion. "Reared in this wild seclusion, yet he has become penetrated with visible consciousness of a Great First Cause." Then, collecting herself, she said aloud: "Methinks 't were pleasant to glide ever thus down the stream of life, hand in hand with the one being whom the soul claims as its affinity. But what am I saying?"—and the delicate-minded girl hid her face in her hands.

A long silence ensued, which was at length broken by her companion.

"Ef you mean you're on the marry," he said thoughtfully, "I ain't in no wise partikler."

"My husband!" faltered the blushing girl; and she fell into his arms.

In ten minutes more the loving couple had landed at Judge Tompkins's.

CHAPTER VI

A year has passed away. Natty Bumpo was returning from Gold Hill, where he had been to purchase provisions. On his way to Donner Lake, rumors of an Indian uprising met his ears. "Dern their pesky skins, ef they dare to touch my Jenny," he muttered between his clenched teeth.

It was dark when he reached the borders of the lake. Around a glittering fire he dimly discerned dusky figures dancing. They were in war paint. Conspicuous among them was the renowned Muck-a-Muck. But why did the fingers of Natty Bumpo tighten convulsively around his rifle?

The chief held in his hand long tufts of raven hair. The heart of the pioneer sickened as he recognized the clustering curls of Genevra. In a moment his rifle was at his shoulder, and with a sharp "ping" Muck-a-Muck leaped into the air a corpse. To knock out the brains of the remaining savages, tear the tresses from the stiffening hand of Muck-a-Muck, and dash rapidly forward to the cottage of Judge Tompkins, was the work of a moment.

He burst open the door. Why did he stand transfixed with open mouth and distended eyeballs? Was the sight too horrible to be borne? On the contrary, before him, in her peerless beauty, stood Genevra Tompkins, leaning on her father's arm.

"Ye'r not scalped, then!" gasped her lover.

"No. I have no hesitation in saying that I am not; but why this abruptness?" responded Genevra.

Bumpo could not speak, but frantically produced the silken tresses. Genevra turned her face aside.

"Why, that's her waterfall!" said the Judge.

Bumpo sank fainting to the floor.

The famous Pike chieftain never recovered from the deceit, and refused to marry Genevra, who died, twenty years afterwards, of a broken heart. Judge Tompkins lost his fortune in Wild Cat. The stage passes twice a week the deserted cottage at Donner Lake. Thus was the death of Muck-a-Muck avenged.

SELINA SEDILIA

BY MISS M. E. B-DD-N AND MRS. H-N-Y W-D.

CHAPTER I

The sun was setting over Sloperton Grange, and reddened the window of the lonely chamber in the western tower, supposed to be haunted by Sir Edward Sedilia, the founder of the Grange. In the dreamy distance arose the gilded mausoleum of Lady Felicia Sedilia, who haunted that portion of Sedilia Manor known as "Stiff-uns Acre." A little to the left of the Grange might have been seen a mouldering ruin, known as "Guy's Keep," haunted by the spirit of Sir Guy Sedilia, who was found, one morning, crushed by one of the fallen battlements. Yet, as the setting sun gilded these objects, a beautiful and almost holy calm seemed diffused about the Grange.

The Lady Selina sat by an oriel window overlooking the park. The sun sank gently in the bosom of the German Ocean, and yet the lady did not lift her beautiful head from the finely curved arm and diminutive hand which supported it. When darkness finally shrouded the landscape she started, for the sound of horse-hoofs clattered over the stones of the avenue. She had scarcely risen, before an aristocratic young man fell on his knees before her.

"My Selina!"

"Edgardo! You here?"

"Yes, dearest."

"And—you—you—have—seen nothing?" said the lady in an agitated voice and nervous manner, turning her face aside to conceal her emotion.

"Nothing—that is, nothing of any account," said Edgardo. "I passed the ghost of your aunt in the park, noticed the spectre of your uncle in the ruined keep, and observed the familiar features of the spirit of your great-grandfather at his usual post. But nothing beyond these trifles, my Selina. Nothing more, love, absolutely nothing."

The young man turned his dark, liquid orbs fondly upon the ingenuous face of his betrothed.

"My own Edgardo!—and you still love me? You still would marry me in spite of this dark mystery which surrounds me? In spite of the fatal history of my race? In spite of the ominous predictions of my aged nurse?"

"I would, Selina;" and the young man passed his arm around her yielding waist. The two lovers gazed at each other's faces in unspeakable bliss. Suddenly Selina started.

"Leave me, Edgardo! leave me! A mysterious something—a fatal misgiving—a dark ambiguity—an equivocal mistrust oppresses me. I would be alone!"

The young man arose, and cast a loving glance on the lady. "Then we will be married on the seventeenth."

"The seventeenth," repeated Selina, with a mysterious shudder.

They embraced and parted. As the clatter of hoofs in the courtyard died away, the Lady Selina sank into the chair she had just quitted.

"The seventeenth," she repeated slowly, with the same fateful shudder. "Ah!—what if he should know that I have another husband living? Dare I reveal to him that I have two legitimate and three natural children? Dare I repeat to him the history of my youth? Dare I confess that at the age of seven I poisoned my sister, by putting verdigris in her cream-tarts,—that I threw my cousin from a swing at the age of twelve? That the lady's maid who incurred the displeasure of my girlhood now lies at the bottom of the horse-pond? No! no! he is too pure,—too good,—too innocent,—to hear such improper conversation!" and her whole body writhed as she rocked to and fro in a paroxysm of grief.

But she was soon calm. Rising to her feet, she opened a secret panel in the wall, and revealed a slow-match ready for lighting.

"This match," said the Lady Selina, "is connected with a mine beneath the western tower, where my three children are confined; another branch of it lies under the parish church, where the record of my first marriage is kept. I have only to light this match and the whole of my past life is swept away!" She approached the match with a lighted candle.

But a hand was laid upon her arm, and with a shriek the Lady Selina fell on her knees before the spectre of Sir Guy.

CHAPTER II

"Forbear, Selina," said the phantom in a hollow voice.

"Why should I forbear?" responded Selina haughtily, as she recovered her courage. "You know the secret of our race?"

"I do. Understand me,—I do not object to the eccentricities of your youth. I know the fearful destiny which, pursuing you, led you to poison your sister and drown your lady's maid. I know the awful doom which I have brought upon this house. But if you make away with these children"—

"Well," said the Lady Selina hastily.

"They will haunt you!"

"Well, I fear them not," said Selina, drawing her superb figure to its full height.

"Yes, but, my dear child, what place are they to haunt? The ruin is sacred to your uncle's spirit. Your aunt monopolizes the park, and, I must be allowed to state, not unfrequently trespasses upon the grounds of others. The horse-pond is frequented by the spirit of your maid, and your murdered sister walks these corridors. To be plain, there is no room at Sloperton Grange for another ghost. I cannot have them in my room,—for you know I don't like children. Think of this, rash girl, and forbear! Would you, Selina," said the phantom mournfully,—"would you force your great-grandfather's spirit to take lodgings elsewhere?"

Lady Selina's hand trembled; the lighted candle fell from her nerveless fingers.

"No," she cried passionately; "never!" and fell fainting to the floor.

CHAPTER III

Edgardo galloped rapidly towards Sloperton. When the outline of the Grange had faded away in the darkness, he reined his magnificent steed beside the ruins of Guy's Keep.

"It wants but a few minutes of the hour," he said, consulting his watch by the light of the moon. "He dare not break his word. He will come." He paused, and peered anxiously into the darkness. "But come what may, she is mine," he continued, as his thoughts reverted fondly to the fair lady he had quitted. "Yet if she knew all. If she knew that I am a disgraced and ruined man,—a felon and an outcast. If she knew that at the age of fourteen I murdered my Latin tutor and forged my uncle's will. If she knew that I had three wives already, and that the fourth victim of misplaced confidence and my unfortunate peculiarity is expected to be at Sloperton by to-night's train with her baby. But no; she must not know it. Constance must not arrive; Burke the Slogger must attend to that.

"Ha! here he is! Well?"

These words were addressed to a ruffian in a slouched hat, who suddenly appeared from Guy's Keep.

"I he's here, measter," said the villain, with a disgracefully low accent and complete disregard of grammatical rules.

"It is well. Listen: I'm in possession of facts that will send you to the gallows. I know of the murder of Bill Smithers, the robbery of the tollgate-keeper, and the making away of the youngest daughter of Sir

Reginald de Walton. A word from me, and the officers of justice are on your track."

Burke the Slogger trembled.

"Hark ye! serve my purpose, and I may yet save you. The 5.30 train from Clapham will be due at Sloperton at 9.25. *It must not arrive!*"

The villain's eyes sparkled as he nodded at Edgardo.

"Enough,—you understand; leave me!"

CHAPTER IV

About half a mile from Sloperton Station the South Clapham and Medway line crossed a bridge over Sloperton-on-Trent. As the shades of evening were closing, a man in a slouched hat might have been seen, carrying a saw and axe under his arm, hanging about the bridge. From time to time he disappeared in the shadow of its abutments, but the sound of a saw and axe still betrayed his vicinity. At exactly nine o'clock he reappeared, and crossing to the Sloperton side, rested his shoulder against the abutment and gave a shove. The bridge swayed a moment, and then fell with a splash into the water, leaving a space of one hundred feet between the two banks. This done, Burke the Slogger,—for it was he,—with a fiendish chuckle seated himself on the divided railway track and awaited the coming of the train.

A shriek from the woods announced its approach. For an instant Burke the Slogger saw the glaring of a red lamp. The ground trembled. The train was going with fearful rapidity. Another second and it had reached the bank. Burke the Slogger uttered a fiendish laugh. But the next moment the train leaped across the chasm, striking the rails exactly even, and dashing out the life of Burke the Slogger, sped away to Sloperton.

The first object that greeted Edgardo, as he rode up to the station on the arrival of the train, was the body of Burke the Slogger hanging on the cowcatcher; the second was the face of his deserted wife looking from the window of a second-class carriage.

CHAPTER V

A nameless terror seemed to have taken possession of Clarissa, Lady Selina's maid, as she rushed into the presence of her mistress.

"Oh, my lady, such news!"

"Explain yourself," said her mistress, rising.

"An accident has happened on the railway, and a man has been killed."

"What—not Edgardo!" almost screamed Selina.

"No, Burke the Slogger, your ladyship!"

"My first husband!" said Lady Selina, sinking on her knees. "Just Heaven, I thank thee!"

CHAPTER VI

The morning of the seventeenth dawned brightly over Sloperton. "A fine day for the wedding," said the sexton to Swipes, the butler of Sloperton Grange. The aged retainer shook his head sadly. "Alas! there's no trusting in signs!" he continued. "Seventy-five years ago, on a day like this, my young mistress"—but he was cut short by the appearance of a stranger.

"I would see Sir Edgardo," said the new-comer impatiently.

The bridegroom, who, with the rest of the wedding-train, was about stepping into the carriage to proceed to the parish church, drew the stranger aside.

"'T's done!" said the stranger, in a hoarse whisper.

"Ah! and you buried her?"

"With the others!"

"Enough. No more at present. Meet me after the ceremony, and you shall have your reward."

The stranger shuffled away, and Edgardo returned to his bride. "A trifling matter of business I had forgotten, my dear Selina; let us proceed." And the young man pressed the timid hand of his blushing bride as he handed her into the carriage. The cavalcade rode out of the courtyard. At the same moment, the deep bell on Guy's Keep tolled ominously.

CHAPTER VII

Scarcely had the wedding-train left the Grange, than Alice Sedilia, youngest daughter of Lady Selina, made her escape from the western tower, owing to a lack of watchfulness on the part of Clarissa. The innocent child, freed from restraint, rambled through the lonely corridors, and finally, opening a door, found herself in her mother's boudoir. For some time she amused herself by examining the various ornaments and elegant trifles with which it was filled. Then, in pursuance of a childish freak, she dressed herself in her mother's laces and ribbons. In this occupation she chanced to touch a peg which proved to be a spring that opened a secret panel in the wall. Alice uttered a cry of delight as she noticed what, to her childish fancy, appeared to be the slow-match of a firework. Taking a lucifer match in her hand she approached the fuse. She hesitated a moment. What would her mother and her nurse say?

Suddenly the ringing of the chimes of Sloperton parish church met her ear. Alice knew that the sound signified that the marriage-party had entered the church, and that she was secure from interruption. With a childish smile upon her lips, Alice Sedilia touched off the slow-match.

CHAPTER VIII

At exactly two o'clock on the seventeenth, Rupert Sedilia, who had just returned from India, was thoughtfully descending the hill toward Sloperton manor. "If I can prove that my aunt, Lady Selina, was married before my father died, I can establish my claim to Sloperton Grange," he uttered, half aloud. He paused, for a sudden trembling of the earth beneath his feet, and a terrific explosion, as of a park of artillery, arrested his progress. At the same moment he beheld a dense cloud of smoke envelop the churchyard of Sloperton, and the western tower of the Grange seemed to be lifted bodily from its foundation. The air seemed filled with falling fragments, and two dark objects struck the earth close at his feet. Rupert picked them up. One seemed to be a heavy volume bound in brass. A cry burst from, his lips.

"The Parish Records." He opened the volume hastily. It contained the marriage of Lady Selina to "Burke the Slogger."

The second object proved to be a piece of parchment. He tore it open with trembling fingers. It was the missing will of Sir James Sedilia!

CHAPTER IX

When the bells again rang on the new parish church of Sloperton it was for the marriage of Sir Rupert Sedilia and his cousin, the only remaining members of the family.

Five more ghosts were added to the supernatural population of Sloperton Grange. Perhaps this was the reason why Sir Rupert sold the property shortly afterward, and that for many years a dark shadow seemed to hang over the ruins of Sloperton Grange.

THE NINETY-NINE GUARDSMEN

BY AL-X-D-R D-M-S

CHAPTER I

SHOWING THE QUALITY OF THE CUSTOMERS OF THE INNKEEPER OF PROVINS

Twenty years after, the gigantic innkeeper of Provins stood looking at a cloud of dust on the highway.

This cloud of dust betokened the approach of a traveler. Travelers had been rare that season on the highway between Paris and Provins.

The heart of the innkeeper rejoiced. Turning to Dame Perigord, his wife, he said, stroking his white apron,—

"St. Denis! make haste and spread the cloth. Add a bottle of Charlevoix to the table. This traveler, who rides so fast, by his pace must be a monseigneur."

Truly the traveler, clad in the uniform of a musketeer, as he drew up to the door of the hostelry, did not seem to have spared his horse. Throwing his reins to the landlord, he leaped lightly to the ground. He was a young man of four and twenty, and spoke with a slight Gascon accent.

"I am hungry, morbleu! I wish to dine!"

The gigantic innkeeper bowed and led the way to a neat apartment, where a table stood covered with tempting viands. The musketeer at once set to work. Fowls, fish, and pates disappeared before him. Perigord sighed as he witnessed the devastations. Only once the stranger paused.

"Wine!" Perigord brought wine. The stranger drank a dozen bottles. Finally he rose to depart. Turning to the expectant landlord, he said,—

"Charge it."

"To whom, your highness?" said Perigord anxiously.

"To his Eminence!"

"Mazarin?" ejaculated the innkeeper.

"The same. Bring me my horse," and the musketeer, remounting his favorite animal, rode away.

The innkeeper slowly turned back into the inn. Scarcely had he reached the courtyard before the clatter of hoofs again called him to the doorway. A young musketeer of a light and graceful figure rode up.

"Parbleu, my dear Perigord, I am famishing. What have you got for dinner?"

"Venison, capons, larks, and pigeons, your excellency," replied the obsequious landlord, bowing to the ground.

"Enough!" The young musketeer dismounted, and entered the inn. Seating himself at the table replenished by the careful Perigord, he speedily swept it as clean as the first comer.

"Some wine, my brave Perigord," said the graceful young musketeer, as soon as he could find utterance.

Perigord brought three dozen of Charlevoix. The young man emptied them almost at a draught.

"By-by, Perigord," he said lightly, waving his hand, as, preceding the astonished landlord, he slowly withdrew.

"But, your highness,—the bill," said the astounded Perigord.

"Ah, the bill. Charge it!"

"To whom?"

"The Queen!"

"What, Madame?"

"The same. Adieu, my good Perigord." And the graceful stranger rode away. An interval of quiet succeeded, in which the innkeeper gazed woefully at his wife. Suddenly he was startled by a clatter of hoofs, and an aristocratic figure stood in the doorway.

"Ah," said the courtier good-naturedly. "What, do my eyes deceive me? No, it is the festive and luxurious Perigord. Perigord, listen. I famish. I languish. I would dine."

The innkeeper again covered the table with viands. Again it was swept clean as the fields of Egypt before the miraculous swarm of locusts. The stranger looked up.

"Bring me another fowl, my Perigord."

"Impossible, your excellency; the larder is stripped clean."

"Another flitch of bacon, then."

"Impossible, your highness; there is no more."

"Well, then, wine!"

The landlord brought one hundred and forty-four bottles. The courtier drank them all.

"One may drink if one cannot eat," said the aristocratic stranger good-humoredly.

The innkeeper shuddered.

The guest rose to depart. The innkeeper came slowly forward with his bill, to which he had covertly added the losses which he had suffered from the previous strangers.

"Ah, the bill. Charge it."

"Charge it! to whom?"

"To the King," said the guest.

"What! his Majesty?"

"Certainly. Farewell, Perigord."

The innkeeper groaned. Then he went out and took down his sign. Then remarked to his wife,—

"I am a plain man, and don't understand politics. It seems, however, that the country is in a troubled state. Between his Eminence the Cardinal, his Majesty the King, and her Majesty the Queen, I am a ruined man."

"Stay," said Dame Perigord, "I have an idea."

"And that is"—

"Become yourself a musketeer."

CHAPTER II

THE COMBAT

On leaving Provins the first musketeer proceeded to Nangis, where he was reinforced by thirty-three followers. The second musketeer, arriving at Nangis at the same moment, placed himself at the head of thirty-three more. The third guest of the landlord of Provins arrived at Nangis in time to assemble together thirty-three other musketeers.

The first stranger led the troops of his Eminence.

The second led the troops of the Queen.

The third led the troops of the King.

The fight commenced. It raged terribly for seven hours. The first musketeer killed thirty of the Queen's troops. The second musketeer killed thirty of the King's troops. The third musketeer killed thirty of his Eminence's troops.

By this time it will be perceived the number of musketeers had been narrowed down to four on each side.

Naturally the three principal warriors approached each other.

They simultaneously uttered a cry.

"Aramis!"

"Athos!"

"D'Artagnan!"

They fell into each other's arms.

"And it seems that we are fighting against each other, my children," said the Count de la Fere mournfully.

"How singular!" exclaimed Aramis and D'Artagnan.

"Let us stop this fratricidal warfare," said Athos.

"We will!" they exclaimed together.

"But how to disband our followers?" queried D'Artagnan.

Aramis winked. They understood each other. "Let us cut 'em down!"

They cut 'em down. Aramis killed three. D'Artagnan three. Athos three.

The friends again embraced. "How like old times!" said Aramis. "How touching!" exclaimed the serious and philosophic Count de la Fere.

The galloping of hoofs caused them to withdraw from each other's embraces. A gigantic figure rapidly approached.

"The innkeeper of Provins!" they cried, drawing their swords.

"Perigord! down with him!" shouted D'Artagnan.

"Stay," said Athos.

The gigantic figure was beside them. He uttered a cry.

"Athos, Aramis, D'Artagnan!"

"Porthos!" exclaimed the astonished trio.

"The same." They all fell in each other's arms.

The Count de la Fere slowly raised his hands to heaven. "Bless you! Bless us, my children! However different our opinion may be in regard to politics, we have but one opinion in regard to our own merits. Where can you find a better man than Aramis?"

"Than Porthos?" said Aramis.

"Than D'Artagnan?" said Porthos.

"Than Athos?" said D'Artagnan.

CHAPTER III

SHOWING HOW THE KING OF
FRANCE WENT UP A LADDER

The King descended into the garden. Proceeding cautiously along the terraced walk, he came to the wall immediately below the windows of Madame. To the left were two windows, concealed by vines. They opened into the apartments of La Valliere.

The King sighed.

"It is about nineteen feet to that window," said the King. "If I had a ladder about nineteen feet long, it would reach to that window. This is logic."

Suddenly the King stumbled over something. "St. Denis!" he exclaimed, looking down. It was a ladder, just nineteen feet long.

The King placed it against the wall. In so doing, he fixed the lower end upon the abdomen of a man who lay concealed by the wall. The man did not utter a cry or wince. The King suspected nothing. He ascended the ladder.

The ladder was too short. Louis the Grand was not a tall man. He was still two feet below the window.

"Dear me!" said the King.

Suddenly the ladder was lifted two feet from below. This enabled the King to leap in the window. At the farther end of the apartment stood a young girl, with red hair and a lame leg. She was trembling with emotion.

"Louise!"

"The King!"

"Ah, my God, mademoiselle."

"Ah, my God, sire."

But a low knock at the door interrupted the lovers. The King uttered a cry of rage; Louise one of despair. The door opened and D'Artagnan entered.

"Good-evening, sire," said the musketeer.

The King touched a bell. Porthos appeared in the doorway.

"Good-evening, sire."

"Arrest M. D'Artagnan."

Porthos looked at D'Artagnan, and did not move.

The King almost turned purple with rage. He again touched the hell. Athos entered. "Count, arrest Porthos and D'Artagnan."

The Count de la Fere glanced at Porthos and D'Artagnan, and smiled sweetly.

"Sacre! Where is Aramis?" said the King violently.

"Here, sire," and Aramis entered.

"Arrest Athos, Porthos, and D'Artagnan."

Aramis bowed and folded his arms.

"Arrest yourself!"

Aramis did not move.

The King shuddered and turned pale. "Am I not King of France?"

"Assuredly, sire, but we are also, severally, Porthos, Aramis, D'Artagnan, and Athos."

"Ah!" said the King.

"Yes, sire."

"What does this mean?"

"It means, your Majesty," said Aramis, stepping forward, "that your conduct as a married man is highly improper. I am an abbe, and I object to these improprieties. My friends here, D'Artagnan, Athos, and Porthos, pure-minded young men, are also terribly shocked. Observe, sire, how they blush!"

Athos, Porthos, and D'Artagnan blushed.

"Ah," said the King thoughtfully. "You teach me a lesson. You are devoted and noble young gentlemen, but your only weakness is your excessive modesty. From this moment I make you all marshals and dukes, with the exception of Aramis."

"And me, sire?" said Aramis.

"You shall be an archbishop!"

The four friends looked up and then rushed into each other's arms. The King embraced Louise de la Valliere, by way of keeping them company. A pause ensued. At last Athos spoke,—

"Swear, my children, that, next to yourselves, you will respect—the King of France; and remember that 'Forty years after' we will meet again."

MISS MIX

BY CH-L-TTE BR-NTE

CHAPTER I

My earliest impressions are of a huge, misshapen rock, against which the hoarse waves beat unceasingly. On this rock three pelicans are standing in a defiant attitude. A dark sky lowers in the background, while two sea-gulls and a gigantic cormorant eye with extreme disfavor the floating corpse of a drowned woman in the foreground. A few bracelets, coral necklaces, and other articles of jewelry, scattered around loosely, complete this remarkable picture.

It is one which, in some vague, unconscious way, symbolizes, to my fancy, the character of a man. I have never been able to explain exactly why. I think I must have seen the picture in some illustrated volume when a baby, or my mother may have dreamed it before I was born.

As a child I was not handsome. When I consulted the triangular bit of looking-glass which I always carried with me, it showed a pale, sandy, and freckled face, shaded by locks like the color of seaweed when the sun strikes it in deep water. My eyes were said to be indistinctive; they were a faint, ashen gray; but above them rose—my only beauty—a high, massive, domelike forehead, with polished temples, like door-knobs of the purest porcelain.

Our family was a family of governesses. My mother had been one, and my sisters had the same occupation. Consequently, when, at the age of thirteen, my eldest sister handed me the advertisement of Mr. Rawjester, clipped from that day's "Times," I accepted it as my destiny. Nevertheless, a mysterious presentiment of an indefinite future haunted me in my dreams that night, as I lay upon my little snow-white bed. The next morning, with two band-boxes tied up in silk handkerchiefs, and a hair trunk, I turned my back upon Minerva Cottage forever.

CHAPTER II

Blunderbore Hall, the seat of James Rawjester, Esq., was encompassed by dark pines and funereal hemlocks on all sides. The wind sang weirdly in the turrets and moaned through the long-drawn avenues of the park. As I approached the house I saw several mysterious figures flit before the windows, and a yell of demoniac laughter answered my summons at the bell. While I strove to repress my gloomy forebodings, the housekeeper, a timid, scared-looking old woman, showed me into the library.

I entered, overcome with conflicting emotions. I was dressed in a narrow gown of dark serge, trimmed with black bugles. A thick green shawl was pinned across my breast. My hands were encased with black half-mittens worked with steel beads; on my feet were large pattens, originally the property of my deceased grandmother. I carried a blue cotton umbrella. As I passed before a mirror I could not help glancing at it, nor could I disguise from myself the fact that I was not handsome.

Drawing a chair into a recess, I sat down with folded hands, calmly awaiting the arrival of my master. Once or twice a fearful yell rang through the house, or the rattling of chains, and curses uttered in a deep, manly voice, broke upon the oppressive stillness. I began to feel my soul rising with the emergency of the moment. "You look alarmed, miss. You don't hear anything, my dear, do you?" asked the housekeeper nervously.

"Nothing whatever," I remarked calmly, as a terrific scream, followed by the dragging of chairs and tables in the room above, drowned for a moment my reply. "It is the silence, on the contrary, which has made me foolishly nervous."

The housekeeper looked at me approvingly, and instantly made some tea for me.

I drank seven cups; as I was beginning the eighth, I heard a crash, and the next moment a man leaped into the room through the broken window.

CHAPTER III

The crash startled me from my self-control. The housekeeper bent toward me and whispered,—

"Don't be excited. It's Mr. Rawjester,—he prefers to come in sometimes in this way. It's his playfulness, ha! ha! ha!"

"I perceive," I said calmly. "It's the unfettered impulse of a lofty soul breaking the tyrannizing bonds of custom." And I turned toward him.

He had never once looked at me. He stood with his back to the fire, which set off the herculean breadth of his shoulders. His face was dark and expressive; his under jaw squarely formed, and remarkably heavy. I was struck with his remarkable likeness to a gorilla.

As he absently tied the poker into hard knots with his nervous fingers, I watched him with some interest. Suddenly he turned toward me:—

"Do you think I'm handsome, young woman?"

"Not classically beautiful," I returned calmly; "but you have, if I may so express myself, an abstract manliness,—a sincere and wholesome barbarity which, involving as it does the naturalness"—But I stopped, for he yawned at that moment,—an action which singularly developed the immense breadth of his lower jaw,—and I saw he had forgotten me. Presently he turned to the housekeeper,—

"Leave us."

The old woman withdrew with a curtsey.

Mr. Rawjester deliberately turned his back upon me and remained silent for twenty minutes. I drew my shawl the more closely around my shoulders and closed my eyes.

"You are the governess?" at length he said.

"I am, sir."

"A creature who teaches geography, arithmetic, and the use of the globes—ha!—a wretched remnant of femininity,—a skimp pattern of girlhood with a premature flavor of tea-leaves and morality. Ugh!"

I bowed my head silently.

"Listen to me, girl!" he said sternly; "this child you have come to teach—my ward—is not legitimate. She is the offspring of my mistress,—a common harlot. Ah! Miss Mix, what do you think of me now?"

"I admire," I replied calmly, "your sincerity. A mawkish regard for delicacy might have kept this disclosure to yourself. I only recognize in your frankness that perfect community of thought and sentiment which should exist between original natures." I looked up; he had already forgotten my presence, and was engaged in pulling off his boots and coat. This done, he sank down in an armchair before the fire, and ran the poker wearily through his hair. I could not help pitying him.

The wind howled dismally without, and the rain beat furiously against the windows. I crept toward him and seated myself on a low stool beside his chair.

Presently he turned, without seeing me, and placed his foot absently in my lap. I affected not to notice it. But he started and looked down.

"You here yet—Carrothead? Ah, I forgot. Do you speak French?"

"Oui, Monsier."

"Taisez-vous!" he said sharply, with singular purity of accent. I complied. The wind moaned fearfully in the chimney, and the light burned dimly. I shuddered in spite of myself. "Ah, you tremble, girl!"

"It is a fearful night."

"Fearful! Call you this fearful? Ha! ha! ha! Look! you wretched little atom, look!" and he dashed forward, and, leaping out of the window, stood like a statue in the pelting storm, with folded arms. He did not stay long, but in a few minutes returned by way of the hall chimney. I saw from the way that he wiped his feet on my dress that he had again forgotten my presence.

"You are a governess. What can you teach?" he asked, suddenly and fiercely thrusting his face in mine.

"Manners!" I replied calmly.

"Ha! teach *me!*"

"You mistake yourself," I said, adjusting my mittens. "Your manners require not the artificial restraint of society. You are radically polite; this impetuosity and ferociousness is simply the sincerity which is the basis of a proper deportment. Your instincts are moral; your better nature, I see, is religious. As St. Paul justly remarks—see chap. 6, 8, 9, and 10 "—

He seized a heavy candlestick, and threw it at me. I dodged it submissively but firmly.

"Excuse me," he remarked, as his under jaw slowly relaxed. "Excuse me, Miss Mix—but I can't stand St. Paul! Enough—you are engaged."

CHAPTER IV

I followed the housekeeper as she led the way timidly to my room. As we passed into a dark hall in the wing, I noticed that it was closed by an iron gate with a grating. Three of the doors on the corridor were likewise grated. A strange noise, as of shuffling feet and the howling of infuriated animals, rang through the hall. Bidding the housekeeper good-night, and taking the candle, I entered my bedchamber.

I took off my dress, and putting on a yellow flannel nightgown, which I could not help feeling did not agree with my complexion, I composed myself to rest by reading Blair's "Rhetoric" and Paley's "Moral Philosophy." I had just put out the light, when I heard voices in the corridor. I listened attentively. I recognized Mr. Rawjester's stern tones.

"Have you fed No. One?" he asked.

"Yes, sir," said a gruff voice, apparently belonging to a domestic.

"How's No. Two?"

"She's a little off her feed, just now, but will pick up in a day or two."

"And No. Three?"

"Perfectly furious, sir. Her tantrums are ungovernable."

"Hush!"

The voices died away, and I sank into a fitful slumber.

I dreamed that I was wandering through a tropical forest. Suddenly I saw the figure of a gorilla approaching me. As it neared me, I recognized the features of Mr. Rawjester. He held his hand to his side as if in pain. I saw that he had been wounded. He recognized me and called me by name, but at the same moment the vision changed to an Ashantee village, where, around the fire, a group of negroes were dancing and participating in some wild Obi festival. I awoke with the strain still ringing in my ears.

"Hokee-pokee wokee fum!"

Good Heavens! could I be dreaming? I heard the voice distinctly on the floor below, and smelt something burning. I arose, with an indistinct presentiment of evil, and hastily putting some cotton in my ears and tying a towel about my head, I wrapped myself in a shawl and rushed downstairs. The door of Mr. Rawjester's room was open. I entered.

Mr. Rawjester lay apparently in a deep slumber, from which even the clouds of smoke that came from the burning curtains of his bed could not rouse him. Around the room a large and powerful negress, scantily attired, with her head adorned with feathers, was dancing wildly, accompanying herself with bone castanets. It looked like some terrible fetich.

I did not lose my calmness. After firmly emptying the pitcher, basin, and slop-jar on the burning bed, I proceeded cautiously to the garden, and returning with the garden engine, I directed a small stream at Mr. Rawjester.

At my entrance the gigantic negress fled. Mr. Rawjester yawned and woke. I explained to him, as he rose dripping from the bed, the reason of my presence. He did not seem to be excited, alarmed, or discomposed. He gazed at me curiously.

"So you risked your life to save mine, eh? you canary-colored teacher of infants."

I blushed modestly, and drew my shawl tightly over my yellow flannel nightgown.

"You love me, Mary Jane,—don't deny it! This trembling shows it!" He drew me closely toward him, and said, with his deep voice tenderly modulated,—"How's her pooty tootens,—did she get her 'ittle tootens wet,—b'ess her?"

I understood his allusion to my feet. I glanced down and saw that in my hurry I had put on a pair of his old india-rubbers. My feet were not small or pretty, and the addition did not add to their beauty.

"Let me go, sir," I remarked quietly. "This is entirely improper; it sets a bad example for your child." And I firmly but gently extricated myself from his grasp. I approached the door. He seemed for a moment buried in deep thought.

"You say this was a negress?"

"Yes, sir."

"Humph, Number One, I suppose."

"Who is Number One, sir?"

"My *first*," he remarked, with a significant and sarcastic smile. Then, relapsing into his old manner, he threw his boots at my head, and bade me begone. I withdrew calmly.

CHAPTER V

My pupil was a bright little girl, who spoke French with a perfect accent. Her mother had been a "French ballet-dancer, which probably accounted for it. Although she was only six years old, it was easy to perceive that she had been several times in love. She once said to me,—

"Miss Mix, did you ever have the grande passion? Did you ever feel a fluttering here?" and she placed her hand upon her small chest, and sighed quaintly; "a kind of distaste for bonbons and caramels, when the world seemed as tasteless and hollow as a broken cordial drop?"

"Then you have felt it, Nina?" I said quietly.

"Oh, dear, yes. There was Buttons,—that was our page, you know,—I loved him dearly, but papa sent him away. Then there was Dick, the groom; but he laughed at me, and I suffered misery!" and she struck a tragic French attitude. "There is to be company here to-morrow," she added, rattling on with childish naivete, "and papa's sweetheart—Blanche Marabout—is to be here. You know they say she is to be my mamma."

What thrill was this shot through me? But I rose calmly, and administering a slight correction to the child, left the apartment.

Blunderbore House, for the next week, was the scene of gayety and merriment. That portion of the mansion closed with a grating was walled up, and the midnight shrieks no longer troubled me.

But I felt more keenly the degradation of my situation. I was obliged to help Lady Blanche at her toilet and help her to look beautiful. For what? To captivate him? Oh—no, no,—but why this sudden thrill and faintness? Did he really love her? I had seen him pinch and swear at her. But I reflected that he had thrown a candlestick at my head, and my foolish heart was reassured.

It was a night of festivity, when a sudden message obliged Mr. Rawjester to leave his guests for a few hours. "Make yourselves merry, idiots," he added, under his breath, as he passed me. The door closed and he was gone.

A half-hour passed. In the midst of the dancing a shriek was heard, and out of the swaying crowd of fainting women and excited men a wild figure strode into the room. One glance showed it to be a highwayman, heavily armed, holding a pistol in each hand.

"Let no one pass out of this room!" he said, in a voice of thunder. "The house is surrounded and you cannot escape. The first one who crosses yonder threshold will be shot like a dog. Gentlemen, I'll trouble you to approach in single file, and hand me your purses and watches."

Finding resistance useless, the order was ungraciously obeyed.

"Now, ladies, please to pass up your jewelry and trinkets."

This order was still more ungraciously complied with. As Blanche handed to the bandit captain her bracelet, she endeavored to conceal a diamond necklace, the gift of Mr. Rawjester, in her bosom. But, with a demoniac grin, the powerful brute tore it from its concealment, and administering a hearty box on the ear of the young girl, flung her aside.

It was now my turn. With a beating heart I made my way to the robber chieftain, and sank at his feet. "Oh, sir, I am nothing but a poor governess, pray let me go."

"Oho! A governess? Give me your last month's wages, then. Give me what you have stolen from your master!" and he laughed fiendishly.

I gazed at him quietly, and said, in a low voice: "I have stolen nothing from you, Mr. Rawjester!"

"Ah, discovered! Hush! listen, girl!" he hissed, in a fierce whisper; "utter a syllable to frustrate my plans, and you die; aid me, and"—But he was gone.

In a few moments the party, with the exception of myself, were gagged and locked in the cellar. The next moment torches were applied to the rich hangings, and the house was in flames. I felt a strong hand seize me, and bear me out in the open air and place me up on the hillside, where I could overlook the burning mansion. It was Mr. Rawjester. "Burn!" he said, as he shook his fist at the flames. Then sinking on his knees before me, he said hurriedly,—

"Mary Jane, I love you; the obstacles to our union are or will be soon removed. In yonder mansion were confined my three crazy wives. One of them, as you know, attempted to kill me! Ha! this is vengeance! But will you be mine?"

I fell, without a word, upon his neck.

MR. MIDSHIPMAN BEEEZY
A NAVAL OFFICER

BY CAPTAIN M-RRY-T, R. N.

CHAPTER I

My father was a north-country surgeon. He had retired, a widower, from her Majesty's navy many years before, and had a small practice in his native village. When I was seven years old he employed me to carry medicines to his patients. Being of a lively disposition, I sometimes amused myself, during my daily rounds, by mixing the contents of the different phials. Although I had no reason to doubt that the general result of this practice was beneficial, yet, as the death of a consumptive curate followed the addition of a strong mercurial lotion to his expectorant, my father concluded to withdraw me from the profession and send me to school.

Grubbins, the schoolmaster, was a tyrant, and it was not long before my impetuous and self-willed nature rebelled against his authority. I soon began to form plans of revenge. In this I was assisted by Tom Snaffle,—a schoolfellow. One day Tom suggested,—

"Suppose we blow him up. I've got two pounds of powder!"

"No, that's too noisy," I replied.

Tom was silent for a minute, and again spoke:—

"You remember how you flattened out the curate, Pills? Couldn't you give Grubbins something—something to make him leathery sick—eh?" A flash of inspiration crossed my mind. I went to the shop of the village apothecary. He knew me; I had often purchased vitriol, which I poured into Grubbins's inkstand to corrode his pens and hum up his coat-tail, on which he was in the habit of wiping them. I boldly asked for an ounce of chloroform. The young apothecary winked and handed me the bottle.

It was Grubbins's custom to throw his handkerchief over his head, recline in his chair, and take a short nap during recess. Watching my opportunity, as he dozed, I managed to slip his handkerchief from his face and substitute my own, moistened with chloroform. In a few minutes he was insensible. Tom and I then quickly shaved his head, beard, and eyebrows, blackened his face with a mixture of vitriol and burnt cork, and fled. There was a row and scandal the next day. My father always excused me by asserting that Grubbins had got drunk,— but somehow found it convenient to procure me an appointment in her Majesty's navy at an early day.

CHAPTER II

An official letter, with the Admiralty seal, informed me that I was expected to join H. M. ship Belcher, Captain Boltrope, at Portsmouth, without delay. In a few days I presented myself to a tall, stern-visaged man, who was slowly pacing the leeward side of the quarter-deck. As I touched my hat he eyed me sternly:—

"So ho! Another young suckling. The service is going to the devil. Nothing but babes in the cockpit and grannies in the board. Boatswain's mate, pass the word for Mr. Cheek!"

Mr. Cheek, the steward, appeared and touched his hat.

"Introduce Mr. Breezy to the young gentlemen. Stop! Where's Mr. Swizzle?"

"At the masthead, sir."

"Where's Mr. Lankey?"

"At the masthead, sir."

"Mr. Briggs?"

"Masthead, too, sir."

"And the rest of the young gentlemen?" roared the enraged officer.

"All masthead, sir."

"Ah!" said Captain Boltrope, as he smiled grimly, "under the circumstances, Mr. Breezy, you had better go to the masthead too."

CHAPTER III

At the masthead I made the acquaintance of two youngsters of about my own age, one of whom informed me that he had been there three hundred and thirty-two days out of the year.

"In rough weather, when the old cock is out of sorts, you know, we never come down," added a young gentleman of nine years, with a dirk nearly as long as himself, who had been introduced to me as Mr. Briggs. "By the way, Pills," he continued, "how did you come to omit giving the captain a naval salute?"

"Why, I touched my hat," I said innocently.

"Yes, but that isn't enough, you know. That will do very well at other times. He expects the naval salute when you first come on board—greeny!"

I began to feel alarmed, and begged him to explain.

"Why, you see, after touching your hat, you should have touched him lightly with your forefinger in his waistcoat, so, and asked, 'How's his nibs?'—you see?"

"How's his nibs?" I repeated.

"Exactly. He would have drawn back a little, and then you should have repeated the salute, remarking, 'How's his royal nibs?' asking cautiously after his wife and family, and requesting to be introduced to the gunner's daughter."

"The gunner's daughter?"

"The same; you know she takes care of us young gentlemen; now don't forget, Pillsy!"

When we were called down to the deck I thought it a good chance to profit by this instruction. I approached Captain Boltrope and repeated the salute without conscientiously omitting a single detail. He remained for a moment livid and speechless. At length he gasped out,—

"Boatswain's mate!"

"If you please, sir," I asked tremulously, "I should like to be introduced to the gunner's daughter!"

"Oh, very good, sir!" screamed Captain Boltrope, rubbing his hands and absolutely capering about the deck with rage. "Oh, d—n you! Of course you shall! Oh, ho! the gunner's daughter! Oh, h—ll! this is too much! Boatswain's mate!" Before I well knew where I was, I was seized, borne to an eight-pounder, tied upon it, and flogged!

CHAPTER IV

As we sat together in the cockpit, picking the weevils out of our biscuit, Briggs consoled me for my late mishap, adding that the "naval salute," as a custom, seemed just then to be honored more in the *breach* than the observance. I joined in the hilarity occasioned by the witticism, and in a few moments we were all friends. Presently Swizzle turned to me:—

"We have just been planning how to confiscate a keg of claret, which Nips, the purser, keeps under his bunk. The old nipcheese lies there drunk half the day, and there's no getting at it."

"Let's get beneath the stateroom and bore through the deck, and so tap it," said Lankey.

The proposition was received with a shout of applause. A long half-inch auger and bit was procured from Chips, the carpenter's mate, and Swizzle, after a careful examination of the timbers beneath the wardroom, commenced operations. The auger at last disappeared, when suddenly there was a slight disturbance on the deck above. Swizzle withdrew the auger hurriedly; from its point a few bright red drops trickled.

"Huzza! send her up again!" cried Lankey.

The auger was again applied. This time a shriek was heard from the purser's cabin. Instantly the light was doused, and the party retreated hurriedly to the cockpit. A sound of snoring was heard as the sentry stuck his head into the door. "All right, sir," he replied in answer to the voice of the officer of the deck.

The next morning we heard that Nips was in the surgeon's hands, with a bad wound in the fleshy part of his leg, and that the auger had *not* struck claret.

CHAPTER V

"Now, Pills, you'll have a chance to smell powder," said Briggs as he entered the cockpit and buckled around his waist an enormous cutlass. "We have just sighted a French ship."

We went on deck. Captain Boltrope grinned as we touched our hats. He hated the purser. "Come, young gentlemen, if you're boring for French claret, yonder's a good quality. Mind your con, sir," he added, turning to the quartermaster, who was grinning.

The ship was already cleared for action. The men, in their eagerness, had started the coffee from the tubs and filled them with shot. Presently the Frenchman yawed, and a shot from a long thirty-two came skipping over the water. It killed the quartermaster and took off both of Lankey's legs. "Tell the purser our account is squared," said the dying boy, with a feeble smile.

The fight raged fiercely for two hours. I remember killing the French admiral, as we boarded, but on looking around for Briggs, after the smoke had cleared away, I was intensely amused at witnessing the following novel sight:

Briggs had pinned the French captain against the mast with his cutlass, and was now engaged, with all the hilarity of youth, in pulling the Captain's coat-tails between his legs, in imitation of a dancing-jack. As the Frenchman lifted his legs and arms, at each jerk of Briggs's, I could not help participating in the general mirth.

"You young devil, what are you doing?" said a stifled voice behind me. I looked up and beheld Captain Boltrope, endeavoring to calm his stern features, but the twitching around his mouth betrayed his intense enjoyment of the scene. "Go to the masthead—up with you, sir!" he repeated sternly to Briggs.

"Very good, sir," said the boy, coolly preparing to mount the shrouds. "Good-by, Johnny Crapaud. Humph!" he added, in a tone intended for my ear, "a pretty way to treat a hero. The service is going to the devil!"

I thought so too.

CHAPTER VI

We were ordered to the West Indies. Although Captain Boltrope's manner toward me was still severe, and even harsh, I understood that my name had been favorably mentioned in the dispatches.

Reader, were you ever at Jamaica? If so, you remember the negresses, the oranges, Port Royal Tom—the yellow fever. After being two weeks at the station, I was taken sick of the fever. In a month I was delirious. During my paroxysms, I had a wild distempered dream of a stern face bending anxiously over my pillow, a rough hand smoothing my hair, and a kind voice saying:—

"B'ess his 'ittle heart! Did he have the naughty fever?" This face seemed again changed to the well-known stern features of Captain Boltrope.

When I was convalescent, a packet edged in black was put in my hand. It contained the news of my father's death, and a sealed letter which he had requested to be given to me on his decease. I opened it tremblingly. It read thus:—

MY DEAR BOY,—I regret to inform you that in all probability you are not my son. Your mother, I am grieved to say, was a highly improper person. Who your father may be, I really cannot say, but perhaps the Honorable Henry Boltrope, Captain R. N., may be able to inform you. Circumstances over which I have no control have deferred this important disclosure. YOUR STRICKEN PARENT.

And so Captain Boltrope was my father. Heavens! Was it a dream? I recalled his stern manner, his observant eye, his ill-concealed uneasiness when in my presence. I longed to embrace him. Staggering to my feet, I rushed in my scanty apparel to the deck, where Captain Boltrope was just then engaged in receiving the Governor's wife and daughter. The ladies shrieked; the youngest, a beautiful girl, blushed deeply. Heeding them not, I sank at his feet, and, embracing them, cried,—

"My father!"

"Chuck him overboard!" roared Captain Boltrope.

"Stay," pleaded the soft voice of Clara Maitland, the Governor's daughter.

"Shave his head! he's a wretched lunatic!" continued Captain Boltrope, while his voice trembled with excitement.

"No, let me nurse and take care of him," said the lovely girl, blushing as she spoke. "Mamma, can't we take him home?"

The daughter's pleading was not without effect. In the meantime I had fainted. When I recovered my senses I found myself in Governor Maitland's mansion.

CHAPTER VII

The reader will guess what followed. I fell deeply in love with Clara Maitland, to whom I confided the secret of my birth. The generous girl asserted that she had detected the superiority of my manner at once. We plighted our troth, and resolved to wait upon events.

Briggs called to see me a few days afterward. He said that the purser had insulted the whole cockpit, and all the midshipmen had called him out. But he added thoughtfully: "I don't see how we can arrange the duel. You see there are six of us to fight him."

"Very easily," I replied. "Let your fellows all stand in a row, and take his fire; that, you see, gives him six chances to one, and he must be a bad shot if he can't hit one of you; while, on the other hand, you see, he gets a volley from you six, and one of you 'll be certain to fetch him."

"Exactly;" and away Briggs went, but soon returned to say that the purser had declined,—"like a d—d coward," he added.

But the news of the sudden and serious illness of Captain Boltrope put off the duel. I hastened to his bedside, but too late,—an hour previous he had given up the ghost.

I resolved to return to England. I made known the secret of my birth, and exhibited my adopted father's letter to Lady Maitland, who at once suggested my marriage with her daughter, before I returned to claim the property. We were married, and took our departure next day.

I made no delay in posting at once, in company with my wife and my friend Briggs, to my native village. Judge of my horror and surprise when my late adopted father came out of his shop to welcome me.

"Then you are not dead!" I gasped.

"No, my dear boy."

"And this letter?"

My father—as I must still call him—glanced on the paper, and pronounced it a forgery. Briggs roared with laughter. I turned to him and demanded an explanation.

"Why, don't you see, Greeny, it's all a joke,—a midshipman's joke!"

"But"—I asked.

"Don't be a fool. You've got a good wife,—be satisfied."

I turned to Clara, and was satisfied. Although Mrs. Maitland never forgave me, the jolly old Governor laughed heartily over the joke, and so well used his influence that I soon became, dear reader, Admiral Breezy, K. C. B.

GUY HEAVYSTONE; OR, "ENTIRE"
A MUSCULAR NOVEL

BY THE AUTHOR OF "SWORD AND GUN"

CHAPTER I

"NEREI REPANDIROSTRUM INCURVICERVICUM PECUS."

A Dingy, swashy, splashy afternoon in October; a school-yard filled with a mob of riotous boys. A lot of us standing outside.

Suddenly came a dull, crashing sound from the schoolroom. At the ominous interruption I shuddered involuntarily, and called to Smithsye,—

"What's up, Smithums?"

"Guy's cleaning out the fourth form," he replied.

At the same moment George de Coverly passed me, holding his nose, from whence the bright Norman blood streamed redly. To him the plebeian Smithsye laughingly,—

"Cully! how's his nibs?"

I pushed the door of the schoolroom open. There are some spectacles which a man never forgets. The burning of Troy probably seemed a large-sized conflagration to the pious Aeneas, and made an impression on him which he carried away with the feeble Anchises.

In the centre of the room, lightly brandishing the piston-rod of a steam-engine, stood Guy Heavystone alone. I say alone, for the pile of small boys on the floor in the corner could hardly be called company.

I will try and sketch him for the reader. Guy Heavystone was then only fifteen. His broad, deep chest, his sinewy and quivering flank, his straight pastern, showed him to be a thoroughbred. Perhaps he was a trifle heavy in the fetlock, but he held his head haughtily erect. His eyes were glittering but pitiless. There was a sternness about the lower part of his face,—the old Heavystone look,—a sternness heightened, perhaps, by the snaffle-bit which, in one of his strange freaks, he wore in his mouth to curb his occasional ferocity. His dress was well adapted to his square-set and herculean frame. A striped knit undershirt, close-fitting striped tights, and a few spangles set off his figure; a neat Glengarry cap adorned his head. On it was displayed the Heavystone crest, a cock *regardant* on a dunghill *or*, and the motto, "Devil a better!"

I thought of Horatius on the bridge, of Hector before the walls. I always make it a point to think of something classical at such times.

He saw me, and his sternness partly relaxed. Something like a smile struggled through his grim lineaments. It was like looking on the Jungfrau after having seen Mont Blanc,—a trifle, only a trifle less sublime and awful. Resting his hand lightly on the shoulder of the headmaster, who shuddered and collapsed under his touch, he strode toward me.

His walk was peculiar. You could not call it a stride. It was like the "crest-tossing Bellerophon,"—a kind of prancing gait. Guy Heavystone pranced toward me.

CHAPTER II

"Lord Lovel he stood at the garden gate,
-combing his milk-white steed."

It was the winter of 186- when I next met Guy Heavystone. He had left the university and had entered the 79th "Heavies." "I have exchanged the gown for the sword, you see," he said, grasping my hand, and fracturing the bones of my little finger, as he shook it.

I gazed at him with unmixed admiration. He was squarer, sterner, and in every way smarter and more remarkable than ever. I began to feel toward this man as Phalaster felt towards Phyrgino, as somebody must have felt toward Archididasculus, as Boswell felt toward Johnson.

"Come into my den," he said; and lifting me gently by the seat of my pantaloons he carried me upstairs and deposited me, before I could apologize, on the sofa. I looked around the room. It was a bachelor's apartment, characteristically furnished in the taste of the proprietor. A few claymores and battleaxes were ranged against the wall, and a culverin, captured by Sir Ralph Heavystone, occupied the corner, the other end of the room being taken up by a light battery. Foils, boxing-gloves, saddles, and fishing-poles lay around carelessly. A small pile of billets-doux lay upon a silver salver. The man was not an anchorite, nor yet a Sir Galahad.

I never could tell what Guy thought of women. "Poor little beasts," he would often say when the conversation turned on any of his fresh conquests. Then, passing his hand over his marble brow, the old look of stern fixedness of purpose and unflinching severity would straighten the lines of his mouth, and he would mutter, half to himself, "S'death!"

"Come with me to Heavystone Grange. The Exmoor hounds throw off to-morrow. I'll give you a mount," he said, as he amused himself by rolling up a silver candlestick between his fingers. "You shall have Cleopatra. But stay," he added thoughtfully; "now I remember, I ordered Cleopatra to be shot this morning."

"And why?" I queried.

"She threw her rider yesterday and fell on him"—

"And killed him?"

"No. That's the reason why I have ordered her to be shot. I keep no animals that are not dangerous—I should add—*deadly!*" He hissed the last sentence between his teeth, and a gloomy frown descended over his calm brow.

I affected to turn over the tradesmen's bills that lay on the table, for, like all of the Heavystone race, Guy seldom paid cash, and said,—

"You remind me of the time when Leonidas"—

"Oh, bother Leonidas and your classical allusions. Come!"

We descended to dinner.

CHAPTER III

"He carries weight, he rides a race,
'Tis for a thousand pound."

"There is Flora Billingsgate, the greatest coquette and hardest rider in the country," said my companion, Ralph Mortmain, as we stood upon Dingleby Common before the meet.

I looked up and beheld Guy Heavystone bending haughtily over the saddle, as he addressed a beautiful brunette. She was indeed a splendidly groomed and high-spirited woman. We were near enough to overhear the following conversation, which any high-toned reader will recognize as the common and natural expression of the higher classes.

"When Diana takes the field the chase is not wholly confined to objects ferae nature," said Guy, darting a significant glance at his companion. Flora did not shrink either from the glance or the meaning implied in the sarcasm.

"If I were looking for an Endymion, now,"—she said archly, as she playfully cantered over a few hounds and leaped a five-barred gate.

Guy whispered a few words, inaudible to the rest of the party, and curveting slightly, cleverly cleared two of the huntsmen in a flying leap, galloped up the front steps of the mansion, and, dashing at full speed through the hall, leaped through the drawing-room window and rejoined me, languidly, on the lawn.

"Be careful of Flora Billingsgate," he said to me, in low stern tones, while his pitiless eye shot a baleful fire. "Gardez-vous!"

"Gnothi seauton," I replied calmly, not wishing to appear to be behind him in perception or verbal felicity.

Guy started off in high spirits. He was well carried. He and the first whip, a ten-stone man, were head and head at the last fence, while the hounds were rolling over their fox a hundred yards farther in the open.

But an unexpected circumstance occurred. Coming back, his chestnut mare refused a ten-foot wall. She reared and fell backward. Again he led her up to it lightly; again she refused, falling heavily from the coping. Guy started to his feet. The old pitiless fire shone in his eyes; the old stern look settled around his mouth. Seizing the mare by the tail and mane he threw her over the wall. She landed twenty feet on the other side, erect and trembling. Lightly leaping the same obstacle himself, he remounted her. She did not refuse the wall the next time.

CHAPTER IV

"He holds him by his glittering eye."

Guy was in the north of Ireland, cock-shooting. So Ralph Mortmain told me, and also that the match between Mary Brandagee and Guy had been broken off by Flora Billingsgate. "I don't like those Billingsgates," said Ralph, "they're a bad stock. Her father, Smithfield de Billingsgate, had an unpleasant way of turning up the knave from the bottom of the pack. But nous varrons; let us go and see Guy."

The next morning we started for Fin-ma-Coul's Crossing. When I reached the shooting-box, where Guy was entertaining a select company of friends, Flora Billingsgate greeted me with a saucy smile. Guy was even squarer and sterner than ever. His gusts of passion were more frequent, and it was with difficulty that he could keep an able-bodied servant in his family. His present retainers were more or less maimed from exposure to the fury of their master. There was a strange cynicism, a cutting sarcasm in his address, piercing through his polished manner. I thought of Timon, etc., etc.

One evening, we were sitting over our Chambertin, after a hard day's work, and Guy was listlessly turning over some letters, when suddenly he uttered a cry. Did you ever hear the trumpeting of a wounded elephant? It was like that.

I looked at him with consternation. He was glancing at a letter which he held at arm's length, and snorting, as it were, at it as he gazed. The lower part of his face was stern, but not as rigid as usual. He was slowly grinding between his teeth the fragments of the glass he had just been drinking from.

Suddenly he seized one of his servants, and forcing the wretch upon his knees, exclaimed, with the roar of a tiger,—

"Dog! why was this kept from me?"

"Why, please sir, Miss Flora said as how it was a reconciliation from Miss Brandagee, and it was to be kept from you where you would not be likely to see it,—and—and"—

"Speak, dog! and you"—

"I put it among your bills, sir!"

With a groan, like distant thunder, Guy fell swooning to the floor.

He soon recovered, for the next moment a servant came rushing into the room with the information that a number of the ingenuous peasantry of the neighborhood were about to indulge that evening in the national pastime of burning a farmhouse and shooting a landlord. Guy smiled a fearful smile, without, however, altering his stern and pitiless expression.

"Let them come," he said calmly; "I feel like entertaining company."

We barricaded the doors and windows, and then chose our arms from the armory. Guy's choice was a singular one: it was a landing-net with a long handle, and a sharp cavalry sabre.

We were not destined to remain long in ignorance of its use. A howl was heard from without, and a party of fifty or sixty armed men precipitated themselves against the door.

Suddenly the window opened. With the rapidity of lightning, Guy Heavystone cast the net over the head of the ringleader, ejaculated "Habet!" and with a backstroke of his cavalry sabre severed the member from its trunk, and drawing the net back again, cast the gory head upon the floor, saying quietly,—

"One."

Again the net was cast, the steel flashed, the net was withdrawn, and an ominous "Two!" accompanied the head as it rolled on the floor.

"Do you remember what Pliny says of the gladiator?" said Guy, calmly wiping his sabre. "How graphic is that passage commencing 'Inter nos,' etc." The sport continued until the heads of twenty desperadoes had been gathered in. The rest seemed inclined to disperse. Guy incautiously showed himself at the door; a ringing shot was heard, and he staggered back, pierced through the heart. Grasping the doorpost in the last unconscious throes of his mighty frame, the whole side of the house yielded to that earthquake tremor, and we had barely time to escape before the whole building fell in ruins. I thought of Samson, the giant judge, etc., etc.; but all was over.

Guy Heavystone had died as he had lived,—*hard*.

JOHN JENKINS OR THE SMOKER REFORMED BY T. S. A-TH-R

CHAPTER I

"One cigar a day!" said Judge Boompointer.

"One cigar a day!" repeated John Jenkins, as with trepidation he dropped his half-consumed cigar under his work-bench.

"One cigar a day is three cents a day," remarked Judge Boompointer gravely; "and do you know, sir, what one cigar a day, or three cents a day, amounts to in the course of four years?"

John Jenkins, in his boyhood, had attended the village school, and possessed considerable arithmetical ability. Taking up a shingle which lay upon his work-bench, and producing a piece of chalk, with a feeling of conscious pride he made an exhaustive calculation.

"Exactly forty-three dollars and eighty cents," he replied, wiping the perspiration from his heated brow, while his face flushed with honest enthusiasm.

"Well, sir, if you saved three cents a day, instead of wasting it, you would now be the possessor of a new suit of clothes, an illustrated Family Bible, a pew in the church, a complete set of Patent Office Reports, a hymnbook, and a paid subscription to 'Arthur's Home Magazine,' which could be purchased for exactly forty-three dollars and eighty cents; and," added the Judge, with increasing sternness, "if you calculate leap-year, which you seem to have strangely omitted, you have three cents more, sir—*three cents more!* What would that buy you, sir?"

"A cigar," suggested John Jenkins; but, coloring again deeply, he hid his face.

"No, sir," said the Judge, with a sweet smile of benevolence stealing over his stern features; "properly invested, it would buy you that which passeth all price. Dropped into the missionary-box, who can tell what heathen, now idly and joyously wantoning in nakedness and sin, might be brought to a sense of his miserable condition, and made, through that three cents, to feel the torments of the wicked?"

With these words the Judge retired, leaving John Jenkins buried in profound thought. "Three cents a day," he muttered. "In forty years I might be worth four hundred and thirty-eight dollars and ten cents,— and then I might marry Mary. Ah, Mary!" The young carpenter sighed, and drawing a twenty-five cent daguerreotype from his vest-pocket, gazed long and fervidly upon the features of a young girl in book muslin and a coral necklace. Then, with a resolute expression, he carefully locked the door of his work-shop, and departed.

Alas! his good resolutions were too late. We trifle with the tide of fortune, which too often nips us in the bud and casts the dark shadow of misfortune over the bright lexicon of youth! That night the half-consumed fragment of John Jenkins's cigar set fire to his work-shop and burned it up, together with all his tools and materials. There was no insurance.

CHAPTER II

THE DOWNWARD PATH

"Then you still persist in marrying John Jenkins?" queried Judge Boompointer, as he playfully, with paternal familiarity, lifted the golden curls of the village belle, Mary Jones.

"I do," replied the fair young girl, in a low voice that resembled rock candy in its saccharine firmness,—"I do. He has promised to reform. Since he lost all his property by fire"—

"The result of his pernicious habit, though he illogically persists in charging it to me," interrupted the Judge.

"Since then," continued the young girl, "he has endeavored to break himself of the habit. He tells me that he has substituted the stalks of the Indian rattan, the outer part of a leguminous plant called the smoking-bean, and the fragmentary and unconsumed remainder of cigars, which occur at rare and uncertain intervals along the road, which, as he informs me, though deficient in quality and strength, are comparatively inexpensive." And blushing at her own eloquence, the young girl hid her curls on the Judge's arm.

"Poor thing!" muttered Judge Boompointer. "Dare I tell her all? Yet I must."

"I shall cling to him," continued the young girl, rising with her theme, "as the young vine clings to some hoary ruin. Nay, nay, chide me not, Judge Boompointer. I will marry John Jenkins!"

The Judge was evidently affected. Seating himself at the table, he wrote a few lines hurriedly upon a piece of paper, which he folded and placed in the fingers of the destined bride of John Jenkins.

"Mary Jones," said the Judge, with impressive earnestness, "take this trifle as a wedding gift from one who respects your fidelity and truthfulness. At the altar let it be a reminder of me." And covering his face hastily with a handkerchief, the stern and iron-willed man left the room. As the door closed, Mary unfolded the paper. It was an order on the corner grocery for three yards of flannel, a paper of needles, four pounds of soap, one pound of starch, and two boxes of matches!

"Noble and thoughtful man!" was all Mary Jones could exclaim, as she hid her face in her hands and burst into a flood of tears.

The bells of Cloverdale are ringing merrily. It is a wedding. "How beautiful they look!" is the exclamation that passes from lip to lip, as Mary Jones, leaning timidly on the arm of John Jenkins, enters the church. But the bride is agitated, and the bridegroom betrays a feverish nervousness. As they stand in the vestibule, John Jenkins fumbles earnestly in his vest-pocket. Can it be the ring he is anxious about? No. He draws a small brown substance from his pocket, and biting off a piece, hastily replaces the fragment and gazes furtively around. Surely no one saw him? Alas! the eyes of two of that wedding party saw the fatal act. Judge Boompointer shook his head sternly. Mary Jones sighed and breathed a silent prayer. Her husband chewed!

CHAPTER III AND LAST

"What! more bread?" said John Jenkins gruffly. "You're always asking for money for bread. D—nation! Do you want to ruin me by your extravagance?" and as he uttered these words he drew from his pocket a bottle of whiskey, a pipe, and a paper of tobacco. Emptying the first at a draught, he threw the empty bottle at the head of his eldest boy, a youth of twelve summers. The missile struck the child full in the temple, and stretched him a lifeless corpse. Mrs. Jenkins, whom the reader will hardly recognize as the once gay and beautiful Mary Jones, raised the dead body of her son in her arms, and carefully placing the unfortunate youth beside the pump in the back yard, returned with saddened step to the house. At another time, and in brighter days, she might have wept at the occurrence. She was past tears now.

"Father, your conduct is reprehensible!" said little Harrison Jenkins, the youngest boy. "Where do you expect to go when you die?"

"Ah!" said John Jenkins fiercely; "this comes of giving children a liberal education; this is the result of Sabbath-schools. Down, viper!"

A tumbler thrown from the same parental fist laid out the youthful Harrison cold. The four other children had, in the mean time, gathered around the table with anxious expectancy. With a chuckle, the now changed and brutal John Jenkins produced four pipes, and filling them with tobacco, handed one to each of his offspring and bade them smoke. "It's better than bread!" laughed the wretch hoarsely.

Mary Jenkins, though of a patient nature, felt it her duty now to speak. "I have borne much, John Jenkins," she said. "But I prefer that the children should not smoke. It is an unclean habit, and soils their clothes. I ask this as a special favor!"

John Jenkins hesitated,—the pangs of remorse began to seize him.

"Promise me this, John!" urged Mary upon her knees.

"I promise!" reluctantly answered John.

"And you will put the money in a savings-bank?"

"I will," repeated her husband; "and I'll give up smoking, too."

"'Tis well, John Jenkins!" said Judge Boompointer, appearing suddenly from behind the door, where he had been concealed during this interview. "Nobly said! my man. Cheer up! I will see that the children are decently buried." The husband and wife fell into each other's arms. And Judge Boompointer, gazing upon the affecting spectacle, burst into tears.

From that day John Jenkins was an altered man.

FANTINE AFTER THE FRENCH OF VICTOR HUGO

PROLOGUE

*As long as there shall exist three paradoxes, a moral
Frenchman, a religious atheist, and a believing skeptic;
so long, in fact, as booksellers shall wait—say twenty-live
years—for a new gospel; so long as paper shall remain
cheap and ink three sous a bottle, I have no hesitation in
saying that such books as these are not utterly profitless.
VICTOR HUGO.*

To be good is to be queer. What is a good man? Bishop Myriel.

My friend, you will possibly object to this. You will say you know
what a good man is. Perhaps you will say your clergyman is a good
man, for instance. Bah! you are mistaken; you are an Englishman, and
an Englishman is a beast.

Englishmen think they are moral when they are only serious. These
Englishmen also wear ill-shaped hats, and dress horribly!

Bah! they are canaille.

Still, Bishop Myriel was a good man,—quite as good as you. Better
than you, in fact.

One day M. Myriel was in Paris. This angel used to walk about the streets like any other man. He was not proud, though fine-looking. Well, three gamins de Paris called him bad names. Says one,—

"Ah, mon Dieu! there goes a priest; look out for your eggs and chickens!" What did this good man do? He called to them kindly.

"My children," said he, "this is clearly not your fault. I recognize in this insult and irreverence only the fault of your immediate progenitors. Let us pray for your immediate progenitors."

They knelt down and prayed for their immediate progenitors.

The effect was touching.

The Bishop looked calmly around.

"On reflection," said he gravely, "I was mistaken; this is clearly the fault of Society. Let us pray for Society."

They knelt down and prayed for Society.

The effect was sublimer yet. What do you think of that? You, I mean.

Everybody remembers the story of the Bishop and Mother Nez Retrousse. Old Mother Nez Retrousse sold asparagus. She was poor; there's a great deal of meaning in that word, my friend. Some people say "poor but honest." I say, Bah!

Bishop Myriel bought six bunches of asparagus. This good man had one charming failing: he was fond of asparagus. He gave her a franc, and received three sous change.

The sous were bad,—counterfeit. What did this good Bishop do? He said: "I should not have taken change from a poor woman."

Then afterwards, to his housekeeper: "Never take change from a poor woman."

Then he added to himself: "For the sous will probably be bad."

II

When a man commits a crime, Society claps him in prison. A prison is one of the worst hotels imaginable.

The people there are low and vulgar. The butter is bad, the coffee is green. Ah, it is horrible!

In prison, as in a bad hotel, a man soon loses, not only his morals, but what is much worse to a Frenchman, his sense of refinement and delicacy.

Jean Valjean came from prison with confused notions of Society. He forgot the modern peculiarities of hospitality. So he walked off with the Bishop's candlesticks.

Let us consider. Candlesticks were stolen; that was evident. Society put Jean Valjean in prison; that was evident, too. In prison, Society took away his refinement; that is evident, likewise.

Who is Society?

You and I are Society.

My friend, you and I stole those candlesticks!

III

The Bishop thought so, too. He meditated profoundly for six days. On the morning of the seventh he went to the Prefecture of Police.

He said: "Monsieur, have me arrested. I have stolen candlesticks."

The official was governed by the law of Society, and refused.

What did this Bishop do?

He had a charming ball and chain made, affixed to his leg, and wore it the rest of his life. This is a fact!

IV

Love is a mystery.

A little friend of mine down in the country, at Auvergne, said to me one day: "Victor, Love is the world,—it contains everything."

She was only sixteen, this sharp-witted little girl, and a beautiful blonde. She thought everything of me.

Fantine was one of those women who do wrong in the most virtuous and touching manner. This is a peculiarity of French grisettes.

You are an Englishman, and you don't understand. Learn, my friend, learn. Come to Paris and improve your morals.

Fantine was the soul of modesty. She always wore high-neck dresses. High-neck dresses are a sign of modesty.

Fantine loved Tholmoyes. Why? My God! What are you to do? It was the fault of her parents, and she hadn't any. How shall you teach her? You must teach the parent if you wish to educate the child. How would you become virtuous?

Teach your grandmother!

V

When Tholmoyes ran away from Fantine,—which was done in a charming, gentlemanly manner,—Fantine became convinced that a rigid sense of propriety might look upon her conduct as immoral. She was a creature of sensitiveness,—and her eyes were opened.

She was virtuous still, and resolved to break off the liaison at once.

So she put up her wardrobe and baby in a bundle, child as she was, she loved them both,—then left Paris.

VI

Fantine's native place had changed.

M. Madeline—an angel, and inventor of jet-work—had been teaching the villagers how to make spurious jet.

This is a progressive age. Those Americans—children of the West,— they make nutmegs out of wood.

I, myself, have seen hams made of pine, in the wigwams of those children of the forest.

But civilization has acquired deception too. Society is made up of deception. Even the best French society.

Still there was one sincere episode.

Eh?

The French Revolution!

VII

M. Madeline was, if anything, better than Myriel.

M. Myriel was a saint. M. Madeline a good man.

M. Myriel was dead. M. Madeline was living.

That made all the difference.

M. Madeline made virtue profitable. I have seen it written,—

"Be virtuous and you will be happy."

Where did I see this written? In the modern Bible? No. In the Koran? No. In Rousseau? No. Diderot? No. Where then?

In a copy-book.

VIII

M. Madeline was M. le Maire.

This is how it came about.

For a long time he refused the honor. One day an old woman, standing on the steps, said,—

"Bah, a good mayor is a good thing.

"You are a good thing.

"Be a good mayor."

This woman was a rhetorician. She understood inductive ratiocination.

IX

When this good M. Madeline, who, the reader will perceive, must have been a former convict, and a very bad man, gave himself up to justice as the real Jean Valjean, about this same time, Fantine was turned away from the manufactory, and met with a number of losses from Society. Society attacked her, and this is what she lost:—

First her lover.

Then her child.

Then her place.

Then her hair.

Then her teeth.

Then her liberty.

Then her life.

What do you think of Society after that? I tell you the present social system is a humbug.

X

This is necessarily the end of Fantine.

There are other things that will be stated in other volumes to follow. Don't be alarmed; there are plenty of miserable people left.

Au revoir—my friend.

"LA FEMME"

HAFTER THE FRENCH OF M. MICHELET

I WOMEN AS AN INSTITUTION

"If it were not for women, few of us would at present be in existence." This is the remark of a cautious and discreet writer. He was also sagacious and intelligent.

Woman! Look upon her and admire her. Gaze upon her and love her. If she wishes to embrace you, permit her. Remember she is weak and you are strong.

But don't treat her unkindly. Don't make love to another woman before her face, even if she be your wife. Don't do it. Always be polite, even should she fancy somebody better than you.

If your mother, my dear Amadis, had not fancied your father better than somebody, you might have been that somebody's son. Consider this. Always be a philosopher, even about women.

Few men understand women. Frenchmen, perhaps, better than any one else. I am a Frenchman.

II
THE INFANT

She is a child—a little thing—an infant.

She has a mother and father. Let us suppose, for example, they are

130

married. Let us be moral if we cannot be happy and free—they are married—perhaps—they love one another—who knows?

But she knows nothing of this; she is an infant—a small thing—a trifle!

She is not lovely at first. It is cruel, perhaps, but she is red, and positively ugly. She feels this keenly, and cries. She weeps. Ah, my God, how she weeps! Her cries and lamentations now are really distressing.

Tears stream from her in floods. She feels deeply and copiously, like M. Alphonse de Lamartine in his "Confessions."

If you are her mother, Madame, you will fancy worms; you will examine her linen for pins, and what not. Ah, hypocrite! you, even *you*, misunderstand her.

Yet she has charming natural impulses. See how she tosses her dimpled arms. She looks longingly at her mother. She has a language of her own. She says, "goo, goo," and "ga, ga." She demands something—this infant!

She is faint, poor thing. She famishes. She wishes to be restored. Restore her, Mother! *It is the first duty of a mother to restore her child!*

III
THE DOLL

She is hardly able to walk; she already totters under the weight of a doll.

It is a charming and elegant affair. It has pink cheeks and purple-black hair. She prefers brunettes, for she has already, with the quick knowledge of a French infant, perceived she is a blonde, and that her doll cannot rival her. Mon Dieu, how touching! Happy child! She spends hours in preparing its toilet. She begins to show her taste in the exquisite details of its dress. She loves it madly, devotedly. She will prefer it to bonbons. She already anticipates the wealth of love she will hereafter pour out on her lover, her mother, her father, and finally, perhaps, her husband.

This is the time the anxious parent will guide these first outpourings. She will read her extracts from Michelet's "L'Amour," Rousseau's "Heloise," and the "Revue des deux Mondes."

IV
THE MUD PIE

She was in tears to-day.

She had stolen away from her bonne and was with some rustic infants. They had noses in the air, and large, coarse hands and feet.

They had seated themselves around a pool in the road, and were fashioning fantastic shapes in the clayey soil with their hands. Her throat swelled and her eyes sparkled with delight as, for the first time, her soft palms touched the plastic mud. She made a graceful and lovely pie. She stuffed it with stones for almonds and plums. She forgot everything. It was being baked in the solar rays, when madame came and took her away.

She weeps. It is night, and she is weeping still.

V
THE FIRST LOVE

She no longer doubts her beauty. She is loved.

She saw him secretly. He is vivacious and sprightly. He is famous. He has already had an affair with Finfin, the fille de chambre, and poor Finfin is desolate. He is noble. She knows he is the son of Madame la Baronne Couturiere. She adores him.

She affects not to notice him. Poor little thing! Hippolyte is distracted—annihilated—inconsolable and charming.

She admires his boots, his cravat, his little gloves—his exquisite pantaloons—his coat, and cane.

She offers to run away with him. He is transported, but magnanimous. He is wearied, perhaps. She sees him the next day offering flowers to the daughter of Madame la Comtesse Blanchisseuse.

She is again in tears.

She reads "Paul et Virginie." She is secretly transported. When she reads how the exemplary young woman laid down her life rather than appear en deshabille to her lover, she weeps again. Tasteful and virtuous Bernardin de Saint-Pierre!—the daughters of France admire you!

All this time her doll is headless in the cabinet. The mud pie is broken on the road.

VI
THE WIFE

She is tired of loving, and she marries.

Her mother thinks it, on the whole, the best thing. As the day approaches, she is found frequently in tears. Her mother will not permit the affianced one to see her, and he makes several attempts to commit suicide.

But something happens. Perhaps it is winter, and the water is cold. Perhaps there are not enough people present to witness his heroism.

In this way her future husband is spared to her. The ways of Providence are indeed mysterious. At this time her mother will talk with her. She will offer philosophy. She will tell her she was married herself.

But what is this new and ravishing light that breaks upon her? The toilet and wedding clothes! She is in a new sphere.

She makes out her list in her own charming writing. Here it is. Let every mother heed it. [Footnote: The delicate reader will appreciate the omission of certain articles for which English synonyms are forbidden.]

She is married. On the day after, she meets her old lover, Hippolyte. He is again transported.

VII
HER OLD AGE

A Frenchwoman never grows old.

THE DWELLER OF THE THRESHOLD

BY SIR ED-D L-TT-N B-LW-R

BOOK I THE PROMPTINGS OF THE IDEAL

It was noon. Sir Edward had stepped from his brougham, and was proceeding on foot down the Strand. He was dressed with his usual faultless taste, but in alighting from his vehicle his foot had slipped, and a small round disk of conglomerated soil, which instantly appeared on his high arched instep, marred the harmonious glitter of his boots. Sir Edward was fastidious. Casting his eyes around, at a little distance he perceived the stand of a youthful bootblack. Thither he sauntered, and carelessly placing his foot on the low stool, he waited the application of the polisher's art. "'Tis true," said Sir Edward to himself, yet half aloud, "the contact of the Foul and the Disgusting mars the general effect of the Shiny and the Beautiful—and, yet, why am I here? I repeat it, calmly and deliberately—why am I here? Ha! Boy!"

The Boy looked up—his dark Italian eyes glanced intelligently at the Philosopher, and as with one hand he tossed back his glossy curls from his marble brow, and with the other he spread the equally glossy Day & Martin over the Baronet's boot, he answered in deep, rich tones: "The Ideal is subjective to the Real. The exercise of apperception gives a distinctiveness to idiocracy, which is, however, subject to the limits of ME. You are an admirer of the Beautiful, sir. You wish your boots blacked. The Beautiful is attainable by means of the Coin."

"Ah," said Sir Edward thoughtfully, gazing upon the almost supernal beauty of the Child before him; "you speak well. You have read Kant."

The Boy blushed deeply. He drew a copy of Kant from his blouse, but in his confusion several other volumes dropped from his bosom on the ground. The Baronet picked them up.

"Ah!" said the Philosopher, "what's this? Cicero's 'De Sonertute,'—at your age, too! Martial's 'Epigrams,' Caesar's 'Commentaries.' What! a classical scholar?"

"E pluribus Unum. Nux vomica. Nil desperandum. Nihil fit!" said the Boy enthusiastically. The Philosopher gazed at the Child. A strange presence seemed to transfuse and possess him. Over the brow of the Boy glittered the pale nimbus of the Student.

"Ah, and Schiller's 'Robbers,' too?" queried the Philosopher.

"Das ist ausgespielt," said the Boy modestly.

"Then you have read my translation of Schiller's 'Ballads'?" continued the Baronet, with some show of interest.

"I have, and infinitely prefer them to the original," said the Boy, with intellectual warmth. "You have shown how in Actual life we strive for a Goal we cannot reach; how in the Ideal the Goal is attainable, and there effort is victory. You have given us the Antithesis which is a key to the Remainder, and constantly balances before us the conditions of the Actual and the privileges of the Ideal."

"My very words," said the Baronet; "wonderful, wonderful!" and he gazed fondly at the Italian boy, who again resumed his menial employment. Alas! the wings of the Ideal were folded. The Student had been absorbed in the Boy.

But Sir Edward's boots were blacked, and he turned to depart. Placing his hand upon the clustering tendrils that surrounded the classic nob of the infant Italian, he said softly, like a strain of distant music,—

"Boy, you have done well. Love the Good. Protect the Innocent. Provide for the Indigent. Respect the Philosopher.... Stay! Can you tell me what *is* The True, The Beautiful, The Innocent, The Virtuous?"

"They are things that commence with a capital letter," said the Boy promptly.

"Enough! Respect everything that commences with a capital letter! Respect ME!" and dropping a halfpenny in the hand of the boy, he departed.

The Boy gazed fixedly at the coin. A frightful and instantaneous change overspread his features. His noble brow was corrugated with baser lines of calculation. His black eye, serpent-like, glittered with suppressed passion. Dropping upon his hands and feet, he crawled to the curbstone, and hissed after the retreating form of the Baronet the single word—

"Bilk!"

BOOK II
IN THE WORLD

"Eleven years ago," said Sir Edward to himself, as his brougham slowly rolled him toward the Committee Room, "just eleven years ago my natural son disappeared mysteriously. I have no doubt in the world but that this little bootblack is he. His mother died in Italy. He resembles his mother very much. Perhaps I ought to provide for him. Shall I disclose myself? No! no! Better he should taste the sweets of Labor. Penury ennobles the mind and kindles the Love of the Beautiful. I will act to him, not like a Father, not like a Guardian, not like a Friend—but like a Philosopher!" With these words, Sir Edward entered the Committee Room. His Secretary approached him. "Sir Edward, there are fears of a division in the House, and the Prime Minister has sent for you."

"I will be there," said Sir Edward, as he placed his hand on his chest and uttered a hollow cough!

No one who heard the Baronet that night, in his sarcastic and withering speech on the Drainage and Sewerage Bill, would have recognized the Lover of the Ideal and the Philosopher of the Beautiful. No one who listened to his eloquence would have dreamed of the

Spartan resolution this iron man had taken in regard to the Lost Boy—his own beloved Lionel. None!

"A fine speech from Sir Edward to-night," said Lord Billingsgate, as, arm and arm with the Premier, he entered his carriage.

"Yes! but how dreadfully he coughs!"

"Exactly. Dr. Bolus says his lungs are entirely gone; he breathes entirely by an effort of will, and altogether independent of pulmonary assistance."

"How strange!" And the carriage rolled away.

BOOK III
THE DWELLER OF THE THRESHOLD

"Adon Ai, appear! appear!"

And as the Seer spoke, the awful Presence glided out of Nothingness, and sat, sphinx-like, at the feet of the Alchemist.

"I am come!" said the Thing.

"You should say, 'I have come,'—it's better grammar," said the Boy-Neophyte, thoughtfully accenting the substituted expression.

"Hush, rash Boy," said the Seer sternly. "Would you oppose your feeble knowledge to the infinite intelligence of the Unmistakable? A word, and you are lost forever."

The Boy breathed a silent prayer, and handing a sealed package to the Seer, begged him to hand it to his father in case of his premature decease.

"You have sent for me," hissed the Presence. "Behold me, Apokatharticon,—the Unpronounceable. In me all things exist that are not already coexistent. I am the Unattainable, the Intangible, the Cause, and the Effect. In me observe the Brahma of Mr. Emerson; not only Brahma himself, but also the sacred musical composition rehearsed by the faithful Hindoo. I am the real Gyges. None others are genuine."

And the veiled Son of the Starbeam laid himself loosely about the room, and permeated Space generally.

"Unfathomable Mystery," said the Rosicrucian in a low, sweet voice. "Brave Child with the Vitreous Optic! Thou who pervadest all things and rubbest against us without abrasion of the cuticle. I command thee, speak!"

And the misty, intangible, indefinite Presence spoke.

BOOK IV
MYSELF

After the events related in the last chapter, the reader will perceive that nothing was easier than to reconcile Sir Edward to his son Lionel, nor to resuscitate the beautiful Italian girl, who, it appears, was not dead, and to cause Sir Edward to marry his first and boyish love, whom he had deserted. They were married in St. George's, Hanover Square. As the bridal party stood before the altar, Sir Edward, with a sweet, sad smile, said in quite his old manner,—

"The Sublime and Beautiful are the Real; the only Ideal is the Ridiculous and Homely. Let us always remember this. Let us through life endeavor to personify the virtues, and always begin 'em with a capital letter. Let us, whenever we can find an opportunity, deliver our sentiments in the form of roundhand copies. Respect the Aged. Eschew Vulgarity. Admire Ourselves. Regard the Novelist."

N N. BEING A NOVEL IN THE FRENCH PARAGRAPHIC STYLE

—Mademoiselle, I swear to you that I love you.

—You who read these pages. You who turn your burning eyes upon these words—words that I trace—ah, heaven! the thought maddens me.

—I will be calm. I will imitate the reserve of the festive Englishman, who wears a spotted handkerchief which he calls a Belchio, who eats biftek, and caresses a bulldog. I will subdue myself like him.

—Ha! Poto-beer! All right—Goddam!

—Or, I will conduct myself as the free-born American—the gay Brother Jonathan. I will whittle me a stick. I will whistle to myself "Yankee Doodle," and forget my passion in excessive expectoration.

—Ho! ho!—wake snakes and walk chalks.

The world is divided into two great divisions,—Paris and the provinces. There is but one Paris. There are several provinces, among which may be numbered England, America, Russia, and Italy.

N N. was a Parisian.

But N N. did not live in Paris. Drop a Parisian in the provinces, and you drop a part of Paris with him. Drop him in Senegambia, and in three days he will give you an omelette soufflee, or a pate de foie gras, served by the neatest of Senegambian filles, whom he will call mademoiselle. In three weeks he will give you an opera.

N N. was not dropped in Senegambia, but in San Francisco,—quite as awkward.

They find gold in San Francisco, but they don't understand gilding.

N N. existed three years in this place. He became bald on the top of his head, as all Parisians do. Look down from your box at the Opera Comique, mademoiselle, and count the bald crowns of the fast young men in the pit. Ah—you tremble! They show where the arrows of love have struck and glanced off.

N N. was almost near-sighted, as all Parisians finally become. This is a gallant provision of nature to spare them the mortification of observing that their lady friends grow old. After a certain age every woman is handsome to a Parisian.

One day, N N. was walking down Washington Street. Suddenly he stopped.

He was standing before the door of a mantua-maker. Beside the counter, at the farther extremity of the shop, stood a young and elegantly formed woman. Her face was turned from N N. He entered. With a plausible excuse and seeming indifference, he gracefully opened conversation with the mantua-maker as only a Parisian can. But he had to deal with a Parisian. His attempts to view the features of the fair stranger by the counter were deftly combated by the shopwoman. He was obliged to retire.

N N. went home and lost his appetite. He was haunted by the elegant basque and graceful shoulders of the fair unknown, during the whole night.

The next day he sauntered by the mantua-maker. Ah! Heavens! A thrill ran through his frame, and his fingers tingled with a delicious electricity. The fair inconnue was there! He raised his hat gracefully. He was not certain, but he thought that a slight motion of her faultless bonnet betrayed recognition. He would have wildly darted into the shop, but just then the figure of the mantua-maker appeared in the doorway.

—Did monsieur wish anything?

—Misfortune! Desperation. N N. purchased a bottle of Prussic acid, a sack of charcoal, and a quire of pink note-paper, and returned home. He wrote a letter of farewell to the closely fitting basque, and opened the bottle of Prussic acid.

Some one knocked at his door. It was a Chinaman, with his weekly linen.

These Chinese are docile, but not intelligent. They are ingenious, but not creative. They are cunning in expedients, but deficient in tact. In love they are simply barbarous. They purchase their wives openly, and not constructively by attorney. By offering small sums for their sweethearts, they degrade the value of the sex.

Nevertheless, N N. felt he was saved. He explained all to the faithful Mongolian, and exhibited the letter he had written. He implored him to deliver it.

The Mongolian assented. The race are not cleanly or sweet-savored, but N N. fell upon his neck. He embraced him with one hand, and closed his nostrils with the other. Through him, he felt he clasped the close-fitting basque.

The next day was one of agony and suspense. Evening came, but no mercy. N N. lit the charcoal. But, to compose his nerves, he closed his door and first walked mildly up and down Montgomery Street. When he returned, he found the faithful Mongolian on the steps.

—All lity!

These Chinese are not accurate in their pronunciation. They avoid the *r*, like the English nobleman.

N N. gasped for breath. He leaned heavily against the Chinaman.

—Then you have seen her, Ching Long?

—Yes. All lity. She cum. Top side of house.

The docile barbarian pointed up the stairs, and chuckled.

—She here—impossible! Ah, Heaven! do I dream?

—Yes. All lity,—top side of house. Good-by, John.

This is the familiar parting epithet of the Mongolian. It is equivalent to our au revoir.

N N. gazed with a stupefied air on the departing servant.

He placed his hand on his throbbing heart. She here,—alone beneath this roof? Oh, heavens,—what happiness!

But how? Torn from her home. Ruthlessly dragged, perhaps, from her evening devotions, by the hands of a relentless barbarian. Could she forgive him?

He dashed frantically up the stairs. He opened the door.

She was standing beside his couch with averted face.

A strange giddiness overtook him. He sank upon his knees at the threshold.

—Pardon, pardon. My angel, can you forgive me?

A terrible nausea now seemed added to the fearful giddiness. His utterance grew thick and sluggish.

—Speak, speak, enchantress. Forgiveness is all I ask. My Love, my Life!

She did not answer. He staggered to his feet. As he rose, his eyes fell on the pan of burning charcoal. A terrible suspicion flashed across his mind. This giddiness—this nausea. The ignorance of the barbarian. This silence. Oh, merciful heavens! she was dying!

He crawled toward her. He touched her. She fell forward with a lifeless sound upon the floor. He uttered a piercing shriek, and threw himself beside her.

A file of gendarmes, accompanied by the Chef Burke, found him the next morning lying lifeless upon the floor. They laughed brutally— these cruel minions of the law—and disengaged his arm from the waist of the wooden dummy which they had come to reclaim, from the mantua-maker.

Emptying a few bucketfuls of water over his form, they finally succeeded in robbing him, not only of his mistress, but of that Death he had coveted without her.

Ah! we live in a strange world, messieurs.

NO TITLE

BY W-LK-E C-LL-NS
PROLOGUE

The following advertisement appeared in the "Times" of the 17th of June, 1845:—

WANTED.—A few young men for a light, genteel employment. Address J. W., P. O.

In the same paper, of same date, in another column:—

TO LET.—That commodious and elegant family mansion, No. 27 Limehouse Road, Pultneyville, will be rented low to a respectable tenant if applied for immediately, the family being about to remove to the Continent.

Under the local intelligence, in another column:—

MISSING.—An unknown elderly gentleman a week ago left his lodgings in the Kent Road, since which nothing has been heard of him. He left no trace of his identity except a portmanteau containing a couple of shirts marked "209, Ward."

To find the connection between the mysterious disappearance of the elderly gentleman and the anonymous communication, the relevancy of both these incidents to the letting of a commodious family mansion, and the dead secret involved in the three occurrences, is the task of the writer of this history.

A slim young man with spectacles, a large hat, drab gaiters, and a notebook, sat late that night with a copy of the "Times" before him, and a pencil which he rattled nervously between his teeth in the coffee-room of the Blue Dragon.

CHAPTER I
MARY JONES'S NARRATIVE

I am upper housemaid to the family that live at No. 27 Limehouse Road, Pultneyville. I have been requested by Mr. Wilkey Collings, which I takes the liberty of here stating is a gentleman born and bred, and has some consideration for the feelings of servants, and is not above rewarding them for their trouble, which is more than you can say for some who ask questions and gets short answers enough, gracious knows, to tell what I know about them. I have been requested to tell my story in my own langwidge, though, being no schollard, mind cannot conceive. I think my master is a brute. Do not know that he has ever attempted to poison my missus,—which is too good for him, and how she ever came to marry him, heart only can tell,—but believe him to be capable of any such hatrosity. Have heard him swear dreadful because of not having his shaving-water at nine o'clock precisely. Do not know whether he ever forged a will or tried to get my missus's property, although, not having confidence in the man, should not be surprised if he had done so. Believe that there was always something mysterious in his conduct. Remember distinctly how the family left home to go abroad. Was putting up my back hair, last Saturday morning, when I heard a ring. Says cook, "That's missus's bell, and mind you hurry or the master 'ill know why." Says I, "Humbly thanking you, mem, but taking advice of them as is competent to give it, I'll take my time." Found missus dressing herself and master growling as usual. Says missus, quite cairn and easy-like, "Mary, we begin to pack to-day." "What for, mem?" says I, taken aback. "What's that hussy asking?" says master from the bedclothes quite savage-like. "For the Continent—Italy," says missus. "Can you go, Mary?" Her voice was quite gentle and saintlike, but I knew the struggle it cost, and says I, "With you, mem, to India's torrid clime, if required, but with African Gorillas," says I, looking toward the bed, "never." "Leave the room," says master, starting up and catching of his bootjack. "Why, Charles!" says missus, "how you talk!" affecting surprise. "Do go, Mary," says she, slipping a half-crown into my hand. I left the room, scorning to take notice of the odious wretch's conduct.

Cannot say whether my master and missus were ever legally married. What with the dreadful state of morals nowadays and them stories in the circulating libraries, innocent girls don't know into what society they might be obliged to take situations. Never saw missus's marriage certificate, though I have quite accidental-like looked in her desk when open, and would have seen it. Do not know of any lovers missus might have had. Believe she had a liking for John Thomas, footman, for she was always spiteful-like—poor lady—when we were together— though there was nothing between us, as cook well knows, and dare not deny, and missus needn't have been jealous. Have never seen arsenic or Prussian acid in any of the private drawers—but have seen paregoric and camphor. One of my master's friends was a Count Moscow, a Russian papist—which I detested.

CHAPTER II
THE SLIM YOUNG MAN'S STORY

I am by profession a reporter, and writer for the press. I live at Pultneyville. I have always had a passion for the marvelous, and have been distinguished for my facility in tracing out mysteries, and solving enigmatical occurrences. On the night of the 17th June, 1845, I left my office and walked homeward. The night was bright and starlight. I was revolving in my mind the words of a singular item I had just read in the "Times." I had reached the darkest portion of the road, and found myself mechanically repeating: "An elderly gentleman a week ago left his lodgings on the Kent Road," when suddenly I heard a step behind me.

I turned quickly, with an expression of horror in my face, and by the light of the newly risen moon beheld an elderly gentleman, with green cotton umbrella, approaching me. His hair, which was snow white, was parted over a broad, open forehead. The expression of his face, which was slightly flushed, was that of amiability verging almost upon imbecility. There was a strange, inquiring look about the widely opened mild blue eye,—a look that might have been intensified to insanity or modified to idiocy. As he passed me, he paused and partly turned his face, with a gesture of inquiry. I see him still, his white locks blowing in the evening breeze, his hat a little on the back of his head, and his figure painted in relief against the dark blue sky.

Suddenly he turned his mild eye full upon me. A weak smile played about his thin lips. In a voice which had something of the tremulousness of age and the self-satisfied chuckle of imbecility in it, he asked, pointing to the rising moon, "Why?—Hush!"

He had dodged behind me, and appeared to be looking anxiously down the road. I could feel his aged frame shaking with terror as he laid his thin hands upon my shoulders and faced me in the direction of the supposed danger.

"Hush! did you not hear them coming?"

I listened; there was no sound but the soughing of the roadside trees in the evening wind. I endeavored to reassure him, with such success that in a few moments the old weak smile appeared on his benevolent face.

"Why?"—But the look of interrogation was succeeded by a hopeless blankness.

"Why?" I repeated with assuring accents.

"Why," he said, a gleam of intelligence flickering over his face, "is yonder moon, as she sails in the blue empyrean, casting a flood of light o'er hill and dale, like—Why," he repeated, with a feeble smile, "is yonder moon, as she sails in the blue empyrean"—He hesitated,— stammered,—and gazed at me hopelessly, with the tears dripping from his moist and widely opened eyes.

I took his hand kindly in my own. "Casting a shadow o'er hill and dale," I repeated quietly, leading him up to the subject, "like—Come, now."

"Ah!" he said, pressing my hand tremulously, "you know it?"

"I do. Why is it like—the—eh—the commodious mansion on the Limehouse Road?"

A blank stare only followed. He shook his head sadly.

"Like the young men wanted for a light, genteel employment?"

He wagged his feeble old head cunningly.

"Or, Mr. Ward," I said, with bold confidence, "like the mysterious disappearance from the Kent Road?" The moment was full of suspense. He did not seem to hear me. Suddenly he turned.

"Ha!"

I darted forward. But he had vanished in the darkness.

CHAPTER III
NO. 27 LIMEHOUSE ROAD

It was a hot midsummer evening. Limehouse Road was deserted save by dust and a few rattling butchers' carts, and the bell of the muffin and crumpet man. A commodious mansion, which stood on the right of the road as you enter Pultneyville, surrounded by stately poplars and a high fence surmounted by a cheval de frise of broken glass, looked to the passing and footsore pedestrian like the genius of seclusion and solitude. A bill announcing in the usual terms that the house was to let hung from the bell at the servants' entrance.

As the shades of evening closed, and the long shadows of the poplars stretched across the road, a man carrying a small kettle stopped and gazed, first at the bill and then at the house. When he had reached the corner of the fence, he again stopped and looked cautiously up and down the road. Apparently satisfied with the result of his scrutiny, he deliberately sat himself down in the dark shadow of the fence, and at once busied himself in some employment, so well concealed as to be invisible to the gaze of passers-by. At the end of an hour he retired cautiously.

But not altogether unseen. A slim young man, with spectacles and notebook, stepped from behind a tree as the retreating figure of the intruder was lost in the twilight, and transferred from the fence to his notebook the freshly stenciled inscription, "S—T—1860—X."

CHAPTER IV
COUNT MOSCOW'S NARRATIVE

I am a foreigner. Observe! To be a foreigner in England is to be mysterious, suspicious, intriguing. M. Collins has requested the history of my complicity with certain occurrences. It is nothing, bah! absolutely nothing. I write with ease and fluency. Why should I not write? Tra-la-la! I am what you English call corpulent. Ha, ha! I am a pupil of Macchiavelli. I find it much better to disbelieve everything, and to approach my subject and wishes circuitously than in a direct manner. You have observed that playful animal, the cat. Call it, and it does not come to you directly, but rubs itself against all the furniture in the room, and reaches you finally—and scratches. Ah, ha, scratches! I am of the feline species. People call me a villain—bah!

I know the family living No. 27 Limehouse Road. I respect the gentleman,—a fine, burly specimen of your Englishman,—and madame, charming, ravishing, delightful. When it became known to me that they designed to let their delightful residence, and visit foreign shores, I at once called upon them. I kissed the hand of madame. I embraced the great Englishman. Madame blushed slightly. The great Englishman shook my hand like a mastiff.

I began in that dexterous, insinuating manner of which I am truly proud. I thought madame was ill. Ah, no. A change, then, was all that was required. I sat down at the piano and sang. In a few minutes madame retired. I was alone with my friend.

Seizing his hand, I began with every demonstration of courteous sympathy. I do not repeat my words, for my intention was conveyed more in accent, emphasis, and manner, than speech. I hinted to him that he had another wife living. I suggested that this was balanced—ha!—by his wife's lover. That, possibly, he wished to fly; hence the letting of his delightful mansion. That he regularly and systematically beat his wife in the English manner, and that she repeatedly deceived him. I talked of hope, of consolation, of remedy. I carelessly produced a bottle of strychnine and a small vial of stramonium from my pocket, and enlarged on the efficiency of drugs. His face, which had gradually become convulsed, suddenly became fixed with a frightful expression. He started to his feet, and roared, "You d—d Frenchman!"

I instantly changed my tactics, and endeavored to embrace him. He kicked me twice, violently. I begged permission to kiss madame's hand. He replied by throwing me downstairs.

I am in bed with my head bound up, and beefsteaks upon my eyes, but still confident and buoyant. I have not lost faith in Macchiavelli. Tra-la-la! as they sing in the opera. I kiss everybody's hands.

CHAPTER V
DR. DIGGS'S STATEMENT

My name is David Diggs. I am a surgeon, living at No. 9 Tottenham Court. On the 15th of June, 1854, I was called to see an elderly gentleman lodging on the Kent Road. Found him highly excited, with strong febrile symptoms, pulse 120, increasing. Repeated incoherently what I judged to be the popular form of a conundrum. On closer examination found acute hydrocephalus, and both lobes of the brain rapidly filling with water. In consultation with an eminent phrenologist, it was further discovered that all the organs were more or less obliterated, except that of Comparison. Hence the patient was enabled to only distinguish the most common points of resemblance between objects, without drawing upon other faculties, such as Ideality or Language, for assistance. Later in the day found him sinking,—being evidently unable to carry the most ordinary conundrum to a successful issue. Exhibited Tinct. Val., Ext. Opii, and Camphor, and prescribed quiet and emollients. On the 17th the patient was missing.

CHAPTER LAST
STATEMENT OF THE PUBLISHER

On the 18th of June, Mr. Wilkie Collins left a roll of manuscript with us for publication, without title or direction, since which time he has not been heard from. In spite of the care of the proof-readers, and valuable literary assistance, it is feared that the continuity of the story has been destroyed by some accidental misplacing of chapters during its progress. How and what chapters are so misplaced, the publisher leaves to an indulgent public to discover.

ANDSOME IS AS HANDSOME DOES

BY CH-S R-DE

CHAPTER I

The Dodds were dead. For twenty years they had slept under the green graves of Kittery churchyard. The townfolk still spoke of them kindly. The keeper of the alehouse, where David had smoked his pipe, regretted him regularly, and Mistress Kitty, Mrs. Dodd's maid, whose trim figure always looked well in her mistress's gowns, was inconsolable. The Hardins were in America. Raby was aristocratically gouty; Mrs. Raby, religious. Briefly, then, we have disposed of—

1. Mr. and Mrs. Dodd (dead).

2. Mr. and Mrs. Hardin (translated).

3. Raby, baron et femme. (Yet I don't know about the former; he came of a long-lived family, and the gout is an uncertain-disease.)

We have active at the present writing (place aux dames)—

1. Lady Caroline Coventry, niece of Sir Frederick.

2. Faraday Huxley Little, son of Henry and Graco Little deceased.

Sequitur to the above, A HERO AND HEROINE.

CHAPTER II

On the death of his parents, Faraday Little was taken to Raby Hall. In accepting his guardianship, Mr. Raby struggled stoutly against two prejudices: Faraday was plain-looking and skeptical.

"Handsome is as handsome does, sweetheart," pleaded Jael, interceding for the orphan with arms that were still beautiful. "Dear knows, it is not his fault if he does not look like—his father," she added with a great gulp. Jael was a woman, and vindicated her womanhood by never entirely forgiving a former rival.

"It's not that alone, madam," screamed Raby, "but, d—m it, the little rascal's a scientist,—an atheist, a radical, a scoffer! Disbelieves in the Bible, ma'am; is full of this Darwinian stuff about natural selection and descent. Descent, forsooth! In my day, madam, gentlemen were content to trace their ancestors back to gentlemen, and not to—monkeys!"

"Dear heart, the boy is clever," urged Jael.

"Clever!" roared Raby; "what does a gentleman want with cleverness?"

CHAPTER III

Young Little *was* clever. At seven he had constructed a telescope; at nine, a flying-machine. At ten he saved a valuable life.

Norwood Park was the adjacent estate,—a lordly domain dotted with red deer and black trunks, but scrupulously kept with graveled roads as hard and blue as steel. There Little was strolling one summer morning, meditating on a new top with concealed springs. At a little distance before him he saw the flutter of lace and ribbons. A young lady, a very young lady,—say of seven summers,—tricked out in the crying abominations of the present fashion, stood beside a low bush. Her nursery-maid was not present, possibly owing to the fact that John the footman was also absent.

Suddenly Little came towards her. "Excuse me, but do you know what those berries are?" He was pointing to the low bush filled with dark clusters of shining—suspiciously shining—fruit.

"Certainly; they are blueberries."

"Pardon me; you are mistaken. They belong to quite another family."

Miss Impudence drew herself up to her full height (exactly three feet nine and a half inches), and, curling an eighth of an inch of scarlet lip, said scornfully, "*Your* family, perhaps."

Faraday Little smiled in the superiority of boyhood over girlhood.

"I allude to the classification. That plant is the belladonna, or deadly nightshade. Its alkaloid is a narcotic poison."

Sauciness turned pale. "I—have—just—eaten—some!" And began to whimper. "Oh dear, what shall I do?" Then did it, i. e., wrung her small fingers, and cried.

"Pardon me one moment." Little passed his arm around her neck, and with his thumb opened widely the patrician-veined lids of her sweet blue eyes. "Thank Heaven, there is yet no dilation of the pupil; it is not too late!" He cast a rapid glance around. The nozzle and about three feet of garden hose lay near him.

"Open your mouth, quick!"

It was a pretty, kissable mouth. But young Little meant business. He put the nozzle down her pink throat as far as it would go.

"Now, don't move."

He wrapped his handkerchief around a hoop-stick. Then he inserted both in the other end of the stiff hose. It fitted snugly. He shoved it in and then drew it back.

Nature abhors a vacuum. The young patrician was as amenable to this law as the child of the lowest peasant. She succumbed. It was all over in a minute. Then she burst into a small fury.

"You nasty, bad—*ugly* boy."

Young Little winced, but smiled.

"Stimulants," he whispered to the frightened nurserymaid, who approached; "good-evening." He was gone.

CHAPTER IV

The breach between young Little and Mr. Raby was slowly widening. Little found objectionable features in the Hall. "This black oak ceiling and wainscoting is not as healthful as plaster; besides, it absorbs the light. The bedroom ceiling is too low; the Elizabethan architects knew nothing of ventilation. The color of that oak paneling which you admire is due to an excess of carbon and the exuvia from the pores of your skin"—

"Leave the house," bellowed Raby, "before the roof falls on your sacrilegious head!"

As Little left the house, Lady Caroline and a handsome boy of about Little's age entered. Lady Caroline recoiled, and then—blushed. Little glared; he instinctively felt the presence of a rival.

CHAPTER V

Little worked hard. He studied night and day. In five years he became a lecturer, then a professor.

He soared as high as the clouds, he dipped as low as the cellars of the London poor. He analyzed the London fog, and found it two parts smoke, one disease, one unmentionable abominations. He published a pamphlet, which was violently attacked. Then he knew he had done something.

But he had not forgotten Caroline. He was walking one day in the Zoological Gardens, and he came upon a pretty picture,—flesh and blood, too.

Lady Caroline feeding buns to the bears! An exquisite thrill passed through his veins. She turned her sweet face and their eyes met. They recollected their first meeting seven years before, but it was his turn to be shy and timid. Wonderful power of age and sex! She met him with perfect self-possession.

"Well meant, but indigestible, I fear" (he alluded to the buns).

"A clever person like yourself can easily correct that" (she, the slyboots, was thinking of something else).

In a few moments they were chatting gayly. Little eagerly descanted upon the different animals; she listened with delicious interest. An hour glided delightfully away.

After this sunshine, clouds.

To them suddenly entered Mr. Raby and a handsome young man. The gentlemen bowed stiffly and looked vicious—as they felt. The lady of this quartette smiled amiably—as she did not feel.

"Looking at your ancestors, I suppose," said Mr. Raby, pointing to the monkeys; "we will not disturb you. Come." And he led Caroline away.

Little was heart-sick. He dared not follow them. But an hour later he saw something which filled his heart with bliss unspeakable.

Lady Caroline, with a divine smile on her face, feeding the monkeys!

CHAPTER VI

Encouraged by love, Little worked hard upon his new flying-machine. His labors were lightened by talking of the beloved one with her French maid Therese, whom he had discreetly bribed. Mademoiselle Therese was venal, like all her class, but in this instance I fear she was not bribed by British gold. Strange as it may seem to the British mind, it was British genius, British eloquence, British thought, that brought her to the feet of this young savan.

"I believe," said Lady Caroline, one day, interrupting her maid in a glowing eulogium upon the skill of "M. Leetell,"—"I believe you are in love with this professor." A quick flush crossed the olive cheek of Therese, which Lady Caroline afterward remembered.

The eventful day of trial came. The public were gathered, impatient and scornful as the pig-headed public are apt to be. In the open area a long cylindrical balloon, in shape like a Bologna sausage, swayed above the machine, from which, like some enormous bird caught in a net, it tried to free itself. A heavy rope held it fast to the ground.

Little was waiting for the ballast, when his eye caught Lady Caroline's among the spectators. The glance was appealing. In a moment he was at her side.

"I should like so much to get into the machine," said the arch-hypocrite demurely.

"Are you engaged to marry young Raby?" said Little bluntly.

"As you please," she said with a curtsy; "do I take this as a refusal?"

Little was a gentleman. He lifted her and her lap-dog into the car.

"How nice! it won't go off?"

"No, the rope is strong, and the ballast is not yet in."

A report like a pistol, a cry from the spectators, a thousand hands stretched to grasp the parted rope, and the balloon darted upward.

Only one hand of that thousand caught the rope,—Little's! But in the same instant the horror-stricken spectators saw him whirled from his feet and borne upward, still clinging to the rope, into space.

CHAPTER VII

[Footnote: The right of dramatization of this and succeeding chapters is reserved by the writer.]

Lady Caroline fainted. The cold, watery nose of her dog on her cheek brought her to herself. She dared not look over the edge of the car; she dared not look up to the bellowing monster above her, bearing her to death. She threw herself on the bottom of the car, and embraced the only living thing spared her,—the poodle. Then she cried. Then a clear voice came apparently out of the circumambient air,—

"May I trouble you to look at the barometer?"

She put her head over the car. Little was hanging at the end of a long rope. She put her head back again.

In another moment he saw her perplexed, blushing face over the edge,—blissful sight.

"Oh, please don't think of coming up! Stay there, do!"

Little stayed. Of course she could make nothing out of the barometer, and said so. Little smiled.

"Will you kindly send it down to me?"

But she had no string or cord. Finally she said, "Wait a moment." Little waited. This time her face did not appear. The barometer came slowly down at the end of—a stay-lace.

The barometer showed a frightful elevation. Little looked up at the valve and said nothing. Presently he heard a sigh. Then a sob. Then, rather sharply,—

"Why don't you do something?"

CHAPTER VIII

Little came up the rope hand over hand. Lady Caroline crouched in the farther side of the car. Fido, the poodle, whined.

"Poor thing," said Lady Caroline, "it's hungry."

"Do you wish to save the dog?" said Little.

"Yes."

"Give me your parasol."

She handed Little a good-sized affair of lace and silk and whalebone. (None of your "sunshades.") Little examined its ribs carefully.

"Give me the dog."

Lady Caroline hurriedly slipped a note under the dog's collar, and passed over her pet.

Little tied the dog to the handle of the parasol and launched them both into space. The next moment they were slowly, but tranquilly, sailing to the earth.

"A parasol and a parachute are distinct, but not different. Be not alarmed, he will get his dinner at some farmhouse."

"Where are we now?"

"That opaque spot you see is London fog. Those twin clouds are North and South America. Jerusalem and Madagascar are those specks to the right."

Lady Caroline moved nearer; she was becoming interested. Then she recalled herself, and said freezingly, "How are we going to descend?"

"By opening the valve."

"Why don't you open it then?"

"BECAUSE THE VALVE-STRING IS BROKEN!"

CHAPTER IX

Lady Caroline fainted. When she revived it was dark. They were apparently cleaving their way through a solid block of black marble. She moaned and shuddered.

"I wish we had a light."

"I have no lucifers." said Little. "I observe, however, that you wear a necklace of amber. Amber under certain conditions becomes highly electrical. Permit me."

He took the amber necklace and rubbed it briskly. Then he asked her to present her knuckle to the gem. Abright spark was the result. This was repeated for some hours. The light was not brilliant, but it was enough for the purposes of propriety, and satisfied the delicately minded girl.

Suddenly there was a tearing, hissing noise and a smell of gas. Little looked up and turned pale. The balloon, at what I shall call the pointed end of the Bologna sausage, was evidently bursting from increased pressure. The gas was escaping, and already they were beginning to descend. Little was resigned but firm.

"If the silk gives way, then we are lost. Unfortunately I have no rope nor material for binding it."

The woman's instinct had arrived at the same conclusion sooner than the man's reason. But she was hesitating over a detail.

"Will you go down the rope for a moment?" she said, with a sweet smile.

Little went down. Presently she called to him. She held something in her hand,—a wonderful invention of the seventeenth century, improved and perfected in this: a pyramid of sixteen circular hoops of light yet strong steel, attached to each other by cloth bands.

With a cry of joy Little seized them, climbed to the balloon, and fitted the elastic hoops over its conical end. Then he returned to the car.

"We are saved." Lady Caroline, blushing, gathered her slim but antique drapery against the other end of the car.

CHAPTER X

They were slowly descending. Presently Lady Caroline distinguished the outlines of Raby Hall.

"I think I will get out here," she said.

Little anchored the balloon, and prepared to follow her.

"Not so, my friend," she said, with an arch smile. "We must not be seen together. People might talk. Farewell."

Little sprang again into the balloon and sped away to America. He came down in California, oddly enough in front of Hardin's door, at Dutch Flat. Hardin was just examining a specimen of ore.

"You are a scientist; can you tell me if that is worth anything?" he said, handing it to Little.

Little held it to the light. "It contains ninety per cent of silver."

Hardin embraced him. "Can I do anything for you, and why are you here?"

Little told his story. Hardin asked to see the rope. Then he examined it carefully.

"Ah, this was cut, not broken!"

"With a knife?" asked Little.

"No. Observe both sides are equally indented. It was done with a *scissors*!"

"Just Heaven!" gasped Little. "Therese!"

CHAPTER XI

Little returned to London. Passing through London one day he met a dog-fancier.

"Buy a nice poodle, sir?"

Something in the animal attracted his attention.

"Fido!" he gasped.

The dog yelped.

Little bought him. On taking off his collar a piece of paper rustled to the floor. He knew the handwriting and kissed it. It ran:—

To THE HONORABLE AUGUSTUS RABY—I cannot marry you. If I marry any one [sly puss] it will be the man who has twice saved my life, Professor Little. CAROLINE COVENTRY.

And she did.

LOTHAW

OR

THE ADVENTURES OF A YOUNG GENTLEMAN IN
SEARCH OF A RELIGION BY MR. BENJAMINS

CHAPTER I

"I remember him a little boy," said the Duchess. "His mother was a dear friend of mine; you know she was one of my bridesmaids."

"And you have never seen him since, mamma?" asked the oldest married daughter, who did not look a day older than her mother.

"Never; he was an orphan shortly after. I have often reproached myself, but it is so difficult to see boys."

This simple yet first-class conversation existed in the morning-room of Plusham, where the mistress of the palatial mansion sat involved in the sacred privacy of a circle of her married daughters. One dexterously applied golden knitting-needles to the fabrication of a purse of floss silk of the rarest texture, which none who knew the almost fabulous wealth of the Duke would believe was ever destined to hold in its silken meshes a less sum than 1,000,000 pounds; another adorned a slipper exclusively with seed pearls; a third emblazoned a page with rare pigments and the finest quality of gold leaf. Beautiful forms leaned over frames glowing with embroidery, and beautiful frames leaned over forms inlaid with mother-of-pearl. Others, more remote, occasionally burst into melody as they tried the passages of a new and exclusive air given to them in MS.

by some titled and devoted friend, for the private use of the aristocracy alone, and absolutely prohibited for publication.

The Duchess, herself the superlative of beauty, wealth, and position, was married to the highest noble in the Three Kingdoms. Those who talked about such matters said that their progeny were exactly like their parents,—a peculiarity of the aristocratic and wealthy. They all looked like brothers and sisters, except their parents, who, such was their purity of blood, the perfection of their manners, and the opulence of their condition, might have been taken for their own children's elder son and daughter. The daughters, with one exception, were all married to the highest nobles in the land. That exception was the Lady Coriander, who, there being no vacancy above a marquis and a rental of 1,000,000 pounds, waited. Gathered around the refined and sacred circle of their breakfast-table, with their glittering coronets, which, in filial respect to their father's Tory instincts and their mother's Ritualistic tastes, they always wore on their regal brows, the effect was dazzling as it was refined. It was this peculiarity and their strong family resemblance which led their brother-in-law, the good-humored St. Addlegourd, to say that, "'Pon my soul, you know, the whole precious mob looked like a ghastly pack of court cards, you know." St. Addlegourd was a radical. Having a rent-roll of 15,000,000 pounds, and belonging to one of the oldest families in Britain, he could afford to be.

"Mamma, I've just dropped a pearl," said the Lady Coriander, bending over the Persian hearth-rug.

"From your lips, sweet friend?" said Lothaw, who came of age and entered the room at the same moment.

"No, from my work. It was a very valuable pearl, mamma; papa gave Isaacs Sons 50,000 pounds for the two."

"Ah, indeed," said the Duchess, languidly rising; "let us go to luncheon."

"But, your Grace," interposed Lothaw, who was still quite young, and had dropped on all fours on the carpet in search of the missing gem, "consider the value"—

"Dear friend," interposed the Duchess with infinite tact, gently lifting him by the tails of his dress coat, "I am waiting for your arm."

CHAPTER II

Lothaw was immensely rich. The possessor of seventeen castles, fifteen villas, nine shooting-boxes, and seven town houses, he had other estates of which he had not even heard.

Everybody at Plusham played croquet, and none badly. Next to their purity of blood and great wealth, the family were famous for this accomplishment. Yet Lothaw soon tired of the game, and after seriously damaging his aristocratically large foot in an attempt to "tight croquet" the Lady Aniseed's ball, he limped away to join the Duchess.

"I'm going to the hennery," she said.

"Let me go with you; I dearly love fowls—broiled," he added thoughtfully.

"The Duke gave Lady Montairy some large Cochins the other day," continued the Duchess, changing the subject with delicate tact.

"Lady Montairy   Quite contrairy, How do your Cochins grow?"

sang Lothaw gayly.

The Duchess looked shocked. After a prolonged silence Lothaw abruptly and gravely said:—

"If you please, ma'am, when I come into my property I should like to build some improved dwellings for the poor, and marry Lady Coriander."

"You amaze me, dear friend; and yet both your aspirations are noble and eminently proper," said the Duchess.

"Coriander is but a child,—and yet," she added, looking graciously upon her companion, "for the matter of that, so are you."

CHAPTER III

Mr. Putney Giles's was Lothaw's first grand dinner-party. Yet, by carefully watching the others, he managed to acquit himself creditably, and avoided drinking out of the finger-bowl by first secretly testing its contents with a spoon. The conversation was peculiar and singularly interesting.

"Then you think that monogamy is simply a question of the thermometer?" said Mrs. Putney Giles to her companion.

"I certainly think that polygamy should be limited by isothermal lines," replied Lothaw.

"I should say it was a matter of latitude," observed a loud, talkative man opposite. He was an Oxford professor with a taste for satire, and had made himself very obnoxious to the company, during dinner, by speaking disparagingly of a former well-known chancellor of the exchequer,—a great statesman and brilliant novelist,—whom he feared and hated.

Suddenly there was a sensation in the room; among the females it absolutely amounted to a nervous thrill. His Eminence, the Cardinal, was announced. He entered with great suavity of manner, and after shaking hands with everybody, asking after their relatives, and chucking the more delicate females under the chin with a high-bred grace peculiar to his profession, he sat down, saying, "And how do we all find ourselves this evening, my dears?" in several different languages, which he spoke fluently.

Lothaw's heart was touched. His deeply religious convictions were impressed. He instantly went up to this gifted being, confessed, and received absolution. "Tomorrow," he said to himself, "I will partake of the communion, and endow the Church with my vast estates. For the present I'll let the improved cottages go."

CHAPTER IV

As Lothaw turned to leave the Cardinal, he was struck by a beautiful face. It was that of a matron, slim but shapely as an Ionic column. Her face was Grecian, with Corinthian temples; Hellenic eyes that looked from jutting eyebrows, like dormer-windows in an Attic forehead, completed her perfect Athenian outline. She wore a black frock-coat tightly buttoned over her bloomer trousers, and a standing collar.

"Your lordship is struck by that face?" said a social parasite.

"I am; who is she?"

"Her name is Mary Ann. She is married to an American, and has lately invented a new religion."

"Ah!" said Lothaw eagerly, with difficulty restraining himself from rushing toward her.

"Yes; shall I introduce you?"

Lothaw thought of Lady Coriander's High Church proclivities, of the Cardinal, and hesitated: "No, I thank you, not now."

CHAPTER V

Lothaw was maturing. He had attended two womens' rights conventions, three Fenian meetings, had dined at White's, and had danced *vis-a-vis* to a prince of the blood, and eaten off gold plates at Crecy House.

His stables were near Oxford, and occupied more ground than the University. He was driving over there one day, when he perceived some rustics and menials endeavoring to stop a pair of runaway horses attached to a carriage in which a lady and gentleman were seated. Calmly awaiting the termination of the accident, with high-bred courtesy Lothaw forbore to interfere until the carriage was overturned, the occupants thrown out, and the runaways secured by the servants, when he advanced and offered the lady the exclusive use of his Oxford stables.

Turning upon him a face whose perfect Hellenic details he remembered, she slowly dragged a gentleman from under the wheels into the light, and presented him with ladylike dignity as her husband, Major-General Camperdown, an American.

"Ah," said Lothaw carelessly, "I believe I have some land there. If I mistake not, my agent, Mr. Putney Giles, lately purchased the State of—Illinois—I think you call it."

"Exactly. As a former resident of the city of Chicago, let me introduce myself as your tenant."

Lothaw bowed graciously to the gentleman, who, except that he seemed better dressed than most Englishmen, showed no other signs of inferiority and plebeian extraction.

"We have met before," said Lothaw to the lady as she leaned on his arm, while they visited his stables, the University, and other places of interest in Oxford, "Pray tell me, what is this new religion of yours?"

"It is Woman Suffrage, Free Love, Mutual Affinity, and Communism. Embrace it and me."

Lothaw did not know exactly what to do. She, however, soothed and sustained his agitated frame, and sealed with an embrace his speechless form. The General approached and coughed slightly with gentlemanly tact.

"My husband will be too happy to talk with you further on this subject," she said with quiet dignity, as she regained the General's side. "Come with us to Oneida. Brook Farm is a thing of the past."

CHAPTER VI

As Lothaw drove toward his country-seat, The Mural Inclosure, he observed a crowd, apparently of the working-class, gathered around a singular-looking man in the picturesque garb of an Ethiopian serenader. "What does he say?" inquired Lothaw of his driver.

The man touched his hat respectfully, and said, "My Mary Ann."

"'My Mary Ann!'" Lothaw's heart beat rapidly. Who was this mysterious foreigner? He had heard from Lady Coriander of a certain Popish plot; but could he connect Mr. Camperdown with it?

The spectacle of two hundred men at arms, who advanced to meet him at the gates of The Mural Inclosure, drove all else from the still youthful and impressible mind of Lothaw. Immediately behind them, on the steps of the baronial halls, were ranged his retainers, led by the chief cook and bottle-washer and head crumb-remover. On either side were two companies of laundry-maids, preceded by the chief crimper and fluter, supporting a long Ancestral Line, on which depended the family linen, and under which the youthful lord of the manor passed into the halls of his fathers. Twenty-four scullions carried the massive gold and silver plate of the family on their shoulders, and deposited it at the feet of their master. The spoons were then solemnly counted by the steward, and the perfect ceremony ended.

Lothaw sighed. He sought out the gorgeously gilded "Taj," or sacred mausoleum erected to his grandfather in the second-story front room, and wept over the man he did not know.

He wandered alone in his magnificent park, and then, throwing himself on a grassy bank, pondered on the Great First Cause and the necessity of religion. "I will send Mary Ann a handsome present," said Lothaw thoughtfully.

CHAPTER VII

"Each of these pearls, my lord, is worth fifty thousand guineas," said Mr. Amethyst, the fashionable jeweler, as he lightly lifted a large shovelful from a convenient bin behind his counter.

"Indeed," said Lothaw carelessly, "I should prefer to see some expensive ones."

"Some number sixes, I suppose," said Mr. Amethyst, taking a couple from the apex of a small pyramid that lay piled on the shelf. "These are about the size of the Duchess of Billingsgate's, but they are in finer condition. The fact is, her Grace permits her two children, the Marquis of Smithfield and the Duke of St. Giles,—two sweet pretty boys, my lord,—to use them as marbles in their games. Pearls require some attention, and I go down there regularly twice a week to clean them. Perhaps your lordship would like some ropes of pearls?"

"About half a cable's length," said Lothaw shortly, "and send them to my lodgings."

Mr. Amethyst became thoughtful. "I am afraid I have not the exact number—that is—excuse me one moment. I will run over to the Tower and borrow a few from the crown jewels." And before Lothaw could prevent him, he seized his hat and left Lothaw alone.

His position certainly was embarrassing. He could not move without stepping on costly gems which had rolled from the counter; the rarest diamonds lay scattered on the shelves; untold fortunes in priceless emeralds lay within his grasp. Although such was the aristocratic purity of his blood and the strength of his religious convictions that he probably would not have pocketed a single diamond, still he could not help thinking that he might be accused of taking some. "You can search me, if you like," he said when Mr. Amethyst returned; "but I assure you, upon the honor of a gentleman, that I have taken nothing."

"Enough, my lord," said Mr. Amethyst, with a low bow; "we never search the aristocracy."

CHAPTER VIII

As Lothaw left Mr. Amethyst's, he ran against General Camperdown. "How is Mary Ann?" he asked hurriedly.

"I regret to state that she is dying," said the General, with a grave voice, as he removed his cigar from his lips, and lifted his hat to Lothaw.

"Dying!" said Lothaw incredulously.

"Alas, too true!" replied the General. "The engagements of a long lecturing season, exposure in traveling by railway during the winter, and the imperfect nourishment afforded by the refreshments along the road, have told on her delicate frame. But she wants to see you before she dies. Here is the key of my lodging. I will finish my cigar out here."

Lothaw hardly recognized those wasted Hellenic outlines as he entered the dimly lighted room of the dying woman. She was already a classic ruin,—as wrecked and yet as perfect as the Parthenon. He grasped her hand silently.

"Open-air speaking twice a week, and Saleratus bread in the rural districts, have brought me to this," she said feebly; "but it is well. The cause progresses. The tyrant man succumbs."

Lothaw could only press her hand.

"Promise me one thing. Don't—whatever you do—become a Catholic."

"Why?"

"The Church does not recognize divorce. And now embrace me. I would prefer at this supreme moment to introduce myself to the next world through the medium of the best society in this. Good-by. When I am dead, be good enough to inform my husband of the fact."

CHAPTER IX

Lothaw spent the next six months on an Aryan island, in an Aryan climate, and with an Aryan race.

"This is an Aryan landscape," said his host, "and that is a Mary Ann statue." It was, in fact, a full-length figure in marble of Mrs. General Camperdown.

"If you please, I should like to become a Pagan," said Lothaw, one day, after listening to an impassioned discourse on Greek art from the lips of his host.

But that night, on consulting a well-known spiritual medium, Lothaw received a message from the late Mrs. General Camperdown, advising him to return to England. Two days later he presented himself at Plusham.

"The young ladies are in the garden," said the Duchess. "Don't you want to go and pick a rose?" she added with a gracious smile, and the nearest approach to a wink that was consistent with her patrician bearing and aquiline nose.

Lothaw went and presently returned with the blushing Coriander upon his arm.

"Bless you, my children," said the Duchess. Then turning to Lothaw, she said: "You have simply fulfilled and accepted your inevitable destiny. It was morally impossible for you to marry out of this family. For the present, the Church of England is safe."

THE HAUNTED MAN

BY CH—R—S D—CK—N—S.
A CHRISTMAS STORY

PART I
THE FIRST PHANTOM

Don't tell me that it wasn't a knocker. I had seen it often enough, and I ought to know. So ought the three-o'clock beer, in dirty high-lows, swinging himself over the railing, or executing a demoniacal jig upon the doorstep; so ought the butcher, although butchers as a general thing are scornful of such trifles; so ought the postman, to whom knockers of the most extravagant description were merely human weaknesses, that were to be pitied and used. And so ought for the matter of that, etc., etc., etc.

But then it was *such* a knocker. A wild, extravagant, and utterly incomprehensible knocker. A knocker so mysterious and suspicious that policeman X 37, first coming upon it, felt inclined to take it instantly in custody, but compromised with his professional instincts by sharply and sternly noting it with an eye that admitted of no nonsense, but confidently expected to detect its secret yet. An ugly knocker; a knocker with a hard human face, that was a type of the harder human face within. A human face that held between its teeth a brazen rod. So hereafter, in the mysterious future should be held, etc., etc.

But if the knocker had a fierce human aspect in the glare of day, you should have seen it at night, when it peered out of the gathering shadows and suggested an ambushed figure; when the light of the street lamps fell upon it, and wrought a play of sinister expression in its hard outlines; when it seemed to wink meaningly at a shrouded figure who, as the night fell darkly, crept up the steps and passed into the mysterious house; when the swinging door disclosed a black passage into which the figure seemed to lose itself and become a part of the mysterious gloom; when the night grew boisterous and the fierce wind made furious charges at the knocker, as if to wrench it off and carry it away in triumph. Such a night as this.

It was a wild and pitiless wind. A wind that had commenced life as a gentle country zephyr, but, wandering through manufacturing towns, had become demoralized, and, reaching the city, had plunged into extravagant dissipation and wild excesses. A roistering wind that indulged in Bacchanalian shouts on the street corners, that knocked off the hats from the heads of helpless passengers, and then fulfilled its duties by speeding away, like all young prodigals,—to sea.

He sat alone in a gloomy library listening to the wind that roared in the chimney. Around him novels and storybooks were strewn thickly; in his lap he held one with its pages freshly cut, and turned the leaves wearily until his eyes rested upon a portrait in its frontispiece. And as the wind howled the more fiercely, and the darkness without fell blacker, a strange and fateful likeness to that portrait appeared above his chair and leaned upon his shoulder. The Haunted Man gazed at the portrait and sighed. The figure gazed at the portrait and sighed too.

"Here again?" said the Haunted Man.

"Here again," it repeated in a low voice.

"Another novel?"

"Another novel."

"The old story?"

"The old story."

"I see a child," said the Haunted Man, gazing from the pages of the book into the fire,—"a most unnatural child, a model infant. It is prematurely old and philosophic. It dies in poverty to slow music. It dies surrounded by luxury to slow music. It dies with an accompaniment of golden water and rattling carts to slow music. Previous to its decease it makes a will; it repeats the Lord's Prayer, it kisses the 'boofer lady.' That child"—

"Is mine," said the phantom.

"I see a good woman, undersized. I see several charming women, but they are all undersized. They are more or less imbecile and idiotic, but always fascinating and undersized. They wear coquettish caps and aprons. I observe that feminine virtue is invariably below the medium height, and that it is always simple and infantine. These women"—

"Are mine."

"I see a haughty, proud, and wicked lady. She is tall and queenly. I remark that all proud and wicked women are tall and queenly. That woman"—

"Is mine," said the phantom, wringing his hands.

"I see several things continually impending. I observe that whenever an accident, a murder, or death is about to happen, there is something in the furniture, in the locality, in the atmosphere, that foreshadows and suggests it years in advance. I cannot say that in real life I have noticed it,—the perception of this surprising fact belongs"—

"To me!" said the phantom. The Haunted Man continued, in a despairing tone,—

"I see the influence of this in the magazines and daily papers; I see weak imitators rise up and enfeeble the world with senseless formula. I am getting tired of it. It won't do, Charles! it won't do!" and the Haunted Man buried his head in his hands and groaned. The figure looked down upon him sternly; the portrait in the frontispiece frowned as he gazed.

"Wretched man," said the phantom, "and how have these things affected you?"

"Once I laughed and cried, but then I was younger. Now, I would forget them if I could."

"Have then your wish. And take this with you, man whom I renounce. From this day henceforth you shall live with those whom I displace. Without forgetting me, 'twill be your lot to walk through life as if we had not met. But first you shall survey these scenes that henceforth must be yours. At one to-night, prepare to meet the phantom I have raised. Farewell!"

The sound of its voice seemed to fade away with the dying wind, and the Haunted Man was alone. But the firelight flickered gayly, and the light danced on the walls, making grotesque figures of the furniture.

"Ha, ha!" said the Haunted Man, rubbing his hands gleefully; "now for a whiskey punch and a cigar."

PART II
THE SECOND PHANTOM

One! The stroke of the far-off bell had hardly died before the front door closed with a reverberating clang. Steps were heard along the passage; the library door swung open of itself, and the Knocker—yes, the Knocker—slowly strode into the room. The Haunted Man rubbed his eyes,—no! there could be no mistake about it,—it was the Knocker's face, mounted on a misty, almost imperceptible body. The brazen rod was transferred from its mouth to its right hand, where it was held like a ghostly truncheon.

"It's a cold evening," said the Haunted Man.

"It is," said the Goblin, in a hard, metallic voice.

"It must be pretty cold out there," said the Haunted Man, with vague politeness. "Do you ever—will you—take some hot water and brandy?"

"No," said the Goblin.

"Perhaps you'd like it cold, by way of change?" continued the Haunted Man, correcting himself, as he remembered the peculiar temperature with which the Goblin was probably familiar.

"Time flies," said the Goblin coldly. "We have no leisure for idle talk. Come!" He moved his ghostly truncheon toward the window, and laid his hand upon the other's arm. At his touch the body of the Haunted Man seemed to become as thin and incorporeal as that of the

Goblin himself, and together they glided out of the window into the black and blowy night.

In the rapidity of their flight the senses of the Haunted Man seemed to leave him. At length they stopped suddenly.

"What do you see?" asked the Goblin.

"I see a battlemented mediaeval castle. Gallant men in mail ride over the drawbridge, and kiss their gauntleted fingers to fair ladies, who wave their lily hands in return. I see fight and fray and tournament. I hear roaring heralds bawling the charms of delicate women, and shamelessly proclaiming their lovers. Stay. I see a Jewess about to leap from a battlement. I see knightly deeds, violence, rapine, and a good deal of blood. I've seen pretty much the same at Astley's."

"Look again."

"I see purple moors, glens, masculine women, bare-legged men, priggish book-worms, more violence, physical excellence, and blood. Always blood,—and the superiority of physical attainments."

"And how do you feel now?" said the Goblin.

The Haunted Man shrugged his shoulders. "None the better for being carried back and asked to sympathize with a barbarous age."

The Goblin smiled and clutched his arm; they again sped rapidly away through the black night, and again halted.

"What do you see?" said the Goblin.

"I see a barrack-room, with a mess-table, and a group of intoxicated Celtic officers telling funny stories, and giving challenges to duel. I see a young Irish gentleman capable of performing prodigies of valor. I learn incidentally that the acme of all heroism is the cornetcy of a dragoon regiment. I hear a good deal of French! No, thank you," said the Haunted Man hurriedly, as he stayed the waving hand of the Goblin; "I would rather *not* go to the Peninsula, and don't care to have a private interview with Napoleon."

Again the Goblin flew away with the unfortunate man, and from a strange roaring below them he judged they were above the ocean. A ship hove in sight, and the Goblin stayed its flight. "Look," he said, squeezing his companion's arm.

The Haunted Man yawned. "Don't you think, Charles, you're rather running this thing into the ground? Of course it's very moral and instructive, and all that. But ain't there a little too much pantomime about it? Come now!"

"Look!" repeated the Goblin, pinching his arm malevolently. The Haunted Man groaned.

"Oh, of course, I see her Majesty's ship Arethusa. Of course I am familiar with her stern First Lieutenant, her eccentric Captain, her one fascinating and several mischievous midshipmen. Of course I know it's a splendid thing to see all this, and not to be seasick. Oh, there, the young gentlemen are going to play a trick on the purser. For God's sake, let us go," and the unhappy man absolutely dragged the Goblin away with him.

When they next halted, it was at the edge of a broad and boundless prairie, in the middle of an oak opening.

"I see," said the Haunted Man, without waiting for his cue, but mechanically, and as if he were repeating a lesson which the Goblin had taught him,—"I see the Noble Savage. He is very fine to look at! But I observe, under his war-paint, feathers, and picturesque blanket, dirt, disease, and an unsymmetrical contour. I observe beneath his inflated rhetoric deceit and hypocrisy; beneath his physical hardihood cruelty, malice, and revenge. The Noble Savage is a humbug. I remarked the same to Mr. Catlin."

"Come," said the phantom.

The Haunted Man sighed, and took out his watch. "Couldn't we do the rest of this another time?"

"My hour is almost spent, irreverent being, but there is yet a chance for your reformation. Come!"

Again they sped through the night, and again halted. The sound of delicious but melancholy music fell upon their ears.

"I see," said the Haunted Man, with something of interest in his manner,—"I see an old moss-covered manse beside a sluggish, flowing river. I see weird shapes: witches, Puritans, clergymen, little children, judges, mesmerized maidens, moving to the sound of melody that thrills me with its sweetness and purity. But, although carried along its calm and evenly flowing current, the shapes are strange and frightful: an eating lichen gnaws at the heart of each. Not only the clergymen, but witch, maiden, judge, and Puritan, all wear Scarlet Letters of some kind burned upon their hearts. I am fascinated and thrilled, but I feel a morbid sensitiveness creeping over me. I—I beg your pardon." The Goblin was yawning frightfully. "Well, perhaps we had better go." "One more, and the last," said the Goblin.

They were moving home. Streaks of red were beginning to appear in the eastern sky. Along the banks of the blackly flowing river by moorland and stagnant fens, by low houses, clustering close to the water's edge, like strange mollusks crawled upon the beach to dry; by misty black barges, the more misty and indistinct seen through its mysterious veil, the river fog was slowly rising. So rolled away and rose from the heart of the Haunted Man, etc., etc.

They stopped before a quaint mansion of red brick. The Goblin waved his hand without speaking.

"I see," said the Haunted Man, "a gay drawing-room. I see my old friends of the club, of the college, of society, even as they lived and moved. I see the gallant and unselfish men whom I have loved, and the snobs whom I have hated. I see strangely mingling with them, and now and then blending with their forms, our old friends Dick Steele, Addison, and Congreve. I observe, though, that these gentlemen have a habit of getting too much in the way. The royal standard of Queen Anne, not in itself a beautiful ornament, is rather too prominent in the picture. The long galleries of black oak, the formal furniture, the old portraits, are picturesque, but depressing. The house is damp. I enjoy myself better here on the lawn, where they are getting up a Vanity Fair. See, the bell rings, the curtain is rising, the puppets are brought out for a new play. Let me see."

The Haunted Man was pressing forward in his eagerness, but the hand of the Goblin stayed him, and pointing to his feet he saw, between him and the rising curtain, a new made grave. And bending above the grave in passionate grief, the Haunted Man beheld the phantom of the previous night. The Haunted Man started, and—woke. The bright sunshine streamed into the room. The air was sparkling with frost. He ran joyously to the window and opened it. A small boy saluted him with "Merry Christmas." The Haunted Man instantly gave him a Bank of England note. "How much like Tiny Tim, Tom, and Bobby that boy looked,—bless my soul, what a genius this Dickens has!"

A knock at the door, and Boots entered.

"Consider your salary doubled instantly. Have you read 'David Copperfield'?"

"Yezzur."

"Your salary is quadrupled. What do you think of the 'Old Curiosity Shop'?"

The man instantly burst into a torrent of tears, and then into a roar of laughter.

"Enough! Here are five thousand pounds. Open a porter-house, and call it 'Our Mutual Friend.' Huzza! I feel so happy!" And the Haunted Man danced about the room.

And so, bathed in the light of that blessed sun, and yet glowing with the warmth of a good action, the Haunted Man, haunted no longer, save by those shapes which make the dreams of children beautiful, reseated himself in his chair, and finished "Our Mutual Friend."

TERENCE DENVILLE

BY CH-L-S L-V-R

CHAPTER I
MY HOME

The little village of Pilwiddle is one of the smallest and obscurest hamlets on the western coast of Ireland. On a lofty crag, overlooking the hoarse Atlantic, stands "Denville's Shot Tower," a corruption by the peasantry of "D'Enville's Chateau," so called from my great-grandfather, Phelim St. Remy d'Enville, who assumed the name and title of a French heiress with whom he ran away. To this fact my familiar knowledge and excellent pronunciation of the French language may be attributed, as well as many of the events which covered my after life.

The Denvilles were always passionately fond of field sports. At the age of four, I was already the boldest rider and the best shot in the country. When only eight, I won the St. Remy Cup at the Pilwiddle races,—riding my favorite blood-mare Hellfire. As I approached the stand amidst the plaudits of the assembled multitude, and cries of, "Thrue for ye, Mashter Terence," and "oh, but it's a Dinville!" there was a slight stir among the gentry, who surrounded the Lord Lieutenant and other titled personages whom the race had attracted thither. "How young he is,—a mere child, and yet how noble-looking," said a sweet low voice, which thrilled my soul.

I looked up and met the full liquid orbs of the Hon. Blanche Fitzroy Sackville, youngest daughter of the Lord Lieutenant. She blushed deeply. I turned pale and almost fainted. But the cold, sneering tones of a masculine voice sent the blood back again into my youthful cheek.

"Very likely the ragged scion of one of these banditti Irish gentry, who has taken naturally to 'the road.' He should be at school—though I warrant me his knowledge of Terence will not extend beyond his own name," said Lord Henry Somerset, aid-de-camp to the Lord Lieutenant.

A moment and I was perfectly calm, though cold as ice. Dismounting, and stepping to the side of the speaker, I said in a low firm voice:—

"Had your lordship read Terence more carefully, you would have learned that banditti are sometimes proficient in other arts beside horsemanship," and I touched his holster significantly with my hand. I had not read Terence myself, but with the skillful audacity of my race I calculated that a vague allusion, coupled with a threat, would embarrass him. It did.

"Ah—what mean you?" he said, white with rage.

"Enough, we are observed," I replied; "Father Tom will wait on you this evening; and to-morrow morning, my lord, in the glen below Pilwiddle, we will meet again."

"Father Tom—glen!" ejaculated the Englishman, with genuine surprise. "What? do priests carry challenges and act as seconds in your infernal country?"

"Yes," I answered scornfully; "why should they not? Their services are more often necessary than those of a surgeon," I added significantly, turning away.

The party slowly rode off, with the exception of the Hon. Blanche Sackville, who lingered for a moment behind. In an instant I was at her side. Bending her blushing face over the neck of her white filly, she said hurriedly:—

"Words have passed between Lord Somerset and yourself. You are about to fight. Don't deny it—but hear me. You will meet him—I know your skill of weapons. He will be at your mercy. I entreat you to spare his life!"

I hesitated. "Never!" I cried passionately; "he has insulted a Denville!"

"Terence," she whispered, "Terence—*for my sake?*"

The blood rushed to my cheeks, and her eyes sought the ground in bashful confusion.

"You love him then?" I cried bitterly.

"No, no," she said agitatedly,—"no, you do me wrong. I—I—cannot explain myself. My father!—the Lady Dowager Sackville—the estate of Sackville—the borough—my uncle, Eitzroy Somerset. Ah! what am I saying? Forgive me. Oh, Terence," she said, as her beautiful head sank on my shoulder, "you know not what I suffer!"

I seized her hand and covered it with passionate kisses.

But the high-bred English girl, recovering something of her former hauteur, said hastily, "Leave me, leave me, but promise!"

"I promise," I replied enthusiastically; "I *will* spare his life!"

"Thanks, Terence,—thanks!" and disengaging her hand from my lips she rode rapidly away.

The next morning, the Hon. Captain Henry Somerset and myself exchanged nineteen shots in the glen, and at each fire I shot away a button from his uniform. As my last bullet shot off the last button from his sleeve, I remarked quietly, "You seem now, my lord, to be almost as ragged as the gentry you sneered at," and rode haughtily away.

CHAPTER II
THE FIGHTING FIFTY-SIXTH

When I was nineteen years old my father sold the Chateau d' Enville, and purchased my commission in the "Fifty-sixth" with the proceeds. "I say, Denville," said young McSpadden, a boy-faced ensign, who had just joined, "you'll represent the estate in the Army, if you won't in the House." Poor fellow, he paid for his meaningless joke with his life, for I shot him through the heart the next morning. "You're a good fellow, Denville," said the poor boy faintly, as I knelt beside him; "good-by!" For the first time since my grandfather's death I wept. I could not help thinking that I would have been a better man if

Blanche—But why proceed? Was she not now in Florence—the belle of the English embassy?

But Napoleon had returned from Elba. Europe was in a blaze of excitement. The Allies were preparing to resist the Man of Destiny. We were ordered from Gibraltar home, and were soon again en route for Brussels. I did not regret that I was to be placed in active service. I was ambitious, and longed for an opportunity to distinguish myself. My garrison life in Gibraltar had been monotonous and dull. I had killed five men in duel, and had an affair with the colonel of my regiment, who handsomely apologized before the matter assumed a serious aspect. I had been twice in love. Yet these were but boyish freaks and follies. I wished to be a man.

The time soon came,—the morning of Waterloo. But why describe that momentous battle, on which the fate of the entire world was hanging? Twice were the Fifty-sixth surrounded by French cuirassiers, and twice did we mow them down by our fire. I had seven horses shot under me, and was mounting the eighth, when an orderly rode up hastily, touched his cap, and, handing me a dispatch, galloped rapidly away.

I opened it hurriedly and read:—

"LET PICTON ADVANCE IMMEDIATELY ON THE RIGHT."

I saw it all at a glance. I had been mistaken for a general officer. But what was to be done? Picton's division was two miles away, only accessible through a heavy cross-fire of artillery and musketry. But my mind was made up.

In an instant I was engaged with an entire squadron of cavalry, who endeavored to surround me. Cutting my way through them, I advanced boldly upon a battery and sabred the gunners before they could bring their pieces to bear. Looking around, I saw that I had in fact penetrated the French centre. Before I was well aware of the locality, I was hailed by a sharp voice in French,—

"Come here, sir!"

I obeyed, and advanced to the side of a little man in a cocked hat.

"Has Grouchy come?"

"Not yet, sire," I replied,—for it was the Emperor.

"Ha!" he said suddenly, bending his piercing eyes on my uniform; "a prisoner?"

"No, sire," I said proudly.

"A spy?"

I placed my hand upon my sword, but a gesture from the Emperor bade me forbear.

"You are a brave man," he said.

I took my snuff-box from my pocket, and, taking a pinch, replied by handing it, with a bow, to the Emperor.

His quick eye caught the cipher on the lid.

"What! a D'Enville? Ha! this accounts for the purity of your accent. Any relation to Roderick d'Enville?"

"My father, sire."

"He was my schoolfellow at the Ecole Polytechnique. Embrace me!" And the Emperor fell upon my neck in the presence of his entire staff. Then, recovering himself, he gently placed in my hand his own magnificent snuff-box, in exchange for mine, and hanging upon my breast the cross of the Legion of Honor which he took from his own, he bade one of his marshals conduct me back to my regiment.

I was so intoxicated with the honor of which I had been the recipient, that on reaching our lines I uttered a shout of joy and put spurs to my horse. The intelligent animal seemed to sympathize with my feelings, and fairly flew over the ground. On a rising eminence a few yards before me stood a gray-haired officer, surrounded by his staff. I don't know what possessed me, but putting spurs to my horse, I rode at him boldly, and with one bound cleared him, horse and all. A shout of indignation arose from the assembled staff. I wheeled suddenly, with the intention of apologizing, but my mare misunderstood me, and, again dashing forward, once more vaulted over the head of the officer, this time unfortunately uncovering him by a vicious kick of her hoof. "Seize him!" roared the entire army. I was seized. As the soldiers led me away, I asked the name of the gray-haired officer. "That—why, that's the DUKE OF WELLINGTON!"

I fainted.

For six months I had brain fever. During my illness ten grapeshot were extracted from my body which I had unconsciously received during the battle. When I opened my eyes I met the sweet glance of a Sister of Charity.

"Blanche!" I stammered feebly.

"The same," she replied.

"You here?"

"Yes, dear; but hush! It's a long story. You see, dear Terence, your grandfather married my great-aunt's sister, and your father again married my grandmother's niece, who, dying without a will, was, according to the French law "—

"But I do not comprehend," I said.

"Of course not," said Blanche, with her old sweet smile; "you've had brain fever; so go to sleep."

I understood, however, that Blanche loved me; and I am now, dear reader, Sir Terence Sackville, K. C. B., and Lady Blanche is Lady Sackville.

MARY MCGILLUP

A SOUTHERN NOVEL
AFTER BELLE BOYD WITH AN
INTRODUCTION BY G. A. S-LA

INTRODUCTION

"Will you write me up?"

The scene was near Temple Bar. The speaker was the famous rebel Mary McGillup,—a young girl of fragile frame, and long, lustrous black hair. I must confess that the question was a peculiar one, and, under the circumstances, somewhat puzzling. It was true I had been kindly treated by the Northerners, and, though prejudiced against them, was to some extent under obligations to them. It was true that I knew little or nothing of American politics, history, or geography. But when did an English writer ever weigh such trifles? Turning to the speaker, I inquired with some caution the amount of pecuniary compensation offered for the work.

"Sir!" she said, drawing her fragile form to its full height, "you insult me,—you insult the South."

"But look ye here, d'ye see—the tin—the blunt—the ready—the stiff, you know. Don't ye see, we can't do without that, you know!"

"It shall be contingent on the success of the story," she answered haughtily. "In the mean time take this precious gem." And drawing a diamond ring from her finger, she placed it with a roll of MSS. in my hands, and vanished.

Although unable to procure more than 1 pound 2s. 6d. from an intelligent pawnbroker to whom I stated the circumstances and with whom I pledged the ring, my sympathies with the cause of a downtrodden and chivalrous people were at once enlisted. I could not help wondering that in rich England, the home of the oppressed and the free, a young and lovely woman like the fair author of those pages should be obliged to thus pawn her jewels—her marriage gift—for the means to procure her bread! With the exception of the English aristocracy,—who much resemble them,—I do not know of a class of people that I so much admire as the Southern planters. May I become better acquainted with both!

Since writing the above, the news of Mr. Lincoln's assassination has reached me. It is enough for me to say that I am dissatisfied with the result. I do not attempt to excuse the assassin. Yet there will be men who will charge this act upon the chivalrous South. This leads me to repeat a remark once before made by me in this connection, which has become justly celebrated. It is this:—

"It is usual, in cases of murder, to look for the criminal among those who expect to be benefited by the crime. In the death of Lincoln, his immediate successor in office alone receives the benefit of his dying."

If her Majesty Queen Victoria were assassinated, which Heaven forbid, the one most benefited by her decease would, of course, be his Royal Highness the Prince of Wales, her immediate successor. It would be unnecessary to state that suspicion would at once point to the real culprit, which would of course be his Royal Highness. This is logic.

But I have done. After having thus stated my opinion in favor of the South, I would merely remark that there is One who judgeth all things,—who weigheth the cause between brother and brother,—and awardeth the perfect retribution; and whose ultimate decision I, as a British subject, have only anticipated.

G. A. S.

CHAPTER I

Every reader of Belle Boyd's narrative will remember an allusion to a "lovely, fragile-looking girl of nineteen," who rivaled Belle Boyd in devotion to the Southern cause, and who, like her, earned the enviable distinction of being a "rebel spy."

I am that "fragile" young creature. Although on friendly terms with the late Miss Boyd, now Mrs. Hardinge, candor compels me to state that nothing but our common politics prevents me from exposing the ungenerous spirit she has displayed in this allusion. To be dismissed in a single paragraph after years of—But I anticipate. To put up with this feeble and forced acknowledgment of services rendered would be a confession of a craven spirit, which, thank God, though "fragile" and only "nineteen," I do not possess. I may not have the "blood of a Howard" in my veins, as some people, whom I shall not disgrace myself by naming, claim to have, but I have yet to learn that the race of McGillup ever yet brooked slight or insult. I shall not say that attention in certain quarters seems to have turned *some people's* heads; nor that it would have been more delicate if certain folks had kept quiet on the subject of their courtship, and the rejection of certain offers, when it is known that their forward conduct was all that procured them a husband! Thank Heaven, the South has some daughters who are above such base considerations! While nothing shall tempt me to reveal the promises to share equally the fame of certain enterprises, which were made by one who shall now be nameless, I have deemed it only just to myself to put my own adventures upon record. If they are not equal to those of another individual, it is because, though "fragile," my education has taught me to have some consideration for the truth. I am done.

CHAPTER II

I was born in Missouri. My dislike for the Northern scum was inherent. This was shown, at an early age, in the extreme distaste I exhibited for Webster's spelling-book,—the work of a well-known Eastern Abolitionist. I cannot be too grateful for the consideration shown by my chivalrous father,—a gentleman of the old school,—who resisted to the last an attempt to introduce Mitchell's Astronomy and Geography into the public school of our district. When I state that this same Mitchell became afterward a hireling helot in the Yankee Army, every intelligent reader will appreciate the prophetic discrimination of this true son of the South.

I was eight years old when I struck the first blow for Southern freedom against the Northern Tyrant. It is hardly necessary to state that in this instance the oppressor was a pale, overworked New England "schoolmarm." The principle for which I was contending, I felt, however, to be the same. Resenting an affront put upon me, I one day heaved a rock [Footnote: NOTE, BY G. A. S.—In the Southwest, any stone larger than a pea is termed "a rock."] at the head of the Vandal schoolmistress. I was seized and overpowered. My pen falters as I reach the climax. English readers will not give credit to this sickening story,—the civilized world will avert its head,—but I, Mary McGillup, was publicly SPANKED!

CHAPTER III

But the chaotic vortex of civil war approached, and fell destruction, often procrastinated, brooded in storm. [Footnote: I make no pretension to fine writing, but perhaps Mrs. Hardinge can lay over that. Oh, of course! M. McG.] As the English people may like to know what was really the origin of the Rebellion, I have no hesitation in giving them the true and only cause. Slavery had nothing to do with it, although the violation of the Declaration of Independence, in the disregard by the North of the Fugitive Slave Law, [Footnote: The Declaration of Independence grants to each subject "the pursuit of life, liberty, and happiness." A fugitive slave may be said to personify "life, liberty, and happiness." Hence his pursuit is really legal. This is logic. G.A.S.] might have provoked a less fiery people than the Southrons. At the inception of the struggle a large amount of Southern indebtedness was held by the people of the North. To force payment from the generous but insolvent debtor—to obtain liquidation from the Southern planter—was really the soulless and mercenary object of the craven Northerners. Let the common people of England look to this. Let the improvident literary hack, the starved impecunious Grub Street debtor, the newspaper frequenter of sponging-houses, remember this in their criticisms of the vile and slavish Yankee.

CHAPTER IV

The roasting of an Abolitionist, by a greatly infuriated community, was my first taste of the horrors of civil war. Heavens! Why will the North persist in this fratricidal warfare? The expulsion of several Union refugees, which soon followed, now fairly plunged my beloved State into the seething vortex.

I was sitting at the piano one afternoon, singing that stirring refrain, so justly celebrated, but which a craven spirit, unworthy of England, has excluded from some of her principal restaurants, and was dwelling with some enthusiasm on the following line:—

"Huzza! she spurns the Northern scum!"

when a fragment of that scum, clothed in that detestable blue uniform which is the symbol of oppression, entered the apartment.

"I have the honor of addressing the celebrated rebel spy, Miss McGillup?" said the Vandal officer.

In a moment I was perfectly calm. With the exception of slightly expectorating twice in the face of the minion, I did not betray my agitation. Haughtily, yet firmly, I replied,—

"I am."

"You looked as if you might be," the brute replied, as he turned on his heel to leave the apartment.

In an instant I threw myself before him. "You shall not leave here thus," I shrieked, grappling him with an energy which no one, seeing my frail figure, would have believed. "I know the reputation of your hireling crew. I read your dreadful purpose in your eye. Tell me not that your designs are not sinister. You came here to insult me,—to kiss me, perhaps. You shan't,—you naughty man. Go away!"

The blush of conscious degradation rose to the cheek of the Lincoln hireling as he turned his face away from mine.

In an instant I drew my pistol from my belt, which, in anticipation of some such outrage, I always carried, and shot him.

CHAPTER V

"Thy forte was less to act than speak, Maryland! Thy politics were changed each week, Maryland! With Northern Vandals thou wast meek, With sympathizers thou wouldst shriek, I know thee—oh, 'twas like thy cheek! Maryland! my Maryland!"

After committing the act described in the preceding chapter, which every English reader will pardon, I went upstairs, put on a clean pair of stockings, and, placing a rose in my lustrous black hair, proceeded at once to the camp of Generals Price and Mosby to put them in possession of information which would lead to the destruction of a portion of the Federal Army. During a great part of my flight I was exposed to a running fire from the Federal pickets of such coarse expressions as, "Go it, Sally Reb," "Dust it, my Confederate Beauty," but I succeeded in reaching the glorious Southern camp uninjured.

In a week afterwards I was arrested, by a lettre de cachet of Mr. Stanton, and placed in the Bastile. British readers of my story will express surprise at these terms, but I assure them that not only these articles but tumbrils, guillotines, and conciergeries were in active use among the Federals. If substantiation be required, I refer to the Charleston "Mercury," the only reliable organ, next to the New York "Daily News," published in the country. At the Bastile I made the acquaintance of the accomplished and elegant author of "Guy Livingstone," [Footnote: The recent conduct of Mr. Livingstone renders him unworthy of my notice. His disgusting praise of Belle Boyd, and complete ignoring of my claims, show the artfulness of some females and puppyism of some men. M. McG.] to whom I presented a curiously carved thigh-bone of a Union officer, and from whom I received the following beautiful acknowledgment:—

DEMOISELLE:—Should I ever win hame to my ain countrie, I make mine avow to enshrine in my reliquaire this elegant bijouterie and offering of La belle Rebelle. Nay, methinks this fraction of man's anatomy were some compensation for the rib lost by the "grand old gardener," Adam.

CHAPTER VI

Released at last from durance vile, and placed on board of an Erie canal-boat, on my way to Canada, I for a moment breathed the sweets of liberty. Perhaps the interval gave me opportunity to indulge in certain reveries which I had hitherto sternly dismissed. Henry Breckinridge Folair, a consistent Copperhead, captain of the canal-boat, again and again pressed that suit I had so often rejected.

It was a lovely moonlight night. We sat on the deck of the gliding craft. The moonbeam and the lash of the driver fell softly on the flanks of the off horse, and only the surging of the tow-rope broke the silence. Folair's arm clasped my waist. I suffered it to remain. Placing in my lap a small but not ungrateful roll of checkerberry lozenges, he took the occasion to repeat softly in my ear the words of a motto he had just unwrapped—with its graceful covering of the tissue paper—from a sugar almond. The heart of the wicked little rebel, Mary McGillup, was won!

The story of Mary McGillup is done. I might have added the journal of my husband, Henry Breckinridge Folair, but as it refers chiefly to his freights and a schedule of his passengers, I have been obliged, reluctantly, to suppress it.

It is due to my friends to say that I have been requested not to write this book. Expressions have reached my ears, the reverse of complimentary. I have been told that its publication will probably insure my banishment for life. Be it so. If the cause for which I labored have been subserved, I am content.

THE HOODLUM BAND

OR
THE BOY CHIEF, THE INFANT POLITICIAN,
AND THE PIRATE PRODIGY

CHAPTER I

It was a quiet New England village. Nowhere in the valley of the Connecticut the autumn sun shone upon a more peaceful, pastoral, manufacturing community. The wooden nutmegs were slowly ripening on the trees, and the white-pine hams for Western consumption were gradually rounding into form under the deft manipulation of the hardy American artisan. The honest Connecticut farmer was quietly gathering from his threshing-floor the shoe-pegs, which, when intermixed with a fair proportion of oats, offered a pleasing substitute for fodder to the effete civilizations of Europe. An almost Sabbath-like stillness prevailed. Doemville was only seven miles from Hartford, and the surrounding landscape smiled with the conviction of being fully insured.

Few would have thought that this peaceful village was the home of the three young heroes whose exploits would hereafter—But we anticipate.

Doemville Academy was the principal seat of learning in the county. Under the grave and gentle administration of the venerable Doctor Context, it had attained just popularity. Yet the increasing infirmities of age obliged the doctor to relinquish much of his trust to his assistants, who, it is needless to say, abused his confidence. Before long their brutal tyranny and deep-laid malevolence became apparent. Boys were absolutely forced to study their lessons. The sickening fact will hardly be believed, but during school-hours they were obliged to remain in their seats with the appearance, at least, of discipline. It is stated by good authority that the rolling of croquet-balls across the floor during recitation was objected to, under the fiendish excuse of its interfering with their studies. The breaking of windows by baseballs, and the beating of small scholars with bats, was declared against. At last, bloated and arrogant with success, the under-teachers threw aside all disguise, and revealed themselves in their true colors. A cigar was actually taken out of a day-scholar's mouth during prayers! A flask of whiskey was dragged from another's desk, and then thrown out of the window. And finally, Profanity, Hazing, Theft, and Lying were almost discouraged.

Could the youth of America, conscious of their power, and a literature of their own, tamely submit to this tyranny? Never! We repeat it firmly. Never! We repeat it to parents and guardians. Never! But the fiendish tutors, chuckling in their glee, little knew what was passing through the cold, haughty intellect of Charles Francis Adams Golightly, aged ten; what curled the lip of Benjamin Franklin Jenkins, aged seven; or what shone in the bold, blue eyes of Bromley Chitterlings, aged six and a half, as they sat in the corner of the playground at recess. Their only other companion and confidant was the negro porter and janitor of the school, known as "Pirate Jim."

Fitly, indeed, was he named, as the secrets of his early wild career—confessed freely to his noble young friends—plainly showed. A slaver at the age of seventeen, the ringleader of a mutiny on the African coast at the age of twenty, a privateersman during the last war with England, the commander of a fire-ship and its sole survivor at twenty-five, with a wild, intermediate career of unmixed piracy, until the Rebellion called him to civil service again as a blockade runner, and peace and a desire for rural repose led him to seek the janitorship of the Doemville Academy, where no questions were asked and references not exchanged—he was, indeed, a fit mentor for our daring youth. Although a man whose days had exceeded the usual space allotted to humanity, the various episodes of his career footing his age up to nearly one hundred and fifty-nine years, he scarcely looked it, and was still hale and vigorous.

"Yes," continued Pirate Jim critically; "I don't think he was any bigger nor you, Master Chitterlings, if as big, when he stood on the fork'stle of my ship and shot the captain o' that East Injyman dead. We used to call him little Weevils, he was so young-like. But, bless your hearts, boys! he wa'n't anything to Little Sammy Barlow, ez once crep' up inter the captain's stateroom on a Rooshin frigate, stabbed him to the heart with a jack-knife, then put on the captain's uniform and his cocked hat, took command of the ship, and fout her hisself."

"Wasn't the captain's clothes big for him?" asked B. Franklin Jenkins anxiously.

The janitor eyed young Jenkins with pained dignity.

"Didn't I say the Rooshin captain was a small, a very small, man? Rooshins is small, likewise Greeks."

A noble enthusiasm beamed in the faces of the youthful heroes.

"Was Barlow as large as me?" asked C. F. Adams Golightly, lifting his curls from his Jove-like brow.

"Yes; but, then, he hed hed, so to speak, experiences. It was allowed that he had pizened his schoolmaster afore he went to sea. But it's dry talking, boys."

Golightly drew a flask from his jacket and handed it to the janitor. It was his father's best brandy. The heart of the honest old seaman was touched.

"Bless ye, my own pirate boy!" he said in a voice suffocating with emotion.

"I've got some tobacco," said the youthful Jenkins, "but it's fine cut; I use only that now."

"I kin buy some plug at the corner grocery," said Pirate Jim, "only I left my portmoney at home."

"Take this watch," said young Golightly; "'tis my father's. Since he became a tyrant and usurper, and forced me to join a corsair's band, I've begun by dividing the property."

"This is idle trifling," said young Chitterlings wildly. "Every moment is precious. Is this an hour to give to wine and wassail? Ha, we want action—action! We must strike the blow for freedom to-night—ay, this very night. The scow is already anchored in the mill-dam, freighted with provisions for a three months' voyage. I have a black flag in my pocket. Why, then, this cowardly delay?"

The two elder youths turned with a slight feeling of awe and shame to gaze on the glowing cheeks and high, haughty crest of their youngest comrade—the bright, the beautiful Bromley Chitterlings. Alas! that very moment of forgetfulness and mutual admiration was fraught with danger. A thin, dyspeptic, half-starved tutor approached.

"It is time to resume your studies, young gentlemen," he said, with fiendish politeness.

They were his last words on earth.

"Down, Tyrant!" screamed Chitterlings.

"Sic him—I mean, sic semper tyrannis!" said the classical Golightly.

A heavy blow on the head from a baseball bat, and the rapid projection of a baseball against his empty stomach, brought the tutor a limp and lifeless mass to the ground. Golightly shuddered. Let not my young readers blame him too rashly. It was his first homicide. "Search his pockets," said the practical Jenkins.

They did so, and found nothing but a Harvard Triennial Catalogue.

"Let us fly," said Jenkins.

"Forward to the boats!" cried the enthusiastic Chitterlings.

But C. F. Adams Golightly stood gazing thoughtfully at the prostrate tutor.

"This," he said calmly, "is the result of a too free government and the common-school system. What the country needs is reform. I cannot go with you, boys."

"Traitor!" screamed the others.

C. F. A. Golightly smiled sadly.

"You know me not. I shall not become a pirate—but a Congressman!"

Jenkins and Chitterlings turned pale.

"I have already organized two caucuses in a baseball club, and bribed the delegates of another. Nay, turn not away. Let us be friends, pursuing through various ways one common end. Farewell!" They shook hands.

"But where is Pirate Jim?" asked Jenkins.

"He left us but for a moment to raise money on the watch to purchase armament for the scow. Farewell!"

And so the gallant, youthful spirits parted, bright with the sunrise of hope.

That night a conflagration raged in Doemville. The Doemville Academy, mysteriously fired, first fell a victim to the devouring element. The candy-shop and cigar-store, both holding heavy liabilities against the academy, quickly followed. By the lurid gleams of the flames, a long, low, sloop-rigged scow, with every mast gone except one, slowly worked her way out of the mill-dam towards the Sound. The next day three boys were missing—C. F. Adams Golightly, B. F. Jenkins, and Bromley Chitterlings. Had they perished in the flames? Who shall say? Enough that never more under these names did they again appear in the homes of their ancestors.

Happy, indeed, would it have been for Doemville had the mystery ended here. But a darker interest and scandal rested upon the peaceful village. During that awful night the boarding-school of Madame Brimborion was visited stealthily, and two of the fairest heiresses of Connecticut—daughters of the president of a savings bank and insurance director—were the next morning found to have eloped. With them also disappeared the entire contents of the savings bank, and on the following day the Flamingo Fire Insurance Company failed.

CHAPTER II

Let my young readers now sail with me to warmer and more hospitable climes. Off the coast of Patagonia a long, low, black schooner proudly rides the seas, that break softly upon the vine-clad shores of that luxuriant land. Who is this that, wrapped in Persian rugs, and dressed in the most expensive manner, calmly reclines on the quarter-deck of the schooner, toying lightly ever and anon with the luscious fruits of the vicinity, held in baskets of solid gold by Nubian slaves? or at intervals, with daring grace, guides an ebony velocipede over the polished black walnut decks, and in and out the intricacies of the rigging? Who is it? well may be asked. What name is it that blanches with terror the cheeks of the Patagonian navy? Who but the Pirate Prodigy—the relentless Boy Scourer of Patagonian seas? Voyagers slowly drifting by the Silurian beach, coasters along the Devonian shore, still shudder at the name of Bromley Chitterlings—the Boy Avenger, late of Hartford, Connecticut.

It has been often asked by the idly curious, Why Avenger, and of what? Let us not seek to disclose the awful secret hidden under that youthful jacket. Enough that there may have been that of bitterness in his past life that they "Whose soul would sicken o'er the heaving wave," or "whose soul would heave above the sickening wave," did not understand. Only one knew him, perhaps too well—a queen of the Amazons taken prisoner off Terra del Fuego a week previous. She loved the Boy Avenger. But in vain; his youthful heart seemed obdurate.

"Hear me," at last he said, when she had for the seventh time wildly proffered her hand and her kingdom in marriage, "and know once and forever why I must decline your flattering proposal. I love another."

With a wild, despairing cry she leaped into the sea, but was instantly rescued by the Pirate Prodigy. Yet, even in that supreme moment, such was his coolness, that on his way to the surface he captured a mermaid, and placing her in charge of his steward, with directions to give her a stateroom, with hot and cold water, calmly resumed his place by the Amazon's side. When the cabin door closed on his faithful servant, bringing champagne and ices to the interesting stranger, Chitterlings resumed his narrative with a choking voice—

"When I first fled from the roof of a tyrannical parent I loved the beautiful and accomplished Eliza J. Sniffen. Her father was president of the Workingmen's Savings Bank, and it was perfectly understood that in the course of time the entire deposits would be his. But, like a vain fool, I wished to anticipate the future, and in a wild moment persuaded Miss Sniffen to elope with me; and with the entire cash assets of the bank, we fled together." He paused, overcome with emotion. "But fate decreed it otherwise. In my feverish haste, I had forgotten to place among the stores of my pirate craft that peculiar kind of chocolate caramel to which Eliza Jane was most partial. We were obliged to put into New Rochelle on the second day out, to enable Miss Sniffen to procure that delicacy at the nearest confectioner's, and match some zephyr worsteds at the first fancy shop. Fatal mistake. She went—she never returned!" In a moment he resumed, in a choking voice, "After a week's weary waiting, I was obliged to put to sea again, bearing a broken heart and the broken bank of her father. I have never seen her since."

"And you still love her?" asked the Amazon queen excitedly.

"Ay, forever!"

"Noble youth. Here, take the reward of thy fidelity; for know, Bromley Chitterlings, that I am Eliza Jane. Wearied with waiting, I embarked on a Peruvian guano ship—it's a long story, dear."

"And altogether too thin," said the Boy Avenger, fiercely releasing himself from her encircling arms. "Eliza Jane's age, a year ago, was only thirteen, and you are forty, if a day."

"True," she returned sadly, "but I have suffered much, and time passes rapidly, and I've grown. You would scarcely believe that this is my own hair."

"I know not," he replied, in gloomy abstraction.

"Forgive my deceit," she returned. "If you are affianced to another, let me at least be—a mother to you."

The Pirate Prodigy started, and tears came to his eyes. The scene was affecting in the extreme. Several of the oldest seamen—men who had gone through scenes of suffering with tearless eyes and unblanched cheeks—now retired to the spirit room to conceal their emotion. A few went into caucus in the forecastle, and returned with the request that the Amazonian queen should hereafter be known as the "Queen of the Pirates' Isle."

"Mother!" gasped the Pirate Prodigy.

"My son!" screamed the Amazonian queen.

They embraced. At the same moment a loud flop was heard on the quarter-deck. It was the forgotten mermaid, who, emerging from her stateroom, and ascending the companion-way at that moment, had fainted at the spectacle. The Pirate Prodigy rushed to her side with a bottle of smelling-salts.

She recovered slowly. "Permit me," she said, rising with dignity, "to leave the ship. I am unaccustomed, to such conduct."

"Hear me—she is my mother!"

"She certainly is old enough to be," replied the mermaid. "And to speak of that being her own hair!" she said, as she rearranged with characteristic grace, a comb, and a small hand-mirror, her own luxuriant tresses.

"If I couldn't afford any other clothes, I might wear a switch, too!" hissed the Amazonian queen. "I suppose you don't dye it on account of the salt water? But perhaps you prefer green, dear?"

"A little salt water might improve your own complexion, love."

"Fishwoman!" screamed the Amazonian queen.

"Bloomerite!" shrieked the mermaid.

In another instant they had seized each other.

"Mutiny! Overboard with them!" cried the Pirate Prodigy, rising to the occasion, and casting aside all human affection in the peril of the moment.

A plank was brought and the two women placed upon it.

"After you, dear," said the mermaid significantly to the Amazonian queen; "you're the oldest."

"Thank you!" said the Amazonian queen, stepping back. "Fish is always served first."

Stung by the insult, with a wild scream of rage the mermaid grappled her in her arms and leaped into the sea.

As the waters closed over them forever, the Pirate Prodigy sprung to his feet. "Up with the black flag, and bear away for New London," he shouted in trumpet-like tones.

"Ha! ha! Once more the Rover is free!"

Indeed it was too true. In that fatal moment he had again loosed himself from the trammels of human feeling and was once more the Boy Avenger.

CHAPTER III

Again I must ask my young readers to mount my hippogriff and hie with me to the almost inaccessible heights of the Rocky Mountains. There, for years, a band of wild and untamable savages, known as the Pigeon Feet, had resisted the blankets and Bibles of civilization. For years the trails leading to their camp were marked by the bones of teamsters and broken wagons, and the trees were decked with the dying scalp-locks of women and children. The boldest of military leaders hesitated to attack them in their fortresses, and prudently left the scalping-knives, rifles, powder, and shot provided by a paternal government for their welfare lying on the ground a few miles from their encampment, with the request that they were not to be used until the military had safely retired. Hitherto, save an occasional incursion into the territory of the Knock-knees, a rival tribe, they had limited their depredations to the vicinity.

But lately a baleful change had come over them. Acting under some evil influence, they now pushed their warfare into the white settlements, carrying fire and destruction with them. Again and again had the Government offered them a free pass to Washington and the privilege of being photographed, but under the same evil guidance they refused. There was a singular mystery in their mode of aggression. Schoolhouses were always burned, the schoolmasters taken into captivity, and never again heard from. A palace car on the Union Pacific Railway, containing an excursion party of teachers en route to San Francisco, was surrounded, its inmates captured, and—their vacancies in the school catalogue never again filled. Even a hoard of educational examiners, proceeding to Cheyenne, were taken prisoners, and obliged to answer questions they themselves had proposed, amidst horrible tortures. By degrees these atrocities were traced to the malign influence of a new chief of the tribe. As yet little was known of him but through his baleful appellations, "Young Man who Goes for His Teacher," and "He Lifts the Hair of the School-Marm." He was said to be small and exceedingly youthful in appearance. Indeed, his earlier appellative, "He Wipes His Nose on His Sleeve," was said to have been given to him to indicate his still boy-like habits.

It was night in the encampment and among the lodges of the Pigeon Toes. Dusky maidens flitted in and out among the campfires like brown moths, cooking the toothsome buffalo-hump, frying the fragrant bear's-meat, and stewing the esculent bean for the braves. For a few favored ones sput grasshoppers were reserved as a rare delicacy, although the proud Spartan soul of their chief scorned all such luxuries.

He was seated alone in his wigwam, attended only by the gentle Mushymush, fairest of the Pigeon Feet maidens. Nowhere were the characteristics of her great tribe more plainly shown than in the little feet that lapped over each other in walking. A single glance at the chief was sufficient to show the truth of the wild rumors respecting his youth. He was scarcely twelve, of proud and lofty bearing, and clad completely in wrappings of various-colored scalloped cloths, which gave him the appearance of a somewhat extra-sized penwiper. An enormous eagle's feather, torn from the wing of a bald eagle who once attempted to carry him away, completed his attire. It was also the memento of one of his most superhuman feats of courage. He would undoubtedly have scalped the eagle but that nature had anticipated him.

"Why is the Great Chief sad?" said Mushymush softly. "Does his soul still yearn for the blood of the palefaced teachers? Did not the scalping of two professors of geology in the Yale exploring party satisfy his warrior's heart yesterday? Has he forgotten that Gardener and King are still to follow? Shall his own Mushymush bring him a botanist to-morrow? Speak, for the silence of my brother lies on my heart like the snow on the mountain, and checks the flow of my speech."

Still the proud Boy Chief sat silent. Suddenly he said, "Hiss!" and rose to his feet. Taking a long rifle from the ground he adjusted its sight. Exactly seven miles away on the slope of the mountain the figure of a man was seen walking. The Boy Chief raised the rifle to his unerring eye and fired. The man fell.

A scout was dispatched to scalp and search the body. He presently returned.

"Who was the paleface?" eagerly asked the chief.

"A life insurance agent."

A dark scowl settled on the face of the chief.

"I thought it was a book peddler."

"Why is my brother's heart sore against the book peddler?" asked Mushymush.

"Because," said the Boy Chief fiercely, "I am again without my regular dime novel—and I thought he might have one in his pack. Hear me, Mushymush. The United States mails no longer bring me my 'Young America' or my 'Boys' and Girls' Weekly.' I find it impossible, even with my fastest scouts, to keep up with the rear of General Howard, and replenish my literature from the sutler's wagon. Without a dime novel or a 'Young America,' how am I to keep up this Injin business?"

Mushymush remained in meditation a single moment. Then she looked up proudly.

"My brother has spoken. It is well. He shall have his dime novel. He shall know the kind of hairpin his sister Mushymush is."

And she arose and gamboled lightly as the fawn out of his presence.

In two hours she returned. In one hand she held three small flaxen scalps, in the other "The Boy Marauder," complete in one volume, price ten cents.

"Three palefaced children," she gasped, "were reading it in the tail-end of an emigrant wagon. I crept up to them softly. Their parents are still unaware of the accident," and she sank helpless at his feet.

"Noble girl!" said the Boy Chief, gazing proudly on her prostrate form; "and these are the people that a military despotism expects to subdue!"

CHAPTER IV

But the capture of several wagon-loads of commissary whiskey, and the destruction of two tons of stationery intended for the general commanding, which interfered with his regular correspondence with the War Department, at last awakened the United States military authorities to active exertion. A quantity of troops were massed before the Pigeon Feet encampment, and an attack was hourly imminent.

"Shine your boots, sir?"

It was the voice of a youth in humble attire, standing before the flap of the commanding general's tent.

The general raised his head from his correspondence.

"Ah," he said, looking down on the humble boy, "I see; I shall write that the appliances of civilization move steadily forward with the army. Yes," he added, "you may shine my military boots. You understand, however, that to get your pay you must first"—

"Make a requisition on the commissary-general, have it certified to by the quartermaster, countersigned by the post-adjutant, and submitted by you to the War Department "—

"And charged as stationery" added the general gently. "You are, I see, an intelligent and thoughtful boy. I trust you neither use whiskey, tobacco, nor are ever profane?"

"I promised my sainted mother"—

"Enough! Go on with your blacking; I have to lead the attack on the Pigeon Feet at eight precisely. It is now half past seven" said the general, consulting a large kitchen clock that stood in the corner of his tent.

The little bootblack looked up—the general was absorbed in his correspondence. The bootblack drew a tin putty-blower from his pocket, took unerring aim, and nailed in a single shot the minute hand to the dial. Going on with his blacking, yet stopping ever and anon to glance over the general's plan of campaign, spread on the table before him, he was at last interrupted by the entrance of an officer.

"Everything is ready for the attack, general. It is now eight o'clock"

"Impossible! It is only half past seven."

"But my watch, and the watches of the staff"—

"Are regulated by my kitchen clock, that has been in my family for years. Enough! it is only half past seven."

The officer retired; the bootblack had finished one boot. Another officer appeared.

"Instead of attacking the enemy, general, we are attacked ourselves. Our pickets are already driven in."

"Military pickets should not differ from other pickets" said the bootblack modestly. "To stand firmly they should be well driven in." "Ha! there is something in that," said the general thoughtfully. "But who are you, who speak thus?"

Rising to his full height, the bootblack threw off his outer rags, and revealed the figure of the Boy Chief of the Pigeon Feet.

"Treason!" shrieked the general. "Order an advance along the whole line."

But in vain. The next moment he fell beneath the tomahawk of the Boy Chief, and within the next quarter of an hour the United States army was dispersed. Thus ended the battle of Bootblack Creek.

CHAPTER V

And yet the Boy Chief was not entirely happy. Indeed, at times he seriously thought of accepting the invitation extended by the Great Chief at Washington immediately after the massacre of his soldiers, and once more revisiting the haunts of civilization, His soul sickened in feverish inactivity; schoolmasters palled on his taste; he had introduced baseball, blind hooky, marbles, and peg-top among his Indian subjects, but only with indifferent success. The squaws persisted in boring holes through the china alleys and wearing them as necklaces; his warriors stuck pipes in their baseball bats, and made war-clubs of them. He could not but feel, too, that the gentle Mushymush, although devoted to her paleface brother, was deficient in culinary education. Her mince-pies were abominable; her jam far inferior to that made by his Aunt Sally of Doemville. Only an unexpected incident kept him equally from the extreme of listless sybaritic indulgence or of morbid cynicism. Indeed, at the age of twelve, he already had become disgusted with existence.

He had returned to his wigwam after an exhausting buffalo hunt, in which he had slain two hundred and seventy-five buffaloes with his own hand, not counting the individual buffalo on which he had leaped, so as to join the herd, and which he afterward led into the camp a captive and a present to the lovely Mushymush. He had scalped two express riders, and a correspondent of the "New York Herald;" had despoiled the Overland Mail stage of a quantity of vouchers which enabled him to draw double rations from the Government, and was reclining on a bearskin, smoking and thinking of the vanity of human endeavor, when a scout entered, saying that a paleface youth had demanded access to his person.

"Is he a commissioner? If so, say that the red man is rapidly passing to the happy hunting-grounds of his fathers, and now desires only peace, blankets, and ammunition; obtain the latter, and then scalp the commissioner."

"But it is only a youth who asks an interview."

"Does he look like an insurance agent? If so, say that I have already policies in three Hartford companies. Meanwhile prepare the stake, and see that the squaws are ready with their implements of torture."

The youth was admitted; he was evidently only half the age of the Boy Chief. As he entered the wigwam, and stood revealed to his host, they both started. In another moment they were locked in each other's arms. "Jenky, old boy!"

"Bromley, old fel!"

B. F. Jenkins, for such was the name of the Boy Chief, was the first to recover his calmness. Turning to his warriors he said proudly,—

"Let my children retire while I speak to the agent of our Great Father in Washington. Hereafter no latch-keys will be provided for the wigwams of the warriors. The practice of late hours must be discouraged."

"How!" said the warriors, and instantly retired.

"Whisper!" said Jenkins, drawing his friend aside. "I am known here only as the Boy Chief of the Pigeon Toes."

"And I," said Bromley Chitterlings proudly, "am known everywhere as the Pirate Prodigy—the Boy Avenger of the Patagonian coast."

"But how came you here?"

"Listen! My pirate brig, the Lively Mermaid, now lies at Meiggs's wharf in San Francisco, disguised as a Mendocino lumber vessel. My pirate crew accompanied me here in a palace car from San Francisco."

"It must have been expensive," said the prudent Jenkins. "It was, hut they defrayed it by a collection from the other passengers, you understand. The papers will be full of it to-morrow. Do you take in the 'New York Sun'?"

"No; I dislike their Indian policy. But why are you here?"

"Hear me, Jenk! 'T is a long and a sad story. The lovely Eliza J. Sniffen, who fled with me from Doemville, was seized by her parents and torn from my arms at New Rochelle. Reduced to poverty by the breaking of the savings bank of which he was president—a failure to which I largely contributed, and the profits of which I enjoyed—I have since ascertained that Eliza Jane Sniffen was forced to become a schoolmistress, departed to take charge of a seminary in Colorado, and since then has never been heard from."

Why did the Boy Chief turn pale, and clutch at the tent-pole for support? Why, indeed?

"Eliza Jane Sniffen," gasped Jenkins,—"aged fourteen, red-haired, with a slight tendency to strabismus?"

"The same."

"Heaven help me! She died by my mandate!"

"Traitor!" shrieked Chitterlings, rushing at Jenkins with a drawn poniard.

But a figure interposed. The slight girlish form of Mushymush with outstretched hands stood between the exasperated Pirate Prodigy and the Boy Chief.

"Forbear," she said sternly to Chitterlings; "you know not what you do."

The two youths paused.

"Hear me," she said rapidly. "When captured in a confectioner's shop at New Rochelle, E. J. Sniffen was taken back to poverty. She resolved to become a schoolmistress. Hearing of an opening in the West, she proceeded to Colorado to take exclusive charge of the pensionnat of Mdme. Choflie, late of Paris. On the way thither she was captured by the emissaries of the Boy Chief"—

"In consummation of a fatal vow I made, never to spare educational instructors," interrupted Jenkins.

"But in her captivity," continued Mushymush, "she managed to stain her face with poke-berry juice, and mingling with the Indian maidens was enabled to pass for one of the tribe. Once undetected, she boldly ingratiated herself with the Boy Chief,—how honestly and devotedly he best can tell,—for I, Mushymush, the little sister of the Boy Chief, am Eliza Jane Sniffen."

The Pirate Prodigy clasped her in his arms. The Boy Chief, raising his hand, ejaculated,—

"Bless you, my children!"

"There is but one thing wanting to complete this reunion," said Chitterlings, after a pause, but the hurried entrance of a scout stopped his utterance.

"A commissioner from the Great Father in Washington."

"Scalp him!" shrieked the Boy Chief; "this is no time for diplomatic trifling."

"We have; but he still insists upon seeing you, and has sent in his card."

The Boy Chief took it, and read aloud, in agonized accents,—

"Charles Francis Adams Golightly, late page in United States Senate, and acting commissioner of United States."

In another moment, Golightly, pale, bleeding, and, as it were, prematurely bald, but still cold and intellectual, entered the wigwam. They fell upon his neck and begged his forgiveness.

"Don't mention it," he said quietly; "these things must and will happen under our present system of government. My story is brief. Obtaining political influence through caucuses, I became at last page in the Senate. Through the exertions of political friends, I was appointed clerk to the commissioner whose functions I now represent. Knowing through political spies in your own camp who you were, I acted upon the physical fears of the commissioner, who was an ex-clergyman, and easily induced him to deputize me to consult with you. In doing so, I have lost my scalp, but as the hirsute signs of juvenility have worked against my political progress, I do not regret it. As a partially bald young man I shall have more power. The terms that I have to offer are simply this: you can do everything you want, go anywhere you choose, if you will only leave this place. I have a hundred-thousand-dollar draft on the United States Treasury in my pocket at your immediate disposal."

"But what's to become of me?" asked Chitterlings.

"Your case has already been under advisement. The Secretary of State, who is an intelligent man, has determined to recognize you as *de jure* and *de facto* the only loyal representative of the Patagonian Government. You may safely proceed to Washington as its envoy extraordinary. I dine with the secretary next week."

"And yourself, old fellow?"

"I only wish that twenty years from now you will recognize by your influence and votes the rights of C. F. A. Golightly to the presidency."

And here ends our story. Trusting that my dear young friends may take whatever example or moral their respective parents and guardians may deem fittest from these pages, I hope in future years to portray further the career of those three young heroes I have already introduced in the springtime of life to their charitable consideration.

EARLIER SKETCHES

M´LISS

AN IDYL OF RED MOUNTAIN

[Pagenote: There are two forms of this tale. The earlier one is that printed originally in *The Golden Era* and afterward and until this time included in Mr. Harte›s collected writings. It is comprised in four chapters and occupies about thirty pages. When the present edition was under consideration, Mr. Harte called his publishers› attention to the fact that the editor of the same paper proposed to him some time later to continue it as a serial. In order to do this, he found himself obliged to make some changes in the earlier incidents. Accordingly he republished the story in its first form, but with some interpolations and alterations, and then proceeded with other chapters, making ten in all, "concluding it," he says, "rather abruptly when I found it was inartistically prolonged." This was in 1863. But even thus the story was not to be let alone. Ten years later, in 1873, another writer took the tale up at the end of the tenth chapter, added fifty more, and issued the whole in *The Golden Era*. When the continuation had been running some time, Mr. Harte discovered the fraud, and inserted a card in the same paper, advising the public that he had nothing whatever to do with this further amplification of his story. Afterward, when the whole was published in book form, he instituted legal proceedings and suppressed the sale.

The present form is Mr. Harte's revision and extension of his first, and is reprinted from *The Golden Era* with his consent. EDITOR.]

CHAPTER I
SMITH'S POCKET

Just where the Sierra Nevada begins to subside in gentle undulations, and the rivers grow less rapid and yellow, on the side of a great red mountain stands Smith's Pocket. Seen from the red road at sunset, in the red light and the red dust, its white houses look like the outcroppings of quartz on the mountain side. The red stage, topped with red-shirted passengers, is lost to view half a dozen times in the tortuous descent, turning up unexpectedly in out-of-the-way places, and vanishing altogether within a hundred yards of the town. It is probably owing to this sudden twist in the road that the advent of a stranger at Smith's Pocket is usually attended with a peculiar circumstance. Dismounting from the vehicle at the stage office the too-confident traveler is apt to walk straight out of town under the impression that it lies in quite another direction. It is related that one of the tunnel men, two miles from town, met one of these self-reliant passengers with a carpetbag, umbrella, "Harper's Magazine," and other evidences of "civilization and refinement," plodding along over the road he had just ridden, vainly endeavoring to find the settlement of Smith's Pocket.

Had he been an observant traveler he might have found some compensation for his disappointment in the weird aspect of that vicinity. There were huge fissures on the hillside, and displacements of the red soil, resembling more the chaos of some primary elementary upheaval than the work of man; while, halfway down, a long flume straddled its narrow body and disproportionate legs over the chasm, like an enormous fossil of some forgotten antediluvian. At every step smaller ditches crossed the road, hiding in their shallow depths unlovely streams that crept away to a clandestine union with the great yellow torrent below. Here and there the ruins of some cabin, with the chimney alone left intact and the hearthstone open to the skies, gave such a flat contradiction to the poetic delusion of Lares and Penates that the heart of the traveler must have collapsed as he gazed, and even the bar-room of the National Hotel have afterward seemed festive, and invested with preternatural comfort and domesticity.

The settlement of Smith's Pocket owed its origin to the finding of a "pocket" on its site by a veritable Smith. Five thousand dollars were taken out of it in one half-hour by Smith. Three thousand dollars were expended by Smith and others in erecting a flume and in tunneling. And then Smith's Pocket was found to be only a pocket, and subject like other pockets to depletion. Although Smith pierced the bowels of the great red mountain, that five thousand dollars was the first and the last return of his labor. The mountain grew reticent of its golden secrets, and the flume steadily ebbed away the remainder of Smith's fortune. Then Smith went into quartz mining. Then into quartz milling. Then into hydraulics and ditching, and then by easy degrees into saloon keeping. Presently it was whispered that Smith was drinking a good deal; then it was known that Smith was an habitual drunkard; and then people began to think, as they are apt to, that he had never been anything else. But the settlement of Smith's Pocket, like that of most discoveries, was happily not dependent on the fortune of its pioneer, and other parties projected tunnels and found pockets. So Smith's Pocket became a settlement with its two fancy stores, its two hotels, its one express office, and its two first families. Occasionally its one long straggling street was overawed by the assumption of the latest San Francisco fashions, imported per express, exclusively to the first families; making outraged nature, in the ragged outline of her furrowed surface, look still more homely, and putting personal insult on that greater portion of the population to whom the Sabbath, with a change of linen, brought merely the necessity of cleanliness without the luxury of adornment. Then there was a Methodist church, and hard by a monte bank, and a little beyond, on the mountain side, a graveyard; and then a little schoolhouse.

"The master," as he was known to his little flock, sat alone one night in the schoolhouse, with some open copybooks before him, carefully making those bold and full characters which are supposed to combine the extremes of chirographical and moral excellence, and had got as far as "Riches are deceitful," and was elaborating the noun with an insincerity of flourish that was quite in the spirit of his text, when he heard a gentle tapping. The woodpeckers had been busy about the roof, during the day, and the noise did not disturb his work. But the opening of the door, and the tapping continuing from the inside, caused him to look up. He was slightly startled by the figure of a young girl, dirty, and shabbily clad. Still her great black eyes, her coarse uncombed lusterless black hair falling over her sunburned face, her red arms and feet streaked with the red soil, were all familiar to him. It was Melissa Smith—Smith's motherless child.

"What can she want here?" thought the master. Everybody knew "M'liss," as she was called, throughout the length and height of Red Mountain. Everybody knew her as an incorrigible girl. Her fierce, ungovernable disposition, her mad freaks and lawless character, were in their way as proverbial as the story of her father's weakness, and as philosophically accepted by the townsfolk. She wrangled with and fought the schoolboys with keener invective and quite as powerful arm. She followed the trails with woodman's craft, and the master had met her before, miles away, shoeless, stockingless, and bareheaded on the mountain road. The miners' camps along the stream supplied her with subsistence during these voluntary pilgrimages, in freely offered alms. Not but that a larger protection had been previously extended to M'liss. The Rev. Joshua McSnagley, "stated" preacher, had placed her in the hotel as servant, by way of preliminary refinement, and had introduced her to his scholars at Sunday-school. But she threw plates occasionally at the landlord, and quickly retorted to the cheap witticisms of the guests, and created in the Sabbath-school a sensation that was so inimical to the orthodox dullness and placidity of that institution, that, with a decent regard for the starched frocks and unblemished morals of the two pink-and-white-faced children of the first families, the reverend gentleman had her ignominiously expelled. Such were the antecedents and such the character of M'liss, as she stood before the master. It was shown in the ragged dress, the unkempt hair and bleeding feet, and asked his pity. It flashed from her black fearless eyes, and commanded his respect.

"I come here to-night," she said rapidly and boldly, keeping her hard glance on his, "because I knew you was alone. I wouldn't come here when them gals was here. I hate 'em and they hates me. That's why. You keep school,—don't you? I want to be teached!"

If to the shabbiness of her apparel and uncomeliness of her tangled hair and dirty face she had added the humility of tears the master would have extended to her the usual moiety of pity, and nothing more. But with the natural though illogical instincts of his species, her boldness awakened in him something of that respect which all original natures pay unconsciously to one another in any grade. And he gazed at her the more fixedly as she went on still rapidly, her hand on the door-latch and her eyes on his.

"My name is M'liss—M'liss Smith! You can bet your life on that. My father's Old Smith—Old Bummer Smith—that's what's the matter with him. M'liss Smith—and I'm comin' to school!"

"Well?" said the master.

Accustomed to be thwarted and opposed, often wantonly and cruelly, for no other purpose than to excite the violent impulses of her nature, the master's phlegm evidently took her by surprise. She stopped. She began to twist a lock of her hair between her fingers; and the rigid line of upper lip, drawn over the wicked little teeth, relaxed and quivered slightly. Then her eyes dropped, and something like a blush struggled up to her cheek, and tried to assert itself through the splashes of redder soil and the sunburn of years. Suddenly she threw herself forward, calling on God to strike her dead, and fell quite weak and helpless, with her face on the master's desk, crying and sobbing as if her heart would break.

The master lifted her gently, and waited for the paroxysm to pass. When, with face still averted, she was repeating between her sobs the mea culpa of childish penitence—that "she'd be good, she didn't mean to," etc., it came to him to ask her why she had left Sabbath-school.

Why had she left Sabbath-school? Why? Oh, yes. What did he (McSnagley) want to tell her she was wicked for? What did he tell her that God hated her for? If God hated her, what did she want to go to

Sabbath school for? *She* didn›t want to be beholden to anybody who hated her.

Had she told McSnagley this?

Yes, she had.

The master laughed. It was a hearty laugh, and echoed so oddly in the little schoolhouse, and seemed so inconsistent and discordant with the sighing of the pines without, that he shortly corrected himself with a sigh. The sigh was quite as sincere in its way, however, and after a moment of serious silence he asked about her father.

Her father. What father? Whose father? What had he ever done for her? Why did the girls hate her? Come, now! What made the folks say, "Old Bummer Smith's M'liss" when she passed? Yes; oh, yes. She wished he was dead—she was dead—everybody was dead; and her sobs broke forth anew.

The master then, leaning over her, told her, as well as he could, what you or I might have said after hearing such unnatural theories from childish lips, only bearing in mind perhaps better than you or I the unnatural facts of her ragged dress, her bleeding feet, and the omnipresent shadow of her drunken father. Then raising her to her feet, he wrapped his shawl around her, and bidding her come early in the morning he walked with her down the road. Then he bade her "goodnight." The moon shone brightly on the narrow path before them. He stood and watched the bent little figure as it staggered down the road, and waited until it had passed the little graveyard and reached the curve of the hill, where it turned and stood for a moment, a mere atom of suffering outlined against the far-off patient stars. Then he went back to his work. But the lines of the copybook thereafter faded into long parallels of never-ending road, over which childish figures seemed to pass sobbing and crying to the night. Then, the little schoolhouse seeming lonelier than before, he shut the door and went home.

The next morning M'liss came to school. Her face had been washed, and her coarse black hair bore evidence of recent struggles with the comb, in which both had evidently suffered. The old defiant look shone occasionally in her eyes, but her manner was tamer and more subdued.

Then began a series of little trials and self-sacrifices in which master and pupil bore an equal part, and which increased the confidence and sympathy between them. Although obedient under the master's eye, at times during recess, if thwarted or stung by a fancied slight, M'liss would rage in ungovernable fury, and many a palpitating young savage, finding himself matched with his own weapons of torment, would seek the master with torn jacket and scratched face, and complaints of the dreadful M'liss. There was a serious division among the townspeople on the subject; some threatening to withdraw their children from such evil companionship, and others as warmly upholding the course of the master in his work of reclamation. Meanwhile, with a steady persistence that seemed quite astonishing to him on looking back afterward, the Master drew M'liss gradually out of the shadow of her past life, as though it were but her natural progress down the narrow path on which he had set her feet the moonlight night of their first meeting. Remembering the experience of the evangelical McSnagley, he carefully avoided that Rock of Ages on which that unskillful pilot had shipwrecked her young faith. But if, in the course of her reading, she chanced to stumble upon those few words which have lifted such as she above the level of the older, the wiser, and the more prudent,—if she learned something of a faith that is symbolized by suffering, and the old light softened in her eyes, it did not take the shape of a lesson. A few of the plainer people had made up a little sum by which the ragged M'liss was enabled to assume the garments of respect and civilization, and often a rough shake of the hand and words of commendation from a red-shirted and burly figure, sent a glow to the cheek of the young master and set him to thinking if it was altogether deserved.

Three months had passed, from the time of their first meeting, and the master was sitting late one evening over the moral and sententious copies, when there came a tap at the door, and again M'liss stood before him. She was neatly clad and clean-faced, and there was nothing perhaps but the long black hair and bright black eyes to remind him of his former apparition. "Are you busy?" she asked; "can you come with me?" and on his signifying his readiness, in her old willful way she said, "Come, then, quick!"

They passed out of the door together and into the dark road. As they entered the town, the master asked her whither she was going. She replied, "to see her father."

It was the first time he had heard her use that filial expression, or, indeed, allude to him in any other way than "Old Smith" or the "Old Man." It was the first time in many weeks that she had spoken of him at all. He had been missed from the settlement for the past fortnight, and the master had credited the rumors of the townsfolk that Smith had "struck something rich" on the "North Fork," about ten miles from the village. As they neared the settlement, the master gathered from M'liss that the rumor was untrue, and that she had seen her father that day. As she grew reticent to further questioning, and as the master was satisfied from her manner that she had some definite purpose beyond her usual willfulness, he passively resigned himself and followed her.

Through remote groggeries, restaurants, and saloons; in gambling-hells and dance-houses, the master, preceded by M'liss, passed and repassed. In the reeking smoke and blasphemous outcries of noisome dens, the child, holding the master's hand, pursued her search with a strange familiarity, perfect self-possession, and implied protection of himself, that even in his anxiety seemed ludicrous. Some of the revelers, recognizing M'liss, called to her to sing and dance for them, and would have forced liquor upon her but for the master's interference. Others mutely made way for them. So an hour slipped by, and as yet their search was fruitless. The master had yawned once or twice and whistled,—two fatal signs of failing interest,—and finally came to a full stop.

"It's half past eleven, Melissa," said he, consulting his watch by a broad pencil of light from an open shutter,—"half past eleven; and it strikes me that our old friends, the woodpeckers, must have gone to bed some hours ago, unless they are waiting up for us. I'm much obliged to you for the evening's entertainment, but I'm afraid that even the pretext of looking for a parent won't excuse further dissipation. We'd better put this off till to-morrow. What do you say, Melissa? Why! what ails the child? What's that noise? Why, a pistol!—You're not afraid of that?"

Few children brought up in the primeval seclusion of Smith's Pocket were unfamiliar with those quick and sharp notes which usually rendered the evening zephyrs of that locality vocal; certainly not M'liss, to have started when that report rang on the clear night air. The echoes caught it as usual, and carried it round and round Red Mountain, and set the dogs to barking all along the streams. The lights seemed to dance and move quickly on the outskirts of the town for a few moments afterward, the stream suddenly rippled quite audibly behind them, a few stones loosened themselves from the hillside and splashed into the stream, a heavy wind seemed to suage the branches of the funereal pines, and then the silence fell again, heavier, deadlier than ever.

When the last echo had died away, the master felt his companion's hand relax its grasp. Taking advantage of this outward expression of tractability, he drew her gently with him until they reached the hotel, which—in her newer aspect of a guest whose board was secured by responsible parties—had forgivingly opened its hospitable doors to the vagrant child. Here the master lingered a moment to assure her that she might count upon his assistance tomorrow; and having satisfied his conscience by this anticipated duty, bade her good-night. In the darkness of the road—going astray several times on his way home, and narrowly escaping the yawning ditches in the trail—he had reason to commend his foresight in dissuading M'liss from a further search that night, and in this pleasant reflection went to hed and slept soundly.

For some hours after a darkness thick and heavy brooded over the settlement. The sombre pines encompassing the village seemed to close threateningly about it as if to reclaim the wilderness that had been wrested from them. A low rustling as of dead leaves, and the damp breath of forest odors filled the lonely street. Emboldened by the darkness other shadows slipped by, leaving strange footprints in the moist ditches for people to point at next day, until the moon, round and full, was lifted above the crest of the opposite hill, and all was magically changed.

The shadows shrank away, leaving the straggling street sleeping in a beauty it never knew by day. All that was unlovely, harsh, and repulsive in its jagged outlines was subdued and softened by that uncertain light. It smoothed the rough furrows and unsightly chasms of the mountain with an ineffable love and tenderness. It fell upon the face of the sleeping M'liss, and left a tear glittering on her black lashes and a smile on her lip, which would have been rare to her at any other time; and fell also on the white upturned face of "Old Smith," with a pistol in his hand and a bullet in his heart, lying dead beside his empty pocket.

CHAPTER II
WHICH CONTAINS A DREAM OF THE JUST ARISTIDES

The opinion which McSnagley expressed in reference to a "change of heart," as experienced by M'liss, was more forcibly described in the gulches and tunnels. It was thought there that M'liss had struck a "good lead." And when there was a new grave added to the little inclosure, and—at the expense of the master—a little board and inscription put above it, the "Red Mountain Banner" came out quite handsomely and did the correct thing for the memory of one of "our oldest pioneers," alluding gracefully to that "bane of noble intellects," touching slightly on the "vicissitudes of fortune," and otherwise assisting our dear brother into genteel obscurity. "He leaves an only child to mourn his loss," said the "Banner," "who is now an exemplary scholar, thanks to the efforts of the Rev. J. McSnagley." That reverend gentleman, in fact, made a strong point of M'liss's conversion, and, indirectly attributing to her former bad conduct the suicide of her father, made affecting allusions in Sunday-school to the beneficial effects of the "silent tomb," and in that cheerful contemplation froze most of the children into speechless horror, and caused the fair-complexioned scions of the first families to howl dismally and refuse to be comforted.

Of the homes that were offered to M'liss when her conversion became known, the master had preferred that of Mrs. Morpher, a womanly and kind-hearted specimen of Southwestern efflorescence, known in her maidenhood as the "Per-ra-rie Rose." By a steady system of struggle and self-sacrifice, she had at last subjugated her naturally careless disposition to principles of "order," which as a pious woman she considered, with Pope, as "Heaven's first law." But she could not entirely govern the orbits of her satellites, however regular her own movements, and her old nature asserted itself in her children. Lycurgus dipped in the cupboard "between meals," and Aristides came home from school without shoes, leaving those important articles at the threshold, for the delights of a barefooted walk down the ditches. Octavia and Cassandra were "keerless" of their clothes. So that with but one exception, however the "Prairie Rose" might have trimmed, pruned, and trained her own natural luxuriance, the little shoots came up defiantly wild and straggling. That one exception was Clytemnestra Morpher, aged fifteen. She was the realization of her mother's most extravagant dream. I stay my hand with difficulty at this moment, for I long to describe this model of deportment; but the progress of my story just at present supplants Clytemnestra in the larger prominence it gives to another member of the family,—the just Aristides.

The long dry summer had come. As each fierce day seemed to burn itself out in little whiffs of pearl gray smoke on the mountain summits, and as the upspringing breeze scattered what might have been its red embers over the landscape, the green wave which, in early spring, had upheaved above Smith's grave grew sere and dry and hard. In those days, the master, strolling in the little churchyard of a Sabbath afternoon, was sometimes surprised to find a few wild flowers, plucked from the damp pine forest, scattered there, and oftener rude wreaths hung upon the little pine cross. Most of these wreaths were formed of a sweet-scented grass which the children loved to keep in their desks, entwined with the pompon-like plumes of the buckeye and syringa, the wood anemone, and here and there the master noticed the dark blue cowl of the monk's-hood or deadly aconite. One day, during a walk, in crossing a wooded ridge, he came upon M'liss in the heart of the forest, perched upon a prostrate pine, on a fantastic throne, formed by the hanging plumes of lifeless branches, her lap full of grasses and pine burrs, and crooning to the just Aristides, who sat humbly at her feet, one of the negro melodies of her younger life. It was perhaps the influence of the season, or the memory of this sylvan enjoyment, which caused Aristides, one midsummer day, to have a singular vision.

The just Aristides had begun that morning with a serious error. Loitering on his way to school, occasionally stopping to inspect the footprints of probable bears, or indulging in cheerful badinage with the tunnel men,—to whom the apparition of a short-legged boy weighed down by a preternaturally large satchel was an object of boisterous solicitude,—Aristides suddenly found that he was an hour and a half too late for school. Whether this circumstance was purely accidental or not is a question of some uncertainty, for Aristides, on finding himself occupying this criminal position, at once resolved to play truant. I shall not stop to inquire by what system of logic this result presented itself to that just youth as a consistent deduction, or whether some indistinct apprehension of another and a better world beyond the settlement, where there were no schools and blackberries were plenty, had not influenced him in taking this fatal step. Enough that he entered on his rash career by instantly eating the dinner which he carried with him, and having propitiated that terrible god whose seat is every small boy's stomach, with a feeling of inexpressible guiltiness creeping over him, he turned his back upon the schoolhouse and ran into the woods.

Away from the glare of the red road, how deliciously cool was the damp breath and twilight dimness of the stately pines. How they seemed to welcome him in their deepest recesses, ranging themselves silently around him as he ran, shutting out the world and its schoolhouses, and the pursuit of indignant parents and vindictive teachers. How in the forest depths the blue jay called to him mockingly, and the kingbird, spreading his tail like a crimson pennant, beckoned him onward. How there was recognition and greeting even in the squirrel that scampered past him, mischievously whisking his ridiculous tail within an inch of his outstretched fingers. And how Aristides, at last flinging away hat, shoes, and satchel, uttered a shrill whoop and dashed forward like a

youthful savage. But are not these things written in the dog's-eared
pages of every boy's memory, even though they seemed afterward to the
just Aristides a part and parcel of his own strange vision?

Yet even such delights had their hour of culmination, and Aristides
found himself at high noon back on the road again in a state of feverish
excitement, carrying a ravished jay's nest, two pine cones, a dead hare,
and a plume of the white syringa. Somewhat overpowered by the weight
of these trophies, which he had collected in the vague belief that they
would be of future service to him, he began to look about for some
convenient place to bestow his booty. It was nearly time for the great
Wingdam stage to go by, and when it came at last with a sharp rattle of
wheels and prancing of horses, and a red pillar of dust hanging over it
that partook of both the fiery and cloudy attributes of the Israelitish sign,
Aristides exchanged epithets with the driver, and, although standing
knee-deep in red dust, felt a thrill of joy in the recognition which no
future honor or dignity might ever give him.

Retracing his steps, the truant presently came to a semicircular
opening in the side of Red Mountain, which inclosed, like the walls of
some vast amphitheatre, what had been the arena of the early struggles
of the gladiators of fortune. There were terrible traces of that struggle
still—in the rock blasted by fire—in the bank furrowed by water—and
in the debris of Red Mountain scattered along the gulch two miles in
extent. Their forgotten engines were lying half buried in the ditches—
the primeval structure which had served them for a banking-house was
roofless, and held the hoards of field-mice and squirrels. The unshapely
stumps of ancient pines dotted the ground, and Aristides remembered
that under the solitary redwood, which of all its brothers remained still
standing, one of those early pioneers lay buried. No wonder that, as the
gentle breeze of that summer day swept through its branches, the just
Aristides might have heard, as part of his wonderful dream, some echo
of its far off brothers of Lebanon, saying, "Since thou art fallen, no feller
has risen up against us!"

But the short legs of Aristides were aching, and he was getting
thirsty. There was a rough cavern close at hand; and as most of these

openings condensed their general dampness somewhere in quiet pools, Aristides turned into the first one. When he had slaked his thirst, he looked around him and recognized Smith's Pocket.

It had undergone little change in the last two years. The winter rains had detached those portions of the wall which were not upheld by decaying timbers. It was certainly a dirty pocket—a pocket filled with rubbish—a shabby pocket—a worn-out and ragged pocket. It was so unpromising in its present exterior, so graphic in its story of misfortune, and so terrible in its recent memories, that the most sanguine prospector would have passed it by, as though the hopeless sentence of Dante had been written over its ragged portal.

The active mind of Aristides, however, saw in the lurking shadows of its arches much promise as a future play-room, to which he intended to induct hereafter his classical brother Lycurgus. In this reflection he threw himself on the ground, and luxuriously burying his bare feet in the cool, loose soil, gave himself up to serene meditation. But the heat and exertion were beginning to exert a certain influence over him, and once or twice his eyes closed. The water rippled beside him with a sleepy sound. The sunlight on the hill without made him wink. The long-drawn cawing of a crow on the opposite hillside, and the buzzing of a bluebottle fly who had sought retreat in the cavern, had a like effect, and he felt himself falling asleep. How long he slept, or if he slept at all, he could not remember, for he started suddenly, and, listening a moment, sprang to his feet. The low, heavy blows of a pick came deadened and muffled from the extremity of the cavern.

At first a terrible fear took possession of him; for an instant the white, rigid face of Smith, as he had seen it on the day of the inquest, when an irresistible curiosity led him to creep into the room where the dead man was lying—for an instant only, this fearful remembrance seemed to rise before him out of the gloom of the pit. The terror passed away.

Ghosts were historically unknown to Aristides, and even had his imaginative faculty been more prominent, the education of Smith's Pocket was not of a kind to foster such weaknesses. Except a twinge of conscience, a momentary recollection of the evil that comes to bad boys through the severe pages of Sunday-school books—with this exception, Aristides was not long in recovering his self-possession. He did not run away, for his curiosity was excited. The same instinct which prompted an examination of bear-tracks gave a fascination to the situation, and a nervous energy to his frame.

The regular blows of the pick still resounded through the cavern. He crept cautiously to the deepest recesses of the pocket, and held his breath and listened. The sound seemed to come from the bowels of the mountain. There was no sign of opening or ingress; an impenetrable veil of quartz was between him and the mysterious laborer. He was creeping back, between the displaced rafters, when a light glanced suddenly in his face, and flashed on the wet roof above him. Looking fearfully down, Aristides beheld between the interstices of the rafters, which formed a temporary flooring, that there was another opening below, and in that opening a man was working. In the queer fantasy of Aristides's dream, it took the aspect of a second pocket and a duplicate Smith!

He had no time to utter his astonishment, for at that moment an ominous rattling of loose soil upon his back made him look up, and he had barely time to spring away before a greater portion of the roof of Smith's Pocket, loosened by the displacement of its supports in his search, fell heavily to the ground. But in the fall a long-handled shovel which had been hidden somewhere in the crevices of the rock above came rattling down with it, and, seizing this as a trophy, Aristides emerged from Smith's Pocket, at a rate of speed which seemed singularly disproportionate with his short legs and round stomach.

When he reached the road the sun was setting. Inspecting his prize by that poetic light, he found that the shovel was a new one, and bore neither mark of use nor exposure. Shouldering it again, with the intention of presenting it as a peace-offering to propitiate the just wrath of his parents, Aristides had gone but a few rods when an unexpected circumstance occurred which dashed his fond hope, and to the conscientious child seemed the shadow of an inevitable Nemesis. At the curve of the road, as the settlement of Smith's Pocket came into view, with its straggling street, and its church spire that seemed a tongue of flame in the setting sun, a broad-shouldered figure sprang, apparently, from out of the bank, and stood in the path of that infelix infant.

"Where are you going with that shovel, you young devil?"

Aristides looked up and saw that his interlocutor was a man of powerful figure, whose face, though partially concealed by a red handkerchief, even in that uncertain light was not prepossessing. Children are quick physiognomists, and Aristides, feeling the presence of evil, from the depths of his mighty little soul then and there took issue with the giant.

"Where are you going with that shovel; d—n you, do you hear?" said he of the red handkerchief impatiently.

"Home," said Aristides stoutly.

"Home, eh!" said the stranger sneeringly. "And where did you steal it, you young thief?"

The Morpher stock not being of a kind to receive opprobrious epithets meekly, Aristides slowly, and with an evident effort, lifted the shovel in a menacing attitude.

A single step was all that separated six feet of Strength from three feet of Valor. The stranger eyed Aristides with an expression of surly amazement, and hesitated. The elephant quailed before the gad-fly. As that precocious infant waved the threatening shovel, his youthful lips slowly fashioned this tremendous sentence:—

"You let me pass and I won't hit you!"

And here I must pause. I would that for the sake of poetry I could leave my hero, bathed in that heroic light, erect and menacing. But alas, in this practical world of ours, the battle is too often to the strong. And I hasten over the humiliating spectacle of Aristides, spanked, cuffed, and kicked, and pick him from the ditch into which he was at last ignominiously tossed, a defeated but still struggling warrior, and so bring him, as the night closes charitably around him, in contrite tears and muddy garments to his father's door.

When the master stopped at Mrs. Morpher's to inquire after his errant pupil that night, he found Aristides in bed, smelling strongly of soap and water, and sinking into a feverish sleep. As he muttered from time to time some incoherent sentence, tossing restlessly in his cot, the master turned to those about him and asked what it was he said.

It was nothing. Aristides had been dreaming, and that was his dream.

That was all. Yet a dream that foreshadowed a slow-coming but unerring justice, that should give the little dreamer in after years some credit to the title of Aristides the Just.

CHAPTER III
UNDER THE GREENWOOD TREE

It was an amiable weakness of Mrs. Morpher to imagine that, of all her classical progeny, Clytemnestra was particularly the model for M'liss. Following this fallacy she threw "Clytie" at the head of M'liss when she was "bad," and set her up before the child for adoration in her penitential moments. It was not therefore surprising to the master to hear that Clytie was coming to school, obviously as a favor to the master and as an example for M'liss and others. For Clytie was quite a young lady. Inheriting her mother's physical peculiarities, and in obedience to the climatic laws of the Red Mountain region, she was an early bloomer. The youth of Smith's Pocket, to whom this kind of flower was rare, sighed for her in April and languished in May. Enamored swains haunted the schoolhouse at the hour of dismissal. A few were jealous of the master.

Perhaps it was this latter circumstance that opened the master's eyes to another. He could not help noticing that Clytie was romantic; that in school she required a great deal of attention; that her pens were uniformly bad and wanted fixing; that she usually accompanied the request with a certain expectation in her eye that was somewhat disproportionate to the quality of service she verbally required; that she sometimes allowed the curves of a round plump white arm to rest on his when he was writing her copies; that she always blushed and flung back her blond curls when she did so. I don't remember whether I have stated that the master was a young man—it's of little consequence, however. He had been severely educated in the school in which Clytie was taking her first lesson, and on the whole withstood the flexible curves and facetious glance like the fine young Spartan that he was. Perhaps an insufficient quality of food may have tended to this asceticism. He generally avoided Clytie; but one evening when she returned to the schoolhouse after something she had forgotten,—and did not find it until the master walked home with her,—I hear that he endeavored to make himself particularly agreeable, partly from the fact, I imagine, that his conduct was adding gall and bitterness to the already overcharged hearts of Clytemnestra's admirers.

The morning after this affecting episode, M'liss did not come to school. Noon came, but not M'liss. Questioning Clytie on the subject, it appeared that they had left for school together, but the willful M'liss had taken another road. The afternoon brought her not. In the evening he called on Mrs. Morpher, whose motherly heart was really alarmed. Mr. Morpher had spent all day in search of her, without discovering a trace that might lead to her discovery. Aristides was summoned as a probable accomplice, but that equitable infant succeeding in impressing the household with his innocence, Mrs. Morpher entertained a vivid impression that the child would yet be found drowned in a ditch, or—what was almost as terrible—mud-dyed and soiled beyond the redemption of soap and water. Sick at heart, the master returned to the schoolhouse. As he lit his lamp and seated himself at his desk, he found a note lying before him, addressed to himself in M'liss's handwriting. It seemed to be written on a leaf torn from some old memorandum-book, and, to prevent sacrilegious trifling, had been sealed with six broken wafers. Opening it almost tenderly, the master read as follows:—

RESPECTED SIR: When you read this, I am run away. Never to come back. Never *Never* NEVER. You can give my beeds to Mary Jennings, and my Amerika's Pride [a, highly colored lithograph from a tobacco box] to Sally Flanders. But don't you give anything to Clytie Morper. Don't you dair to. Do you know what my opinnion is of her,

it is this, she is perfekly disgustin. That is all and no more at present
from MELISSA SMITH.

The master mused for some time over this characteristic epistle.
As he was mechanically refolding it his eye caught a sentence written
on the back in pencil, in another handwriting, somewhat blurred and
indistinct from the heavy incisive strokes of M'liss's pen on the other
side. It seemed to be a memorandum belonging to the book from which
the leaf was originally torn:—

July 17th. 5 hours in drift—dipping west—took out 20 oz.; cleaned
up 40 oz. Mem.—saw M. S.

"July 17th," said the master, opening his desk and taking out a file of
the "Red Mountain Banner." "July 17th," he repeated, running over the
pages till he came to a paragraph headed "DISTRESSING SUICIDE."
"July 17th—why, that's the day Smith killed himself. That's funny!"

In a strict etymological sense there was nothing so very ludicrous in
this coincidence, nor did the master's face betray any expression of the
kind. Perhaps the epithet was chosen to conceal the vague uneasiness
which it produced in his mind. We are all of us more affected by these
coincidences than we care to confess to one another. If the most matter-
of-fact reader of these pages were to find a hearse standing in front of his
door for three consecutive mornings, although the circumstance might
be satisfactorily explained,—shall I go further and say, *because* the
circumstance might be satisfactorily explained,—he would vaguely
wish it hadn›t happened. Philosophize as we may, the simple fact of
two remote lines crossing each other always seems to us of tremendous
significance, and quite overshadows the more important truth that the
real parallels of life›s journey are the lines that never meet. It will do us
good to remember these things, and look more kindly on our brothers
of Borrioboola-Gha and their fetich superstitions, when we drop our
silver in the missionary box next Sabbath.

"I wonder where that memorandum came from," said the master, as
he rose at last and buttoned up his coat. "Who is 'M. S.'? M. S. stands
for manuscript and Melissa Smith. Why don't"—But checking an
impulsive query as to why people don't make their private memoranda

generally intelligible, the master put the letter in his pocket and went home.

At sunrise the next morning he was picking his way through the palm-like fern and thick underbrush of the pine forest, starting the hare from its form, and awakening a querulous protest from a few dissipated crows, who had evidently been making a night of it, and so came to the wooded ridge where he had once found M'liss. There he found the prostrate pine and tessellated branches, but the throne was vacant. As he drew nearer, what might have been some frightened animal started through the crackling limbs. It ran up the tossed arms of the fallen monarch, and sheltered itself in some friendly foliage. The master, reaching the old seat, found the nest still warm; looking up in the intertwining branches, he met the black eyes of the errant M'liss. They gazed at each other without speaking. She was first to break the silence.

"What do you want?" she asked curtly.

The master had decided on a course of action. "I want some crab apples," he said humbly.

"Shan't have 'em! go away! Why don't you get 'em of Clytemnerestera?" It seemed to be a relief to M'liss to express her contempt in additional syllables to that classical young woman's already long-drawn title. "Oh, you wicked thing!"

"I am hungry, Lissy. I have eaten nothing since dinner yesterday. I am famished!" and the young man, in a state of remarkable exhaustion, leaned against the tree.

Melissa's heart was touched. In the bitter days of her gypsy life she had known the sensation he so artfully simulated. Overcome by his heartbroken tone, but not entirely divested of suspicion, she said:—

"Dig under the tree near the roots, and you 'll find lots: but mind you don't tell," for M'liss had *her* hoards as well as the rats and squirrels.

But the master of course was unable to find them, the effects of hunger probably blinding his senses. M'liss grew uneasy. At length she peered at him through the leaves in an elfish way, and questioned:—

"If I come down and give you some, you'll promise you won't touch me?"

The master promised.

"Hope you'll die if you do?"

The master accepted instant dissolution as a forfeit. M'liss slid down the tree. The duties of hospitality fulfilled, she seated herself at a little distance and eyed the master with extreme caution.

"Why didn't you eat your breakfast, you bad man?"

"Because I've run away."

"Where to?" said M'liss, her eyes twinkling.

"Anywhere—anywhere, away from here!" responded that deceitful wretch with tragic wildness of demeanor.

"What made you?—bad boy!" said M'liss, with a sudden respect of conventionalities, and a rare touch of tenderness in her tones. "You'd better go back where your vittals are."

"What are victuals to a wounded spirit?" asked the young man dramatically. He had reached the side of M'liss during this dialogue, and had taken her unresisting hand. He was too wise to notice his victory, however; and drawing Melissa's note from his pocket, opened it before her.

"Couldn't you find any paper in the schoolhouse without tearing a leaf out of my memorandum book, Melissa?" he asked.

"It ain't out of your memorandum book," responded M'liss fiercely.

"Indeed," said the master, turning to the lines in pencil; "I thought it was my handwriting."

M'liss, who had been looking over his shoulder, suddenly seized the paper and snatched it out of his hand.

"It's father's writing!" she said, after a pause, in a softer tone.

"Where did you get it, M'liss?"

"Aristides gave it to me."

"Where did he get it?"

"Don't know. He had the book in his pocket when I told him I was going to write to you, and he tore the leaf out. There now—don't bother me any more." M'liss had turned her face away, and the black hair had hid her downcast eyes.

Something in her gesture and expression reminded him of her

father. Something, and more that was characteristic to her at such moments, made him fancy another resemblance, and caused him to ask impulsively, and less cautiously than was his wont:—

"Do you remember your mother, M'liss?"

"No."

"Did you never see her?"

"No—didn't I tell you not to bother, and you're a-goin' and doin' it," said M'liss savagely.

The master was silent a moment. "Did you ever think you would like to have a mother, M'liss?" he asked again.

"No-o-o-o!"

The master rose; M'liss looked up.

"Does Aristides come to school to-day?"

"I don't know."

"Are you going back? You'd better," she said.

"Well!—perhaps I may. Good-by!"

He had proceeded a few steps when, as he expected, she called him back. He turned. She was standing by the tree, with tears glistening in her eyes. The master felt the right moment had come. Going up to her, he took both her hands in his, and looking in her tearful eyes, said gravely:—

"M'liss, do you remember the first evening you came to see me?"

M'liss remembered.

"You asked me if you might come to school, and I said—"

"Come!" responded the child softly.

"If I told you I was lonely without my little scholar, and that I wanted her to come, what would you say?"

The child hung her head in silence. The master waited patiently. Tempted by the quiet, a hare ran close to the couple, and raising her bright eyes and velvet fore paws, gazed at them fearlessly. A squirrel ran halfway down the furrowed bark of the fallen tree, and there stopped.

"*We* are waiting, Lissy," said the master in a whisper, and the child smiled. Stirred by a passing breeze, the treetops rocked, and a slanting sunbeam stole through their interlaced boughs and fell on the doubting face and irresolute little figure. But a step in the dry branches and a rustling in the underbrush broke the spell.

A man dressed as a miner, carrying a long-handled shovel, came slowly through the woods. A red handkerchief tied around his head under his hat, with the loose ends hanging from beneath, did not add much favor to his unprepossessing face. He did not perceive the master and M'liss until he was close upon them. When he did, he stopped suddenly and gazed at them with an expression of lowering distrust. M'liss drew nearer to the master.

"Good-mornin'—picknickin', eh?" he asked, with an attempt at geniality that was more repulsive than his natural manner.

"How are you—prospecting, eh?" said the master quietly, after the established colloquial formula of Red Mountain.

"Yes—a little in that way."

The stranger still hesitated, apparently waiting for them to go first, a matter which M'liss decided by suddenly taking the master's hand in her quick way. What she said was scarcely audible, but the master, parting her hair over her forehead, kissed her, and so, hand in hand, they passed out of the damp aisles and forest odors into the open sunlit road. But M'liss, looking back, saw that her old seat was occupied by the hopeful prospector, and fancied that in the shadows of her former throne something of a gratified leer overspread his face. "He'll have to dig deep to find the crab apples," said the child to the master, as they came to the Red Mountain road.

When Aristides came to school that day he was confronted by M'liss. But neither threats nor entreaties could extract from that reticent youth the whereabout of the memorandum book nor where he got it. Two or three days afterward, during recess, he approached M'liss, and beckoned her one side.

"Well," said M'liss impatiently.

"Did you ever read the story of 'Ali Baba'?"

"Yes."

"Do you believe it?"

"No."

"Well," said that sage infant, wheeling around on his stout legs, "*it's true!*"

CHAPTER IV
WHICH HAS A GOOD MORAL TENDENCY

Somewhat less spiteful in her intercourse with the other scholars, M'liss still retained an offensive attitude toward Clytemnestra. Perhaps the jealous element was not entirely stilled in her passionate little breast. Perhaps it was that Clytemnestra's round curves and plump outlines afforded an extensive pinching surface. But while these ebullitions were under the master's control, her enmity occasionally took a new and irresponsible form.

In his first estimate of the child's character he could not conceive that she had ever possessed a doll. But the master, like many other professed readers of character, was safer in *a posteriori* than *a priori* reasoning, for M'liss had a doll. But then it was a peculiar doll,—a frightful perversion of wax and sawdust,—a doll fearfully and wonderfully made,—a smaller edition of M'liss. Its unhappy existence had been a secret discovered accidentally by Mrs. Morpher. It had been the oldtime companion of M'liss's wanderings, and bore evident marks of suffering. Its original complexion was long since washed away by the weather, and anointed by the slime of ditches. It looked very much as M'liss had in days past. Its one gown of faded stuff was dirty and ragged as hers had been. M'liss had never been known to apply to it any childish term of endearment. She never exhibited it in the presence of other children. It was put severely to bed in a hollow tree near the schoolhouse, and only allowed exercise during M'liss's rambles. Fulfilling a stern duty to her doll—as she would to herself—it knew no luxuries.

Now, Mrs. Morpher, obeying a commendable impulse, bought another doll and gave it to M'liss. The child received it gravely and curiously. The master, on looking at it one day, fancied he saw a slight resemblance in its round red cheeks and mild blue eyes to Clytemnestra.

It became evident before long that M'liss had also noticed the same resemblance. Accordingly she hammered its waxen head on the rocks when she was alone, and sometimes dragged it with a string round its neck to and from school. At other times, setting it up on her desk, she made a pincushion of its patient and inoffensive body. Whether this was done in revenge of what she considered a second figurative obtrusion of Clytie's excellencies upon her; or whether she had an intuitive appreciation of the rites of certain other heathens, and indulging in that "fetich" ceremony imagined that the original of her wax model would pine away and finally die, is a metaphysical question I shall not now consider.

In spite of these moral vagaries, the master could not help noticing in her different tasks the workings of a quick, restless, and vigorous perception. She knew neither the hesitancy nor the doubts of childhood. Her answers in class were always slightly dashed with audacity. Of course she was not infallible. But her courage and daring in venturing beyond her own depth and that of the floundering little swimmers around her, in their minds outweighed all errors of judgment. Children are no better than grown people in this respect, I fancy; and whenever the little red hand flashed above her desk, there was a wondering silence, and even the master was sometimes oppressed with a doubt of his own experience and judgment.

Nevertheless, certain attributes which at first amused and entertained his fancy began to affect him with grave doubts. He could not but see that M'liss was revengeful, irreverent, and willful. But there was one better quality which pertained to her semi-savage disposition—the faculty of physical fortitude and self-sacrifice, and another—though not always an attribute of the noble savage—truth. M'liss was both fearless and sincere—perhaps in such a character the adjectives were synonymous.

The master had been doing some hard thinking on this subject, and had arrived at that conclusion quite common to all who think sincerely, that he was generally the slave of his own prejudices, when he determined to call on the Rev. Mr. McSnagley for advice. This decision was somewhat humiliating to his pride, as he and McSnagley were not friends. But he thought of M'liss, and the evening of their first meeting; and perhaps with a pardonable superstition that it was not chance alone that had guided her willful feet to the schoolhouse, and perhaps with a complacent consciousness of the rare magnanimity of the act, he choked back his dislike and went to McSnagley.

The reverend gentleman was glad to see him. Moreover, he observed that the master was looking "peartish" and hoped he had got over the "neuralgy" and "rheumatiz." He himself had been troubled with a dumb "ager" since last conference. But he had learned to "rastle and pray."

Pausing a moment to enable the master to write this certain method of curing the dumb "ager" upon the book and volume of his brain, Mr. McSnagley proceeded to inquire after Sister Morpher. "She is an adornment to Christewanity, and has a likely, growin' young family," added Mr. McSnagley; "and there is that mannerly young gal—so well behaved—Miss Clytie." In fact, Clytie's perfections seemed to affect him to such an extent that he dwelt for several minutes upon them. The master was doubly embarrassed. In the first place, there was an enforced contrast with poor M'liss in all this praise of Clytie. Secondly, there was something unpleasantly confidential in his tone of speaking of Morpher's earliest born. So that the master, after a few futile efforts to say something natural, found it convenient to recall another engagement and left without asking the information required, but in his after reflections somewhat unjustly giving the Rev. Mr. McSnagley the full benefit of having refused it.

But the master obtained the advice in another and unexpected direction.

The resident physician of Smith's Pocket was a Dr. Duchesne, or as he was better known to the locality, "Dr. Doochesny." Of a naturally refined nature and liberal education, he had steadily resisted the aggressions and temptations of Smith's Pocket, and represented to the master a kind of connecting link between his present life and the past. So that an intimacy sprang up between the two men, involving prolonged interviews in the doctor's little back shop, often to the exclusion of other suffering humanity and their physical ailments. It was in one of these interviews that the master mentioned the coincidence of the date of the memoranda on the back of M'liss's letter and the day of Smith's suicide.

"If it were Smith's own handwriting, as the child says it is," said the master, "it shows a queer state of mind that could contemplate suicide and indite private memoranda within the same twenty-four hours."

Dr. Duchesne removed his cigar from his lips and looked attentively at his friend.

"The only hypothesis," continued the master, "is that Smith was either drunk or crazy, and the fatal act was in a measure unpremeditated."

"Every man who commits suicide," returned the doctor gravely, "is in my opinion insane, or, what is nearly the same thing, becomes through suffering an irresponsible agent. In my professional experience I have seen most of the forms of mental and physical agony, and know what sacrifices men will make to preserve even an existence that to me seemed little better than death, so long as their intellect remained unclouded. When you come to reflect on the state of mind that chooses death as a preferable alternative, you generally find an exaltation and enthusiasm that differs very little from the ordinary diagnosis of delirium. Smith was not drunk," added the doctor in his usual careless tone; "I saw his body."

The master remained buried in reflection. Presently the doctor removed his cigar.

"Perhaps I might help you to explain the coincidence you speak of."

"How?"

"Very easily. But this is a professional secret, you understand."

"Yes, I understand," said the master hastily, with an ill-defined uneasiness creeping over him.

"Do you know anything of the phenomena of death by gunshot wounds?"

"No!"

"Then you must take certain facts as granted. Smith, you remember, was killed *instantly!* The nature of his wound and the manner of his death were such as would have caused an instantaneous and complete relaxation of *all* the muscles. Rigidity and contraction would have supervened of course, but only after life was extinct and consciousness fled. Now Smith was found with his hand tightly grasping a pistol."

"Well?"

"Well, my dear boy, he must have grasped it after he was dead, or have prevailed on some friend to stiffen his fingers round it."

"Do you mean that he was murdered?"

Dr. Duchesne rose and closed the door. "We have different names for these things in Smith's Pocket. I mean to say that he didn't kill himself—that's all."

"But, doctor," said the master earnestly; "do you think you have done right in concealing this fact? Do you think it just—do you think it consistent with your duty to his orphan child?"

"That's why I have said nothing about it," replied the doctor coolly,—"because of my consideration for his orphan child."

The master breathed quickly, and stared at the doctor.

"Doctor! you don't think that M'liss"—

"Hush!—don't get excited, my young friend. Remember I am not a lawyer—only a doctor."

"But M'liss was with me the very night he must have been killed. We were walking together when we heard the report—that is—a report—which must have been the one"—stammered the master.

"When was that?"

"At half past eleven. I remember looking at my watch."

"Humph!—when did you meet her first?"

"At half past eight. Come, doctor, you have made a mistake here at least," said the young man with an assumption of ease he was far from feeling. "Give M'liss the benefit of the doubt."

Dr. Duchesne replied by opening a drawer of his desk. After rummaging among the powders and mysterious looking instruments with which it was stored, he finally brought forth a longitudinal slip of folded white paper. It was appropriately labeled "*Poison.*"

"Look here," said the doctor, opening the paper. It contained two or three black coarse hairs. "Do you know them?"

"No."

"Look again!"

"It looks something like Melissa's hair," said the master, with a fathomless sinking of the heart.

"When I was called to look at the body," continued the doctor with the deliberate cautiousness of a professional diagnosis, "my suspicions were aroused by the circumstance I told you of. I managed to get possession of the pistol, and found these hairs twisted around the lock as though they had been accidentally caught and violently disentangled. I don't think that any one else saw them. I removed them without observation, and—they are at your service."

The master sank back in his seat and pressed his hand to his forehead. The image of M'liss rose before him with flashing eye and long black hair, and seemed to beat down and resist defiantly the suspicion that crept slowly over his heart.

"I forbore to tell you this, my friend," continued the doctor slowly and gravely, "because when I learned that you had taken this strange child under your protection I did not wish to tell you that which—though I contend does not alter her claims to man's sympathy and kindness— still might have prejudiced her in your eyes. Her improvement under your care has proven my position correct. I have, as you know, peculiar ideas of the extent to which humanity is responsible. I find in my heart—looking back over that child's career—no sentiment but pity. I am mistaken in you if I thought this circumstance aroused any other feeling in yours."

Still the figure of M'liss stood before the master as he bent before the doctor's words, in the same defiant attitude, with something of scorn in the great dark eyes, that made the blood tingle in his cheeks, and seemed to make the reasoning of the speaker but meaningless and empty words. At length he rose. As he stood with his hand on the latch he turned to Dr. Duchesne, who was watching him with careful solicitude.

"I don't know but that you have done well to keep this from me. At all events it has not—cannot, and should not alter my opinion toward

M'liss. You will of course keep it a secret. In the mean time you must not blame me if I cling to my instincts in preference to your judgment. I still believe that you are mistaken in regard to her."

"Stay, one moment," said the doctor; "promise me you will not say anything of this, nor attempt to prosecute the matter further till you have consulted with me."

"I promise. Good-night."

"Good-night;" and so they parted.

True to that promise and his own instinctive promptings the master endeavored to atone for his momentary disloyalty by greater solicitude for M'liss. But the child had noticed some change in the master's thoughtful manner, and in one of their long post-prandial walks she stopped suddenly, and mounting a stump, looked full in his face with big searching eyes.

"You ain't mad?" said she, with an interrogative shake of the black braids.

"No."

"Nor bothered?"

"No."

"Nor hungry?" (Hunger was to M'liss a sickness that might attack a person at any moment.)

"No."

"Nor thinking of her?"

"Of whom, Lissy?"

"That white girl." (This was the latest epithet invented by M'liss, who was a very dark brunette, to express Clytemnestra.)

"No."

"Upon your word?" (A substitute for "Hope you 'll die!" proposed by the master.)

"Yes."

"And sacred honor?"

"Yes."

Then M'liss gave him a fierce little kiss, and hopping down, fluttered off. For two or three days after that she condescended to appear like other children and be, as she expressed it, "good."

When the summer was about spent, and the last harvest had been gathered in the valleys, the master bethought him of gathering in a few ripened shoots of the young idea, and of having his Harvest Home, or Examination. So the savans and professionals of Smith's Pocket were gathered to witness that time-honored custom of placing timid children in a constrained position, and bullying them as in a witness-box. As usual in such cases, the most audacious and self-possessed were the lucky recipients of the honors. The reader will imagine that in the present instance M'liss and Clytie were preeminent and divided public attention: M'liss with her clearness of material perception and self-reliance, and Clytie with her placid self-esteem and saintlike correctness of deportment. The other little ones were timid and blundering. M'liss's readiness and brilliancy, of course, captivated the greatest number, and provoked the greatest applause, and M'liss's antecedents had unconsciously awakened the strongest sympathies of the miners, whose athletic forms were ranged against the walls, or whose handsome bearded faces looked in at the window. But M'liss's popularity was overthrown by an unexpected circumstance.

McSnagley had invited himself, and had been going through the pleasing entertainment of frightening the more timid pupils by the vaguest and most ambiguous questions, delivered in an impressive, funereal tone; and M'liss had soared into astronomy, and was tracking the course of our "spotted ball" through space, and defining the "tethered orbits" of the planets, when McSnagley deliberately arose.

"Meelissy, ye were speaking of the revolutions of this yer yearth, and its movements with regard to the sun, and I think you said it had been a-doin' of it since the creation, eh?"

M'liss nodded a scornful affirmative.

"Well, was that the truth?" said McSnagley, folding his arms.

"Yes," said M'liss, shutting up her little red lips tightly.

The handsome outlines at the windows peered further into the schoolroom, and a saintly, Raphael-like face, with blond beard and soft blue eyes, belonging to the biggest scamp in the diggings, turned toward the child and whispered:—

"Stick to it, M'liss! It's only a big bluff of the parson."

The reverend gentleman heaved a deep sigh, and cast a compassionate glance at the master, then at the children, and then rested his eye on Clytemnestra. That young woman softly elevated her round, white arm. Its seductive curves were enhanced by a gorgeous and massive specimen bracelet, the gift of one of her humblest worshipers, worn in honor of the occasion. There was a momentary pause. Clytie's round cheeks were very pink and soft. Clytie's big eyes were very bright and blue. Clytie's low-necked white book-muslin rested softly on Clytie's white, plump shoulders. Clytie looked at the master, and the master nodded. Then Clytie spoke softly:

"Joshua commanded the sun to stand still, and it obeyed him."

There was a low hum of applause in the schoolroom, a triumphant expression on McSnagley's face, a grave shadow on the master's, and a comical look of disappointment reflected from the windows. M'liss skimmed rapidly over her astronomy, and then shut the book with a loud snap. A groan burst from McSnagley, an expression of astonishment from the schoolroom, and a yell from the windows, as M'liss brought her red fist down on the desk, with the emphatic declaration:—

"It's a d—n lie. I don't believe it!"

CHAPTER V
"OPEN SESAME"

The long wet season had drawn near its close. Signs of spring were visible in the swelling buds and rushing torrents. The pine forests exhaled a fresher spicery. The azaleas were already budding; the ceanothus getting ready its lilac livery for spring. On the green upland which climbed the Red Mountain at its southern aspect, the long spike of the monk's-hood shot up from its broad-leaved stool and once more shook its dark blue bells. Again the billow above Smith's grave was soft and green, its crest just tossed with the foam of daisies and buttercups. The little graveyard had gathered a few new dwellers in the past year, and the mounds were placed two by two by the little paling until they reached Smith's grave, and there, there was but one. General superstition had shunned the enforced companionship. The plot beside Smith was vacant.

It was the custom of the driver of the great Wingdam stage to whip up his horses at the foot of the hill, and soenter Smith's Pocket at that remarkable pace which the woodcuts in the hotel bar-room represented to credulous humanity as the usual rate of speed of that conveyance. At least, Aristides Morpher thought so as he stood one Sunday afternoon, uneasily conscious of his best jacket and collar, waiting its approach. Nor could anything shake his belief that regularly on that occasion the horses ran away with the driver, and that that individual from motives of deep policy pretended not to notice it until they were stopped.

"Anybody up from below, Bill?" said the landlord as the driver slowly descended from his perch.

"Nobody for you," responded Bill shortly. "Dusenberry kem up as usual, and got off at the old place. You can't make a livin' off him, I reckon."

"Have you found out what his name is yet?" continued the landlord, implying that "Dusenberry" was simply a playful epithet of the driver.

"He says his name is Waters," returned Bill. "Jake said he saw him at the North Fork in '50—called himself Moore then. Guess he ain't no good, nowhow. What's he doin' round here?"

"Says he's prospectin'," replied the landlord. "He has a claim somewhere in the woods. Gambles a little too, I reckon. He don't travel on his beauty anyhow."

"If you had seen him makin' up to a piece of calico inside, last trip, and she a-makin' up to him quite confidential-like, I guess you'd think he was a lady-killer. My eye, but wasn't she a stunner! Clytie Morpher wasn't nowhere to begin with her."

"Who was she, Bill?" asked half a dozen masculine voices.

"Don't know. We picked her up this side of 'Coyote.' Fancy? I tell you!—pretty little hat and pink ribbings—eyes that ud bore you through at a hundred yards—white teeth—brown gaiters, and such an ankle! She didn't want to show it,—oh, no!" added the sarcastic Bill with deep significance.

"Where did you leave her, Bill?" asked a gentle village swain who had been fired by the glowing picture of the fair unknown.

"That's what's the matter. You see after we picked her up, she said she was goin' through to Wingdam. Of course there wasn't anything in the stage or on the road too good to offer her. Old Major Spaffler wanted to treat her to lemonade at every station. Judge Plunkett kep' a-pullin' down the blinds and a-h'istin' of them up to keep out the sun and let in the air. Blest if old McSnagley didn't want to carry her travelin'-bag. There wasn't any attention, boys, she didn't get—but it wasn't no use—bless you! She never so much as passed the time of day with them."

"But where did she go?" inquired another anxious auditor.

"Keep your foot off the drag, and I 'll tell you. Arter we left Ring Tail Canon, Dusenberry, as usual, got on. Presently one of the outsides turned round to me, and says he, 'D—d if Ugly Mug ain't got the inside track of all of you this time!' I looked down, and dern my skin if there wasn't Dusenberry a-sittin' up alongside of the lady, quite comfortable, as if they had ben children together. At the next station Dusenberry gets off. So does the lady. 'Ain't you goin' on to Wingdam,' says I. 'No,' says she. 'Mayn't we have the pleasure of your kempany further?' says the judge, taking off his hat. 'No, I've changed my mind,' says she, and off she got, and off she walked arm in arm with him as cool as you please."

"Wonder if that wa'n't the party that passed through here last July?" asked the blacksmith, joining the loungers in front of the stage-office. "Waters brought up a buggy to get the axle bolted. There was a woman setting in the buggy, but the hood was drawn down, and I didn't get to see her face." During this conversation Aristides, after a long, lingering glance at the stage, had at last torn himself away from its fascinations, and was now lounging down the long straggling street in a peculiarly dissipated manner, with his hat pushed on the back part of his head, his right hand and a greater portion of his right arm buried in his trousers pocket. This might have been partly owing to the shortness of his legs

243

and the comparative amplitude of his trousers, which to the casual observer seemed to obviate the necessity of any other garment. But when he reached the bottom of the street, and further enlivened his progress by whistling shrilly between his fingers, and finally drew a fragment of a cigar from his pocket and placed it between his teeth, it was evident that there was a moral as well as physical laxity in his conduct. The near fact was that Aristides had that afternoon evaded the Sunday-school, and was open to any kind of infant iniquity.

The main street of Smith's Pocket gradually lost its civilized character, and after one or two futile attempts at improvement at its lower extremity, terminated impotently in a chaos of ditches, races, and trailings. Out of this again a narrow trail started along the mountain side, and communicated with that vast amphitheatre which still exhibited the pioneer efforts of the early settlers. It was this trail that Aristides took that Sunday afternoon, and which he followed until he reached the hillside a few rods below the yawning fissure of Smith's Pocket. After a careful examination of the vicinity, he cleared away the underbrush beside a fallen pine that lay near, and sat down in the attitude of patient and deliberate expectancy.

Five minutes passed—ten, twenty—and finally a half-hour was gone. Aristides threw away his cigar, which he had lacked determination to light, and peeled small slips from the inner bark of the pine-tree, and munched them gravely. Another five, ten, and twenty minutes passed, and the sun began to drop below the opposite hillside. Another ten minutes, and the whole of the amphitheatre above was in heavy shadow. Ten minutes more, and the distant windows in the settlement flamed redly. Five minutes, and the spire of the Methodist church caught the glow—and then the underbrush crackled.

Aristides, looking up, saw the trunk of the prostrate pine slowly lifting itself before him.

A second glance showed the fearless and self-possessed boy that the apparent phenomenon was simply and easily explained. The tree had fallen midway and at right angles across the trunk of another prostrate monarch. So accurately and evenly was it balanced that the child was satisfied, from a liberal experience of the application of these principles to the game of "seesaw," that a very slight impulse to either end was sufficient to destroy the equilibrium. That impulse proceeded from his end of the tree, as he saw when the uplifted trunk disclosed an opening in the ground beneath it, and the head and shoulders of a man emerging therefrom.

Aristides threw himself noiselessly on his stomach. The thick clump of an azalea hid him from view, though it did not obstruct his survey of the stranger, whom he at once recognized as his former enemy,—the man with the red handkerchief,—the hopeful prospector of Red Mountain, and the hypothetical "Dusenberry" of the stage-driver.

The stranger looked cautiously round, and Aristides shrank close behind the friendly azalea.

Satisfied that he was unobserved, the subterranean proprietor returned to the opening and descended, reappearing with a worn black enameled traveling-bag which he carried with difficulty. This he again enveloped in a blanket and strapped tightly on his back, and a long-handled shovel, brought up from the same mysterious storehouse, completed his outfit. As he stood for a moment leaning on the shovel, it was the figure of the hopeful prospector in the heart of the forest. A very slight effort was sufficient to replace the fallen tree in its former position. Raising the shovel to his shoulder, he moved away, brushing against the azalea bush which hid the breathless Aristides. The sound of his footsteps retreating through the crackling brush presently died out, and a drowsy Sabbath stillness succeeded.

Aristides rose. There was a wonderful brightness in his gray eyes, and a flush on his sunburned cheek. Seizing a root of the fallen pine he essayed to move it. But it defied his endeavors. Aristides looked round.

"There's some trick about it, but I'll find it yet," said that astute child. Breaking off the limb of a buckeye, he extemporized a lever. The first attempt failed. The second succeeded, and the long roots of the tree again, ascended. But as it required prolonged effort to keep the tree up, before the impetus was lost Aristides seized the opportunity to jump into the opening. At the same moment the tree slowly returned to its former position.

In the sudden change from the waning light to complete darkness, Aristides was for a moment confounded. Recovering himself, he drew a match from his capacious pocket, and striking it against the sole of his shoe, by the upspringing flash perceived a candle stuck in the crevices of the rock beside him. Lighting it, he glanced curiously around him. He was at the entrance of a long gallery at the further extremity of which he could faintly see the glimmering of the outer daylight. Following this gallery cautiously he presently came to an antechamber, and by the glimmering of the light above him at once saw that it was the same he had seen in his wonderful dream.

The antechamber was about fourteen feet square, with walls of decomposed quartz, mingling with flaky mica that reflected here and there the gleam of Aristides's candle with a singular brilliancy. It did not need much observation on his part to determine the reason of the stranger's lonely labors. On a rough rocker beside him were two fragments of ore taken from the adjacent wall, the smallest of which the two arms of Aristides could barely clasp. To his dazzled eyes they seemed to be almost entirely of pure gold. The great strike of '56 at Ring Tail Canon had brought to the wonderful vision of Smith's Pocket no such nuggets as were here.

Aristides turned to the wall again, which had been apparently the last scene of the stranger's labors, and from which the two masses of ore were taken. Even to his inexperienced eye it represented a wealth almost incalculable. Through the loose, red soil everywhere glittering star points of the precious metal threw back the rays of his candle. Aristides turned pale and trembled.

Here was the realization of his most extravagant fancy. Ever since his strange dream and encounter with the stranger, he had felt an irresistible desire to follow up his adventure, and discover the secrets of the second cavern. But when he had returned to Smith's Pocket, a few days after, the wreck of the fallen roof had blocked up that part of the opening from which he had caught sight of the hidden workman below. During his visit he had picked up from among the rubbish the memorandum book which had supplied M'liss with letter paper. Still haunting the locality after school hours, he had noticed that regularly at sunset the man with the red handkerchief appeared in some mysterious way from the hillside below Smith's Pocket, and went away in the direction of the settlement. By careful watching, Aristides had fixed the location of his mysterious appearance to a point a few rods below the opening of Smith's Pocket. Flushed by this discovery, he had been betrayed from his usual discretion so far as to intimate a hinting of the suspicion that possessed him in the few mysterious words he had whispered to M'liss at school. The accident we have described above determined the complete discovery of the secret.

Who was the stranger, and why did he keep the fact of this immense wealth hidden from the world? Suppose he, Aristides, were to tell? Wouldn't the schoolboys look up at him with interest as the hero and discoverer of this wonderful cavern, and wouldn't the stage-driver feel proud of his acquaintance and offer him rides for nothing?

Why hadn't Smith discovered it—who was poor and wanted money, whom Aristides had liked, who was the father of M'liss, for whom Aristides confessed a secret passion, who belonged to the settlement and helped to build it up—instead of the stranger? Had Smith never a suspicion that gold was so near him, and if so, why had he killed himself? But did Smith kill himself? And at this thought and its correlative fancy, again the cheek of Aristides blanched, and the candle shook in his nerveless fingers.

Apart and distinct from these passing conjectures one idea remained firm and dominant in his mind: the man with the red handkerchief had no right to this treasure! The mysterious instinct which directed this judicial ruling of Aristides had settled this fact as indubitably as though proven by the weight of the strongest testimony. For an instant a wild thought sprang up in his heart, and he seized the nearest mass of ore with the half-formed intention of bearing it directly to the feet of M'liss as her just and due inheritance. But Aristides could not lift it, and the idea passed out of his mind with the frustrated action.

At the further end of the gallery a few blankets were lying, and with some mining implements, a kettle of water, a few worn flannel shirts, were the only articles which this subterranean habitation possessed. In turning over one of the blankets Aristides picked up a woman's comb. It was a tortoise-shell, and bright with some fanciful ornamentation. Without a moment's hesitation Aristides pocketed it as the natural property of M'liss. A pocketbook containing a few old letters in the breast pocket of one of the blue shirts was transferred to that of Aristides with the same coolness and sentiment of instinctive justice.

Aristides wisely reflected that these unimportant articles would excite no suspicion if found in his possession. A fragment of the rock, which, if he had taken it as he felt impelled, would have precipitated the discovery that Aristides had decided to put off until he had perfected a certain plan. The light from the opening above had gradually faded, and Aristides knew that night had fallen. To prevent suspicion he must return home. He reentered the gallery and reached the opening of the egress. One of the roots of the tree projected into the opening.

He seized it and endeavored to lift it, but in vain. Panting with exertion, he again and again exerted the fullest power of his active sinews, but the tree remained immovable—the opening remained sealed as firmly as with Solomon's signet. Raising his candle towards it, Aristides saw the reason of its resistance. In his hurried ingress he had allowed the tree to revolve sufficiently to permit one of its roots to project into the opening, which held it firmly down. In the shock of the discovery the excitement which had sustained him gave way, and with a hopeless cry the just Aristides fell senseless on the floor of the gallery.

CHAPTER VI
THE TRIALS OF MRS. MORPHER

"Now, where on earth can that child be?" said Mrs. Morpher, shading her eyes with her hand, as she stood at the door of the "Mountain

Ranch," looking down the Wingdam road at sunset. "With his best things on; too. Goodness!—what *were* boys made for?"

Mr. Morpher, without replying to this question, apparently addressed to himself as an adult representative of the wayward species, appeared at the door, and endeavored to pour oil on the troubled waters.

"Oh, *he's* all right, Sue! Don›t fuss about *him,*" said Mr. Morpher with an imbecile sense of conveying comfort in the emphasized pronoun. "He's down the gulch, or in the tunnel, or over to the claim. He'll turn up by bedtime. Don't you worry about *him*. I›ll look him up in a minit," and Mr. Morpher, taking his hat, sauntered down the road in the direction of the National Hotel.

Mrs. Mopher gazed doubtfully after her liege. "Looking up" Aristides, in her domestic experience, implied a prolonged absence in the bar-room of the hotel, the tedium whereof was beguiled by seven-up or euchre. But she only said: "Don't be long, James," and sighed hopelessly as she turned back into the house.

Once again within her own castle walls Mrs. Morpher dropped her look of patient suffering and glanced defiantly around for a fresh grievance.

The decorous little parlor offered nothing to provoke the hostility of her peculiar instincts. Spotless were the white curtains; the bright carpet guiltless of stain or dust. The chairs were placed arithmetically in twos, and added up evenly on the four sides with nothing to carry over. Two bunches of lavender and fennel breathed an odor of sanctified cleanliness through the room. Five daguerreotypes on the mantelpiece represented the Morpher family in the progressive stages of petrifaction, and had the Medusa-like effect of freezing visitors into similar attitudes in their chairs. The walls were further enlivened with two colored engravings of scenes in the domestic history of George Washington, in which the Father of his Country seemed to look blandly from his own correct family circle into Morpher's, and to breathe quite audibly from his gilt frame a dignified blessing.

Lingering a moment in this sacred inclosure to readjust the tablecloth, Mrs. Morpher passed into the dining-room, where the correct Crytie presided at the supper-table, at which the rest of the family were seated. Mrs. Morpher's quick eyes caught the spectacle of M'liss with her chin resting on her hands, and her elbows on the table, sardonically surveying the model of deportment opposite to her.

"M'liss!"

"Well?"

"Where's your elbows?"

"Here's one and there's the other," said M'liss quietly, indicating their respective localities by smartly tapping them with the palm of her hand.

"Take them off the table, instantly, you bold, forward girl—and you, sir, quit that giggling and eat your supper, if you don't want to be put to bed without it!" added Mrs. Morpher to Lycurgus, to whom M'liss's answer had afforded boundless satisfaction. "You're getting to be just as bad as her, and mercy knows you never were a seraphim!"

"What's a seraphim, mother, and what do they do?" asked Lycnrgus, with growing interest.

"They don't ask questions when they should be eating their supper, and thankful for it," interposed Clytie, authoritatively, as one to whom the genteel attributes and social habits of the seraphim had been a privileged revelation.

"But, mother"—

"Hush—and don't be a heathen—run and see who is coming in," said Mrs. Morpher, as the sound of footsteps was heard in the passage.

The door opened and McSnagley entered.

"Why, bless my soul—how do you do?" said Mrs. Morpher, with genteel astonishment. "Quite a stranger, I declare."

This was a polite fiction. M'liss knew the fact to be that Mrs. Morpher was reputed to "set the best table" in Smith's Pocket, and McSnagley always called in on Sunday evenings at supper to discuss the current gossip, and "nag" M'liss with selected texts. The verbal McSnagley as usual couldn't stop a moment—and just dropped in "in passin'." The actual McSnagley deposited his hat in the corner, and placed himself, in the flesh, on a chair by the table.

"And how's Brother James, and the fammerly?"

"They're all well—except 'Risty;' he's off again,—as if my life weren't already pestered out with one child," and Mrs. Morpher glanced significantly at M'liss.

"Ah, well, we all of us have our trials," said McSnagley. "I've been ailin' again. That ager must be in my bones still. I've been rather onsettled myself to-day."

There was the appearance of truth in this statement; Mr. McSnagley's voice had a hollow resonant sound, and his eyes were nervous and fidgety. He had an odd trick, too, of occasionally stopping in the middle of a sentence, and listening as though he heard some distant sound. These things, which Mrs. Morpher recalled afterwards, did not, in the undercurrent of uneasiness about Aristides which she felt the whole of that evening, so particularly attract her notice.

"I know something," said Lycurgus, during one of these pauses, from the retirement of his corner.

"If you dare to—Kerg!" said M'liss.

"M'liss says she knows where Risty is, but she won't tell," said the lawgiver, not heeding the warning. The words were scarcely uttered before M'liss's red hand flashed in the air and descended with a sounding box on the traitor's ear. Lycurgus howled, Mrs. Morpher darted into the corner, and M'liss was dragged defiant and struggling to the light.

"Oh, you wicked, wicked child—why don't you say where, if you know?" said Mrs. Morpher, shaking her, as if the information were to be dislodged from some concealed part of her clothing.

"I didn't say I knew for sure," at last responded M'liss. "I said I thought I knew."

"Well, where do you think he is?"

But M'liss was firm. Even the gloomy picture of the future state devised by McSnagley could not alter her determination. Mrs. Morpher, who had a wholesome awe for this strange child, at last had recourse to entreaty. Finally M'liss offered a compromise.

"I'll tell the master, but I won't tell you—partikerly him," said M'liss, indicating the parson with a bodkin-like dart of her forefinger.

251

Mrs. Morpher hesitated. Her maternal anxiety at length overcame her sense of dignity and discipline.

"Who knows where the master is, or where he is to be found to-night?" she asked hastily.

"He's over to Dr. Duchesne's," said Clytie eagerly; "that is," she stammered, a rich color suddenly flushing from her temples to her round shoulders, "he's usually there in the evenings, I mean."

"Run over, there's a dear, and ask him to come here," said Mrs. Morpher, without noticing a sudden irregularity of conduct in her firstborn. "Run quick!"

Clytie did not wait for a second command. Without availing herself of the proffered company of McSnagley she hastily tied the strings of her school hat under her plump chin, and slipped out of the house. It was not far to the doctor's office, and Clytie walked quickly, overlooking in her haste and preoccupation the admiring glances which several of the swains of Smith's Pocket cast after her as she passed. But on arriving at the doctor's door, so out of breath and excited was this usual model of deportment that, on finding herself in the presence of the master and his friend, she only stood in embarrassed silence, and made up for her lack of verbal expression by a succession of eloquent blushes.

Let us look at her for a moment as she stands there. Her little straw hat, trimmed with cherry-colored ribbons, rests on the waves of her blonde hair. There are other gay ribbons on her light summer dress, clasping her round waist, girdling her wrist, and fastening her collar about her white throat. Her large blue eyes are very dark and moist—it may be with excitement or a tearful thought of the lost Aristides—or the tobacco smoke, with which I regret to say the room is highly charged. But certainly as she stands leaning against the doorway, biting her moist scarlet lip, and trying to pull down the broad brim of her hat over the surging waves of color that *will* beat rhythmically up to her cheeks and temples, she is so dangerously pretty that I am glad for the masters sake he is the philosopher he has just described himself to his friend the doctor, and that he prefers to study human physiology from the inner surfaces.

When Clytie had recovered herself sufficiently to state her message, the master offered to accompany her back. As Clytie took his arm with some slight trepidation Dr. Duchesne, who had taken sharp notes of these "febrile" symptoms, uttered a prolonged whistle and returned thoughtfully to his office.

Although Clytie found the distance returning no further than the distance going, with the exhaustion of her first journey it was natural that her homeward steps should be slower, and that the master should regulate his pace to accommodate her. It was natural, too, that her voice should be quite low and indistinct, so that the master was obliged to bring his hat nearer the cherry-colored ribbons in the course of conversation. It was also natural that he should offer the sensitive young girl such comfort as lay in tenderly modulated tones and playful epithets. And if in the irregularities of the main street it was necessary to take Clytie's hand or to put his arm around her waist in helping her up declivities, that the master saw no impropriety in the act was evident from the fact that he did not remove his arm when the difficulty was surmounted. In this way Clytie's return occupied some moments more than her going, and Mrs. Morpher was waiting anxiously at the door when the young people arrived. As the master entered the rooom, M'liss called him to her. "Bend down your head" she said, "and I'll whisper. But mind, now, I don't say I know for truth where Risty is, I only reckon."

The master bent down his head. As usual in such cases, everybody else felt constrained to listen, and McSnagley's curiosity was awakened to its fullest extent. When the master had received the required information, he said quietly:—

"I think I'll go myself to this place which M'liss wishes to make a secret of and see if the boy is there. It will save trouble to any one else, if she should be mistaken."

"Hadn't you better take some one with you?" said Mrs. Morpher.

"By all means. I 'll go!" said Mr. McSnagley, with feverish alacrity.

The master looked inquiringly at M'liss.

"He can go if he wants to, but he'd better not," said M'liss, looking directly into McSnagley's eyes.

"What do you mean by that, you little savage?" said McSnagley quickly.

M'liss turned scornfully away. "Go," she said,—"go if you want to," and resumed her seat in the corner.

The master hesitated. But he could not withstand the appeal in the eyes of the mother and daughter, and after a short inward struggle he turned to McSnagley and bade him briefly "Come."

When they had left the house and stood in the road together, McSnagley stopped.

"Where are you goin'?"

"To Smith's Pocket."

McSnagley still lingered. "Do you ever carry any weppings?" he at length asked.

"Weapons? No. What do you want with weapons to go a mile on a starlit road to a deserted claim. Nonsense, man, what are you thinking of? We're hunting a lost child, not a runaway felon. Come along," and the master dragged him away.

Mrs. Morpher watched them from the door until their figures were lost in the darkness. When she returned to the dining-room, Clytie had already retired to her room, and Mrs. Morpher, overruling M'liss's desire to sit up until the master returned, bade her follow that correct example. "There's Clytie, now, gone to bed like a young lady, and do you do like her," and Mrs. Morpher, with this one drop of balm in the midst of her trials, trimmed the light and sat down in patience to wait for Aristides, and console herself with the reflection of Clytie's excellence. "Poor Clytie!" mused that motherly woman; "how excited and worried she looks about her brother. I hope she'll be able to get to sleep."

It did not occur to Mrs. Morpher that there were seasons in the life of young girls when younger brothers ceased to become objects of extreme solicitude. It did not occur to her to go upstairs and see how her wish was likely to be gratified. It was well in her anxiety that she did not, and that the crowning trial of the day's troubles was spared her then. For at that moment Clytie was lying on the bed where she had flung herself without undressing, the heavy masses of her blond hair tumbled about her neck, and her hot face buried in her hands.

Of what was the correct Clytie thinking?

She was thinking, lying there with her burning cheeks pressed against the pillow, that she loved the master! She was recalling step by step every incident that had occurred in their lonely walk. She was repeating to herself his facile sentences, wringing and twisting them to extract one drop to assuage the strange thirst that was growing up in her soul. She was thinking—silly Clytie!—that he had never appeared so kind before, and she was thinking—sillier Clytie!—that no one had ever before felt as she did then.

How soft and white his hands were! How sweet and gentle were the tones of his voice! How easily he spoke—so unlike her father, McSnagley, or the young men whom she met at church or on picnics! How tall and handsome he looked as he pressed her hand at the door! Did he press her hand, or was it a mistake? Yes, he must have pressed her hand, for she remembers now to have pressed his in return. And he put his arm around her waist once, and she feels it yet, and the strange perfume as he drew her closer to him. (Mem.—The master had been smoking. Poor Clytie!)

When she had reached this point she raised herself and sat up, and began the process of undressing, mechanically putting each article away in the precise, methodical habit of her former life. But she found herself soon sitting again on the bed, twisting her hair, which fell over her plump white shoulders, idly between her fingers, and patting the carpet with her small white foot. She had been sitting thus some minutes when she heard the sound of voices without, the trampling of many feet, and a loud rapping at the door below. She sprang to the door and looked out in the passage. Something white passed by her like a flash and crouched down at the head of the stairs. It was M'liss.

Mrs. Morpher opened the door.

"Is Mr. Morpher in?" said a half dozen strange, hoarse voices.

"No!"

"Where is he?"

"He's at some of the saloons. Oh, tell me, has anything happened? Is it about Aristides? Where is he—is he safe?" said Mrs. Morpher, wringing her hands in agony.

"He's all right," said one of the men, with Mr. Morpher's old emphasis; "but"—

"But what?"

M'liss moved slowly down the staircase, and Clytie from the passage above held her breath.

"There's been a row down to Smith's old Pocket—a fight—a man killed."

"Who?" shouted M'liss from the stairs.

"McSnagley—shot dead."

CHAPTER VII
THE PEOPLE vs. JOHN DOE WATERS.
Before Chief Justice LYNCH.

The hurried statement of the messenger was corroborated in the streets that night. It was certain that McSnagley was killed. Smith's Pocket, excited but skeptical, had seen the body, had put its fingers in the bullethole, and was satisfied. Smith's Pocket, albeit hoarse with shouting and excitement, still discussed details with infinite relish in bar-rooms and saloons, and in the main street in clamorous knots that in front of the jail where the prisoner was confined seemed to swell into a mob. Smith's Pocket, bearded, blue-shirted, and belligerent, crowding about this locality, from time to time uttered appeals to justice that swelled on the night wind, not infrequently coupling these invocations with the name of that eminent jurist—Lynch.

Let not the simple reader suppose that the mere taking off of a fellow mortal had created this uproar. The tenure of life in Smith's Pocket was vain and uncertain at the best, and as such philosophically accepted, and the blowing out of a brief candle here and there seldom left a permanent shadow with the survivors. In such instances, too, the victims had received their quietus from the hands of brother townsmen, socially, as it were, in broad day, in the open streets, and under other mitigating circumstances. Thus, when Judge Starbottle of Virginia and "French Pete" exchanged shots with each other across the plaza until their revolvers were exhausted, and the luckless Pete received a bullet through the lungs, half the town witnessed it, and were struck with the gallant and chivalrous bearing of these gentlemen, and to this day point with feelings of pride and admiration to the bulletholes in the door of the National Hotel, as they explain how narrow was the escape of the women in the parlor. But here was a man murdered at night, in a lonely place, and by a stranger—a man unknown to the saloons of Smith's Pocket—a wretch who could not plead the excitement of monte or the delirium of whiskey as an excuse. No wonder that Smith's Pocket surged with virtuous indignation beneath the windows of his prison, and clamored for his blood.

And as the crowd thickened and swayed to and fro, the story of his crime grew exaggerated by hurried and frequent repetition. Half a dozen speakers volunteered to give the details with an added horror to every sentence. How one of Morpher's children had been missing for a week or more. How the schoolmaster and the parson were taking a walk that evening, and coming to Smith's Pocket heard a faint voice from its depths which they recognized as belonging to the missing child. How they had succeeded in dragging him out and gathered from his infant lips the story of his incarceration by the murderer, Waters, and his enforced labors in the mine. How they were interrupted by the appearance of Waters, followed by a highly colored and epithet-illustrated account of the interview and quarrel. How Waters struck the schoolmaster, who returned the blow with a pick. How Waters thereupon drew a derringer and fired, missing the schoolmaster, but killing McSnagley behind him. How it was believed that Waters was one of Joaquin's gang, that he had killed Smith, etc., etc. At each pause the crowd pushed and panted, stealthily creeping around the doors and windows of the jail like some strange beast of prey, until the climax was reached, and a hush fell, and two men were silently dispatched for a rope, and a critical examination was made of the limbs of a pine-tree in the vicinity.

The man to whom these incidents had the most terrible significance might have seemed the least concerned as he sat that night but a few feet removed from the eager crowd without, his hands lightly clasped together between his knees, and the expression on his face of one whose thoughts were far away. A candle stuck in a tin sconce on the wall flickered as the night wind blew freshly through a broken pane of the window. Its uncertain light revealed a low room whose cloth ceiling was stained and ragged, and from whose boarded walls the torn paper hung in strips; a lumber-room partitioned from the front office, which was occupied by a justice of the peace. If this temporary dungeon had an appearance of insecurity, there was some compensation in the spectacle of an armed sentinel who sat upon a straw mattress in the doorway, and another who patrolled the narrow hall which led to the street. That the prisoner was not placed in one of the cells in the floor below may have been owing to the fact that the law recognized his detention as only temporary, and while providing the two guards as a preventive against the egress of crime within, discreetly removed all unnecessary and provoking obstacles to the ingress of justice from without.

Since the prisoner's arrest he had refused to answer any interrogatories. Since he had been placed in confinement he had not moved from his present attitude. The guard, finding all attempts at conversation fruitless, had fallen into a reverie, and regaled himself with pieces of straw plucked from the mattress. A mouse ran across the floor. The silence contrasted strangely with the hum of voices in the street.

The candle-light, falling across the prisoner's forehead, showed the features which Smith's Pocket knew and recognized as Waters, the strange prospector. Had M'liss or Aristides seen him then they would have missed that sinister expression which was part of their fearful remembrance. The hard, grim outlines of his mouth were relaxed, the broad shoulders were bent and contracted, the quick, searching eyes were fixed on vacancy. The strong man—physically strong only—was

258

breaking up. The fist that might have felled an ox could do nothing more than separate its idle fingers with childishness of power and purpose. An hour longer in this condition, and the gallows would have claimed a figure scarcely less limp and impotent than that it was destined to ultimately reject.

He had been trying to collect his thoughts. Would they hang him? No, they must try him first, legally, and he could prove—he could prove—But what could he prove? For whenever he attempted to consider the uncertain chances of his escape, he found his thoughts straying wide of the question. It was of no use for him to clasp his fingers or knit his brows. Why did the recollection of a school-fellow, long since forgotten, blot out all the fierce and feverish memories of the night and the terrible certainty of the future? Why did the strips of paper hanging from the wall recall to him the pattern of a kite he had flown forty years ago. In a moment like this, when all his energies were required and all his cunning and tact would be called into service, could he think of nothing better than trying to match the torn paper on the wall, or to count the cracks in the floor? And an oath rose to his lips, but from very feebleness died away without expression.

Why had he ever come to Smith's Pocket? If he had not been guided by that hell-cat, this would not have happened. What if he were to tell *all* he knew? What if he should accuse *her*? But would they be willing to give up the bird they had already caught? Yet he again found himself cursing his own treachery and cowardice, and this time an exclamation burst from his lips and attracted the attention of the guard.

"Hello, there! easy, old fellow; thar ain't any good in that," said the sentinel, looking up. "It's a bad fix you're in, *sure*, but rarin' and pitchin' won't help things. 'T ain't no use cussin'—leastways, 't ain't that kind o' swearing that gets a chap out o' here", he added, with a conscientious reservation. "Now, ef I was in your place, I'd kinder reflect on my sins, and make my peace with God Almighty, for I tell you the looks o' them people outside ain't pleasant. You're in the hands of the law, and the law will protect you as far as it can,—as far as two men can stand agin a hundred; sabe? That's what's the matter; and it's as well that you knowed that now as any time."

But the prisoner had relapsed into his old attitude, and was surveying the jailor with the same abstracted air as before. That individual resumed his seat on the mattress, and now lent his ear to a colloquy which seemed to be progressing at the foot of the stairs. Presently he was hailed by his brother turnkey from below.

"Oh, Bill," said fidus Achates from the passage, with the usual Californian prefatory ejaculation.

"Well?"

"Here's M'liss! Says she wants to come up. Shall I let her in?"

The subject of inquiry, however, settled the question of admission by darting past the guard below in this moment of preoccupation, and bounded up the stairs like a young fawn. The guards laughed.

"Now, then, my infant phenomenon," said the one called Bill, as M'liss stood panting before him, "wot 's up? and nextly, wot's in that bottle?"

M'liss whisked the bottle which she held in her hand smartly under her apron, and said curtly, "Where's him that killed the parson?"

"Yonder," replied the man, indicating the abstracted figure with his hand. "Wot do *you* want with him? None o› your tricks here, now," he added threateningly.

"I want to see him!"

"Well, look! make the most of your time, and *his* too, for the matter of that; but mind, now, no nonsense, M›liss, he won›t stand it!" repeated the guard with an emphasis in the caution.

M'liss crossed the room, until opposite the prisoner. "Are you the chap that killed the parson?" she said, addressing the motionless figure.

Something in the tone of her voice startled the prisoner from the reverie. He raised his head and glanced quickly, and with his old sinister expression, at the child.

"What's that to you?" he asked, with the grim lines setting about his mouth again, and the old harshness of his voice.

"Didn't I tell you he wouldn't stand any of your nonsense, M'liss?" said the guard testily.

M'liss only repeated her question.

"And what if I did kill him?" said the prisoner savagely; "what's that to you, you young hell-cat? Guard!—damnation!—what do you let her come here for? Do you hear? Guard!" he screamed, rising in a transport of passion, "take her away! fling her downstairs! What the h—ll is she doing here?"

"If you was the man that killed McSnagley," said M'liss, without heeding the interruption, "I've brought you something;" and she drew the bottle from under her apron and extended it to Waters, adding, "It's brandy—Cognac—A1."

"Take it away, and take yourself with it," returned Waters, without abating his angry accents. "Take it away! do you hear?"

"Well, that's what I call ongrateful, dog-gone my skin if it ain't," said the guard, who had been evidently struck with M'liss's generosity. "Pass the licker this way, my beauty, and I'll keep it till he changes his mind. He's naturally a little flustered just now, but he'll come round after you go."

But M'liss didn't accede to this change in the disposition of the gift, and was evidently taken aback by her reception and the refusal of the proffered comfort.

"Come, hand the bottle here!" repeated the guard. "It's agin rules to bring the pris'ner anything, anyway, and it's confiscated to the law. It's agin the rules, too, to ask a pris'ner any question that'll criminate him, and on the whole you'd better go, M'liss," added the guard, to whom the appearance of the bottle had been the means of provoking a spasm of discipline.

But M'liss refused to make over the coveted treasure. Bill arose half jestingly and endeavored to get possession of the bottle. A struggle ensued, good-naturedly on the part of the guard, but characterized on the part of M'liss by that half-savage passion which any thwarted whim or instinct was sure to provoke in her nature. At last with a curse she freed herself from his grasp, and seizing the bottle by the neck aimed it with the full strength of her little arm fairly at his head. But he was quick enough to avert that important object, if not quick enough to save his shoulder from receiving the strength of the blow, which shattered the thin glass and poured the fiery contents of the bottle over his shirt and breast, saturating his clothes, and diffusing a sharp alcoholic odor through the room.

A forced laugh broke from his lips, as he sank back on the mattress, not without an underlying sense of awe at this savage girl who stood panting before him, and from whom he had just escaped a blow which might have been fatal. "It's a pity to waste so much good licker," he added, with affected carelessness, narrowly watching each movement of the young pythoness, whose rage was not yet abated.

"Come, M'liss," he said at last, "we'll say quits. You've lost your brandy, and I've got some of the pieces of yonder bottle sticking in my shoulder yet. I suppose brandy is good for bruises, though. Hand me the light!"

M'liss reached the candle from the sconce and held it by the guard as he turned back the collar of his shirt to lay bare his shoulder. "So," he muttered, "black and blue; no bones broken, though no fault of yours, eh? my young cherub, if it wasn't. There—why, what are you looking at in that way, M'liss, are you crazy?—Hell's furies, don't hold the light so near! What are you doing; Hell—ho, there! Help!"

Too late, for in an instant he was a sheet of living flame. When or how the candle had touched his garments, saturated with the inflammable fluid, Waters, the only inactive spectator in the room, could never afterward tell. He only knew that the combustion was instantaneous and complete, and before the cry had died from his lips, not only the guard, but the straw mattress on which he had been sitting, and the loose strips of paper hanging from the walls, and the torn cloth ceiling above were in flames.

"Help! Help! Fire! Fire!"

With a superhuman effort, M'liss dragged the prisoner past the blazing mattress, through the doorway into the passage, and drew the door, which opened outwardly, against him. The unhappy guard, still blazing like a funeral pyre, after wildly beating the air with his arms for a few seconds, dashed at the broken window, which gave way with his weight, and precipitated him, still flaming, into the yard below. A column of smoke and a licking tongue of flame leaped from the open window at the same moment, and the cry of fire was reechoed from a hundred voices in the street. But scarcely had M'liss closed the open door against Waters, when the guard from the doorway mounted the stairs in time to see a flaming figure leap from the window. The room was filled with smoke and fire. With an instinct of genius, M'liss, pointing to the open window, shouted hoarsely in his ear:—

"Waters has escaped!"

A cry of fury from the guard was echoed from the stairs, even now crowded by the excited mob, who feared the devastating element might still cheat them of their intended victim. In another moment the house was emptied, and the front street deserted, as the people rushed to the rear of the jail—climbing fences and stumbling over ditches in pursuit of the imagined runaway. M'liss seized the hat and coat of the luckless "Bill," and dragging the prisoner from his place of concealment hurriedly equipped him, and hastened through the blinding smoke of the staircase boldly on the heels of the retiring crowd. Once in the friendly darkness of the street, it was easy to mingle with the pushing throng until an alley crossing at right angles enabled them to leave the main thoroughfare. A few moments' rapid flight, and the outskirts of the town were reached, the tall pines opened their abysmal aisles to the fugitives, and M'liss paused with her companion. Until daybreak, at least, here they were safe!

From the time they had quitted the burning room to that moment, Waters had passed into his listless, abstracted condition, so helpless and feeble that he retained the grasp of M'liss's hand more through some instinctive prompting rather than the dictates of reason. M'liss had found it necessary to almost drag him from the main street and the hurrying crowd, which seemed to exercise a strange fascination over his bewildered senses. And now he sat down passively beside her, and seemed to submit to the guidance of her superior nature.

"You're safe enough now till daylight," said M'liss, when she had recovered her breath, "but you must make the best time you can through these woods to-night, keeping the wind to your back, until you come to the Wingdam road. There! do you hear?" said M'liss, a little vexed at her companion's apathy.

Waters released the hand of M'liss, and commenced mechanically to button his coat around his chest with fumbling, purposeless fingers. He then passed his hand across his forehead as if to clear his confused and bewildered brain; all this, however, to no better result than to apparently root his feet to the soil and to intensify the stupefaction which seemed to be creeping over him.

"Be quick, now! You've no time to lose! Keep straight on through the woods until you see the stars again before you, and you're on the other side of the ridge. What are you waiting for?" And M'liss stamped her little foot impatiently.

An idea which had been struggling for expression at last seemed to dawn in his eyes. Something like a simpering blush crept over his face as he fumbled in his pocket. At last, drawing forth a twenty-dollar piece, he bashfully offered it to M'liss. In a twinkling the extended arm was stricken up, and the bright coin flew high in the air, and disappeared in the darkness.

"Keep your money! I don't want it. Don't do that again!" said M'liss, highly excited, "or I'll—I'll—bite you!"

Her wicked little white teeth flashed ominously as she said it.

"Get off while you can. Look!" she added, pointing to a column of flame shooting up above the straggling mass of buildings in the village, "the jail is burning; and if that goes, the block will go with it. Before morning these woods will be filled with people. Save yourself while you can!"

Waters turned and moved away in the darkness. "Keep straight on, and don't waste a moment," urged the child, as the man seemed still disposed to linger. "Trot now!" and in another moment he seemed to melt into the forest depths.

M'liss threw her apron around her head, and coiled herself up at the root of a tree in something of her old fashion. She had prophesied truly of the probable extent of the fire. The fresh wind, whirling the sparks over the little settlement, had already fanned the single flame into the broad sheet which now glowed fiercely, defining the main street along its entire length. The breeze which fanned her cheek bore the crash of falling timbers and the shouts of terrified and anxious men. There were no engines in Smith's Pocket, and the contest was unequal. Nothing but a change of wind could save the doomed settlement.

The red glow lit up the dark cheek of M'liss and kindled a savage light in her black eyes. Relieved by the background of the sombre woods, she might have been a red-handed Nemesis looking over the city of Vengeance. As the long tongues of flame licked the broad colonnade of the National Hotel, and shot a wreathing pillar of fire and smoke high into the air, M'liss extended her tiny fist and shook it at the burning building with an inspiration that at the moment seemed to transfigure her.

So the night wore away until the first red bars of morning light gleamed beyond the hill, and seemed to emulate the dying embers of the devastated settlement. M'liss for the first time began to think of the home she had quitted the night before, and looked with some anxiety in the direction of "Mountain Ranch." Its white walls and little orchard were untouched, and looked peacefully over the blackened and deserted village. M'liss rose, and, stretching her cramped limbs, walked briskly toward the town. She had proceeded but a short distance when she heard the sound of cautious and hesitating footsteps behind her, and, facing quickly about, encountered the figure of Waters.

"Are you drunk?" said M'liss passionately, "or what do you mean by this nonsense?"

The man approached her with a strange smile on his face, rubbing his hands together, and shivering as with cold. When he had reached her side he attempted to take her hand. M'liss shrank away from him with an expression of disgust.

"What are you doing here again?" she demanded.

"I want to go with you. It's dark in there," he said, motioning to the wood he had just quitted, "and I don't like to be alone. You'll let me be with you, won't you? I won't be any trouble;" and a feeble smile flickered on his lips.

M'liss darted a quick look into his face. The grim outlines of his mouth were relaxed, and his lips moved again impotently. But his eyes were bright and open,—bright with a look that was new to M'liss— that imparted a strange softness and melancholy to his features,—the incipient gleam of insanity!

CHAPTER VIII
THE AUTHOR TO THE READER—EXPLANATORY

If I remember rightly, in one of the admirable tragedies of Tsien Tsiang at a certain culminating point of interest an innocent person is about to be sacrificed. The knife is raised and the victim meekly awaits the stroke. At this moment the author of the play appears on the stage, and, delivering an excellent philosophical dissertation on the merits of the "situation," shows that by the purest principles of art the sacrifice is necessary, but at the same time offers to the audience the privilege of changing the denouement. Such, however, is the nice aesthetic sense of a Chinese auditory, and so universal the desire of bloodshed in the heathen breast, that invariably at each representation of this remarkable tragedy the cause of humanity gives way to the principles of art.

I offer this precedent as an excuse for digressing at a moment when I have burned down a small settlement, dispatched a fellow being, and left my heroine alone in the company of an escaped convict who has just developed insanity as a new social quality. My object in thus digressing is to confer with the reader in regard to the evolution of this story,—a familiarity not without precedent, as I might prove from most of the old Greek comedies, whose *parabasis* permits the poet to mingle freely with the *dramatis personae*, to address the audience and descant at length in regard to himself, his play, and his own merits.

The fact is that, during the progress of this story, I have received many suggestions from intimate friends in regard to its incidents and construction. I have also been in the receipt of correspondence from distant readers, one letter of which I recall signed by an "Honest Miner," who advises me to "do the right thing by M'liss," or intimates somewhat obscurely that he will "bust my crust for me," which, though complimentary in its abstract expression of interest, and implying a taste for euphonism, evinces an innate coarseness which I fear may blunt his perceptions of delicate shades and Greek outlines.

Again, the practical nature of Californians and their familiarity with scenes and incidents which would be novel to other people have occasioned me great uneasiness. In the course of the last three chapters of M'liss I have received some twenty or thirty communications from different parts of the State corroborating incidents of my story, which I solemnly assure the reader is purely fictitious. Some one has lately sent me a copy of an interior paper containing an old obituary of Smith of Smith's Pocket. Another correspondent writes to me that he was acquainted with the schoolmaster in the fall of '49, and that they "grubbed together." The editors of the serial in which this story appears assure me that they have received an advertisement from the landlord of the "National Hotel" contingent upon an editorial notice of its having been at one time the abode of M'liss; while an aunt of the heroine, alluding in excellent terms to the reformed character of her niece M'liss, clenches her sincerity by requesting the loan of twenty dollars to buy clothes for the desolate orphan.

Under these circumstances I have hesitated to go on. What were the bodiless creatures of my fancy—the pale phantoms of thought, evoked in the solitude of my chamber, and sometimes even midst the hum of busy streets—have suddenly grown into flesh and blood, living people, protected by the laws of society, and having their legal right to actions for slander in any court. Worse than that, I have sometimes thought with terror of the new responsibility which might attach to my development of their characters. What if I were obliged to support and protect these Frankenstein monsters? What if the original of the principal villain of my story should feel impelled through aesthetic principles of art to work out in real life the supposititious denouement I have sketched for him?

I have therefore concluded to lay aside my pen for this week, leaving the catastrophe impending, and await the suggestion of my correspondents. I do so the more cheerfully as it enables the editors of this weekly to publish twenty-seven more columns of Miss Braddon's "Outcasts of Society" and the remainder of the "Duke's Motto,"—two works which in the quiet simplicity of their home-like pictures and household incidents are attended with none of the difficulties which beset my unhappy story.

CHAPTER IX
CLEANING UP

As the master, wan-eyed and unrefreshed by slumber, strayed the next morning among the blackened ruins of the fire, he was conscious of having undergone some strange revulsion of sentiment. What he remembered of the last evening's events, though feverish and indistinct as a dream, and though, like a dream, without coherency or connected outline, had nevertheless seriously impressed him. How frivolous and trifling his past life and its pursuits looked through the lightning vista opened to his eyes by the flash of Waters's pistol! "Suppose I had been killed," ruminated the master, "what then? A paragraph in the 'Banner,' headed 'Fatal Affray,' and my name added to the already swollen list of victims to lawless violence and crime! Humph! A pretty scrape, truly!" And the master ground his teeth with vexation.

Let not the reader judge him too hastily. In the best regulated mind, thankfulness for deliverance from danger is apt to be mingled with some doubts as to the necessity of the trial.

In this frame of mind the last person he would have cared to meet was Clytie. That young woman's evil genius, however, led her to pass the burnt district that morning. Perhaps she had anticipated the meeting. At all events, he had proceeded but a few steps before he was confronted by the identical round hat and cherry colored ribbons. But in his present humor the cheerful color somehow reminded him of the fire and of a ruddy stain over McSnagley's heart, and invested the innocent Clytie with a figurative significance. Now Clytie's reveries at that moment were pleasant, if the brightness of her eyes and the freshened color on her cheeks were any sign, and, as she had not seen the master since then, she naturally expected to take up the thread of romance where it had been dropped. But it required all her feminine tact to conceal her embarrassment at his formal greeting and constrained manner.

"He is bashful," reasoned Clytie to herself.

"This girl is a tremendous fool," growled the master inwardly.

An awkward pause ensued. Finally, Clytie *loquitur*:—

"M'liss has been missing since the fire!"

"Missing?" echoed the master in his natural tone.

Clytie bit her lip with vexation. "Yes, she's always running away. She'll be back again. But you look interested. Do you know," she continued with exceeding archness, "I sometimes think, Mr. Gray, if M'liss were a little older"—

"Well?"

"Well, putting this and that together, you know!"

"Well?"

"People will talk, you know," continued Clytie, with that excessive fondness weak people exhibit in enveloping in mystery the commonest affairs of life.

"People are d——-d fools!" roared the master.

The correct Clytie was a little shocked. Perhaps underneath it was a secret admiration of the transgressor. Force even of this cheap quality goes a good way with some natures.

"That is," continued the master, with an increase of dignity in inverse proportion to the lapse he had made, "people are apt to be mistaken, Miss Morpher, and without meaning it, to do infinite injustice to their fellow mortals. But I see I am detaining you. I will try and find Melissa. I wish you good-morning." And Don Whiskerandos stalked solemnly away.

Clytie turned red and white by turns, and her eyes filled with tears. This denouement to her dreams was utterly unexpected. While a girl of stronger character and active intelligence would have employed the time in digesting plans of future retaliation and revenge, Clytie's dull brain and placid nature were utterly perplexed and shaken.

"Dear me!" said Clytie to herself, as she started home, "if he don't love me, why don't he say so?"

The master, or Mr. Gray, as we may now call him as he draws near the close of his professional career, took the old trail through the forest, which led to M'liss's former hiding-place. He walked on briskly, revolving in his mind the feasibility of leaving Smith's Pocket. The late disaster, which would affect the prosperity of the settlement for some time to come, offered an excuse to him to give up his situation. On searching his pockets he found his present capital to amount to ten dollars. This increased by forty dollars, due him from the trustees, would make fifty dollars; deduct thirty dollars for liabilities, and he would have twenty dollars left to begin the world anew. Youth and hope added an indefinite number of ciphers to the right hand of these figures, and in this sanguine mood our young Alnaschar walked on until he had reached the old pine throne in the bank of the forest. M'liss was not there. He sat down on the trunk of the tree, and for a few moments gave himself up to the associations it suggested. What would become of M'liss after he was gone? But he quickly dropped the subject as one too visionary and sentimental for his then fiercely practical consideration, and, to prevent the recurrence of such distracting fancies, began to retrace his steps toward the settlement. At the edge of the woods, at a point where the trail forked toward the old site of Smith's Pocket, he saw M'liss coming toward him. Her ordinary pace on such occasions was a kind of Indian trot; to his surprise she was walking slowly, with her apron thrown over her head,—an indication of meditation with M'liss and the usual way in which she excluded the outer world in studying her lessons. When she was within a few feet of him he called her by name. She started as she recognized him. There was a shade of seriousness in

270

her dark eyes, and the hand that took his was listless and totally unlike her old frank, energetic grasp.

"You look worried, M'liss," said Mr. Gray soothingly, as the old sentimental feeling crept over his heart. "What's the matter now?"

M'liss replied by seating herself on the bank beside the road, and pointed to a place by her side. Mr. Gray took the proffered seat. M'liss then, fixing her eyes on some distant part of the view, remained for some moments in silence. Then, without turning her head or moving her eyes, she asked:—

"What's that they call a girl that has money left her?"

"An heiress, M'liss?"

"Yes, an heiress."

"Well?" said Mr. Gray.

"Well," said M'liss, without moving her eyes, "I'm one,—I'm a heiress!"

"What's that, M'liss?" said Mr. Gray laughingly.

M'liss was silent again. Suddenly turning her eyes full upon him, she said:—

"Can you keep a secret?"

"Yes," said Mr. Gray, beginning to be impressed by the child's manner. "Listen, then."

In short quick sentences, M'liss began. How Aristides had several times hinted of the concealed riches of Smith's Pocket. How he had last night repeated the story to her of a strange discovery he had made. How she remembered to have heard her father often swear that there was money "in that hole," if he only had means to work it. How, partly impressed by this statement and partly from curiosity and pity for the prisoner, she had visited him in confinement. An account of her interview, the origin of the fire, her flight with Waters. (*Questions* by Mr. Gray: What was your object in assisting this man to escape? *Ans.* They were going to kill him. *Ques.* Hadn't he killed McSnagley. *Ans.* Yes, but McSnagley ought to have been killed long ago.) How she had taken leave of him that morning. How he had come back again "silly." How she had dragged him on toward the Wingdam road, and how he had told her that all the hidden wealth of Smith's Pocket had belonged to her father. How she had found out, from some questions, that he had known her father. But how all his other answers were "silly."

"And where is he now?" asked Mr. Gray.

"Gone," said M'liss. "I left him at the edge of the wood to go back and get some provisions, and when I returned he was gone. If he had any senses left, he's miles away by this time. When he was off I went back to Smith's Pocket. I found the hidden opening and saw the gold."

Mr. Gray looked at her curiously. He had, in his more intimate knowledge of her character, noticed the unconcern with which she spoke of the circumstances of her father's death and the total lack of any sentiment of filial regard. The idea that this man whom she had aided in escaping had ever done her injury had not apparently entered her mind, nor did Mr. Gray think it necessary to hint the deeper suspicion he had gathered from Dr. Duchesne that Waters had murdered her father. If the story of the concealed treasures of Smith's Pocket were exaggerated he could easily satisfy himself on that point. M'liss met his suggestion to return to the Pocket with alacrity, and the two started away in that direction.

It was late in the afternoon when Mr. Gray returned. His heightened color and eager inquiry for Dr. Duchesne provoked the usual hope from the people that he met "that it was nothing serious." No, nothing was the matter, the master answered with a slight laugh, but would they send the doctor to his schoolhouse when he returned? "That young chap's worse than he thinks," was one sympathizing suggestion; "this kind of life's too rough for his sort."

To while away the interim, Mr. Gray stopped on his way to the schoolhouse at the stage office as the Wingdam stage drew up and disgorged its passengers. He was listlessly watching the passengers as they descended when a soft voice from the window addressed him, "May I trouble you for your arm as I get down?" Mr. Gray looked up. It was a singular request, as the driver was at that moment standing by the door, apparently for that purpose. But the request came from a handsome woman, and with a bow the young man stepped to the door.

The lady laid her hand lightly on his arm, sprang from the stage with a dexterity that showed the service to have been merely ceremonious, thanked him with an elaboration of acknowledgment which seemed equally gratuitous, and disappeared in the office.

"That's what I call a dead set," said the driver, drawing a long breath, as he turned to Mr. Gray, who stood in some embarrassment. "Do you know her?"

"No," said Mr. Gray laughingly, "do you?"

"Nary time! But take care of yourself, young man; she's after you, sure!"

But Mr. Gray was continuing his walk to the schoolhouse, unmindful of the caution. For the momentary glimpse he had caught of this woman's face, she appeared to be about thirty. Her dress, though tasteful and elegant, in the present condition of California society afforded no criterion of her social status. But the figure of Dr. Duchesne waiting for him at the schoolhouse door just then usurped the place of all others, and she dropped out of his mind.

"Now then," said the doctor, as the young man grasped his hand, "you want me to tell you why your eyes are bloodshot, why your cheeks burn, and your hand is dry and hot?"

"Not exactly! Perhaps you'll understand the symptoms better when you've heard my story. Sit down here and listen."

The doctor took the proffered seat on top of a desk, and Mr. Gray, after assuring himself that they were entirely alone, related the circumstances he had gathered from M'liss that morning.

"You see, doctor, how unjust were your surmises in regard to this girl," continued Mr. Gray. "But let that pass now. At the conclusion of her story, I offered to go with her to this Ali Baba cave. It was no easy job finding the concealed entrance, but I found it at last, and ample corroboration of every item of this wild story. The pocket is rich with the most valuable ore. It has evidently been worked for some time since the discovery was made, but there is still a fortune in its walls, and several thousand dollars of ore sacked up in its galleries. Look at that!" continued Mr. Gray, as he drew an oblong mass of quartz and metal from his pocket. "Think of a secret of this kind having been intrusted for three weeks to a penniless orphan girl of twelve and an eccentric schoolboy of ten, and undivulged except when a proper occasion offered."

Dr. Duchesne smiled. "And Waters is really clear?"

"Yes," said Mr. Gray.

"And M'liss assisted him to escape?"

"Yes."

"Well, you are an innocent one! And you see nothing in this but an act of thoughtless generosity? No assisting of an old accomplice to escape?"

"I see nothing but truth in her statement," returned Mr. Gray stoutly. "If there has been any wrong committed, I believe her to be innocent of its knowledge."

"Well, I'm glad at least the money goes to her and not to him. But how are you to establish her right to this property?"

"That was my object in conferring with you. At present the claim is abandoned. I have taken up the ground in my own name (for her), and this afternoon I posted up the usual notice."

"Go on. You are not so much of a fool, after all."

"Thank you! This will hold until a better claim is established. Now, if Smith had discovered this lead, and was, as the lawyers say, 'seized and possessed' of it at the time of his death, M'liss, of course, as next of kin, inherits it."

"But how can this be proved? It is the general belief that Smith committed suicide through extreme poverty and destitution."

Mr. Gray drew a letter from his pocket.

"You remember the memorandum I showed you, which came into my possession. Here it is; it is dated the day of his death."

Dr. Duchesne took it and read:—

"July 17th. Five hours in drift—dipping west. Took out 20 oz.—cleaned up 40 oz.—Mem. Saw M. S."

"This evidently refers to actual labor in the mine at the time," said Dr. Duchesne. "But is it legally sufficient to support a claim of this

274

magnitude? That is the only question now. You say this paper was the leaf of an old memorandum, torn off and used for a letter by M'liss; do you know where the orignal book can be found?"

"Aristides has it, or knows where it is," answered Mr. Gray.

"Find it by all means. And get legal advice before you do anything. Go this very evening to Judge Plunkett and state your case to him. The promise of a handsome contingent fee won't hurt M'liss's prospects any. Remember, our ideas of abstract justice and the letter of the law in this case may be entirely different. Take Judge Plunkett your proofs; that is," said the Doctor, stopping and eyeing his friend keenly, "if you have no fears for M'liss if this matter should be thoroughly ventilated."

Mr. Gray did not falter.

"I go at once," said he gayly, "if only to prove the child's claim to a good name if we fail in getting her property."

The two men left the schoolhouse together. As they reached the main street, the doctor paused:—

"You are still determined?"

"I am," responded the young man.

"Good-night, and God speed you, then," and the doctor left him.

The fire had been particularly severe on the legal fraternity in the settlement, and Judge Plunkett's office, together with those of his learned brethren, had been consumed with the courthouse on the previous night. The judge's house was on the outskirts of the village, and thither Mr. Gray proceeded. The judge was at home, but engaged at that moment. Mr. Gray would wait, and was ushered into a small room evidently used as a kitchen, but just then littered with law books, bundles of papers, and blanks that had been hastily rescued from the burning building. The sideboard groaned with the weight of several volumes of New York Reports, that seemed to impart a dusty flavor to the adjoining victual. Mr. Gray picked up a volume of supreme court decisions from the coal-scuttle, and was deep in an interesting case, when the door of the adjoining room opened and Judge Plunkett appeared.

He was an oily man of about fifty, with spectacles. He was glad to see

275

the schoolmaster. He hoped he was not suffering from the excitement of the previous evening. For his part, the spectacle of sober citizens rising in a body to vindicate the insulted majesty of the laws of society, and of man, had always something sublime in it. And the murderer had really got away after all. And it was a narrow escape the schoolmaster had, too, at Smith's Pocket.

Mr. Gray took advantage of the digression to state his business. He briefly recounted the circumstances of the discovery of the hidden wealth of Smith's Pocket, and exhibited the memorandum he had shown the doctor. When he had concluded, Judge Plunkett looked at him over his spectacles, and rubbed his hands with satisfaction.

"You apprehend," said the judge eagerly, "that you will have no difficulty in procuring this book from which the leaf was originally torn?"

"None," replied Mr. Gray.

"Then, sir, I should give as my professional opinion that the case was already won."

Mr. Gray shook the hand of the little man with great fervor, and thanked him for his belief. "And so this property will go entirely to M'liss?" he asked again.

"Well—ah—no—not exactly," said Judge Plunkett, with some caution. "She will benefit by it undoubtedly—undoubtedly," and he rubbed his hands again.

"Why not M'liss alone? There are no other claimants!" said Mr. Gray.

"I beg your pardon—you mistake," said Judge Plunkett, with a smile. "You surely would not leave out the widow and mother?"

"Why, M'liss is an orphan," said Mr. Gray in utter bewilderment.

"A sad mistake, sir,—a painful though natural mistake. Mr. Smith, though separated from his wife, was never divorced. A very affecting history—the old story, you know—an injured and loving woman deserted by her natural protector, but disdaining to avail herself of our legal aid. By a singular coincidence that I should have told you, I am anticipating you in this very case. Your services, however, I feel will be invaluable. Your concern for her amiable and interesting daughter Narcissa—ah, no, Melissa—will, of course, make you with us. You have never seen Mrs. Smith? A fine-looking, noble woman, sir,—though still disconsolate,—still thinking of the departed one. By another singular coincidence that I should have told you, she is here now. You shall see her, sir. Pray, let me introduce you;" and still rubbing his hands, Judge Plunkett led the way to the adjoining room.

Mr. Gray followed him mechanically. A handsome woman rose from the sofa as they entered. It was the woman he assisted to alight from the Wingdam stage.

CHAPTER X
THE RED ROCK

In the strong light that fell upon her face, Mr. Gray had an opportunity to examine her features more closely. Her eyes, which were dark and singularly brilliant, were half closed, either from some peculiar conformation of the lids, or an habitual effort to conceal expression. Her skin was colorless with that satin-like lustre that belongs to some brunettes, relieved by one or two freckles that were scarcely blemishes. Her face was squared a little at the lower angles, but the chin was round and soft, and the curves about the mouth were full and tender enough to destroy the impression left by contemplation of those rigid outlines. The effect of its general contour was that of a handsome woman of thirty. In detail, as the eye dwelt upon any particular feature, you could have added a margin of ten years either way.

"Mrs. Smith—Mr. Gray," said the lawyer briskly. "Mr. Gray is the gentleman who, since the decease of your husband, has taken such a benevolent interest in our playful Narcissa—Melissa, I should say. He is the preceptor of our district school, and beside his relation as teacher to your daughter has, I may say in our legal fashion, stood *in loco parentis*—in other words, has been a parent, a—a—father to her."

At the conclusion of this speech Mrs. Smith darted a quick glance at Mr. Gray, which was unintelligible to any but a woman. As there were none of her own keen-witted sex present to make an ungracious interpretation of it, it passed unnoticed, except the slight embarrassment and confusion it caused the young man from its apparent gratuity.

"We have met before, I believe," said Mrs. Smith, with her bright eyes half hid and her white teeth half disclosed. "I can easily imagine Mr. Gray's devotion to a friend from his courtesy to a stranger. Let me thank you again for both my daughter and myself."

In the desperate hope of saying something natural, Mr. Gray asked if she had seen Melissa yet.

"Oh, dear, no! Think how provoking! Judge Plunkett says it is absolutely impossible till some tiresome formalities are over. There are so many stupid forms to go through with first. But how is she? You have seen her, have you not? you will see her again to-night, perhaps? How I long to embrace her again! She was a mere baby when she left me. Tell her how I long to fly to her."

Her impassioned utterance and the dramatic gestures that accompanied these words afforded a singular contrast to the cool way with which she rearranged the folds of her dress when she had finished, folding her hands over her lap and settling herself unmistakably back again on the sofa. Perhaps it was this that made Mr. Gray think she had, at some time, been an actress. But the next moment he caught her eye again and felt pleased,—and again vexed with himself for being so,— and in this mental condition began to speak in favor of his old pupil. His embarrassment passed away as he warmed with his subject, dwelling at length on M'liss's better qualities, and did not return until in a breathless pause he became aware that this woman's bright eyes were bent upon him. The color rose in his cheek, and with a half-muttered apology for his prolixity he offered his excuses to retire.

"Stay a moment, Mr. Gray," said the lawyer. "You are going to town, and will not think it a trouble to see Mrs. Smith safely back to her hotel. You can talk these things over with our fair friend on the way. To-morrow, at ten, I trust to see you both again."

"Perhaps I am taxing Mr. Gray's gallantry too much," interposed the lady with a very vivid disclosure of eyes and teeth. "Mr. Gray would be only too happy." After he had uttered this civility, there was a slight consciousness of truth about it that embarrassed him again. But Mrs. Smith took his proffered arm, and they bade the lawyer good-night and passed out in the starlit night together.

Four weeks have elapsed since the advent of Mrs. Smith to the settlement,—four weeks that might have been years in any other but a California mining camp, for the wonderful change that has been wrought in its physical aspect. Each stage has brought its load of fresh adventurers; another hotel, which sprang up on the site of the National, has its new landlord, and a new set of faces about its hospitable board, where the conventional bean appears daily as a modest vegetable or in the insincerer form of coffee. The sawmills have been hard at work for the last month, and huge gaps appear in the circling files of redwood where the fallen trees are transmuted to a new style of existence in the damp sappy tenements that have risen over the burnt district. The "great strike" at Smith's Pocket has been heralded abroad, and above and below, and on either side of the crumbling tunnel that bears that name, as other tunnels are piercing the bowels of the mountain, shafts are being sunk, and claims are taken up even to the crest of Red Mountain, in the hope of striking the great Smith lead. Already an animated discussion has sprung up in the columns of the "Red Mountain Banner" in regard to the direction of the famous lead,—a discussion assisted by correspondents who have assumed all the letters of the alphabet in their anonymous arguments, and have formed the opposing "angle" and "dip" factions of Smith's Pocket. But whatever be the direction of the lead, the progress of the settlement has been steadily onward, with an impetus gained by the late disaster. That classical but much abused bird, the Phoenix, has been invoked from its ashes in several editorials in the "Banner," to sit as a type of resuscitated Smith's Pocket, while in the homelier phrase of an honest miner "it seemed as if the fire kem to kinder clean out things for a fresh start."

Meanwhile the quasi-legal administration of the estate of Smith is drawing near a termination that seems to credit the prophetic assertion of Judge Plunkett. One fact has been evolved in the process of examination, viz., that Smith had discovered the new lead before he was murdered. It was a fair hypothesis that the man who assumed the benefit of his discovery was the murderer, but as this did not immediately involve the settlement of the estate it excited little comment or opposition. The probable murderer had escaped. Judicial investigations even in the hands of the people had been attended with disastrous public results, and there was no desire on the part of justice to open the case and deal with an abstract principle when there was no opportunity of making an individual example. The circumstances were being speedily forgotten in the new excitement; even the presence of Mrs. Smith lost its novelty. The "Banner," when alluding to her husband, spoke of him as the "late J. Smith, Esq.," attributing the present activity of business as the result of his lifelong example of untiring energy, and generally laid the foundation of a belief, which thereafter obtained, that he died comfortably in the bosom of his family, surrounded by disconsolate friends. The history of all pioneer settlements has this legendary basis, and M'liss may live to see the day when her father's connection with the origin of the settlement shall become apocryphal, and contested like that of Romulus and Remus and their wolfish wet-nurse.

It is to the everlasting credit and honor of Smith's Pocket that the orphan and widow meet no opposition from the speculative community, and that the claim's utmost boundaries are liberally rendered. How far this circumstance may be owing to the rare personal attractions of the charming widow or to M'liss's personal popularity, I shall not pretend to say. It is enough that when the brief of Judge Plunkett's case is ready there are clouds of willing witnesses to substantiate and corroborate doubtful points to an extent that is more creditable to their generosity than their veracity.

M'liss has seen her mother. Mr. Gray, with his knowledge of his pupil's impulsiveness, has been surprised to notice that the new relationship seems to awaken none of those emotions in the child's nature that he confidently looked for. On the occasion of their first meeting, to which Mr. Gray was admitted, M'liss maintained a guarded shyness totally different from her usual frank boldness,—a shyness that was the more remarkable from its contrast with the unrepressed and somewhat dramatic emotions of Mrs. Smith. Now, under her mother's protection and care, he observes another radical change in M'liss's appearance. She is dressed more tastefully and neatly—not entirely the result of a mother's influence, but apparently the result of some natural instinct now for the first time indulged, and exhibited in a ribbon or a piece of jewelry, worn with a certain air of consciousness. There is a more strict attention to the conventionalities of life; her speech is more careful and guarded; her walk, literally, more womanly and graceful. Those things Mr. Gray naturally attributes to the influence of the new relation, though he cannot help recalling his meeting with M'liss in the woods, on the morning of the fire, and of dating many of these changes from thence.

It is a pleasant morning, and Mr. Gray is stirring early. He has been busied in preparation the night previous, for this is his last day in Smith's Pocket. He lingers for some time about the schoolhouse, gathering up those little trifles which lie about his desk, which have each a separate history in his experience of Smith's Pocket, and are a part of the incrustations of his life. Lastly, a file of the "Red Mountain Banner," is taken from the same receptacle and packed away in his bag. He walks to the door and turns to look back. Has he forgotten anything? No, nothing. But still he lingers. He wonders who will take his place at the desk, and for the first time in his pedagogue experience, perhaps, feels something of an awful responsibility as he thinks of his past influence over the wretched little beings who used to tremble at his nod, and whose future, ill or good, he may have helped to fashion. At last he closes the door, almost tenderly, and walks thoughtfully down the road. He has to pass the cabin of an Irish miner, whose little boy is toddling in the ditch, with a pinafore, hands, and face in a chronic state of untidiness. Mr. Gray seizes him with an hilarious impulse, and after a number of rapid journeys to Banbury Cross, in search of an old woman who mounted a mythical white horse, he kisses the cleanest place on his broad expanse of cheek, presses some silver into his chubby fist, tells him to be a good boy, and deposits him in the ditch again. Having in this youthful way atoned for certain sins of omission a little further back, he proceeds, with a sense of perfect absolution, on his way to the settlement.

A few hours lie between him and his departure, to be employed in friendly visits to Mrs. Morpher, Dr. Duchesne, M'liss, and her mother. The Mountain Ranch is nearest, and thither Mr. Gray goes first. Mrs. Morpher, over a kneading-trough, with her bare arm whitened with flour, is genuinely grieved at parting with the master, and, in spite of Mr. Gray's earnest remonstrances, insists upon conducting him into the chill parlor, leaving him there until she shall have attired herself in a manner becoming to "company." "I don't want you to go at all—no more I don't," says Mrs. Morpher, with all sincerity, as she seats herself finally on the shining horsehair sofa. "The children will miss you. I don't believe that any one will do for Risty, Kerg, and Clytie what you have done. But I suppose you know best what's best. Young men like to see the world, and it ain't expected one so young as you should settle down yet. That's what I was telling Clytie this morning. That was just the way with my John afore he was married. I suppose you'll see M'liss and *her* before you go. They say that she is going to San Francisco soon. Is it so?"

Mr. Gray understands the personal pronoun to refer to Mrs. Smith, a title Mrs. Morpher has never granted M'liss's mother, for whom she entertains an instinctive dislike. He answers in the affirmative, however, with the consciousness of uneasiness under the inquiry; and as the answer does not seem to please Mrs. Morpher, he is constrained to commend M'liss's manifest improvement under her mother's care.

"Well" says Mrs. Morpher, with a significant sigh, "I hope it's so; but bless us, where's Clytie? You mustn't go without saying 'good-by' to her" and Mrs. Morpher starts away in search of her daughter.

The dining-room door scarcely closes before the bedroom door opens, and Clytie crosses the parlor softly with something in her hands. "You are going now?" she says hurriedly.

"Yes."

"Will you take this?" putting a sealed package into his hand, "and keep it without opening it until"—

"Until when, Clytie?"

"Until you are married."

Mr. Gray laughs.

"Promise me," repeats Clytie.

"But I may expire in the mean time, through sheer curiosity."

"Promise!" says Clytie gravely.

"I promise, then."

Mr. Gray receives the package. "Good-by," says Clytie softly.

Clytie's rosy cheek is very near Mr. Gray. There is nobody by. He is going away. It is the last time. He kisses her just before the door opens again to Mrs. Morpher.

Another shake of hands all around, and Mr. Gray passes out of the Mountain Ranch forever.

Dr. Duchesne's office is near at hand; but for some reason, that Mr. Gray cannot entirely explain to himself, he prefers to go to Mrs. Smith's first. The little cottage which they have taken temporarily is soon reached, and as the young man stands at the door he re-knots the bow of his cravat, and passes his fingers through his curls,—trifles that to Dr. Duchesne or any other critical, middle-aged person might look bad.

M'liss and Mrs. Smith are both at home. They have been waiting for him so long. Was it that pretty daughter of Mrs. Morpher—the fair young lady with blond curls,—who caused the detention? Is not Mr. Gray a sly young fellow for all his seeming frankness? So he must go to-day? He cannot possibly wait a few days, and go with them? Thus Mrs. Smith, between her red lips and white teeth, and under her half-closed eyes; for M'liss stands quietly apart without speaking. Her reserve during the interview contrasts with the vivacity of her mother as though they had changed respective places in relationship. Mr. Gray is troubled by this, and as he rises to go, he takes M'liss's hand in his.

"Have you nothing to say to me before I go?" he asks.

"Good-by," answers M'liss.

"Nothing more?"

"That's enough," rejoins the child simply.

Mr. Gray bites his lips. "I may never see you again, you know, Melissa," he continues.

"You will see us again," says M'liss quietly, raising her great dark eyes to his.

The blood mounted to his cheek and crimsoned his forehead. He was conscious, too, that the mother's face had taken fire at his own, as she walked away toward the window.

"Good-by, then," said Mr. Gray pettishly, as he stooped to kiss her.

M'liss accepted the salute stoically. Mr. Gray took Mrs. Smith's hand; her face had resumed its colorless, satin-like sheen.

"M'liss knows the strength of your good will, and makes her calculations accordingly. I hope she may not be mistaken," she said, with a languid tenderness of voice and eye. The young man bent over her outstretched hand, and withdrew as the Wingdam stage noisily rattled up before the National Hotel.

There was but little time left to spend with Dr. Duchesne, so the physician walked with him to the stage office. There were a few of the old settlers lounging by the stage, who had discerned, just as the master was going away, how much they liked him. Mr. Gray had gone through the customary bibulous formula of leave-taking; with a hearty shake of the doctor's hand, and a promise to write, he climbed to the box of the stage. "All aboard!" cried the driver, and with a preliminary bound, the stage rolled down Main Street.

Mr. Gray remained buried in thought as they rolled through the town, each object in passing recalling some incident of his past experience. The stage had reached the outskirts of the settlement when he detected a well-known little figure running down a by-trail to intersect the road before the stage had passed. He called the driver's attention to it, and as they drew up at the crossing Aristides's short legs and well-known features were plainly discernible through the dust. He was holding in his hand a letter.

"Well, my little man, what is it?" said the driver impatiently.

"A letter for the master," gasped the exhausted child.

"Give it here!—Any answer?"

"Wait a moment," said Mr. Gray.

"Look sharp, then, and get your billet duxis before you go next time."

Mr. Gray hurriedly broke the seal and read these words:

Judge Plunkett has just returned from the county seat.   Our case is won. We leave here next week.   J.S.

P.S. Have you got my address in San Francisco?

"Any answer?" said the driver.

"None."

"Get up!"

And the stage rolled away from Smith's Pocket, leaving the just Aristides standing in the dust of its triumphal wheels.

HIGH-WATER MARK

When the tide was out on the Dedlow Marsh, its extended dreariness was patent. Its spongy, low-lying surface, sluggish, inky pools, and tortuous sloughs, twisting their slimy way, eel-like, toward the open bay, were all hard facts. So were the few green tussocks, with their scant blades, their amphibious flavor, and unpleasant dampness. And if you chose to indulge your fancy,—although the flat monotony of the Dedlow Marsh was not inspiring,—the wavy line of scattered drift gave an unpleasant consciousness of the spent waters, and made the dead certainty of the returning tide a gloomy reflection, which no present sunshine could dissipate. The greener meadow-land seemed oppressed with this idea, and made no positive attempt at vegetation until the work of reclamation should be complete. In the bitter fruit of the low cranberry bushes one might fancy he detected a naturally sweet disposition curdled and soured by an injudicious course of too much regular cold water.

The vocal expression of the Dedlow Marsh was also melancholy and depressing. The sepulchral boom of the bittern, the shriek of the curlew, the scream of passing brant, the wrangling of quarrelsome teal, the sharp querulous protest of the startled crane, and syllabled complaint of the "killdeer" plover were beyond the power of written expression. Nor was the aspect of these mournful fowls at all cheerful and inspiring. Certainly not the blue heron, standing midleg deep in the water, obviously catching cold in a reckless disregard of wet feet and consequences; nor the mournful curlew, the dejected plover, or the low-spirited snipe, who saw fit to join him in his suicidal contemplation;

nor the impassive kingfisher—an ornithological Marius—reviewing the desolate expanse; nor the black raven that went to and fro over the face of the marsh continually, but evidently couldn't make up his mind whether the waters had subsided, and felt low-spirited in the reflection that after all this trouble he wouldn't be able to give a definite answer. On the contrary, it was evident at a glance that the dreary expanse of Dedlow Marsh told unpleasantly on the birds, and that the season of migration was looked forward to with a feeling of relief and satisfaction by the full grown, and of extravagant anticipation by the callow brood. But if Dedlow Marsh was cheerless at the slack of the low tide, you should have seen it when the tide was strong and full. When the damp air blew chilly over the cold glittering expanse, and came to the faces of those who looked seaward like another tide; when a steel-like glint marked the low hollows and the sinuous line of slough; when the great shell-incrusted trunks of fallen trees arose again, and went forth on their dreary purposeless wanderings, drifting hither and thither, but getting no farther toward any goal at the falling tide or the day's decline than the cursed Hebrew in the legend; when the glossy ducks swung silently, making neither ripple nor furrow on the shimmering surface; when the fog came in with the tide and shut out the blue above, even as the green below had been obliterated; when boatmen, lost in that fog, paddling about in a hopeless way, started at what seemed the brushing of mermen's fingers on the boat's keel, or shrank from the tufts of grass spreading around like the floating hair of a corpse, and knew by these signs that they were lost upon Dedlow Marsh, and must make a night of it, and a gloomy one at that,—then you might know something of Dedlow Marsh at high water.

Let me recall a story connected with this latter view which never failed to recur to my mind in my long gunning excursions upon Dedlow Marsh. Although the event was briefly recorded in the county paper, I had the story, in all its eloquent detail, from the lips of the principal actor. I cannot hope to catch the varying emphasis and peculiar coloring of feminine delineation, for my narrator was a woman; but I'll try to give at least its substance.

She lived midway of the great slough of Dedlow Marsh and a good-sized river, which debouched four miles beyond into an estuary formed by the Pacific Ocean, on the long sandy peninsula which constituted the southwestern boundary of a noble bay. The house in which she lived was a small frame cabin raised from the marsh a few feet by stout piles, and was three miles distant from the settlements upon the river. Her husband was a logger,—a profitable business in a county where the principal occupation was the manufacture of lumber.

It was the season of early spring, when her husband left on the ebb of a high tide with a raft of logs for the usual transportation to the lower end of the bay. As she stood by the door of the little cabin when the voyagers departed, she noticed a cold look in the southeastern sky, and she remembered hearing her husband say to his companions that they must endeavor to complete their voyage before the coming of the south-westerly gale which he saw brewing. And that night it began to storm and blow harder than she had ever before experienced, and some great trees fell in the forest by the river, and the house rocked like her baby's cradle.

But however the storm might roar about the little cabin, she knew that one she trusted had driven bolt and bar with his own strong hand, and that had he feared for her he would not have left her. This, and her domestic duties, and the care of her little sickly baby, helped to keep her mind from dwelling on the weather, except, of course, to hope that he was safely harbored with the logs at Utopia in the dreary distance. But she noticed that day, when she went out to feed the chickens and look after the cow, that the tide was up to the little fence of their garden patch, and the roar of the surf on the south beach, though miles away, she could hear distinctly. And she began to think that she would like to have some one to talk with about matters, and she believed that if it had not been so far and so stormy, and the trail so impassable, she would have taken the baby and have gone over to Ryekman's, her nearest neighbor. But then, you see, he might have returned in the storm, all wet, with no one to see to him; and it was a long exposure for baby, who was croupy and ailing.

But that night, she never could tell why, she didn't feel like sleeping or even lying down. The storm had somewhat abated, but she still "sat and sat," and even tried to read. I don't know whether it was a Bible or some profane magazine that this poor woman read, but most probably the latter, for the words all ran together and made such sad nonsense that she was forced at last to put the book down and turn to that dearer volume which lay before her in the cradle, with its white initial leaf as yet unsoiled, and try to look forward to its mysterious future. And, rocking the cradle, she thought of everything and everybody, but still was wide awake as ever.

It was nearly twelve o'clock when she at last lay down in her clothes. How long she slept she could not remember, but she awoke with a dreadful choking in her throat, and found herself standing, trembling all over, in the middle of the room, with her baby clasped to her breast, and she was "saying something." The baby cried and sobbed, and she walked up and down trying to hush it, when she heard a scratching at the door. She opened it fearfully, and was glad to see it was only old Pete, their dog, who crawled, dripping with water, into the room. She would have liked to look out, not in the faint hope of her husband's coming, but to see how things looked; but the wind shook the door so savagely that she could hardly hold it. Then she sat down a little while, and then walked up and down a little while, and then she lay down again a little while. Lying close by the wall of the little cabin, she thought she heard once or twice something scrape slowly against the clapboards, like the scraping of branches. Then there was a little gurgling sound, "like the baby made when it was swallowing;" then something went "click-click" and "cluck-cluck," so that she sat up in bed. When she did so she was attracted by something else that seemed creeping from the back door toward the centre of the room. It wasn't much wider than her little finger, but soon it swelled to the width of her hand, and began spreading all over the floor. It was water!

She ran to the front door and threw it wide open, and saw nothing but water. She ran to the back door and threw it open, and saw nothing but water. She ran to the side window, and throwing that open, she saw nothing but water. Then she remembered hearing her husband once say that there was no danger in the tide, for that fell regularly, and people could calculate on it, and that he would rather live near the bay than the river, whose banks might overflow at any time. But was it the tide? So she ran again to the back door, and threw out a stick of wood. It drifted away towards the bay. She scooped up some of the water and put it eagerly to her lips. It was fresh and sweet. It was the river, and not the tide!

It was then—oh, God be praised for his goodness! she did neither faint nor fall; it was then—blessed be the Saviour, for it was his merciful hand that touched and strengthened her in this awful moment—that fear dropped from her like a garment, and her trembling ceased. It was then and thereafter that she never lost her self-command, through all the trials of that gloomy night.

She drew the bedstead toward the middle of the room, and placed a table upon it, and on that she put the cradle. The water on the floor was already over her ankles, and the house once or twice moved so perceptibly, and seemed to be racked so, that the closet doors all flew open. Then she heard the same rasping and thumping against the wall, and, looking out, saw that a large uprooted tree, which had lain near the road at the upper end of the pasture, had floated down to the house. Luckily its long roots dragged in the soil and kept it from moving as rapidly as the current, for had it struck the house in its full career, even the strong nails and bolts in the piles could not have withstood the shock. The hound had leaped upon its knotty surface, and crouched near the roots, shivering and whining. A ray of hope flashed across her mind. She drew a heavy blanket from the bed, and, wrapping it about the babe, waded in the deepening waters to the door. As the tree swung again, broadside on, making the little cabin creak and tremble, she leaped on to its trunk. By God's mercy she succeeded in obtaining a footing on its slippery surface, and, twining an arm about its roots, she held in the other her moaning child. Then something cracked near the front porch, and the whole front of the house she had just quitted fell forward,—just as cattle fall on their knees before they lie down,—and at the same moment the great redwood tree swung round and drifted away with its living cargo into the black night.

For all the excitement and danger, for all her soothing of her crying babe, for all the whistling of the wind, for all the uncertainty of her situation, she still turned to look at the deserted and water-swept cabin. She remembered oven then, and she wondered how foolish she was to think of it at that time, that she wished she had put on another dress and the baby's best clothes; and she kept praying that the house would be spared so that he, when he returned, would have something to come to, and it wouldn't be quite so desolate, and—how could he ever know what had become of her and baby? And at the thought she grew sick and faint. But she had something else to do besides worrying, for whenever the long roots of her ark struck an obstacle the whole trunk made half a revolution, and twice dipped her in the black water. The hound, who kept distracting her by running up and down the tree and howling, at last fell off at one of these collisions. He swam for some time beside her, and she tried to get the poor beast upon the tree, but he "acted silly" and wild, and at last she lost sight of him forever. Then she and her baby were left alone. The light which had burned for a few minutes in the deserted cabin was quenched suddenly. She could not then tell whither she was drifting. The outline of the white dunes on the peninsula showed dimly ahead, and she judged the tree was moving in a line with the river. It must be about slack water, and she had probably reached the eddy formed by the confluence of the tide and the overflowing waters of the river. Unless the tide fell soon, there was present danger of her drifting to its channel, and being carried out to sea or crushed in the floating drift. That peril averted, if she were carried out on the ebb toward the bay, she might hope to strike one of the wooded promontories of the peninsula, and rest till daylight. Sometimes she thought she heard voices and shouts from the river, and the bellowing of cattle and bleating of sheep. Then again it was only the ringing in her ears and throbbing of her heart. She found at about this time that she was so chilled and stiffened in her cramped position that she could scarcely move, and the baby cried so when she put it to her breast that she noticed the milk refused to flow; and she was so frightened at that that she put her head under her shawl, and for the first time cried bitterly.

When she raised her head again the boom of the surf was behind her, and she knew that her ark had again swung round. She dipped up the water to cool her parched throat, and found that it was salt as her tears. There was a relief, though, for by this sign she knew that she was drifting with the tide. It was then the wind went down, and the great and awful silence oppressed her. There was scarcely a ripple against the furrowed sides of the great trunk on which she rested, and around her all was black gloom and quiet. She spoke to the baby just to hear herself speak, and to know that she had not lost her voice. She thought then—it was queer, but she could not help thinking it—how awful must have been the night when the great ship swung over the Asiatic peak, and the sounds of creation were blotted out from the world. She thought, too, of mariners clinging to spars, and of poor women who were lashed to rafts and beaten to death by the cruel sea. She tried to thank God that she was thus spared, and lifted her eyes from the baby who had fallen into a fretful sleep. Suddenly, away to the southward, a great light lifted itself out of the gloom, and flashed and flickered, and flickered and flashed again. Her heart fluttered quickly against the baby's cold cheek. It was the lighthouse at the entrance of the bay. As she was yet wondering the tree suddenly rolled a little, dragged a little, and then seemed to lie quiet and still. She put out her hand and the current gurgled against it. The tree was aground, and, by the position of the light and the noise of the surf, aground upon the Dedlow Marsh.

Had it not been for her baby, who was ailing and croupy, had it not been for the sudden drying up of that sensitive fountain, she would have felt safe and relieved. Perhaps it was this which tended to make all her impressions mournful and gloomy. As the tide rapidly fell, a great flock of black brant fluttered by her, screaming and crying. Then the plover flew up and piped mournfully as they wheeled around the trunk, and at last fearlessly lit upon it like a gray cloud. Then the heron flew over and around her, shrieking and protesting, and at last dropped its gaunt legs only a few yards from her. But, strangest of all, a pretty white bird, larger than a dove,—like a pelican, but not a pelican,—circled around and around her. At last it lit upon a rootlet of the tree quite over her shoulder. She put out her hand and stroked its beautiful white neck, and it never appeared to move. It stayed there so long that she thought she would lift up the baby to see it and try to attract her attention. But when she did so, the child was so chilled and cold, and had such a blue look under the little lashes, which it didn't raise at all, that she screamed aloud, and the bird flew away, and she fainted.

Well, that was the worst of it, and perhaps it was not so much, after all, to any but herself. For when she recovered her senses it was bright sunlight and dead low water. There was a confused noise of guttural voices about her, and an old squaw, singing an Indian "hushaby," and rocking herself from side to side before a fire built on the marsh, before which she, the recovered wife and mother, lay weak and weary. Her first thought was for her baby, and she was about to speak when a young squaw, who must have been a mother herself, fathomed her thought and brought her the "mowitch," pale but living, in such a queer little willow cradle, all bound up, just like the squaw's own young one, that she laughed and cried together, and the young squaw and the old squaw showed their big white teeth and glinted their black eyes, and said, "Plenty get well, skeena mowitch," "Wagee man come plenty soon," and she could have kissed their brown faces in her joy. And then she found that they had been gathering berries on the marsh in heir queer comical baskets, and saw the skirt of her gown fluttering on the tree from afar, and the old squaw couldn't resist the temptation of procuring a new garment, and came down and discovered the "wagee" woman and child. And of course she gave the garment to the old squaw, as you may imagine, and when *he* came at last and rushed up to her, looking about ten years older in his anxiety, she felt so faint again that they had to carry her to the canoe. For, you see, he knew nothing about the flood until he met the Indians at Utopia, and knew by the signs that the poor woman was his wife. And at the next high tide he towed the tree away back home, although it wasn't worth the trouble, and built another house, using the old tree for the foundation and props, and called it after her, "Mary›s Ark!" But you may guess the next house was built above high-water mark. And that›s all.

Not much, perhaps, considering the malevolent capacity of the Dedlow Marsh. But you must tramp over it at low water, or paddle over it at high tide, or get lost upon it once or twice in the fog, as I have, to understand properly Mary's adventure, or to appreciate duly the blessings of living beyond high-water mark.

A LONELY RIDE

As I stepped into the Slumgullion stage I saw that it was a dark night, a lonely road, and that I was the only passenger. Let me assure the reader that I have no ulterior design in making this assertion. A long course of light reading has forewarned me what every experienced intelligence must confidently look for from such a statement. The story-teller who willfully tempts fate by such obvious beginnings, who is to the expectant reader in danger of being robbed or half-murdered, or frightened by an escaped lunatic, or introduced to his lady-love for the first time, deserves to be detected. I am relieved to say that none of these things occurred to me. The road from Wingdam to Slumgullion knew no other banditti than the regularly licensed hotel-keepers; lunatics had not yet reached such depth of imbecility as to ride of their own free will in Californian stages; and my Laura, amiable and long-suffering as she always is, could not, I fear, have borne up against these depressing circumstances long enough to have made the slightest impression on me.

I stood with my shawl and carpetbag in hand, gazing doubtingly on the vehicle. Even in the darkness the red dust of Wingdam was visible on its roof and sides, and the red slime of Slumgullion clung tenaciously to its wheels. I opened the door; the stage creaked uneasily, and in the gloomy abyss the swaying straps beckoned me, like ghostly hands, to come in now, and have my sufferings out at once.

I must not omit to mention the occurrence of a circumstance which struck me as appalling and mysterious. A lounger on the steps of the hotel, who I had reason to suppose was not in any way connected with the stage company, gravely descended, and, walking toward the conveyance, tried the handle of the door, opened it, expectorated in the carriage, and returned to the hotel with a serious demeanor. Hardly had he resumed his position, when another individual, equally disinterested, impassively walked down the steps, proceeded to the back of the stage, lifted it, expectorated carefully on the axle, and returned slowly and pensively to the hotel. A third spectator wearily disengaged himself from one of the Ionic columns of the portico and walked to the box, remained for a moment in serious and expectorative contemplation of the boot, and then returned to his column. There was something so weird in this baptism that I grew quite nervous.

Perhaps I was out of spirits. A number of infinitesimal annoyances, winding up with the resolute persistency of the clerk at the stage office to enter my name misspelt on the way-bill, had not predisposed me to cheerfulness. The inmates of the Eureka House, from a social view-point, were not attractive. There was the prevailing opinion—so common to many honest people—that a serious style of deportment and conduct toward a stranger indicates high gentility and elevated station. Obeying this principle, all hilarity ceased on my entrance to supper, and general remark merged into the safer and uncompromising chronicle of several bad cases of diphtheria, then epidemic at Wingdam. When I left the dining-room, with an odd feeling that I had been supping exclusively on mustard and tea leaves, I stopped a moment at the parlor door. A piano, harmoniously related to the dinner-bell, tinkled responsive to a diffident and uncertain touch. On the white wall the shadow of an old and sharp profile was bending over several symmetrical and shadowy curls. "I sez to Mariar, 'Mariar' sez I, 'praise to the face is open disgrace" I heard no more. Dreading some susceptibility to sincere expression on the subject of female loveliness, I walked away, checking the compliment that otherwise might have risen unbidden to my lips, and have brought shame and sorrow to the household.

It was with the memory of these experiences resting heavily upon me that I stood hesitatingly before the stage door. The driver, about to mount, was for a moment illuminated by the open door of the hotel. He had the wearied look which was the distinguishing expression of

Wingdam. Satisfied that I was properly way-billed and receipted for, he took no further notice of me. I looked longingly at the box-seat, but he did not respond to the appeal. I flung my carpetbag into the chasm, dived recklessly after it, and—before I was fairly seated—with a great sigh, a creaking of unwilling springs, complaining bolts, and harshly expostulating axle, we moved away. Rather the hotel door slipped behind, the sound of the piano sank to rest, and the night and its shadows moved solemnly upon us.

To say it was dark expressed but faintly the pitchy obscurity that encompassed the vehicle. The roadside trees were scarcely distinguishable as deeper masses of shadow; I knew them only by the peculiar sodden odor that from time to time sluggishly flowed in at the open window as we rolled by. We proceeded slowly; so leisurely that, leaning from the carriage, I more than once detected the fragrant sigh of some astonished cow, whose ruminating repose upon the highway we had ruthlessly disturbed. But in the darkness our progress, more the guidance of some mysterious instinct than any apparent volition of our own, gave an indefinable charm of security to our journey, that a moment's hesitation or indecision on the part of the driver would have destroyed.

I had indulged a hope that in the empty vehicle I might obtain that rest so often denied me in its crowded condition. It was a weak delusion. When I stretched out my limbs it was only to find that the ordinary conveniences for making several people distinctly uncomfortable were distributed throughout my individual frame. At last, resting my arms on the straps, by dint of much gymnastic effort I became sufficiently composed to be aware of a more refined species of torture. The springs of the stage, rising and falling regularly, produced a rhythmical beat, which began to painfully absorb my attention. Slowly this thumping merged into a senseless echo of the mysterious female of the hotel parlor, and shaped itself into this awful and benumbing axiom: "Praise-to-the-face-is-open-disgrace. Praise-to-the-face-is-open-disgrace." Inequalities of the road only quickened its utterance or drawled it to an exasperating length.

It was of no use to seriously consider the statement. It was of no use to except to it indignantly. It was of no use to recall the many instances where praise to the face had redounded to the everlasting honor of praiser and bepraised; of no use to dwell sentimentally on modest genius and courage lifted up and strengthened by open commendation; of no use to except to the mysterious female,—to picture her as rearing a thin-blooded generation on selfish and mechanically repeated axioms,—all this failed to counteract the monotonous repetition of this sentence. There was nothing to do but to give in, and I was about to accept it weakly, as we too often treat other illusions of darkness and necessity, for the time being, when I became aware of some other annoyance that had been forcing itself upon me for the last few moments. How quiet the driver was!

Was there any driver? Had I any reason to suppose that he was not lying gagged and bound on the roadside, and the highwayman, with blackened face, who did the thing so quietly, driving me—whither? The thing is perfectly feasible. And what is this fancy now being jolted out of me? A story? It's of no use to keep it back, particularly in this abysmal vehicle, and here it comes: I am a marquis—a French marquis; French, because the peerage is not so well known, and the country is better adapted to romantic incident—a marquis, because the democratic reader delights in the nobility. My name is something ligny. I am coming from Paris to my country-seat at St. Germain. It is a dark night, and I fall asleep and tell my honest coachman, Andre, not to disturb me, and dream of an angel. The carriage at last stops at the chateau. It is so dark that, when I alight, I do not recognize the face of the footman who holds the carriage-door. But what of that?—peste! I am heavy with sleep. The same obscurity also hides the old familiar indecencies of the statues on the terrace; but there is a door, and it opens and shuts behind me smartly. Then I find myself in a trap, in the presence of the brigand who has quietly gagged poor Andre and conducted the carriage thither. There is nothing for me to do, as a gallant French marquis, but to say, "Parbleu!" draw my rapier, and die valorously! I am found, a week or two after, outside a deserted cabaret near the barrier, with a hole through my ruffled linen, and my pockets stripped. No; on second thoughts, I am rescued,—rescued by the angel I have been dreaming of, who is the assumed daughter of the brigand, but the real daughter of an intimate friend.

Looking from the window again, in the vain hope of distinguishing the driver, I found my eyes were growing accustomed to the darkness. I could see the distant horizon, defined by India-inky woods relieving a lighter sky. A few stars, widely spaced in this picture, glimmering sadly. I noticed again the infinite depth of patient sorrow in their serene faces; and I hope that the Vandal who first applied the flippant "twinkle" to them may not be driven melancholy mad by their reproachful eyes. I noticed again the mystic charm of space, that imparts a sense of individual solitude to each integer of the densest constellation, involving the smallest star with immeasurable loneliness. Something of this calm and solitude crept over me, and I dozed in my gloomy cavern. When I awoke the full moon was rising. Seen from my window, it had an indescribably unreal and theatrical effect. It was the full moon of Norma—that remarkable celestial phenomenon which rises so palpably to a hushed audience and a sublime andante chorus, until the Casta Diva is sung—the "inconstant moon" that then and thereafter remains fixed in the heavens as though it were a part of the solar system inaugurated by Joshua. Again the white-robed Druids filed past me, again I saw that improbable mistletoe cut from that impossible oak, and again cold chills ran down my back with the first strain of the recitative. The thumping springs essayed to beat time, and the private box-like obscurity of the vehicle lent a cheap enchantment to the view. But it was a vast improvement upon my past experience, and I hugged the fond delusion.

My fears for the driver were dissipated with the rising moon. A familiar sound had assured me of his presence in the full possession of at least one of his most important functions. Frequent and full expectoration convinced me that his lips were as yet not sealed by the gag of highwaymen, and soothed my anxious ear. With this load lifted from my mind, and assisted by the mild presence of Diana, who left, as when she visited Endymion, much of her splendor outside my cavern,—I looked around the empty vehicle. On the forward seat lay a woman's hairpin. I picked it up with an interest that, however, soon abated. There was no scent of the roses to cling to it still, not even of hair-oil. No bent or twist in its rigid angles betrayed any trait of its wearer's character. I tried to think that it might have been "Mariar's." I tried to imagine that, confining the symmetrical curls of that girl, it might have heard the soft compliments whispered in her ears which provoked the wrath of the aged female. But in vain. It was reticent and unswerving in its upright fidelity, and at last slipped listlessly through my fingers.

I had dozed repeatedly,—waked on the threshold of oblivion by contact with some of the angles of the coach, and feeling that I was unconsciously assuming, in imitation of a humble insect of my childish recollection, that spherical shape which could best resist those impressions, when I perceived that the moon, riding high in the heavens, had begun to separate the formless masses of the shadowy landscape. Trees isolated, in clumps, and assemblages, changed places before my window. The sharp outlines of the distant hills came back as in daylight, but little softened in the dry, cold, dewless air of a California summer night. I was wondering how late it was, and thinking that if the horses of the night traveled as slowly as the team before us, Faustus might have been spared his agonizing prayer, when a sudden spasm of activity attacked my driver. A succession of whip-snappings, like a pack of Chinese crackers, broke from the box before me. The stage leaped forward, and when I could pick myself from under the seat, a long white building had in some mysterious way rolled before my window. It must be Slumgullion! As I descended from the stage I addressed the driver:—

"I thought you changed horses on the road?"

"So we did. Two hours ago."

"That's odd. I didn't notice it."

"Must have been asleep, sir. Hope you had a pleasant nap. Bully place for a nice quiet snooze, empty stage, sir!"

300

THE MAN OF NO ACCOUNT

His name was Fagg,—David Fagg. He came to California in '52 with us, in the Skyscraper. I don't think he did it in an adventurous way. He probably had no other place to go to. When a knot of us young fellows would recite what splendid opportunities we resigned to go, and how sorry our friends were to have us leave, and show daguerreotypes and locks of hair, and talk of Mary and Susan, the man of no account used to sit by and listen with a pained, mortified expression on his plain face, and say nothing. I think he had nothing to say. He had no associates, except when we patronized him; and, in point of fact, he was a good deal of sport to us. He was always seasick whenever we had a capful of wind. He never got his sea-legs on either. And I never shall forget how we all laughed when Eattler took him the piece of pork on a string, and—But you know that time-honored joke. And then we had such a splendid lark with him. Miss Fanny Twinkler couldn't bear the sight of him, and we used to make Fagg think that she had taken a fancy to him, and sent him little delicacies and books from the cabin. You ought to have witnessed the rich scene that took place when he came up, stammering and very sick, to thank her! Didn't she flash up grandly, and beautifully, and scornfully? So like "Medora," Rattler said,—Rattler knew Byron by heart,—and wasn't Old Fagg awfully cut up? But he got over it, and when Rattler fell sick at Valparaiso, Old Fagg used to nurse him. You see he was a good sort of fellow, but he lacked manliness and spirit. He had absolutely no idea of poetry. I've seen him sit stolidly by, mending his old clothes, when Rattler delivered that stirring apostrophe of Byron's to the ocean. He asked Rattler once, quite seriously, if he thought Byron was ever seasick. I don't remember Rattler's reply, but I know we all laughed very much, and I have no doubt it was something good, for Rattler was smart.

When the Skyscraper arrived at San Francisco we had a grand "feed." We agreed to meet every year and perpetuate the occasion. Of course we didn't invite Fagg. Fagg was a steerage passenger, and it was necessary, you see, now we were ashore, to exercise a little discretion. But Old Fagg, as we called him,—he was only about twenty-five years old, by the way,—was the source of immense amusement to us that day. It appeared that he had conceived the idea that he could walk to Sacramento, and actually started off afoot. We had a good time, and shook hands with one another all around, and so parted. Ah, me! only eight years ago, and yet some of those hands, then clasped in amity, have been clenched at each other, or have dipped furtively in one another's pockets. I know that we didn't dine together the next year, because young Barker swore he wouldn't put his feet under the same mahogany with such a very contemptible scoundrel as that Mixer; and Nibbles, who borrowed money at Valparaiso of young Stubbs, who was then a waiter in a restaurant, didn't like to meet such people.

When I bought a number of shares in the Coyote Tunnel at Mugginsville, in '54, I thought I'd take a run up there and see it. I stopped at the Empire Hotel, and after dinner I got a horse and rode round the town and out to the claim. One of those individuals whom newspaper correspondents call "our intelligent informant," and to whom in all small communities the right of answering questions is tacitly yielded, was quietly pointed out to me. Habit had enabled him to work and talk at the same time, and he never pretermitted either. He gave me a history of the claim, and added: "You see, stranger (he addressed the bank before him), gold is sure to come outer that theer claim (he put in a comma with his pick), but the old pro-pri-e-tor (he wriggled out the word and the point of his pick) warn't of much account (a long stroke of the pick for a period). He was green, and let the boys about here jump him,"—and the rest of his sentence was confided to his hat, which he had removed to wipe his manly brow with his red bandana.

I asked him who was the original proprietor.

"His name war Fagg."

I went to see him. He looked a little older and plainer. He had worked hard, he said, and was getting on "so-so." I took quite a liking to him and patronized him to some extent. Whether I did so because I was beginning to have a distrust for such fellows as Rattler and Mixer is not necessary for me to state.

You remember how the Coyote Tunnel went in, and how awfully we shareholders were done! Well, the next thing I heard was that Rattler, who was one of the heaviest shareholders, was up at Mugginsville keeping bar for the proprietor of the Mugginsville Hotel, and that Old Fagg had struck it rich, and didn't know what to do with his money. All this was told me by Mixer, who had been there settling up matters, and likewise that Eagg was sweet upon the daughter of the proprietor of the aforesaid hotel. And so by hearsay and letter I eventually gathered that old Robins, the hotel man, was trying to get up a match between Nellie Robins and Fagg. Nellie was a pretty, plump, and foolish little thing, and would do just as her father wished. I thought it would be a good thing for—Fagg if he should marry and settle down; that as a married man he might be of some account. So I ran up to Mugginsville one day to look after things. It did me an immense deal of good to make Rattler mix my drinks for me,—Rattler! the gay, brilliant, and unconquerable Rattler, who had tried to snub me two years ago! I talked to him about Old Fagg and Nellie, particularly as I thought the subject was distasteful. He never liked Fagg, and he was sure, he said, that Nellie did n't. Did Nellie like anybody else? He turned round to the mirror behind the bar and brushed up his hair. I understood the conceited wretch. I thought I'd put Fagg on his guard, and get him to hurry up matters. I had a long talk with him. You could see by the way the poor fellow acted that he was badly stuck. He sighed, and promised to pluck up courage to hurry matters to a crisis. Nellie was a good girl, and I think had a sort of quiet respect for Old Fagg's unobtrusiveness.

But her fancy was already taken captive by Rattler's superficial qualities, which were obvious and pleasing. I don't think Nellie was any worse than you or I. We are more apt to take acquaintances at their apparent value than their intrinsic worth. It's less trouble, and except when we want to trust them, quite as convenient. The difficulty with women is that their feelings are apt to get interested sooner than ours, and then, you know, reasoning is out of the question. This is what Old Fagg would have known had he been of any account. But he was n't. So much the worse for him.

It was a few months afterward, and I was sitting in my office when in walked Old Fagg. I was surprised to see him down, but we talked over the current topics in that mechanical manner of people who know that they have something else to say, but are obliged to get at it in that formal way. After an interval, Fagg in his natural manner said,—

"I'm going home!"

"Going home?"

"Yes,—that is, I think I'll take a trip to the Atlantic States. I came to see you, as you know I have some little property, and I have executed a power of attorney for you to manage my affairs. I have some papers I'd like to leave with you. Will you take charge of them?"

"Yes," I said. "But what of Nellie?"

His face fell. He tried to smile, and the combination resulted in one of the most startling and grotesque effects I ever beheld. At length he said,—

"I shall not marry Nellie,—that is,"—he seemed to apologize internally for the positive form of expression,—"I think that I had better not."

"David Fagg," I said with sudden severity, "you're of no account!"

To my astonishment, his face brightened.

"Yes," said he, "that's it!—I'm of no account! But I always knew it. You see, I thought Rattler loved that girl as well as I did, and I knew she liked him better than she did me, and would be happier, I dare say, with him. But then I knew that old Robins would have preferred me to him, as I was better off,—and the girl would do as he said,—and, you see,

I thought I was kinder in the way,—and so I left. But," he continued, as I was about to interrupt him, "for fear the old man might object to Rattler, I've lent him enough to set him up in business for himself in Dogtown. A pushing, active, brilliant fellow, you know, like Rattler can get along, and will soon be in his old position again,—and you needn't be hard on him, you know, if he doesn't. Good-by."

I was too much disgusted with his treatment of that Rattler to be at all amiable, but as his business was profitable, I promised to attend to it, and he left. A few weeks passed. The return steamer arrived, and a terrible incident occupied the papers for days afterwards. People in all parts of the State conned eagerly the details of an awful shipwreck, and those who had friends aboard went away by themselves, and read the long list of the lost under their breath. I read of the gifted, the gallant, the noble, and loved ones who had perished, and among them I think I was the first to read the name of David Fagg. For the "man of no account" had "gone home!"

NOTES BY FLOOD AND FIELD

PART I
IN THE FIELD

It was near the close of an October day that I began to be disagreeably conscious of the Sacramento Valley. I had been riding since sunrise, and my course through the depressing monotony of the long level landscape affected me more like a dull, dyspeptic dream than a business journey, performed under that sincerest of natural phenomena,—a California sky. The recurring stretches of brown and baked fields, the gaping fissures in the dusty trail, the hard outline of the distant hills, and the herds of slowly moving cattle, seemed like features of some glittering stereoscopic picture that never changed. Active exercise might have removed this feeling, but my horse by some subtle instinct had long since given up all ambitious effort, and had lapsed into a dogged trot.

It was autumn, but not the season suggested to the Atlantic reader under that title. The sharply defined boundaries of the wet and dry seasons were prefigured in the clear outlines of the distant hills. In the dry atmosphere the decay of vegetation was too rapid for the slow hectic which overtakes an Eastern landscape, or else Nature was too practical for such thin disguises. She merely turned the Hippocratic face to the spectator, with the old diagnosis of death in her sharp, contracted features.

In the contemplation of such a prospect there was little to excite any but a morbid fancy. There were no clouds in the flinty blue heavens, and the setting of the sun was accompanied with as little ostentation as was consistent with the dryly practical atmosphere. Darkness soon followed, with a rising wind, which increased as the shadows deepened on the plain. The fringe of alder by the watercourse began to loom up as I urged my horse forward. A half-hour's active spurring brought me to a corral, and a little beyond a house, so low and broad, it seemed at first sight to be half buried in the earth.

My second impression was that it had grown out of the soil like some monstrous vegetable, its dreary proportions were so in keeping with the vast prospect. There were no recesses along its roughly boarded walls for vagrant and unprofitable shadows to lurk in the daily sunshine. No projection for the wind by night to grow musical over, to wail, whistle, or whisper to; only a long wooden shelf containing a chilly-looking tin basin and a bar of soap. Its uncurtained windows were red with the sinking sun, as though bloodshot and inflamed from a too long unlidded existence. The tracks of cattle led to its front door, firmly closed against the rattling wind.

To avoid being confounded with this familiar element, I walked to the rear of the house, which was connected with a smaller building by a slight platform. A grizzled, hard-faced old man was standing there, and met my salutation with a look of inquiry, and, without speaking, led the way to the principal room. As I entered, four young men who were reclining by the fire slightly altered their attitudes of perfect repose, but beyond that betrayed neither curiosity nor interest. A hound started from a dark corner with a growl, but was immediately kicked by the old man into obscurity and silenced again. I can't tell why, but I instantly received the impression that for a long time the group by the fire had not uttered a word or moved a muscle. Taking a seat, I briefly stated my business. Was a United States surveyor. Had come on account of the Espiritu Santo rancho. Wanted to correct the exterior boundaries of township lines, so as to connect with the near exteriors of private grants. There had been some intervention to the old survey by a Mr. Tryan, who had preempted adjacent—"Settled land warrants," interrupted the old man. "Ah, yes! land warrants,—and then this was Mr. Tryan?"

I had spoken mechanically, for I was preoccupied in connecting other public lines with private surveys, as I looked in his face. It was certainly a hard face, and reminded me of the singular effect of that mining operation known as "ground sluicing;" the harder lines of underlying character were exposed, and what were once plastic curves and soft outlines were obliterated by some powerful agency.

There was a dryness in his voice not unlike the prevailing atmosphere of the valley, as he launched into an ex parte statement of the contest, with a fluency which, like the wind without, showed frequent and unrestrained expression. He told me—what I had already learned—that the boundary line of the old Spanish grant was a creek, described in the loose phraseology of the deseno as beginning in the valda or skirt of the hill, its precise location long the subject of litigation. I listened and answered with little interest, for my mind was still distracted by the wind which swept violently by the house, as well as by his odd face, which was again reflected in the resemblance that the silent group by the fire bore toward him. He was still talking, and the wind was yet blowing, when my confused attention was aroused by a remark addressed to the recumbent figures.

"Now, then, which on ye'll see the stranger up the creek to Altascar's to-morrow?"

There was a general movement of opposition in the group, but no decided answer.

"Kin you go, Kerg?"

"Who's to look up stock in Strarberry per-ar-ie?"

This seemed to imply a negative, and the old man turned to another hopeful, who was pulling the fur from a mangy bearskin on which he was lying, with an expression as though it were somebody's hair.

"Well, Tom, wot's to hinder you from goin'?"

"Mam's goin' to Brown's store at sun-up, and I s'pose I've got to pack her and the baby again."

I think the expression of scorn this unfortunate youth exhibited for the filial duty into which he had been evidently beguiled was one of the finest things I had ever seen.

"Wise?"

Wise deigned no verbal reply, but figuratively thrust a worn and patched boot into the discourse. The old man flushed quickly.

"I told ye to get Brown to give you a pair the last time you war down the river."

"Said he wouldn't without an order. Said it was like pulling gum-teeth to get the money from you even then."

There was a grim smile at this local hit at the old man's parsimony, and Wise, who was clearly the privileged wit of the family, sank back in honorable retirement.

"Well, Joe, ef your boots are new, and you aren't pestered with wimmin and children, p'r'aps you'll go," said Tryan, with a nervous twitching, intended for a smile, about a mouth not remarkably mirthful.

Tom lifted a pair of bushy eyebrows and said shortly,—

"Got no saddle."

"Wot's gone of your saddle?"

"Kerg, there!" indicating his brother with a look such as Cain might have worn at the sacrifice.

"You lie!" returned Kerg cheerfully.

Tryan sprang to his feet, seizing the chair, flourishing it around his head and gazing furiously in the hard young faces which fearlessly met his own. But it was only for a moment; his arm soon dropped by his side, and a look of hopeless fatality crossed his face. He allowed me to take the chair from his hand, and I was trying to pacify him by the assurance that I required no guide, when the irrepressible Wise again lifted his voice—

"Theer's George comin'! Why don't ye ask him? He'll go and introduce you to Don Fernandy's darter, too, ef you ain't perticklar."

The laugh which followed this joke, which evidently had some domestic allusion (the general tendency of rural pleasantry), was followed by a light step on the platform, and the young man entered. Seeing a stranger present, he stopped and colored, made a shy salute and colored again, and then, drawing a box from the corner, sat down, his hands clasped tightly together and his very handsome bright blue eyes turned frankly on mine.

Perhaps I was in a condition to receive the romantic impression he made upon me, and I took it upon myself to ask his company as guide, and he cheerfully assented. But some domestic duty called him presently away.

The fire gleamed brightly on the hearth, and, no longer resisting the prevailing influence, I silently watched the spirting flame, listening to the wind which continually shook the tenement. Besides the one chair, which had acquired a new importance in my eyes, I presently discovered a crazy table in one corner, with an inkbottle and pen, the latter in that greasy state of decomposition peculiar to country taverns and farmhouses. A goodly array of rifles and double-barreled guns stocked the corner; half a dozen saddles and blankets lay near, with a mild flavor of the horse about them. Some deer and bear skins completed the inventory. As I sat there, with the silent group around me, the shadowy gloom within and the dominant wind without, I found it difficult to believe I had ever known a different existence. My profession had often led me to wilder scenes, but rarely among those whose unrestrained habits and easy unconsciousness made me feel so lonely and uncomfortable. I shrank closer to myself, not without grave doubts—which I think occur naturally to people in like situations— that this was the general rule of humanity, and I was a solitary and somewhat gratuitous exception.

It was a relief when a laconic announcement of supper by a weak-eyed girl caused a general movement in the family. We walked across the dark platform, which led to another low-ceiled room. Its entire length was occupied by a table, at the further end of which a weak-eyed woman was already taking her repast as she at the same time gave nourishment to a weak-eyed baby. As the formalities of introduction had been dispensed with, and as she took no notice of me, I was enabled to slip into a seat without discomposing or interrupting her. Tryan extemporized a grace, and the attention of the family became absorbed in bacon, potatoes, and dried apples.

The meal was a sincere one. Gentle gurglings at the upper end of the table often betrayed the presence of the "wellspring of pleasure." The conversation generally referred to the labors of the day, and comparing notes as to the whereabouts of missing stock. Yet the supper was such a vast improvement upon the previous intellectual feast, that when a chance allusion of mine to the business of my visit brought out the elder Tryan, the interest grew quite exciting. I remember he inveighed bitterly against the system of ranch-holding by the "Greasers," as he was pleased to term the native Californians. As the same ideas have been sometimes advanced under more pretentious circumstances, they may be worthy of record.

"Look at 'em holdin' the finest grazin' land that ever lay outer doors? Whar's the papers for it? Was it grants? Mighty fine grants,—most of 'em made arter the 'Merrikans got possession. More fools the 'Merrikans for lettin' 'em hold 'em. Wat paid for 'em? 'Merrikan blood and money.

"Didn't they oughter have suthin' out of their native country? Wot for? Did they ever improve? Got a lot of yaller-skinned diggers, not so sensible as niggers, to look arter stock, and they a-sittin' home and smokin'. With their gold and silver candlesticks, and missions, and crucifixens, priests and graven idols, and sich? Them sort things wuren't allowed in Mizzoori."

At the mention of improvements I involuntarily lifted my eyes, and met the half-laughing, half-embarrassed look of George. The act did not escape detection, and I had at once the satisfaction of seeing that the rest of the family had formed an offensive alliance against us.

"It was agin nater and agin God," added Tryan. "God never intended gold in the rocks to be made into heathen candlesticks and crucifixens. That's why he sent 'Merrikans here. Nater never intended such a climate for lazy lopers. She never gi'n six months' sunshine to be slept and smoked away."

How long he continued, and with what further illustration, I could not say, for I took an early opportunity to escape to the sitting-room. I was soon followed by George, who called me to an open door leading to a smaller room, and pointed to a bed.

"You'd better sleep there to-night," he said; "you'll be more comfortable, and I'll call you early."

I thanked him, and would have asked him several questions which were then troubling me, but he shyly slipped to the door and vanished.

A shadow seemed to fall on the room when he had gone. The "boys" returned, one by one, and shuffled to their old places. A larger log was thrown on the fire, and the huge chimney glowed like a furnace, but it did not seem to melt or subdue a single line of the hard faces that it lit. Half an hour later, the furs which had served as chairs by day undertook the nightly office of mattresses, and each received its owner's full-length figure. Mr. Tryan had not returned, and I missed George. I sat there until, wakeful and nervous, I saw the fire fall and shadows mount the wall. There was no sound but the rushing of the wind and the snoring of the sleepers. At last, feeling the place insupportable, I seized my hat, and, opening the door, ran out briskly into the night.

The acceleration of my torpid pulse in the keen fight with the wind, whose violence was almost equal to that of a tornado, and the familiar faces of the bright stars above me, I felt as a blessed relief. I ran, not knowing whither, and when I halted, the square outline of the house was lost in the alder-bushes. An uninterrupted plain stretched before me, like a vast sea beaten flat by the force of the gale. As I kept on I noticed a slight elevation toward the horizon, and presently my progress was impeded by the ascent of an Indian mound. It struck me forcibly as resembling an island in the sea. Its height gave me a better view of the expanding plain. But even here I found no rest. The ridiculous interpretation Tryan had given the climate was somehow sung in my ears and echoed in my throbbing pulse as, guided by the stars, I sought the house again.

But I felt fresher and more natural as I stepped upon the platform. The door of the lower building was open, and the old man was sitting beside the table, thumbing the leaves of a Bible with a look in his face as though he were hunting up prophecies against the "Greaser." I turned to enter, but my attention was attracted by a blanketed figure lying beside the house on the platform. The broad chest heaving with healthy slumber, and the open, honest face were familiar. It was George, who had given up his bed to the stranger among his people. I was about to wake him, but he lay so peaceful and quiet, I felt awed and hushed. And I went to bed with a pleasant impression of his handsome face and tranquil figure soothing me to sleep.

I was awakened the next morning from a sense of lulled repose and grateful silence by the cheery voice of George, who stood beside my bed ostentatiously twirling a riata, as if to recall the duties of the day to my sleep-bewildered eyes. I looked around me. The wind had been magically laid, and the sun shone warmly through the windows. A dash of cold water, with an extra chill on, from the tin basin, helped to brighten me. It was still early, but the family had already breakfasted and dispersed, and a wagon winding far in the distance showed that the unfortunate Tom had already "packed" his relatives away. I felt more cheerful,—there are few troubles Youth cannot distance with the start of a good night's rest. After a substantial breakfast, prepared by George, in a few moments we were mounted and dashing down the plain.

We followed the line of alder that defined the creek, now dry and baked with summer's heat, but which in winter, George told me, overflowed its banks. I still retain a vivid impression of that morning's ride; the far-off mountains, like silhouettes, against the steel-blue sky; the crisp, dry air, and the expanding track before me, animated often by the well-knit figure of George Tryan, musical with jingling spurs and picturesque with flying riata. He rode a powerful native roan, wild-eyed, untiring in stride, and unbroken in nature. Alas! the curves of beauty were concealed by the cumbrous machillas of the Spanish saddle, which levels all equine distinctions. The single rein lay loosely on the cruel bit that can gripe and, if need be, crush the jaw it controls.

Again the illimitable freedom of the valley rises before me as we again bear down into sunlit space. Can this be Chu-Chu, staid and respectable filly of American pedigree,—Chu-Chu, forgetful of plank-roads and cobble stones, wild with excitement, twinkling her small white feet beneath me? George laughs out of a cloud of dust, "Give her

her head; don't you see she likes it?" and Chu-Chu seems to like it, and, whether bitten by native tarantula into native barbarism or emulous of the roan, "blood" asserts itself, and in a moment the peaceful servitude of years is beaten out in the music of her clattering hoofs. The creek widens to a deep gully. We dive into it and up on the opposite side, carrying a moving cloud of impalpable powder with us. Cattle are scattered over the plain, grazing quietly or banded together in vast restless herds. George makes a wide, indefinite sweep with the riata, as if to include them all in his vaquero's loop, and says, "Ours!"

"About how many, George?"

"Don't know."

"How many?"

"Well, p'r'aps three thousand head," says George, reflecting. "We don't know; takes five men to look 'em up and keep run."

"What are they worth?"

"About thirty dollars a head."

I make a rapid calculation, and look my astonishment at the laughing George. Perhaps a recollection of the domestic economy of the Tryan household is expressed in that look, for George averts his eye and says apologetically,—

"I've tried to get the old man to sell and build, but you know he says it ain't no use to settle down just yet. We must keep movin'. In fact, he built the shanty for that purpose, lest titles should fall through, and we'd have to get up and move stakes farther down," Suddenly his quick eye detects some unusual sight in a herd we are passing, and with an exclamation he puts his roan into the centre of the mass. I follow, or rather Chu-Chu darts after the roan, and in a few moments we are in the midst of apparently inextricable horns and hoofs. "Toro!" shouts George, with vaquero enthusiasm, and the band opens a way for the swinging riata. I can feel their steaming breaths, and their spume is cast on Chu-Chu's quivering flank.

Wild, devilish-looking beasts are they; not such shapes as Jove might have chosen to woo a goddess, nor such as peacefully range the downs of Devon, but lean and hungry Cassius-like bovines, economically got up to meet the exigencies of a six-months' rainless climate, and accustomed to wrestle with the distracting wind and the blinding dust.

"That's not our brand," says George; "they're strange stock," and he points to what my scientific eye recognizes as the astrological sign of Venus deeply seared in the brown flanks of the bull he is chasing. But the herd are closing round us with low mutterings, and George has again recourse to the authoritative "Toro," and with swinging riata divides the "bossy bucklers" on either side. When we are free, and breathing somewhat more easily, I venture to ask George if they ever attack any one.

"Never horsemen,—sometimes footmen. Not through rage, you know, but curiosity. They think a man and his horse are one, and if they meet a chap afoot, they run him down and trample him under hoof, in the pursuit of knowledge. But," adds George, "here's the lower bench of the foothills, and here's Altascar's corral, and that white building you see yonder is the casa."

A whitewashed wall inclosed a court containing another adobe building, baked with the solar beams of many summers. Leaving our horses in the charge of a few peons in the courtyard, who were basking lazily in the sun, we entered a low doorway, where a deep shadow and an agreeable coolness fell upon us, as sudden and grateful as a plunge in cool water, from its contrast with the external glare and heat. In the centre of a low-ceiled apartment sat an old man with a black silk handkerchief tied about his head, the few gray hairs that escaped from its folds relieving his gamboge-colored face. The odor of cigarritos was as incense added to the cathedral gloom of the building.

As Senor Altascar rose with well-bred gravity to receive us, George advanced with such a heightened color, and such a blending of tenderness and respect in his manner, that I was touched to the heart by so much devotion in the careless youth. In fact, my eyes were still dazzled by the effect of the outer sunshine, and at first I did not see the white teeth and black eyes of Pepita, who slipped into the corridor as we entered.

It was no pleasant matter to disclose particulars of business which would deprive the old senor of the greater part of that land we had just ridden over, and I did it with great embarrassment. But he listened calmly,—not a muscle of his dark face stirring,—and the smoke curling placidly from his lips showed his regular respiration. When I had finished, he offered quietly to accompany us to the line of demarcation. George had meanwhile disappeared, but a suspicious conversation in broken Spanish and English in the corridor betrayed his vicinity. When he returned again, a little absent-minded, the old man, by far the coolest and most self-possessed of the party, extinguished his black silk cap beneath that stiff, uncomely sombrero which all native Californians affect. A serapa thrown over his shoulders hinted that he was waiting. Horses are always ready saddled in Spanish ranchos, and in half an hour from the time of our arrival we were again loping in the staring sunlight. But not as cheerfully as before. George and myself were weighed down by restraint, and Altascar was gravely quiet. To break the silence, and by way of a consolatory essay, I hinted to him that there might be further intervention or appeal, but the proffered oil and wine were returned with a careless shrug of the shoulders and a sententious "Que bueno? Your courts are always just."

The Indian mound of the previous night's discovery was a bearing monument of the new line, and there we halted. We were surprised to find the old man Tryan waiting us. For the first time during our interview the old Spaniard seemed moved, and the blood rose in his yellow cheek. I was anxious to close the scene, and pointed out the corner boundaries as clearly as my recollection served.

"The deputies will be here to-morrow to run the lines from this initial point, and there will be no further trouble, I believe, gentlemen."

Senor Altascar had dismounted and was gathering a few tufts of dried grass in his hands. George and I exchanged glances. He presently arose from his stooping posture, and advancing to within a few paces of Joseph Tryan, said in a voice broken with passion,—

"And I, Fernando Jesus Maria Altascar, put you in possession of my land in the fashion of my country."

He threw a sod to each of the cardinal points.

"I don't know your courts, your judges, or your corregidores. Take the llano!—and take this with it. May the drought seize your cattle till their tongues hang down as long as those of your lying lawyers! May it be the curse and torment of your old age, as you and yours have made it of mine!"

We stepped between the principal actors in this scene, which only the passion of Altascar made tragical, but Tryan, with a humility but ill concealing his triumph, interrupted,—

"Let him curse on. He 'll find 'em coming home to him sooner than the cattle he has lost through his sloth and pride. The Lord is on the side of the just, as well as agin all slanderers and revilers."

Altascar but half guessed the meaning of the Missourian, yet sufficiently to drive from his mind all but the extravagant power of his native invective.

"Stealer of the sacrament! Open not!—open not, I say, your lying Judas lips to me! Ah! half-breed, with the soul of a coyote!—Car-r-r-ramba!" With his passion reverberating among the consonants like distant thunder, he laid his hand upon the mane of his horse as though it had been the gray locks of his adversary, swung himself into the saddle, and galloped away.

George turned to me.

"Will you go back with us to-night?"

I thought of the cheerless walls, the silent figures by the fire, and the roaring wind, and hesitated.

"Well, then, good-by."

"Good-by, George."

Another wring of the hands, and we parted. I had not ridden far, when I turned and looked back. The wind had risen early that afternoon, and was already sweeping across the plain. A cloud of dust traveled before it, and a picturesque figure occasionally emerging therefrom was my last indistinct impression of George Tryan.

PART II
IN THE FLOOD

Three months after the survey of the Espiritu Santo rancho I was again in the valley of the Sacramento. But a general and terrible visitation had erased the memory of that event as completely as I supposed it had obliterated the boundary monuments I had planted. The great flood of 1861-62 was at its height when, obeying some indefinite yearning, I took my carpetbag and embarked for the inundated valley.

There was nothing to be seen from the bright cabin windows of the Golden City but night deepening over the water. The only sound was the pattering rain, and that had grown monotonous for the past two weeks, and did not disturb the national gravity of my countrymen as they silently sat around the cabin stove. Some on errands of relief to friends and relatives wore anxious faces, and conversed soberly on the one absorbing topic. Others like myself, attracted by curiosity, listened eagerly to newer details. But, with that human disposition to seize upon any circumstance that might give chance event the exaggerated importance of instinct, I was half conscious of something more than curiosity as an impelling motive.

The dripping of rain, the low gurgle of water, and a leaden sky greeted us the next morning as we lay beside the half-submerged levee of Sacramento. Here, however, the novelty of boats to convey us to the hotels was an appeal that was irresistible. I resigned myself to a dripping rubber-cased mariner called Joe, and wrapping myself in a shining cloak of the like material, about as suggestive of warmth as court-plaster might have been, took my seat in the stern sheets of his boat. It was no slight inward struggle to part from the steamer, that to most of the passengers was the only visible connecting link between us and the dry and habitable earth, but we pulled away and entered the city, stemming a rapid current as we shot the levee.

We glided up the long level of K Street,—once a cheerful busy thoroughfare, now distressing in its silent desolation. The turbid water, which seemed to meet the horizon edge before us, flowed at right angles in sluggish rivers through the streets. Nature had revenged herself on the local taste by disarraying the regular rectangles by huddling houses on street corners, where they presented abrupt gables to the current, or by capsizing them in compact ruin. Crafts of all kinds were gliding in and out of low-arched doorways. The water was over the top of the fences surrounding well-kept gardens, in the first stories of hotels and private dwellings, trailing its slime on velvet carpets as well as roughly boarded floors. And a silence quite as suggestive as the visible desolation was in the voiceless streets that no longer echoed to carriage-wheel or footfall. The low ripple of water, the occasional splash of oars, or the warning cry of boatmen were the few signs of life and habitation.

With such scenes before my eyes and such sounds in my ears, as I lie lazily in the boat, is mingled the song of my gondolier, who sings to the music of his oars. It is not quite as romantic as his brother of the Lido might improvise, but my Yankee Giuseppe has the advantage of earnestness and energy, and gives a graphic description of the terrors of the past week and of noble deeds of self-sacrifice and devotion, occasionally pointing out a balcony from which some California Bianca or Laura had been snatched, half-clothed and famished. Giuseppe is otherwise peculiar, and refuses the proffered fare, for—am I not a citizen of San Francisco, which was first to respond to the suffering cry of Sacramento? and is not he, Giuseppe, a member of the Howard Society? No, Giuseppe is poor, but cannot take my money. Still, if I must spend it, there is the Howard Society, and the women and children without food and clothing at the Agricultural Hall. I thank the generous gondolier, and we go to the Hall,—a dismal, bleak place, ghastly with the memories of last year's opulence and plenty,—and here Giuseppe's fare is swelled by the stranger's mite. But here Giuseppe tells me of the "Relief Boat" which leaves for the flooded district in the interior, and here, profiting by the lesson he has taught me, I make the resolve to turn my curiosity to the account of others, and am accepted of those who go forth to succor and help the afflicted. Giuseppe takes charge of my carpetbag, and does not part from me until I stand on the slippery deck of Relief Boat No. 3.

An hour later I am in the pilot-house, looking down upon what was once the channel of a peaceful river. But its banks are only defined by tossing tufts of willow washed by the long swell that breaks over a vast inland sea. Stretches of tule land fertilized by its once regular channel, and dotted by nourishing ranchos, are now cleanly erased. The cultivated profile of the old landscape had faded. Dotted lines in symmetrical perspective mark orchards that are buried and chilled in the turbid flood. The roofs of a few farmhouses are visible, and here and there the smoke curling from chimneys of half-submerged tenements shows an undaunted life within. Cattle and sheep are gathered on Indian mounds, waiting the fate of their companions, whose carcases drift by us or swing in eddies with the wrecks of barns and outhouses. Wagons are stranded everywhere where the tide could carry them. As I wipe the moistened glass, I see nothing but water, pattering on the deck from the lowering clouds, dashing against the window, dripping from the willows, hissing by the wheels, everywhere washing, coiling, sapping, hurrying in rapids, or swelling at last into deeper and vaster lakes, awful in their suggestive quiet and concealment.

As day fades into night the monotony of this strange prospect grows oppressive. I seek the engine-room, and in the company of some of the few half-drowned sufferers we have already picked up from temporary rafts, I forget the general aspect of desolation in their individual misery. Later we meet the San Francisco packet, and transfer a number of our passengers. From them we learn how inward-bound vessels report to having struck the well-defined channel of the Sacramento fifty miles beyond the bar. There is a voluntary contribution taken among the generous travelers for the use of our afflicted, and we part company with a hearty "God speed" on either side. But our signal lights are not far distant before a familiar sound comes back to us,—an indomitable Yankee cheer,—which scatters the gloom.

Our course is altered, and we are steaming over the obliterated banks far in the interior. Once or twice black objects loom up near us,—the wrecks of houses floating by. There is a slight rift in the sky towards the north, and a few bearing stars to guide us over the waste.

As we penetrate into shallower water, it is deemed advisable to divide our party into smaller boats, and diverge over the submerged prairie. I borrow a pea-coat of one of the crew, and in that practical disguise am doubtfully permitted to pass into one of the boats. We give way northerly. It is quite dark yet, although the rift of cloud has widened.

It must have been about three o'clock, and we were lying upon our oars in an eddy formed by a clump of cottonwood, and the light of the steamer is a solitary bright star in the distance, when the silence is broken by the "bow oar":—

"Light ahead."

All eyes are turned in that direction. In a few seconds a twinkling light appears, shines steadily, and again disappears, as if by the shifting position of some black object apparently drifting close upon us.

"Stern, all!—a steamer!"

"Hold hard, there! Steamer be d—-d!" is the reply of the coxswain. "It's a house, and a big one too."

It is a big one, looming in the starlight like a huge fragment of the darkness. The light comes from a single candle which shines through a window as the great shape swings by. Some recollection is drifting back to me with it, as I listen with beating heart.

"There's some one in it, by heavens! Give way, boys,—lay her alongside. Handsomely, now! The door's fastened; try the window; no! here's another!"

In another moment we are trampling in the water, which washes the floor to the depth of several inches. It is a large room, at the farther end of which an old man is sitting, wrapped in a blanket, holding a candle in one hand, and apparently absorbed in the book he holds with the other. I spring toward him with an exclamation:—

"Joseph Tryan!"

He does not move. We gather closer to him, and I lay my hand gently on his shoulder, and say,—

"Look up, old man, look up! Your wife and children, where are they? The boys,—George! Are they here? are they safe?"

He raises his head slowly, and turns his eyes to mine, and we

321

involuntarily recoil before his look. It is a calm and quiet glance, free from fear, anger, or pain; but it somehow sends the blood curdling through our veins. He bowed his head over his book again, taking no further notice of us. The men look at me compassionately and hold their peace. I make one more effort:—

"Joseph Tryan, don't you know me—the surveyor who surveyed your ranch,—the Espiritu Santo? Look up, old man!"

He shuddered and wrapped himself closer in his blanket. Presently he repeated to himself, "The surveyor who surveyed your ranch, Espiritu Santo," over and over again, as though it were a lesson he was trying to fix in his memory.

I was turning sadly to the boatmen, when he suddenly caught me fearfully by the hand, and said:—

"Hush!"

We were silent.

"Listen!" He puts his arm around my neck, and whispers in my ear, "I'm *a-moving off!*"

"Moving off?"

"Hush! Don't speak so loud. Moving off! Ah! wot's that? Don't you hear?—there!—listen!"

We listen, and hear the water gurgle and click beneath the floor.

"It's them wot he sent I—old Altascar sent. They've been here all night. I heard 'em first in the creek, when they came to tell the old man to move farther off. They came nearer and nearer. They whispered under the door, and I saw their eyes on the step,—their cruel, hard eyes. Ah! why don't they quit?"

I tell the men to search the room and see if they can find any farther traces of the family, while Tryan resumes his old attitude. It is so much like the figure I remember on the breezy night, that a superstitious feeling is fast overcoming me. When they have returned, I tell them briefly what I know of him, and the old man murmurs again,—

"Why don't they quit, then? They have the stock,—all gone—gone,—gone for the hides and hoofs," and he groans bitterly.

"There are other boats below us. The shanty cannot have drifted far, and perhaps the family are safe by this time," says the coxswain hopefully.

We lift the old man up, for he is quite helpless, and carry him to the boat. He is still grasping the Bible in his right hand, though its strengthening grace is blank to his vacant eye, and he cowers in the stern as we pull slowly to the steamer, while a pale gleam in the sky shows the coming day.

I was weary with excitement, and when we reached the steamer, and I had seen Joseph Tryan comfortably bestowed, I wrapped myself in a blanket near the boiler and presently fell asleep. But even then the figure of the old man often started before me, and a sense of uneasiness about George made a strong undercurrent to my drifting dreams. I was awakened at about eight o'clock in the morning by the engineer, who told me one of the old man's sons had been picked up and was now on board.

"Is it George Tryan?" I ask quickly.

"Don't know; but he's a sweet one, whoever he is," adds the engineer, with a smile at some luscious remembrance. "You'll find him for'ard."

I hurry to the bow of the boat, and find not George, but the irrepressible Wise, sitting on a coil of rope, a little dirtier and rather more dilapidated than I can remember having seen him.

He is examining, with apparent admiration, some rough, dry clothes that have been put out for his disposal. I cannot help thinking that circumstances have somewhat exalted his usual cheerfulness. He puts me at ease by at once addressing me:—

"These are high old times, ain't they? I say, what do you reckon's become o' them thar bound'ry moniments you stuck? Ah!"

The pause which succeeds this outburst is the effect of a spasm of admiration at a pair of high boots, which, by great exertion, he has at last pulled on his feet.

"So you've picked up the ole man in the shanty, clean crazy? He must have been soft to have stuck there instead o' leavin' with the old woman. Did n't know me from Adam; took me for George!"

At this affecting instance of paternal forgetfulness, Wise was

evidently divided between amusement and chagrin. I took advantage
of the contending emotions to ask about George.

"Don't know whar he is! If he'd tended stock instead of running
about the prairie, packin' off wimmin and children, he might have saved
suthin'. He lost every hoof and hide, I'll bet a cooky! Say, you," to a
passing boatman, "when are you goin' to give us some grub? I'm hungry
'nough to skin and eat a hoss. Reckon I'll turn butcher when things is
dried up, and save hides, horns, and taller."

I could not but admire this indomitable energy, which under softer
climatic influences might have borne such goodly fruit.

"Have you any idea what you'll do, Wise?" I ask.

"Thar ain't much to do now," says the practical young man. "I'll
have to lay over a spell, I reckon, till things comes straight. The land
ain't worth much now, and won't be, I dessay, for some time. Wonder
whar the ole man'll drive stakes next."

"I meant as to your father and George, Wise."

"Oh, the ole man and I'll go on to Miles's, whar Tom packed the
old woman and babies last week. George'll turn up somewhar atween
this and Altascar's, ef he ain't thar now."

I ask how the Altascars have suffered.

"Well, I reckon he ain't lost much in stock. I shouldn't wonder
if George helped him drive 'em up the foothills. And his casa's built
too high. Oh, thar ain't any water thar, you bet. Ah!" says Wise, with
reflective admiration, "those Greasers ain't the darned fools people
thinks 'em. I'll bet thar ain't one swamped out in all 'er Californy." But
the appearance of "grub" cut this rhapsody short.

"I shall keep on a little farther," I say, "and try to find George."

Wise stared a moment at this eccentricity until a new light dawned
upon him.

"I don't think you'll save much. What's the percentage,—workin'
on shares, eh?"

I answer that I am only curious, which I feel lessens his opinion
of me, and with a sadder feeling than his assurance of George's safety
might warrant, I walked away.

From others whom we picked up from time to time we heard of George's self-sacrificing devotion, with the praises of the many he had helped and rescued. But I did not feel disposed to return until I had seen him, and soon prepared myself to take a boat to the lower valda of the foothills, and visit Altascar. I soon perfected my arrangements, bade farewell to Wise, and took a last look at the old man, who was sitting by the furnace fires quite passive and composed. Then our boat-head swung round, pulled by sturdy and willing hands.

It was again raining, and a disagreeable wind had risen. Our course lay nearly west, and we soon knew by the strong current that we were in the creek of the Espiritu Santo. From time to time the wrecks of barns were seen, and we passed many half-submerged willows hung with farming implements.

We emerge at last into a broad silent sea. It is the llano de Espiritu Santo. As the wind whistles by me, piling the shallower fresh water into mimic waves, I go back, in fancy, to the long ride of October over that boundless plain, and recall the sharp outlines of the distant hills which are now lost in the lowering clouds. The men are rowing silently, and I find my mind, released from its tension, growing benumbed and depressed as then. The water, too, is getting more shallow as we leave the banks of the creek, and with my hand dipped listlessly over the thwarts, I detect the tops of chimisal, which shows the tide to have somewhat fallen. There is a black mound, bearing to the north of the line of alder, making an adverse current, which, as we sweep to the right to avoid it, I recognize. We pull close alongside, and I call to the men to stop.

There was a stake driven near its summit with the initials, "L. E. S. I." Tied halfway down was a curiously worked riata. It was George's. It had been cut with some sharp instrument, and the loose gravelly soil of the mound was deeply dented with horse's hoofs. The stake was covered with horsehairs. It was a record, but no clue.

The wind had grown more violent, as we still fought our way forward, resting and rowing by turns, and oftener "poling" the shallower surface, but the old valda, or bench, is still distant. My recollection of the old survey enables me to guess the relative position of the meanderings of the creek, and an occasional simple professional experiment to determine the distance gives my crew the fullest faith in my ability. Night overtakes us in our impeded progress. Our condition looks more dangerous than it really is, but I urge the men, many of whom are still new in this mode of navigation, to greater exertion by assurance of perfect safety and speedy relief ahead. We go on in this way until about eight o'clock, and ground by the willows. We have a muddy walk for a few hundred yards before we strike a dry trail, and simultaneously the white walls of Altascar's appear like a snow-bank before us. Lights are moving in the courtyard; but otherwise the old tomb-like repose characterizes the building.

One of the peons recognized me as I entered the court, and Altascar met me on the corridor.

I was too weak to do more than beg his hospitality for the men who had dragged wearily with me. He looked at my hand, which still unconsciously held the broken riata. I began, wearily, to tell him about George and my fears, but with a gentler courtesy than was even his wont, he gravely laid his hand on my shoulder.

"Poco a poco, senor,—not now. You are tired, you have hunger, you have cold. Necessary it is you should have peace."

He took us into a small room and poured out some French cognac, which he gave to the men that had accompanied me. They drank, and threw themselves before the fire in the larger room. The repose of the building was intensified that night, and I even fancied that the footsteps on the corridor were lighter and softer. The old Spaniard's habitual gravity was deeper; we might have been shut out from the world as well as the whistling storm, behind those ancient walls with their time-worn inheritor.

Before I could repeat my inquiry he retired. In a few minutes two smoking dishes of chupa with coffee were placed before us, and my men ate ravenously. I drank the coffee, but my excitement and weariness kept down the instincts of hunger.

I was sitting sadly by the fire when he reentered.

"You have eat?"

I said, "Yes," to please him.

"Bueno, eat when you can,—food and appetite are not always."

He said this with that Sancho-like simplicity with which most of his countrymen utter a proverb, as though it were an experience rather than a legend, and, taking the riata from the floor, held it almost tenderly before him.

"It was made by me, senor."

"I kept it as a clue to him, Don Altascar," I said. "If I could find him"—

"He is here."

"Here! and"—but I could not say, "well!" I understood the gravity of the old man's face, the hushed footfalls, the tomb-like repose of the building, in an electric flash of consciousness: I held the clue to the broken riata at last. Altascar took my hand, and we crossed the corridor to a sombre apartment. A few tall candles were burning in sconces before the window.

In an alcove there was a deep bed with its counterpane, pillows, and sheets heavily edged with lace, in all that splendid luxury which the humblest of these strange people lavish upon this single item of their household. I stepped beside it and saw George lying, as I had seen him one before, peacefully at rest. But a greater sacrifice than that he had known was here, and his generous heart was stilled forever.

"He was honest and brave," said the old man, and turned away.

There was another figure in the room; a heavy shawl drawn over her graceful outline, and her long black hair hiding the hands that buried her downcast face. I did not seem to notice her, and, retiring presently, left the loving and loved together.

When we were again beside the crackling fire, in the shifting shadows of the great chamber, Altascar told me how he had that morning met the horse of George Tryan swimming on the prairie; how that, farther on, he found him lying, quite cold and dead, with no marks or bruises on his person; that he had probably become exhausted in fording the creek, and that he had as probably reached the mound only to die for want of that help he had so freely given to others; that, as a last act, he had freed his horse. These incidents were corroborated by many who collected in the great chamber that evening,—women and children,— most of them succored through the devoted energies of him who lay cold and lifeless above.

He was buried in the Indian mound,—the single spot of strange perennial greenness, which the poor aborigines had raised above the dusty plain. A little slab of sandstone with the initials "G. T." is his monument, and one of the bearings of the initial corner of the new survey of the Espiritu Santo rancho.

WAITING FOR THE SHIP

A FORT POINT IDYL

About an hour's ride from the Plaza there is a high bluff with the ocean breaking uninterruptedly along its rocky beach. There are several cottages on the sands, which look as if they had recently been cast up by a heavy sea. The cultivated patch behind each tenement is fenced in by bamboos, broken spars, and driftwood. With its few green cabbages and turnip-tops, each garden looks something like an aquarium with the water turned off. In fact you would not be surprised to meet a merman digging among the potatoes, or a mermaid milking a sea-cow hard by.

Near this place formerly arose a great semaphoric telegraph, with its gaunt arms tossed up against the horizon. It has been replaced by an observatory, connected with an electric nerve to the heart of the great commercial city. From this point the incoming ships are signaled, and again checked off at the City Exchange. And while we are here, looking for the expected steamer, let me tell you a story.

Not long ago, a simple, hard-working mechanic had amassed sufficient by diligent labor in the mines to send home for his wife and two children. He arrived in San Francisco a month before the time the ship was due, for he was a Western man, and had made the overland journey, and knew little of ships or seas or gales. He procured work in the city, but as the time approached he would go to the shipping office regularly every day. The month passed, but the ship came not; then a month and a week, two weeks, three weeks, two months, and then a year. The rough, patient face, with soft lines overlying its hard

329

features, which had become a daily apparition at the shipping-agent's, then disappeared. It turned up one afternoon at the observatory as the setting sun relieved the operator from his duties. There was something so childlike and simple in the few questions asked by this stranger, touching his business, that the operator spent some time to explain. When the mystery of signals and telegraphs was unfolded, the stranger had one more question to ask. "How long might a vessel be absent before they would give up expecting her?" The operator couldn't tell; it would depend on circumstances. Would it be a year? Yes, it might be a year, and vessels had been given up for lost after two years and had come home. The stranger put his rough hand on the operator's, and thanked him for his "troubil," and went away.

Still the ship came not. Stately clippers swept into the Gate, and merchantmen went by with colors flying, and the welcoming gun of the steamer often reverberated among the hills. Then the patient face, with the old resigned expression, but a brighter, wistful look in the eye, was regularly met on the crowded decks of the steamer as she disembarked her living freight. He may have had a dimly defined hope that the missing ones might yet come this way, as only another road over that strange unknown expanse. But he talked with ship captains and sailors, and even this last hope seemed to fail. When the careworn face and bright eyes were presented again at the observatory, the operator, busily engaged, could not spare time to answer foolish interrogatories, so he went away. But as night fell, he was seen sitting on the rocks with his face turned seaward, and was seated there all that night. When he became hopelessly insane, for that was what the physicians said made his eyes so bright and wistful, he was cared for by a fellow craftsman who had known his troubles. He was allowed to indulge his fancy of going out to watch for the ship, in which she "and the children" were, at night, when no one else was watching. He had made up his mind that the ship would come in at night. This, and the idea that he would relieve the operator, who would be tired with watching all day, seemed to please him. So he went out and relieved the operator every night!

For two years the ships came and went. He was there to see the outward-bound clipper, and greet her on her return. He was known only by a few who frequented the place. When he was missed at last from his accustomed spot, a day or two elapsed before any alarm was felt. One Sunday, a party of pleasure-seekers clambering over the rocks were attracted by the barking of a dog that had run on before them. When they came up they found a plainly dressed man lying there dead. There were a few papers in his pocket,—chiefly slips cut from different journals of old marine memoranda,—and his face was turned towards the distant sea.

A NIGHT AT WINGDAM

I had been stage-ridden and bewildered all day, and when we swept down with the darkness into the Arcadian hamlet of Wingdam I resolved to go no farther, and rolled out in a gloomy and dyspeptic state. The effects of a mysterious pie, and some sweetened carbonic acid known to the proprietor of the Half-way House as "lemming sody," still oppressed me. Even the facetia of the gallant expressman, who knew everybody's Christian name along the route, who rained letters, newspapers, and bundles from the top of the stage, whose legs frequently appeared in frightful proximity to the wheels, who got on and off while we were going at full speed, whose gallantry, energy, and superior knowledge of travel crushed all us other passengers to envious silence, and who just then was talking with several persons and manifestly doing something else at the same time,—even this had failed to interest me. So I stood gloomily, clutching my shawl and carpetbag, and watched the stage roll away, taking a parting look at the gallant expressman as he hung on the top rail with one leg, and lit his cigar from the pipe of a running footman. I then turned toward the Wingdam Temperance Hotel.

It may have been the weather, or it may have been the pie, but I was not impressed favorably with the house. Perhaps it was the name extending the whole length of the building, with a letter under each window, making the people who looked out dreadfully conspicuous. Perhaps it was that "Temperance" always suggested to my mind rusks and weak tea. It was uninviting. It might have been called the "Total Abstinence" Hotel, from the lack of anything to intoxicate or inthrall the senses. It was designed with an eye to artistic dreariness. It was so much too large for the settlement that it appeared to be a very slight improvement on outdoors. It was unpleasantly new. There was the forest flavor of dampness about it, and a slight spicing of pine. Nature outraged, but not entirely subdued, sometimes broke out afresh in little round, sticky, resinous tears on the doors and windows. It seemed to me that boarding there must seem like a perpetual picnic. As I entered the door, a number of the regular boarders rushed out of a long room, and set about trying to get the taste of something out of their mouths, by the application of tobacco in various forms. A few immediately ranged themselves around the fireplace, with their legs over each other's chairs, and in that position silently resigned themselves to indigestion. Remembering the pie, I waived the invitation of the landlord to supper, but suffered myself to be conducted into the sitting-room. "Mine host" was a magnificent-looking, heavily bearded specimen of the animal man. He reminded me of somebody or something connected with the drama. I was sitting beside the fire, mutely wondering what it could be, and trying to follow the particular chord of memory thus touched into the intricate past, when a little delicate-looking woman appeared at the door, and, leaning heavily against the casing, said in an exhausted tone, "Husband!" As the landlord turned toward her, that particular remembrance flashed before me in a single line of blank verse. It was this: "Two souls with but one single thought, two hearts that beat as one."

It was Ingomar and Parthenia his wife. I imagined a different denouement from the play. Ingomar had taken Parthenia back to the mountains, and kept a hotel for the benefit of the Alemanni, who resorted there in large numbers. Poor Parthenia was pretty well fagged out, and did all the work without "help." She had two "young barbarians," a boy and a girl. She was faded, but still good-looking.

I sat and talked with Ingomar, who seemed perfectly at home, and told me several stories of the Alemanni, all bearing a strong flavor of the wilderness, and being perfectly in keeping with the house. How he, Ingomar, had killed a certain dreadful "b'ar," whose skin was just up "yar," over his bed. How he, Ingomar, had killed several "bucks," whose skins had been prettily fringed and embroidered by Parthenia, and even now clothed him. How he, Ingomar, had killed several "Injins," and was once nearly scalped himself. All this with that ingenious candor which is perfectly justifiable in a barbarian, but which a Greek might feel inclined to look upon as "blowing." Thinking of the wearied Parthenia, I began to consider for the first time that perhaps she had better married the old Greek. Then she would at least have always looked neat. Then she would not have worn a woolen dress flavored with all the dinners of the past year. Then she would not have been obliged to wait on the table with her hair half down. Then the two children would not have hung about her skirts with dirty fingers, palpably dragging her down day by day. I suppose it was the pie which put such heartless and improper ideas in my head, and so I rose up and told Ingomar I believed I'd go to bed. Preceded by that redoubtable barbarian and a flaring tallow candle, I followed him upstairs to my room. It was the only single room he had, he told me; he had built it for the convenience of married parties who might stop here, but, that event not happening yet, he had left it half furnished. It had cloth on one side, and large cracks on the other. The wind, which always swept over Wingdam at night-time, puffed through the apartment from different apertures. The window was too small for the hole in the side of the house where it hung, and rattled noisily. Everything looked cheerless and dispiriting. Before Ingomar left me, he brought that "b'arskin," and throwing it over the solemn bier which stood in one corner, told me he reckoned that would keep me warm, and then bade me good-night. I undressed myself, the light blowing out in the middle of that ceremony, crawled under the "b'arskin," and tried to compose myself to sleep.

But I was staringly wide awake. I heard the wind sweep down the mountain-side, and toss the branches of the melancholy pine, and then enter the house, and try all the doors along the passage. Sometimes strong currents of air blew my hair all over the pillow, as with strange whispering breaths. The green timber along the walls seemed to be sprouting, and sent a dampness even through the "b'arskin." I felt like Robinson Crusoe in his tree, with the ladder pulled up,—or like the rocked baby of the nursery song. After lying awake half an hour, I regretted having stopped at Wingdam; at the end of the third quarter, I wished I had not gone to bed; and when a restless hour passed, I got up and dressed myself. There had been a fire down in the big room. Perhaps it was still burning. I opened the door and groped my way along the passage, vocal with the snores of the Alemanni and the whistling of the night wind; I partly fell downstairs, and at last entering the big room, saw the fire still burning. I drew a chair toward it, poked it with my foot, and was astonished to see, by the upspringing flash, that Parthenia was sitting there also, holding a faded-looking baby.

I asked her why she was sitting up.

"She did not go to bed on Wednesday night before the mail arrived, and then she awoke her husband, and there were passengers to 'tend to."

"Did she not get tired sometimes?"

"A little, but Abner" (the barbarian's Christian name) "had promised to get her more help next spring, if business was good."

"How many boarders had she?"

"She believed about forty came to regular meals, and there was transient custom, which was as much as she and her husband could 'tend to. But *he* did a great deal of work."

"What work?"

"Oh, bringing in the wood, and looking after the traders' things."

"How long had she been married?"

"About nine years. She had lost a little girl and boy. Three children living. *He* was from Illinois. She from Boston. Had an education (Boston Female High School,—Geometry, Algebra, a little Latin and Greek). Mother and father died. Came to Illinois alone, to teach school. Saw *him*—yes—a love match." ("Two souls," etc., etc.) "Married and emigrated to Kansas. Thence across the Plains to California. Always on the outskirts of civilization. *He* liked it.

"She might sometimes have wished to go home. Would like to on account of her children. Would like to give them an education. Had taught them a little herself, but couldn't do much on account of other work. Hoped that the boy would be like his father, strong and hearty.

Was fearful the girl would be more like her. Had often thought she was not fit for a pioneer's wife."

"Why?"

"Oh, she was not strong enough, and had seen some of his friends' wives in Kansas who could do more work. But he never complained,— he was so kind." ("Two souls," etc.)

Sitting there with her head leaning pensively on one hand, holding the poor, wearied, and limp-looking baby wearily on the other arm, dirty, drabbled, and forlorn, with the firelight playing upon her features no longer fresh or young, but still refined and delicate, and even in her grotesque slovenliness still bearing a faint reminiscence of birth and breeding, it was not to be wondered that I did not fall into excessive raptures over the barbarian's kindness. Emboldened by my sympathy, she told me how she had given up, little by little, what she imagined to be the weakness of her early education, until she found that she acquired but little strength in her new experience. How, translated to a backwoods society, she was hated by the women, and called proud and "fine," and how her dear husband lost popularity on that account with his fellows. How, led partly by his roving instincts, and partly from other circumstances, he started with her to California. An account of that tedious journey. How it was a dreary, dreary waste in her memory, only a blank plain marked by a little cairn of stones,—a child's grave. How she had noticed that little Willie failed. How she had called Abner's attention to it, but, man-like, he knew nothing about children, and pooh-poohed it, and was worried by the stock. How it happened that after they had passed Sweetwater she was walking beside the wagon one night, and looking at the western sky, and she heard a little voice say "Mother." How she looked into the wagon and saw that little Willie was sleeping comfortably and did not wish to wake him. How that in a few moments more she heard the same voice saying "Mother." How she came back to the wagon and leaned down over him, and felt his breath upon her face, and again covered him up tenderly, and once more resumed her weary journey beside him, praying to God for his recovery. How with her face turned to the sky she heard the same voice saying

336

"Mother," and directly a great bright star shot away from its brethren and expired. And how she knew what had happened, and ran to the wagon again only to pillow a little pinched and cold white face upon her weary bosom. The thin red hands went up to her eyes here, and for a few moments she sat still. The wind tore round the house and made a frantic rush at the front door, and from his couch of skins in the inner room Ingomar, the barbarian, snored peacefully.

"Of course she always found a protector from insult and outrage in the great courage and strength of her husband?"

"Oh, yes; when Ingomar was with her she feared nothing. But she was nervous and had been frightened once!"

"How?"

"They had just arrived in California. They kept house then, and had to sell liquor to traders. Ingomar was hospitable, and drank with everybody, for the sake of popularity and business, and Ingomar got to like liquor, and was easily affected by it. And how one night there was a boisterous crowd in the bar-room; she went in and tried to get him away, but only succeeded in awakening the coarse gallantry of the half-crazed revelers. And how, when she had at last got him in the room with her frightened children, he sank down on the bed in a stupor, which made her think the liquor was drugged. And how she sat beside him all night, and near morning heard a step in the passage, and, looking toward the door, saw the latch slowly moving up and down, as if somebody were trying it. And how she shook her husband, and tried to waken him, but without effect. And how at last the door yielded slowly at the top (it was bolted below), as if by a gradual pressure without; and how a hand protruded through the opening. And how as quick as lightning she nailed that hand to the wall with her scissors (her only weapon), but the point broke, and somebody got away with a fearful oath. How she never told her husband of it, for fear he would kill that somebody; but how on one day a stranger called here, and as she was handing him his coffee, she saw a queer triangular scar on the back of his hand." She was still talking, and the wind was still blowing, and Ingomar was still snoring from his couch of skins, when there was a shout high up the straggling street, and a clattering of hoofs and rattling of wheels. The mail had arrived. Parthenia ran with the faded baby to awaken Ingomar, and almost simultaneously the gallant expressman stood again before me, addressing me by my Christian name, and invited me to drink out of a mysterious black bottle. The horses were speedily watered, and the business of the gallant expressman concluded, and, bidding Parthenia good by, I got on the stage, and immediately fell asleep, and dreamt of calling on Parthenia and Ingomar, and being treated with pie to an unlimited extent, until I woke up the next morning in Sacramento. I have some doubts as to whether all this was not a dyspeptic dream, but I never witness the drama, and hear that noble sentiment concerning "Two souls," etc., without thinking of Wingdam and poor Parthenia.

SPANISH AND AMERICAN LEGENDS

THE LEGEND OF MONTE DEL DIABLO

The cautious reader will detect a lack of authenticity in the following pages. I am not a cautious reader myself, yet I confess with some concern to the absence of much documentary evidence in support of the singular incident I am about to relate. Disjointed memoranda, the proceedings of ayuntamientos and early departmental juntas, with other records of a primitive and superstitious people, have been my inadequate authorities. It is but just to state, however, that though this particular story lacks corroboration, in ransacking the Spanish archives of Upper California I have met with many more surprising and incredible stories, attested and supported to a degree that would have placed this legend beyond a cavil or doubt. I have, also, never lost faith in the legend myself, and in so doing have profited much from the examples of divers grant-claimants, who have often jostled me in their more practical researches, and who have my sincere sympathy at the skepticism of a modern hard-headed and practical world.

For many years after Father Junipero Serro first rang his bell in the wilderness of Upper California, the spirit which animated that adventurous priest did not wane. The conversion of the heathen went on rapidly in the establishment of missions throughout the land. So sedulously did the good Fathers set about their work, that around their isolated chapels there presently arose adobe huts, whose mud-plastered and savage tenants partook regularly of the provisions, and occasionally of the Sacrament, of their pious hosts. Nay, so great was their progress, that one zealous Padre is reported to have administered the Lord's Supper one Sabbath morning to "over three hundred heathen salvages."

It was not to be wondered that the Enemy of Souls, being greatly incensed thereat, and alarmed at his decreasing popularity, should have grievously tempted and embarrassed these holy Fathers, as we shall presently see.

Yet they were happy, peaceful days for California. The vagrant keels of prying Commerce had not as yet ruffled the lordly gravity of her bays. No torn and ragged gulch betrayed the suspicion of golden treasure. The wild oats drooped idly in the morning heat or wrestled with the afternoon breezes. Deer and antelope dotted the plain. The watercourses brawled in their familiar channels, nor dreamed of ever shifting their regular tide. The wonders of the Yosemite and Calaveras were as yet unrecorded. The holy Fathers noted little of the landscape beyond the barbaric prodigality with which the quick soil repaid the sowing. A new conversion, the advent of a saint's day, or the baptism of an Indian baby, was at once the chronicle and marvel of their day.

At this blissful epoch there lived at the Mission of San Pablo Father Jose Antonio Haro, a worthy brother of the Society of Jesus. He was of tall and cadaverous aspect. A somewhat romantic history had given a poetic interest to his lugubrious visage. While a youth, pursuing his studies at famous Salamanca, he had become enamored of the charms of Dona Carmen de Torrencevara, as that lady passed to her matutinal devotions. Untoward circumstances, hastened, perhaps, by a wealthier suitor, brought this amour to a disastrous issue, and Father Jose entered a monastery, taking upon himself the vows of celibacy. It was here that his natural fervor and poetic enthusiasm conceived expression as a missionary. A longing to convert the uncivilized heathen succeeded his frivolous earthly passion, and a desire to explore and develop unknown fastnesses continually possessed him. In his flashing eye and sombre exterior was detected a singular commingling of the discreet Las Casas and the impetuous Balboa.

Fired by this pious zeal, Father Jose went forward in the van of Christian pioneers. On reaching Mexico he obtained authority to establish the Mission of San Pablo. Like the good Junipero, accompanied only by an acolyte and muleteer, he unsaddled his mules in a dusky canon, and rang his bell in the wilderness. The savages—a peaceful, inoffensive, and inferior race—presently flocked around him. The nearest military post was far away, which contributed much to the security of these pious pilgrims, who found their open trustfulness and amiability better fitted to repress hostility than the presence of an armed, suspicious, and brawling soldiery. So the good Father Jose said matins and prime, mass and vespers, in the heart of sin and heathenism, taking no heed to himself, but looking only to the welfare of the Holy Church. Conversions soon followed, and on the 7th of July, 1760, the first Indian baby was baptized,—an event which, as Father Jose piously records, "exceeds the richnesse of gold or precious jewels or the chancing upon the Ophir of Solomon." I quote this incident as best suited to show the ingenious blending of poetry and piety which distinguished Father Jose's record.

The Mission of San Pablo progressed and prospered, until the pious founder thereof, like the infidel Alexander, might have wept that there were no more heathen worlds to conquer. But his ardent and enthusiastic spirit could not long brook an idleness that seemed begotten of sin; and one pleasant August morning in the year of grace 1770 Father Jose issued from the outer court of the mission building, equipped to explore the field for new missionary labors.

Nothing could exceed the quiet gravity and unpretentiousness of the little cavalcade. First rode a stout muleteer, leading a pack-mule laden with the provisions of the party, together with a few cheap crucifixes and hawks' bells. After him came the devout Padre Jose, bearing his breviary and cross, with a black serapa thrown around his shoulders; while on either side trotted a dusky convert, anxious to show a proper sense of his regeneration by acting as guide into the wilds of his heathen brethren. Their new condition was agreeably shown by the absence of the usual mud-plaster, which in their unconverted state they assumed to keep away vermin and cold. The morning was bright and propitious. Before their departure, mass had been said in the chapel, and the protection of St. Ignatius invoked against all contingent evils, but especially against bears, which, like the fiery dragons of old, seemed to cherish unconquerable hostility to the Holy Church.

As they wound through the canon, charming birds disported upon boughs and sprays, and sober quails piped from the alders; the willowy watercourses gave a musical utterance, and the long grass whispered on the hillside. On entering the deeper defiles, above them towered dark green masses of pine, and occasionally the madrono shook its bright scarlet berries. As they toiled up many a steep ascent, Father Jose sometimes picked up fragments of scoria, which spake to his imagination of direful volcanoes and impending earthquakes. To the less scientific mind of the muleteer Ignacio they had even a more terrifying significance; and he once or twice snuffed the air suspiciously, and declared that it smelt of sulphur. So the first day of their journey wore away, and at night they encamped without having met a single heathen face. It was on this night that the Enemy of Souls appeared to Ignacio in an appalling form. He had retired to a secluded part of the camp and had sunk upon his knees in prayerful meditation, when he looked up and perceived the Arch-Fiend in the likeness of a monstrous bear. The Evil One was seated on his hind legs immediately before him, with his fore paws joined together just below his black muzzle. Wisely conceiving this remarkable attitude to be in mockery and derision of his devotions, the worthy muleteer was transported with fury. Seizing an arquebus, he instantly closed his eyes and fired. When he had recovered from the effects of the terrific discharge, the apparition had disappeared. Father Jose, awakened by the report, reached the spot only in time to chide the muleteer for wasting powder and ball in a contest with one whom a single ave would, have been sufficient to utterly discomfit. What further reliance he placed on Ignacio's story is not known; but, in commemoration of a worthy Californian custom, the place was called "La Canada de la Tentacion del Pio Muletero," or "The Glen of the Temptation of the Pious Muleteer," a name which it retains to this day.

The next morning the party, issuing from a narrow gorge, came upon a long valley, sear and burnt with the shadeless heat. Its lower extremity was lost in a fading line of low hills, which, gathering might and volume toward the upper end of the valley, upheaved a stupendous bulwark against the breezy north. The peak of this awful spur was just touched by a fleecy cloud that shifted to and fro like a banneret. Father Jose gazed at it with mingled awe and admiration. By a singular coincidence, the muleteer Ignacio uttered the simple ejaculation "Diablo!"

As they penetrated the valley, they soon began to miss the agreeable life and companionable echoes of the canon they had quitted. Huge fissures in the parched soil seemed to cane as with thirsty mouths. A few squirrels darted from the earth and disappeared as mysteriously before the jingly mules. A gray wolf trotted leisurely along just ahead. But whichever way Father Jose turned, the mountain always asserted itself and arrested his wandering eye. Out of the dry and arid valley it seemed to spring into cooler and bracing life. Deep cavernous shadows dwelt along its base; rocky fastnesses appeared midway of its elevation; and on either side huge black hills diverged like massy roots from a central trunk. His lively fancy pictured these hills peopled with a majestic and intelligent race of savages; and looking into futurity, he already saw a monstrous cross crowning the dome-like summit. Far different were the sensations of the muleteer, who saw in those awful solitudes only fiery dragons, colossal bears, and breakneck trails. The converts, Concepcion and Incarnacion, trotting modestly beside the Padre, recognized, perhaps, some manifestation of their former weird mythology.

At nightfall they reached the base of the mountain. Here Father Jose unpacked his mules, said vespers, and, formally ringing his bell, called upon the Gentiles within hearing to come and accept the holy faith. The echoes of the black frowning hills around him caught up the pious invitation and repeated it at intervals; but no Gentiles appeared that night. Nor were the devotions of the muleteer again disturbed, although he afterward asserted that, when the Father's exhortation was ended, a mocking peal of laughter came from the mountain. Nothing daunted by these intimations of the near hostility of the Evil One, Father Jose declared his intention to ascend the mountain at early dawn, and before the sun rose the next morning he was leading the way.

The ascent was in many places difficult and dangerous. Huge fragments of rock often lay across the trail, and after a few hours' climbing they were forced to leave their mules in a little gully and continue the ascent afoot. Unaccustomed to such exertion, Father Jose often stopped to wipe the perspiration from his thin cheeks. As the day wore on a strange silence oppressed them. Except the occasional pattering of a squirrel, or a rustling in the chimisal bushes, there were no signs of life. The half-human print of a bear's foot sometimes appeared before them, at which Ignacio always crossed himself piously. The eye was sometimes cheated by a dripping from the rocks, which on closer inspection proved to be a resinous oily liquid with an abominable sulphurous smell. When they were within a short distance of the summit, the discreet Ignacio, selecting a sheltered nook for the camp, slipped aside and busied himself in preparations for the evening, leaving the holy Father to continue the ascent alone. Never was there a more thoughtless act of prudence, never a more imprudent piece of caution. Without noticing the desertion, buried in pious reflection, Father Jose pushed mechanically on, and, reaching the summit, cast himself down and gazed upon the prospect.

Below him lay a succession of valleys opening into each other like gentle lakes, until they were lost to the southward. Westerly the distant range hid the bosky canada which sheltered the Mission of San Pablo. In the farther distance the Pacific Ocean stretched away, bearing a cloud of fog upon its bosom, which crept through the entrance of the bay, and rolled thickly between him and the northeastward; the same fog hid the base of the mountain and the view beyond. Still from time to time the fleecy veil parted, and timidly disclosed charming glimpses of mighty rivers, mountain defiles, and rolling plains, sear with ripened oats and bathed in the glow of the setting sun. As father Jose gazed, he was penetrated with a pious longing. Already his imagination, filled with enthusiastic conceptions, beheld all that vast expanse gathered under the mild sway of the holy faith and peopled with zealous converts. Each little knoll in fancy became crowned with a chapel; from each dark canon gleamed the white walls of a mission building. Growing bolder in his enthusiasm and looking farther into futurity, he beheld a new Spain rising on these savage shores. He already saw the spires of stately cathedrals, the domes of palaces, vineyards, gardens, and groves. Convents, half hid among the hills, peeping from plantations of branching limes, and long processions of chanting nuns wound through the denies. So completely was the good Father's conception of the future confounded with the past, that even in their choral strain the well-remembered accents of Carmen struck his ear. He was busied in these fanciful imaginings, when suddenly over that extended prospect the faint distant tolling of a bell rang sadly out and died. It was the Angelus. Father Jose listened with superstitious exaltation. The Mission of San Pablo was far away, and the sound must have been some miraculous omen. But never before, to his enthusiastic sense, did the sweet seriousness of this angelic symbol come with such strange significance. With the last faint peal his glowing fancy seemed to cool; the fog closed in below him, and the good Father remembered he had not had his supper. He had risen and was wrapping his serapa around him, when he perceived for the first time that he was not alone.

Nearly opposite, and where should have been the faithless Ignacio, a grave and decorous figure was seated. His appearance was that of an elderly hidalgo, dressed in mourning, with mustaches of iron-gray carefully waxed and twisted round a pair of lantern-jaws. The monstrous hat and prodigious feather, the enormous ruff and exaggerated trunk-hose, contrasted with a frame shriveled and wizened, all belonged to a century previous. Yet Father Jose was not astonished. His adventurous life and poetic imagination, continually on the look-out for the marvelous, gave him a certain advantage over the practical and material-minded. He instantly detected the diabolical quality of his visitant, and was prepared. With equal coolness and courtesy he met the cavalier's obeisance.

"I ask your pardon, Sir Priest," said the stranger, "for disturbing your meditations. Pleasant they must have been, and right fanciful, I imagine, when occasioned by so fair a prospect."

"Worldly, perhaps, Sir Devil,—for such I take you to be," said the

345

holy Father, as the stranger bowed his black plumes to the ground; "worldly, perhaps; for it hath pleased Heaven to retain even in our regenerated state much that pertaineth to the flesh, yet still, I trust, not without some speculation for the welfare of the Holy Church. In dwelling upon yon fair expanse, mine eyes have been graciously opened with prophetic inspiration, and the promise of the heathen as an inheritance hath marvelously recurred to me. For there can be none lack such diligence in the true faith but may see that even the conversion of these pitiful salvages hath a meaning. As the blessed St. Ignatius discreetly observes," continued Father Jose, clearing his throat and slightly elevating his voice, "'the heathen is given to the warriors of Christ, even as the pearls of rare discovery which gladden the hearts of shipmen.' Nay, I might say"—

But here the stranger, who had been wrinkling his brows and twisting his mustaches with well-bred patience, took advantage of an oratorical pause.

"It grieves me, Sir Priest, to interrupt the current of your eloquence as discourteously as I have already broken your meditations; but the day already waneth to night. I have a matter of serious import to make with you, could I entreat your cautious consideration a few moments."

Father Jose hesitated. The temptation was great, and the prospect of acquiring some knowledge of the Great Enemy's plans not the least trifling object. And, if the truth must be told, there was a certain decorum about the stranger that interested the Padre. Though well aware of the Protean shapes the Arch-Fiend could assume, and though free from the weaknesses of the flesh, Father Jose was not above the temptations of the spirit. Had the Devil appeared, as in the case of the pious St. Anthony, in the likeness of a comely damsel, the good Father, with his certain experience of the deceitful sex, would have whisked her away in the saying of a paternoster. But there was, added to the security of age, a grave sadness about the stranger,—a thoughtful consciousness, as of being at a great moral disadvantage, which at once decided him on a magnanimous course of conduct.

The stranger then proceeded to inform him that he had been

diligently observing the holy Father's triumphs in the valley. That, far from being greatly exercised thereat, he had been only grieved to see so enthusiastic and chivalrous an antagonist wasting his zeal in a hopeless work. For, he observed, the issue of the great battle of Good and Evil had been otherwise settled, as he would presently show him. "It wants but a few moments of night," he continued, "and over this interval of twilight, as you know, I have been given complete control. Look to the west."

As the Padre turned, the stranger took his enormous hat from his head and waved it three times before him. At each sweep of the prodigious feather the fog grew thinner, until it melted impalpably away, and the former landscape returned, yet warm with the glowing sun. As Father Jose gazed a strain of martial music arose from the valley, and issuing from a deep canon the good Father beheld a long cavalcade of gallant cavaliers, habited like his companion. As they swept down the plain, they were joined by like processions, that slowly defiled from every ravine and canon of the mysterious mountain. From time to time the peal of a trumpet swelled fitfully upon the breeze; the cross of Santiago glittered, and the royal banners of Castile and Aragon waved over the moving column. So they moved on solemnly toward the sea, where, in the distance, Father Jose saw stately caravels, bearing the same familiar banner, awaiting them. The good Padre gazed with conflicting emotions, and the serious voice of the stranger broke the silence.

"Thou hast beheld, Sir Priest, the fading footprints of adventurous Castile. Thou hast seen the declining glory of old Spain,—declining as yonder brilliant sun. The sceptre she hath wrested from the heathen is fast dropping from her decrepit and fleshless grasp. The children she hath fostered shall know her no longer. The soil she hath acquired shall be lost to her as irrevocably as she herself hath thrust the Moor from her own Granada."

The stranger paused, and his voice seemed broken by emotion; at the same time, Father Jose, whose sympathizing heart yearned toward the departing banners, cried in poignant accents,—

"Farewell, ye gallant cavaliers and Christian soldiers! Farewell, thou,

Juries de Balboa! thou, Alonzo de Ojeda! and thou, most venerable Las Casas! farewell, and may Heaven prosper still the seed ye left behind!"

Then turning to the stranger, Father Jose beheld him gravely draw his pocket-handkerchief from the basket-hilt of his rapier and apply it decorously to his eyes. "Pardon this weakness, Sir Priest," said the cavalier apologetically; "but these worthy gentlemen were ancient friends of mine, and have done me many a delicate service,—much more, perchance, than these poor sables may signify," he added, with a grim gesture toward the mourning suit he wore.

Father Jose was too much preoccupied in reflection to notice the equivocal nature of this tribute, and, after a few moments' silence, said, as if continuing his thought,—

"But the seed they have planted shall thrive and prosper on this fruitful soil."

As if answering the interrogatory, the stranger turned to the opposite direction, and, again waving his hat, said, in the same serious tone, "Look to the east!"

The Father turned, and, as the fog broke away before the waving plume, he saw that the sun was rising. Issuing with its bright beams through the passes of the snowy mountains beyond appeared a strange and motley crew. Instead of the dark and romantic visages of his last phantom train, the Father beheld with strange concern the blue eyes and flaxen hair of a Saxon race. In place of martial airs and musical utterance, there rose upon the ear a strange din of harsh gutturals and singular sibilation. Instead of the decorous tread and stately mien of the cavaliers of the former vision, they came pushing, bustling, panting, and swaggering. And as they passed, the good Father noticed that giant trees were prostrated as with the breath of a tornado, and the bowels of the earth were torn and rent as with a convulsion. And Father Jose looked in vain for holy cross or Christian symbol; there was but one that seemed an ensign, and he crossed himself with holy horror as he perceived it bore the effigy of a bear.

"Who are these swaggering Ishmaelites?" he asked, with something of asperity in his tone.

The stranger was gravely silent.

"What do they here, with neither cross nor holy symbol?" he again demanded.

"Have you the courage to see, Sir Priest?" responded the stranger quietly.

Father Jose felt his crucifix, as a lonely traveler might his rapier, and assented.

"Step under the shadow of my plume," said the stranger.

Father Jose stepped beside him and they instantly sank through the earth.

When he opened his eyes, which had remained closed in prayerful meditation during his rapid descent, he found himself in a vast vault, bespangled overhead with luminous points like the starred firmament. It was also lighted by a yellow glow that seemed to proceed from a mighty sea or lake that occupied the centre of the chamber. Around this subterranean sea dusky figures flitted, bearing ladles filled with the yellow fluid, which they had replenished from its depths. From this lake diverging streams of the same mysterious flood penetrated like mighty rivers the cavernous distance. As they walked by the banks of this glittering Styx, Father Jose perceived how the liquid stream at certain places became solid. The ground was strewn with glittering flakes. One of these the Padre picked up and curiously examined. It was virgin gold.

An expression of discomfiture overcast the good Father's face at this discovery; but there was trace neither of malice nor satisfaction in the stranger's air, which was still of serious and fateful contemplation. When Father Jose recovered his equanimity, he said bitterly,—

"This, then, Sir Devil, is your work! This is your deceitful lure for the weak souls of sinful nations! So would you replace the Christian grace of Holy Spain!"

"This is what must be," returned the stranger gloomily. "But listen, Sir Priest. It lies with you to avert the issue for a time. Leave me here in peace. Go back to Castile, and take with you your bells, your images, and your missions. Continue here, and you only precipitate results. Stay! promise me you will do this, and you shall not lack that which will render your old age an ornament and a blessing;" and the stranger motioned significantly to the lake.

It was here, the legend discreetly relates, that the Devil showed—as he always shows sooner or later—his cloven hoof. The worthy Padre, sorely perplexed by this threefold vision, and, if the truth must be told, a little nettled at this wresting away of the glory of holy Spanish discovery, had shown some hesitation. But the unlucky bribe of the Enemy of Souls touched his Castilian spirit. Starting hack in deep disgust, he brandished his crucifix in the face of the unmasked Fiend, and in a voice that made the dusky vault resound cried,—

"Avaunt thee, Sathanas! Diaholus, I defy thee! What! wouldst thou bribe me,—me, a brother of the Sacred Society of the Holy Jesus, Licentiate of Cordova and Inquisitor of Guadalaxara? Thinkest thou to buy me with thy sordid treasure? Avaunt!"

What might have been the issue of this rupture, and how complete might have been the triumph of the holy Father over the Arch-Fiend, who was recoiling aghast at these sacred titles and the nourishing symbol, we can never know, for at that moment the crucifix slipped through his fingers.

Scarcely had it touched the ground before Devil and holy Father simultaneously cast themselves toward it. In the struggle they clinched, and the pious Jose, who was as much the superior of his antagonist in bodily as in spiritual strength, was about to treat the Great Adversary to a back somersault, when he suddenly felt the long nails of the stranger piercing his flesh. A new fear seized his heart, a numbing chillness crept through his body, and he struggled to free himself, but in vain. A strange roaring was in his ears; the lake and cavern danced before his eyes and vanished, and with a loud cry he sank senseless to the ground.

When he recovered his consciousness, he was aware of a gentle swaying motion of his body. He opened his eyes, and saw it was high noon, and that he was being carried in a litter through the valley. He felt stiff, and looking down, perceived that his arm was tightly bandaged to his side.

He closed his eyes, and, after a few words of thankful prayer, thought how miraculously he had been preserved, and made a vow of candlesticks to the blessed Saint Jose. He then called in a faint voice, and presently the penitent Ignacio stood beside him.

The joy the poor fellow felt at his patron's returning consciousness for some time choked his utterance. He could only ejaculate, "A miracle! Blessed Saint Jose, he lives!" and kiss the Padre's bandaged hand. Father Jose, more intent on his last night's experience, waited for his emotion to subside, and asked where he had been found.

"On the mountain, your Reverence, but a few varas from where he attacked you."

"How?—you saw him then?" asked the Padre in unfeigned astonishment.

"Saw him, your Reverence! Mother of God! I should think I did! And your Reverence shall see him too, if he ever comes again within range of Ignacio's arquebus."

"What mean you, Ignacio?" said the Padre, sitting bolt-upright in his litter.

"Why, the bear, your Reverence,—the bear, holy Father, who attacked your worshipful person while you were meditating on the top of yonder mountain."

"Ah!" said the holy Father, lying down again. "Chut, child! I would be at peace."

When he reached the mission he was tenderly cared for, and in a few weeks was enabled to resume those duties from which, as will be seen, not even the machinations of the Evil One could divert him. The news of his physical disaster spread over the country, and a letter to the Bishop of Guadalaxara contained a confidential and detailed account of the good Father's spiritual temptation. But in some way the story leaked out; and long after Jose was gathered to his fathers, his mysterious encounter formed the theme of thrilling and whispered narrative. The mountain was generally shunned. It is true that Senor Joaquin Pedrillo afterward located a grant near the base of the mountain; but as Senora Pedrillo was known to be a termagant half-breed, the senor was not supposed to be over-fastidious.

Such is the legend of Monte del Diablo. As I said before, it may seem to lack essential corroboration. The discrepancy between the Father's narrative and the actual climax has given rise to some skepticism on the part of ingenious quibblers. All such I would simply refer to that part of the report of Senor Julio Serro, Sub-Prefect of San Pablo, before whom attest of the above was made. Touching this matter, the worthy Prefect observes, "That although the body of Father Jose doth show evidence of grievous conflict in the flesh, yet that is no proof that the Enemy of Souls, who could assume the figure of a decorous elderly caballero, could not at the same time transform himself into a bear for his own vile purposes."

THE RIGHT EYE OF THE COMMANDER

The year of grace 1797 passed away on the coast of California in a southwesterly gale. The little bay of San Carlos, albeit sheltered by the headlands of the Blessed Trinity, was rough and turbulent; its foam clung quivering to the seaward wall of the mission garden; the air was filled with flying sand and spume, and as the Senor Comandante, Hermenegildo Salvatierra, looked from the deep embrasured window of the presidio guardroom, he felt the salt breath of the distant sea buffet a color into his smoke-dried cheeks.

The commander, I have said, was gazing thoughtfully from the window of the guardroom. He may have been reviewing the events of the year now about to pass away. But, like the garrison at the Presidio, there was little to review. The year, like its predecessors, had been uneventful,—the days had slipped by in a delicious monotony of simple duties, unbroken by incident or interruption. The regularly recurring feasts and saints' days, the half-yearly courier from San Diego, the rare transport-ship and rarer foreign vessel, were the mere details of his patriarchal life. If there was no achievement, there was certainly no failure. Abundant harvests and patient industry amply supplied the wants of presidio and mission. Isolated from the family of nations, the wars which shook the world concerned them not so much as the last earthquake; the struggle that emancipated their sister colonies on the other side of the continent to them had no suggestiveness. In short, it was that glorious Indian summer of Californian history around which so much poetical haze still lingers,—that bland, indolent autumn of

Spanish rule, so soon to be followed by the wintry storms of Mexican independence and the reviving spring of American conquest.

The commander turned from the window and walked toward the fire that burned brightly on the deep oven-like hearth. A pile of copy-books, the work of the presidio school, lay on the table. As he turned over the leaves with a paternal interest, and surveyed the fair round Scripture text,—the first pious pothooks of the pupils of San Carlos, an audible commentary fell from his lips: "'Abimelech took her from Abraham'—ah, little one, excellent!—'Jacob sent to see his brother'—body of Christ! that upstroke of thine, Paquita, is marvelous; the governor shall see it!" A film of honest pride dimmed the commander's left eye,—the right, alas! twenty years before had been sealed by an Indian arrow. He rubbed it softly with the sleeve of his leather jacket, and continued: "'The Ishmaelites having arrived'"—

He stopped, for there was a step in the courtyard, a foot upon the threshold, and a stranger entered. With the instinct of an old soldier, the commander, after one glance at the intruder, turned quickly toward the wall, where his trusty Toledo hung, or should have been hanging. But it was not there, and as he recalled that the last time he had seen that weapon it was being ridden up and down the gallery by Pepito, the infant son of Bautista, the tortilio-maker, he blushed, and then contented himself with frowning upon the intruder.

But the stranger's air, though irreverent, was decidedly peaceful. He was unarmed, and wore the ordinary cape of tarpaulin and sea-boots of a mariner. Except a villainous smell of codfish, there was little about him that was peculiar.

His name, as he informed the commander in Spanish that was more fluent than elegant or precise,—his name was Peleg Scudder. He was master of the schooner General Court, of the port of Salem, in Massachusetts, on a trading voyage to the South Seas, but now driven by stress of weather into the bay of San Carlos. He begged permission to ride out the gale under the headlands of the Blessed Trinity, and no more. Water he did not need, having taken in a supply at Bodega. He knew the strict surveillance of the Spanish port regulations in regard to foreign vessels, and would do nothing against the severe discipline and good order of the settlement. There was a slight tinge of sarcasm in his tone as he glanced toward the desolate parade ground of the presidio and the open unguarded gate. The fact was that the sentry, Felipe Gomez, had discreetly retired to shelter at the beginning of the storm, and was then sound asleep in the corridor.

The commander hesitated. The port regulations were severe, but he was accustomed to exercise individual authority, and beyond an old order issued ten years before, regarding the American ship Columbia, there was no precedent to guide him. The storm was severe, and a sentiment of humanity urged him to grant the stranger's request. It is but just to the commander to say that his inability to enforce a refusal did not weigh with his decision. He would have denied with equal disregard of consequences that right to a seventy-four-gun ship which he now yielded so gracefully to this Yankee trading schooner. He stipulated only that there should be no communication between the ship and shore. "For yourself, Senor Captain," he continued, "accept my hospitality. The fort is yours as long as you shall grace it with your distinguished presence," and with old-fashioned courtesy he made the semblance of withdrawing from the guardroom.

Master Peleg Scudder smiled as he thought of the half-dismantled fort, the two mouldy brass cannon, cast in Manila a century previous, and the shiftless garrison. A wild thought of accepting the commander's offer literally, conceived in the reckless spirit of a man who never let slip an offer for trade, for a moment filled his brain, but a timely reflection of the commercial unimportance of the transaction checked him. He only took a capacious quid of tobacco, as the commander gravely drew a settle before the fire, and in honor of his guest untied the black silk handkerchief that bound his grizzled brows.

What passed between Salvatierra and his guest that night it becomes me not, as a grave chronicler of the salient points of history, to relate. I have said that Master Peleg Scudder was a fluent talker, and under the influence of divers strong waters, furnished by his host, he became still more loquacious. And think of a man with a twenty years' budget of gossip! The commander learned, for the first time, how Great Britain lost her colonies; of the French Revolution; of the great Napoleon, whose achievements, perhaps, Peleg colored more highly than the commander's superiors would have liked. And when Peleg turned questioner, the commander was at his mercy. He gradually made himself master of the gossip of the mission and presidio, the "small beer" chronicles of that pastoral age, the conversion of the heathen, the presidio schools, and even asked the commander how he had lost his eye. It is said that at this point of the conversation Master Peleg produced from about his person divers small trinkets, kickshaws and new-fangled trifles, and even forced some of them upon his host. It is further alleged that under the malign influence of Peleg and several glasses of aguardiente the commander lost somewhat of his decorum, and behaved in a manner unseemly for one in his position, reciting high-flown Spanish poetry, and even piping in a thin high voice divers madrigals and heathen canzonets of an amorous complexion, chiefly in regard to a "little one" who was his, the commander's, "soul." These allegations, perhaps unworthy the notice of a serious chronicler, should be received with great caution, and are introduced here as simple hearsay. That the commander, however, took a handkerchief and attempted to show his guest the mysteries of the sembi cuacua, capering in an agile but indecorous manner about the apartment, has been denied. Enough for the purposes of this narrative, that at midnight Peleg assisted his host to bed with many protestations of undying friendship, and then, as the gale had abated, took his leave of the presidio, and hurried aboard the General Court. When the day broke the ship was gone.

I know not if Peleg kept his word with his host. It is said that the holy Fathers at the mission that night heard a loud chanting in the plaza, as of the heathens singing psalms through their noses; that for many days after an odor of salt codfish prevailed in the settlement; that a dozen hard nutmegs, which were unfit for spice or seed, were found in the possession of the wife of the baker, and that several bushels of shoe-pegs, which bore a pleasing resemblance to oats, but were quite inadequate to the purposes of provender, were discovered in the stable of the blacksmith.

But when the reader reflects upon the sacredness of a Yankee trader's word, the stringent discipline of the Spanish port regulations, and the proverbial indisposition of my countrymen to impose upon the confidence of a simple people, he will at once reject this part of the story.

A roll of drums, ushering in the year 1798, awoke the commander. The sun was shining brightly, and the storm had ceased. He sat up in bed, and through the force of habit rubbed his left eye. As the remembrance of the previous night came back to him, he jumped from his couch and ran to the window. There was no ship in the bay. A sudden thought seemed to strike him, and he rubbed both of his eyes. Not content with this, he consulted the metallic mirror which hung beside his crucifix. There was no mistake; the commander had a visible second eye,—a right one,—as good, save for the purposes of vision, as the left.

Whatever might have been the true secret of this transformation, but one opinion prevailed at San Carlos. It was one of those rare miracles vouchsafed a pious Catholic community as an evidence to the heathen, through the intercession of the blessed San Carlos himself. That their beloved commander, the temporal defender of the Faith, should be the recipient of this miraculous manifestation was most fit and seemly. The commander himself was reticent; he could not tell a falsehood,—he dared not tell the truth. After all, if the good folk of San Carlos believed that the powers of his right eye were actually restored, was it wise and discreet for him to undeceive them? For the first time in his life the commander thought of policy,—for the first time he quoted that text which has been the lure of so many well-meaning but easy Christians, of being "all things to all men." Infeliz Hermenegildo Salvatierra!

For by degrees an ominous whisper crept through the little settlement. The right eye of the commander, although miraculous, seemed to exercise a baleful effect upon the beholder. No one could look at it without winking. It was cold, hard, relentless, and unflinching. More than that, it seemed to be endowed with a dreadful prescience,—a faculty of seeing through and into the inarticulate thoughts of those it looked upon. The soldiers of the garrison obeyed the eye rather than the voice of their commander, and answered his glance rather than his lips in questioning. The servants could not evade the ever-watchful but cold attention that seemed to pursue them. The children of the presidio school smirched their copy-books under the awful supervision, and poor Paquita, the prize pupil, failed utterly in that marvelous up-stroke when her patron stood beside her. Gradually distrust, suspicion, self-accusation, and timidity took the place of trust, confidence, and security throughout San Carlos. Wherever the right eye of the commander fell, a shadow fell with it.

Not was Salvatierra entirely free from the baleful influence of his miraculous acquisition. Unconscious of its effect upon others, he only saw in their actions evidence of certain things that the crafty Peleg had hinted on that eventful New Year's eve. His most trusty retainers stammered, blushed, and faltered before him. Self-accusations, confessions of minor faults and delinquencies, or extravagant excuses and apologies met his mildest inquiries. The very children that he loved—his pet pupil, Paquita—seemed to be conscious of some hidden sin. The result of this constant irritation showed itself more plainly. For the first half-year the commander's voice and eye were at variance. He was still kind, tender, and thoughtful in speech. Gradually, however, his voice took upon itself the hardness of his glance and its skeptical, impassive quality, and as the year again neared its close it was plain that the commander had fitted himself to the eye, and not the eye to the commander.

It may be surmised that these changes did not escape the watchful solicitude of the Fathers. Indeed, the few who were first to ascribe the right eye of Salvatierra to miraculous origin and the special grace of the blessed San Carlos, now talked openly of witchcraft and the agency of Luzbel, the evil one. It would have fared ill with Hermenegildo Salvatierra had he been aught but commander or amenable to local authority. But the reverend Father, Friar Manuel de Cortes, had no power over the political executive, and all attempts at spiritual advice failed signally. He retired baffled and confused from his first interview with the commander, who seemed now to take a grim satisfaction in the fateful power of his glance. The holy Father contradicted himself, exposed the fallacies of his own arguments, and even, it is asserted, committed himself to several undoubted heresies. When the commander stood up at mass, if the officiating priest caught that skeptical and searching eye, the service was inevitably ruined. Even the power of the Holy Church seemed to be lost, and the last hold upon the affections of the people and the good order of the settlement departed from San Carlos.

As the long dry summer passed, the low hills that surrounded the white walls of the presidio grew more and more to resemble in hue the leathern jacket of the commander, and Nature herself seemed to have borrowed his dry, hard glare. The earth was cracked and seamed with drought; a blight had fallen upon the orchards and vineyards, and the rain, long delayed and ardently prayed for, came not. The sky was as tearless as the right eye of the commander. Murmurs of discontent, insubordination, and plotting among the Indians reached his ear; he only set his teeth the more firmly, tightened the knot of his black silk handkerchief, and looked up his Toledo.

The last day of the year 1798 found the commander sitting, at the hour of evening prayers, alone in the guardroom. He no longer attended the services of the Holy Church, but crept away at such times to some solitary spot, where he spent the interval in silent meditation. The firelight played upon the low beams and rafters, but left the bowed figure of Salvatierra in darkness. Sitting thus, he felt a small hand touch his arm, and, looking down, saw the figure of Paquita, his little Indian pupil, at his knee. "Ah! littlest of all," said the commander, with something of his old tenderness, lingering over the endearing diminutives of his native speech,—"sweet one, what doest thou here? Art thou not afraid of him whom every one shuns and fears?"

"No," said the little Indian readily, "not in the dark. I hear your voice,—the old voice; I feel your touch,—the old touch; but I see not your eye, Senor Comandante. That only I fear,—and that, O senor, O my father," said the child, lifting her little arms towards his,—"that I know is not thine own!"

The commander shuddered and turned away. Then, recovering himself, he kissed Paquita gravely on the forehead and bade her retire. A few hours later, when silence had fallen upon the presidio, he sought his own couch and slept peacefully.

At about the middle watch of the night a dusky figure crept through the low embrasure of the commander's apartment. Other figures were flitting through the parade-ground, which the commander might have seen had he not slept so quietly. The intruder stepped noiselessly to the couch and listened to the sleeper's deep-drawn respiration. Something glittered in the firelight as the savage lifted his arm; another moment and the sore perplexities of Hermenegildo Salvatierra would have been over, when suddenly the savage started and fell back in a paroxysm of terror. The commander slept peacefully, but his right eye, widely opened, fixed and unaltered, glared coldly on the would-be assassin. The man fell to the earth in a fit, and the noise awoke the sleeper.

To rise to his feet, grasp his sword, and deal blows thick and fast upon the mutinous savages who now thronged the room, was the work of a moment. Help opportunely arrived, and the undisciplined Indians were speedily driven beyond the walls; but in the scuffle the commander received a blow upon his right eye, and, lifting his hand to that mysterious organ, it was gone. Never again was it found, and never again, for bale or bliss, did it adorn the right orbit of the commander.

With it passed away the spell that had fallen upon San Carlos. The rain returned to invigorate the languid soil, harmony was restored between priest and soldier, the green grass presently waved over the sere hillsides, the children flocked again to the side of their martial preceptor, a Te Deum was sung in the mission church, and pastoral content once more smiled upon the gentle valleys of San Carlos. And far southward crept the General Court with its master. Peleg Scudder, trafficking in heads and peltries with the Indians, and offering glass eyes, wooden legs, and other Boston notions to the chiefs.

THE LEGEND OF DEVIL'S POINT

On the northerly shore of San Francisco Bay, at a point where the Golden Gate broadens into the Pacific, stands a bluff promontory. It affords shelter from the prevailing winds to a semicircular bay on the east. Around this bay the hillside is bleak and barren, but there are traces of former habitation in a weather-beaten cabin and deserted corral. It is said that these were originally built by an enterprising squatter, who for some unaccountable reason abandoned them shortly after. The "jumper" who succeeded him disappeared one day quite as mysteriously. The third tenant, who seemed to be a man of sanguine, hopeful temperament, divided the property into building lots, staked off the hillside, and projected the map of a new metropolis. Failing, however, to convince the citizens of San Francisco that they had mistaken the site of their city, he presently fell into dissipation and despondency. He was frequently observed haunting the narrow strip of beach at low tide or perched upon the cliff at high water. In the latter position a sheep-tender one day found him, cold and pulseless, with a map of his property in his hand, and his face turned toward the distant sea.

Perhaps these circumstances gave the locality its infelicitous reputation. Vague rumors were bruited of a supernatural influence that had been exercised on the tenants. Strange stories were circulated of the origin of the diabolical title by which the promontory was known. By some it was believed to be haunted by the spirit of one of Sir Francis Drake's sailors, who had deserted his ship in consequence of stories told by the Indians of gold discoveries, but who had perished by starvation on the rocks. A vaquero who had once passed a night in the ruined cabin related how a strangely dressed and emaciated figure had knocked at the door at midnight and demanded food. Other story-tellers, of more historical accuracy, roundly asserted that Sir Francis himself had been little better than a pirate, and had chosen this spot to conceal quantities of ill-gotten booty taken from neutral bottoms, and had protected his hiding-place by the orthodox means of hellish incantation and diabolic agencies. On moonlight nights a shadowy ship was sometimes seen standing off and on, or when fogs encompassed sea and shore, the noise of oars rising and falling in their rowlocks could be heard muffled and indistinctly during the night. Whatever foundation there might have been for these stories, it was certain that a more weird and desolate-looking spot could not have been selected for their theatre. High hills, verdureless and enfiladed with dark canadas, cast their gaunt shadows on the tide. During a greater portion of the day the wind, which blew furiously and incessantly, seemed possessed with a spirit of fierce disquiet and unrest. Toward nightfall the sea-fog crept with soft step through the portals of the Golden Gate, or stole in noiseless marches down the hillside, tenderly soothing the wind-buffeted face of the cliff, until sea and sky were hid together. At such times the populous city beyond and the nearer settlement seemed removed to an infinite distance. An immeasurable loneliness settled upon the cliff. The creaking of a windlass, or the monotonous chant of sailors on some unseen, outlying ship, came faint and far, and full of mystic suggestion.

About a year ago a well-to-do middle-aged broker of San Francisco found himself at nightfall the sole occupant of a plunger, encompassed in a dense fog, and drifting toward the Golden Gate. This unexpected termination of an afternoon's sail was partly attributable to his want of nautical skill, and partly to the effect of his usually sanguine nature. Having given up the guidance of his boat to the wind and tide, he had trusted too implicitly for that reaction which his business experience assured him was certain to occur in all affairs, aquatic as well as terrestrial. "The tide will turn soon," said the broker confidently, "or something will happen." He had scarcely settled himself back again in the stern-sheets, before the bow of the plunger, obeying some mysterious impulse, veered slowly around and a dark object loomed up before him. A gentle eddy carried the boat farther in shore, until at last it was completely embayed under the lee of a rocky point now faintly discernible through the fog. He looked around him in the vain hope of recognizing some familiar headland. The tops of the high hills which rose on either side were hidden in the fog. As the boat swung around, he succeeded in fastening a line to the rocks, and sat down again with a feeling of renewed confidence and security.

It was very cold. The insidious fog penetrated his tightly buttoned coat, and set his teeth to chattering in spite of the aid he sometimes drew from a pocket-flask. His clothes were wet, and the stern-sheets were covered with spray. The comforts of fire and shelter continually rose before his fancy as he gazed wistfully on the rocks. In sheer despair he finally drew the boat toward the most accessible part of the cliff and essayed to ascend. This was less difficult than it appeared, and in a few moments he had gained the hill above. A dark object at a little distance attracted his attention, and on approaching it proved to be a deserted cabin. The story goes on to say that, having built a roaring fire of stakes pulled from the adjoining corral, with the aid of a flask of excellent brandy, he managed to pass the early part of the evening with comparative comfort. There was no door in the cabin, and the windows were simply square openings, which freely admitted the searching fog. But in spite of these discomforts,—being a man of cheerful, sanguine temperament,—he amused himself by poking the fire and watching the ruddy glow which the flames threw on the fog from the open door. In this innocent occupation a great weariness overcame him, and he fell asleep.

He was awakened at midnight by a loud "halloo," which seemed to proceed directly from the sea. Thinking it might be the cry of some boatman lost in the fog, he walked to the edge of the cliff, but the thick veil that covered sea and land rendered all objects at the distance of a few feet indistinguishable. He heard, however, the regular strokes of oars rising and falling on the water. The halloo was repeated. He was clearing his throat to reply, when to his surprise an answer came apparently from the very cabin he had quitted. Hastily retracing his steps, he was the more amazed, on reaching the open door, to find a stranger warming himself by the fire. Stepping back far enough to conceal his own person, he took a good look at the intruder.

He was a man of about forty, with a cadaverous face. But the oddity of his dress attracted the broker's attention more than his lugubrious physiognomy. His legs were hid in enormously wide trousers descending to his knee, where they met long boots of sealskin. A pea-jacket with exaggerated cuffs, almost as large as the breeches, covered his chest, and around his waist a monstrous belt, with a buckle like a dentist's sign, supported two trumpet-mouthed pistols and a curved hanger. He wore a long queue, which depended halfway down his back. As the firelight fell on his ingenuous countenance the broker observed with some concern that this queue was formed entirely of a kind of tobacco known as pigtail or twist. Its effect, the broker remarked, was much heightened when in a moment of thoughtful abstraction the apparition bit off a portion of it and rolled it as a quid into the cavernous recesses of his jaws.

Meanwhile the nearer splash of oars indicated the approach of the unseen boat. The broker had barely time to conceal himself behind the cabin before a number of uncouth-looking figures clambered up the hill toward the ruined rendezvous. They were dressed like the previous comer, who, as they passed through the open door, exchanged greetings with each in antique phraseology, bestowing at the same time some familiar nickname. Flash-in-the-Pan, Spitter-of-Frogs, Malmsey Butt, Latheyard Will, and Mark-the-Pinker, were the few sobriquets the broker remembered. Whether these titles were given to express some peculiarity of their owner he could not tell, for a silence followed as they slowly ranged themselves upon the floor of the cabin in a semicircle around their cadaverous host.

At length Malmsey Butt, a spherical-bodied man-of-war's-man, with a rubicund nose, got on his legs somewhat unsteadily, and addressed himself to the company. They had met that evening, said the speaker, in accordance with a time-honored custom. This was simply to relieve that one of their number who for fifty years had kept watch and ward over the locality where certain treasures had been buried. At this point the broker pricked up his ears. "If so be, camarados and brothers all," he continued, "ye are ready to receive the report of our excellent and well-beloved brother, Master Slit-the-Weazand, touching his search for this treasure, why, marry, to 't and begin."

A murmur of assent went around the circle as the speaker resumed his seat. Master Slit-the-Weazand slowly opened his lantern jaws and began. He had spent much of his time in determining the exact location of the treasure. He believed—nay, he could state positively—that its position was now settled. It was true he had done some trifling little business outside. Modesty forbade his mentioning the particulars, but he would simply state that of the three tenants who had occupied the cabin during the past ten years, none were now alive. [Applause, and cries of "Go to! thou wast always a tall fellow!" and the like.]

Mark-the-Pinker next arose. Before proceeding to business he had a duty to perform in the sacred name of friendship. It ill became him to pass a eulogy upon the qualities of the speaker who had preceded him, for he had known him from "boyhood's hour." Side by side they had wrought together in the Spanish war. For a neat hand with a Toledo he challenged his equal, while how nobly and beautifully he had won his present title of Slit-the-Weazand all could testify. The speaker, with some show of emotion, asked to be pardoned if he dwelt too freely on passages of their early companionship; he then detailed, with a fine touch of humor, his comrade's peculiar manner of slitting the ears and lips of a refractory Jew who had been captured in one of their previous voyages. He would not weary the patience of his hearers, but would briefly propose that the report of Slit-the-Weazand be accepted, and that the thanks of the company be tendered him.

A breaker of strong spirits was then rolled into the hut, and cans of grog were circulated freely from hand to hand. The health of Slit-the-Weazand was proposed in a neat speech by Mark-the-Pinker, and responded to by the former gentleman in a manner that drew tears to the eyes of all present. To the broker, in his concealment, this momentary diversion from the real business of the meeting occasioned much anxiety. As yet nothing had been said to indicate the exact locality of the treasure to which they had mysteriously alluded. Fear restrained him from open inquiry, and curiosity kept him from making good his escape during the orgy which followed. But his situation was beginning to become critical. Flash-in-the-Pan, who seemed to have been a man of choleric humor, taking fire during some hotly contested argument, discharged both his pistols at the breast of his opponent. The balls passed through on each side immediately below his armpits, making a clean hole, through which the horrified broker could see the firelight behind him. The wounded man, without betraying any concern, excited the laughter of the company by jocosely putting his arms akimbo, and inserting his thumbs into the orifices of the wounds as if they had been armholes. This having in a measure restored good humor, the party joined hands and formed a circle preparatory to dancing. The dance was commenced by some monotonous stanzas hummed in a very high key by one of the party, the rest joining in the following chorus, which seemed to present a familiar sound to the broker's ear:—

Her Majesty is very sicke, Lord Essex hath the measles, Our Admiral hath licked ye French—Poppe! saith ye weasel!"

At the regular recurrence of the last line, the party discharged their loaded pistols in all directions, rendering the position of the unhappy broker one of extreme peril and perplexity.

When the tumult had partially subsided, Flash-in-the-Pan called the meeting to order, and most of the revelers returned to their places, Malmsey Butt, however, insisting upon another chorus, and singing at the top of his voice:—

"I am ycleped J. Keyser—I was born at Spring, hys Garden, My father toe make me ane clerke erst did essaye, But a fico

*for ye offis—I spurn ye losels offeire; For I fain would be
ane butcher by'r ladykin alwaye."*

Flash-in-the-Pan drew a pistol from his belt, and bidding some
one gag Malmsey Butt with the stock of it, proceeded to read from a
portentous roll of parchment that he held in his hand. It was a semi-legal
document, clothed in the quaint phraseology of a bygone period. After
a long preamble, asserting their loyalty as lieges of her most bountiful
Majesty and Sovereign Lady the Queen, the document declared that
they then and there took possession of the promontory, and all the
treasure-trove therein contained, formerly buried by Her Majesty's most
faithful and devoted Admiral Sir Francis Drake, with the right to search,
discover, and appropriate the same; and for the purpose thereof they did
then and there form a guild or corporation to so discover, search for, and
disclose said treasures, and by virtue thereof they solemnly subscribed
their names. But at this moment the reading of the parchment was
arrested by an exclamation from the assembly, and the broker was seen
frantically struggling at the door in the strong arms of Mark-the-Pinker.

"Let me go!" he cried, as he made a desperate attempt to reach the
side of Master Flash-in-the-Pan. "Let me go! I tell you, gentlemen, that
document is not worth the parchment it is written on. The laws of the
State, the customs of the country, the mining ordinances, are all against
it. Don't, by all that's sacred, throw away such a capital investment
through ignorance and informality. Let me go! I assure you, gentlemen,
professionally, that you have a big thing,—a remarkably big thing, and
even if I ain't in it, I'm not going to see it fall through. Don't, for God's
sake, gentlemen, I implore you, put your names to such a ridiculous
paper. There isn't a notary"—

He ceased. The figures around him, which were beginning to
grow fainter and more indistinct as he went on, swam before his eyes,
flickered, reappeared again, and finally went out. He rubbed his eyes
and gazed around him. The cabin was deserted. On the hearth the red
embers of his fire were fading away in the bright beams of the morning
sun, that looked aslant through the open window. He ran out to the

cliff. The sturdy sea-breeze fanned his feverish cheeks and tossed the white caps of waves that beat in pleasant music on the beach below. A stately merchantman with snowy canvas was entering the Gate. The voices of sailors came cheerfully from a bark at anchor below the point. The muskets of the sentries gleamed brightly on Alcatraz, and the rolling of drums swelled on the breeze. Farther on, the hills of San Francisco, cottage-crowned and bordered with wharves and warehouses, met his longing eye.

Such is the legend of Devil's Point. Any objections to its reliability may be met with the statement that the broker who tells the story has since incorporated a company under the title of "Flash-in-the-Pan Gold and Silver Treasure Mining Company," and that its shares are already held at a stiff figure. A copy of the original document is said to be on record in the office of the company, and on any clear day the locality of the claim may be distinctly seen from the hills of San Francisco.

THE ADVENTURE OF
PADRE VICENTIO

A LEGEND OF SAN FRANCISCO

One pleasant New Year's eve, about forty years ago, Padre Yicentio was slowly picking his way across the sand-hills from the Mission Dolores. As he climbed the crest of the ridge beside Mission Creek, his broad, shining face might have been easily mistaken for the beneficent image of the rising moon, so bland was its smile and so indefinite its features. For the Padre was a man of notable reputation and character; his ministration at the Mission of San Jose bad been marked with cordiality and unction; he was adored by the simple-minded savages, and had succeeded in impressing his individuality so strongly upon them, that the very children were said to have miraculously resembled him in feature.

As the holy man reached the loneliest portion of the road, he naturally put spurs to his mule as if to quicken that decorous pace which the obedient animal had acquired through long experience of its master's habits. The locality had an unfavorable reputation. Sailors—deserters from whale-ships—had been seen lurking about the outskirts of the town, and low scrub oaks which everywhere beset the trail might have easily concealed some desperate runaway. Besides these material obstructions, the Devil, whose hostility to the Church was well known, was said to sometimes haunt the vicinity in the likeness of a spectral whaler, who had met his death in a drunken bout from a harpoon in the hands of a companion. The ghost of this unfortunate mariner was frequently observed sitting on the hill toward the dusk of evening, armed with his favorite weapon and a tub containing a coil of line, looking out for some belated traveler on whom to exercise his professional skill. It is related that the good Father Jose Maria of the Mission Dolores had been twice attacked by this phantom sportsman; that once, on returning from San Francisco, and panting with exertion from climbing the hill, he was startled by a stentorian cry of "There she blows!" quickly followed by a hurtling harpoon, which buried itself in the sand beside him; that on another occasion he narrowly escaped destruction, his serapa having been transfixed by the diabolical harpoon and dragged away in triumph. Popular opinion seems to have been divided as to the reason for the Devil's particular attention to Father Jose, some asserting that the extreme piety of the Padre excited the Evil One's animosity, and others that his adipose tendency simply rendered him, from a professional view-point, a profitable capture.

Had Father Vicentio been inclined to scoff at this apparition as a heretical innovation, there was still the story of Concepcion, the Demon Vaquero, whose terrible riata was fully as potent as the whaler's harpoon. Concepcion, when in the flesh, had been a celebrated herder of cattle and wild horses, and was reported to have chased the Devil in the shape of a fleet pinto colt all the way from San Luis Obispo to San Francisco, vowing not to give up the chase until he had overtaken the disguised Arch-Enemy. This the Devil prevented by resuming his own shape, but kept the unfortunate vaquero to the fulfillment of his rash vow; and Concepcion still scoured the coast on a phantom steed, beguiling the monotony of his eternal pursuit by lassoing travelers, dragging them at the heels of his unbroken mustang until they were eventually picked up, half strangled, by the roadside. The Padre listened attentively for the tramp of this terrible rider. But no footfall broke the stillness of the night; even the hoofs of his own mule sank noiselessly in the shifting sand. Now and then a rabbit bounded lightly by him, or a quail ran into the bushes. The melancholy call of plover from the adjoining marshes of Mission Creek came to him so faintly and fitfully that it seemed almost a recollection of the past rather than a reality of the present.

To add to his discomposure, one of those heavy sea-fogs peculiar to the locality began to drift across the hills and presently encompassed him. While endeavoring to evade its cold embraces, Padre Vicentio incautiously drove his heavy spurs into the flanks of his mule as that puzzled animal was hesitating on the brink of a steep declivity. Whether the poor beast was indignant at this novel outrage, or had been for some time reflecting on the evils of being priest-ridden, has not transpired; enough that he suddenly threw up his heels, pitching the reverend man over his head, and, having accomplished this feat, coolly dropped on his knees and tumbled after his rider.

Over and over went the Padre, closely followed by his faithless mule. Luckily the little hollow which received the pair was of sand, that yielded to the superincumbent weight, half burying them without further injury. For some moments the poor man lay motionless, vainly endeavoring to collect his scattered senses. A hand irreverently laid upon his collar and a rough shake assisted to recall his consciousness. As the Padre staggered to his feet he found himself confronted by a stranger.

Seen dimly through the fog, and under circumstances that to say the least were not prepossessing, the new-comer had an inexpressibly mysterious and brigand-like aspect. A long boat-cloak concealed his figure, and a slouched hat hid his features, permitting only his eyes to glisten in the depths. With a deep groan the Padre slipped from the stranger's grasp and subsided into the soft sand again.

"Gad's life!" said the stranger, pettishly, "hast no more bones in thy fat carcass than a jellyfish? Lend a hand, here! Yo, heave ho!" and he dragged the Padre into an upright position. "Now, then, who and what art thou?"

The Padre could not help thinking that the question might have more properly been asked by himself; but with an odd mixture of dignity and trepidation he began enumerating his different titles, which were by no means brief, and would have been alone sufficient to strike awe in the bosom of an ordinary adversary. The stranger irreverently broke in upon his formal phrases, and assuring him that a priest was the very person he was looking for, coolly replaced the old man's hat, which had tumbled off, and bade him accompany him at once on an errand of spiritual counsel to one who was even then lying in extremity. "To think," said the stranger, "that I should stumble upon the very man I was seeking! Body of Bacchus! but this is lucky! Follow me quickly, for there is no time to lose."

Like most easy natures, the positive assertion of the stranger, and withal a certain authoritative air of command, overcame what slight objections the Padre might have feebly nurtured during this remarkable interview. The spiritual invitation was one, also, that he dared not refuse; not only that, but it tended somewhat to remove the superstitious dread with which he had begun to regard the mysterious stranger. But, following at a respectful distance, the Padre could not help observing with a thrill of horror that the stranger's footsteps made no impression on the sand, and his figure seemed at times to blend and incorporate itself with the fog, until the holy man was obliged to wait for its reappearance. In one of these intervals of embarrassment he heard the ringing of the far-off mission bell proclaiming the hour of midnight. Scarcely had the last stroke died away before the announcement was taken up and repeated by a multitude of bells of all sizes, and the air was filled with the sound of striking clocks and the pealing of steeple chimes. The old man uttered a cry of alarm. The stranger sharply demanded the cause. "The bells! did you not hear them?" gasped Padre Vicentio. "Tush! tush!" answered the stranger, "thy fall hath set triple bob-majors ringing in thine ears. Come on!"

The Padre was only too glad to accept the explanation conveyed in this discourteous answer. But he was destined for another singular experience. When they had reached the summit of the eminence now known as Russian Hill, an exclamation again burst from the Padre. The stranger turned to his companion with an impatient gesture, but the Padre heeded him not. The view that burst upon his sight was such as might well have engrossed the attention of a more enthusiastic temperament. The fog had not yet reached the hill, and the long valleys and hillsides of the embarcadero below were glittering with the light of a populous city. "Look!" said the Padre, stretching his hand over the spreading landscape. "Look! dost thou not see the stately squares and brilliantly lighted avenues of a mighty metropolis? Dost thou not see, as it were, another firmament below?"

"Avast heaving, reverend man, and quit this folly," said the stranger, dragging the bewildered Padre after him. "Behold rather the stars knocked out of thy hollow noddle by the fall thou hast had. Prithee, get over thy visions and rhapsodies, for the time is wearing apace."

The Padre humbly followed without another word. Descending the hill toward the north, the stranger leading the way, in a few moments the Padre detected the wash of waves, and presently his feet struck the firmer sand of the beach. Here the stranger paused, and the Padre perceived a boat lying in readiness hard by. As he stepped into the stern-sheets', in obedience to the command of his companion, he noticed that the rowers seemed to partake of the misty incorporeal texture of his companion, a similarity that became the more distressing when he perceived also that their oars in pulling together made no noise. The stranger, assuming the helm, guided the boat on quietly, while the fog, settling over the face of the water and closing around them, seemed to interpose a muffled wall between themselves and the rude jarring of the outer world. As they pushed further into this penetralia, the Padre listened anxiously for the sound of creaking blocks and the rattling of cordage, but no vibration broke the veiled stillness or disturbed the warm breath of the fleecy fog. Only one incident occurred to break the monotony of their mysterious journey. A one-eyed rower, who sat in front of the Padre, catching the devout Father's eye, immediately grinned such a ghastly smile, and winked his remaining eye with such diabolical intensity of meaning, that the Padre was constrained to utter a pious ejaculation, which had the disastrous effect of causing the marine Cocles to "catch a crab," throwing his heels in the air and his head into the bottom of the boat. But even this accident did not disturb the gravity of the rest of the ghastly boat's crew.

When, as it seemed to the Padre, ten minutes had elapsed, the outline of a large ship loomed up directly across their bow. Before he could utter the cry of warning that rose to his lips, or brace himself against

the expected shock, the boat passed gently and noiselessly through the
sides of the vessel, and the holy man found himself standing on the
berth-deck of what seemed to be an ancient caravel. The boat and boat's
crew had vanished. Only his mysterious friend, the stranger, remained.
By the light of a swinging-lamp the Padre beheld him standing beside
a hammock, whereon, apparently, lay the dying man to whom he had
been so mysteriously summoned. As the Padre, in obedience to a sign
from his companion, stepped to the side of the sufferer, he feebly opened
his eyes and thus addressed him:—

"Thou seest before thee, reverend Father, a helpless mortal, struggling
not only with the last agonies of the flesh, but beaten down and tossed
with sore anguish of the spirit. It matters little when or how I became
what thou now seest me. Enough that my life has been ungodly and
sinful, and that my only hope of absolution lies in my imparting to thee
a secret which is of vast importance to the Holy Church, and affects
greatly her power, wealth, and dominion on these shores. But the terms
of this secret and the conditions of my absolution are peculiar. I have
but five minutes to live. In that time I must receive the extreme unction
of the Church."

"And thy secret?" said the holy Father.

"Shall be told afterwards," answered the dying man. "Come, my
time is short. Shrive me quickly."

The Padre hesitated. "Couldst thou not tell this secret first?"

"Impossible!" said the dying man, with what seemed to the Padre a
momentary gleam of triumph. Then, as his breath grew feebler, he called
impatiently, "Shrive me! shrive me!"

"Let me know at least what this secret concerns?" suggested the
Padre insinuatingly.

"Shrive me first," said the dying man.

But the priest still hesitated, parleying with the sufferer until the
ship's bell struck, when, with a triumphant mocking laugh from the
stranger, the vessel suddenly fell to pieces, amid the rushing of waters
which at once involved the dying man, the priest, and the mysterious
stranger.

The Padre did not recover his consciousness until high noon the next day, when he found himself lying in a little hollow between the Mission Hills, and his faithful mule a few paces from him, cropping the sparse herbage. The Padre made the best of his way home, but wisely abstained from narrating the facts mentioned above until after the discovery of gold, when the whole of this veracious incident was related, with the assertion of the Padre that the secret which was thus mysteriously snatched from his possession was nothing more than the discovery of gold, years since, by the runaway sailors from the expedition of Sir Francis Drake.

THE DEVIL AND THE BROKER

A MEDIAEVAL LEGEND

The church clocks in San Francisco were striking ten. The Devil, who had been flying over the city that evening, just then alighted on the roof of a church near the corner of Bush and Montgomery streets. It will be perceived that the popular belief that the Devil avoids holy edifices, and vanishes at the sound of a credo or paternoster, is long since exploded. Indeed, modern skepticism asserts that he is not averse to these orthodox discourses, which particularly bear reference to himself, and in a measure recognize his power and importance.

I am inclined to think, however, that his choice of a resting-place was a good deal influenced by its contiguity to a populous thoroughfare. When he was comfortably seated, he began pulling out the joints of a small rod which he held in his hand, and which presently proved to be an extraordinary fishing-pole, with a telescopic adjustment that permitted its protraction to a marvelous extent. Affixing a line thereto, he selected a fly of a particular pattern from a small box which he carried with him, and, making a skillful cast, threw his line into the very centre of that living stream which ebbed and flowed through Montgomery Street.

Either the people were very virtuous that evening, or the bait was not a taking one. In vain the Devil whipped the stream at an eddy in front of the Occidental, or trolled his line into the shadows of the Cosmopolitan; five minutes passed without even a nibble. "Dear me!" quoth the Devil, "that's very singular; one of my most popular flies, too!

Why, they'd have risen by shoals in Broadway or Beacon Street for that. Well, here goes another." And fitting a new fly from his well-filled box, he gracefully recast his line.

For a few moments there was every prospect of sport. The line was continually bobbing and the nibbles were distinct and gratifying. Once or twice the bait was apparently gorged and carried off to the upper stories of the hotels, to be digested at leisure. At such times the professional manner in which the Devil played out his line would have thrilled the heart of Izaak Walton. But his efforts were unsuccessful; the bait was invariably carried off without hooking the victim, and the Devil finally lost his temper. "I've heard of these San Franciscans before," he muttered. "Wait till I get hold of one, that's all!" he added malevolently, as he rebaited his hook. A sharp tug and a wriggle followed his next trial, and finally, with considerable effort, he landed a portly two-hundred-pound broker upon the church roof.

As the victim lay there gasping, it was evident that the Devil was in no hurry to remove the hook from his gills; nor did he exhibit in this delicate operation that courtesy of manner and graceful manipulation which usually distinguished him.

"Come," he said gruffly, as he grasped the broker by the waistband, "quit that whining and grunting. Don't flatter yourself that you're a prize, either. I was certain to have had you. It was only a question of time."

"It is not that, my lord, which troubles me," whined the unfortunate wretch, as he painfully wriggled his head, "but that I should have been fooled by such a paltry bait. What will they say of me down there? To have let 'bigger things' go by, and to be taken in by this cheap trick," he added, as he groaned and glanced at the fly which the Devil was carefully rearranging, "is what,—pardon me, my lord,—is what gets me!"

"Yes," said the Devil philosophically, "I never caught anybody yet who didn't say that; but tell me, ain't you getting somewhat fastidious down there? Here is one of my most popular flies, the greenback," he continued, exhibiting an emerald-looking insect, which he drew from his box. "This, so generally considered excellent in election season, has not even been nibbled at. Perhaps your sagacity, which, in spite of this unfortunate contretemps, no one can doubt," added the Devil, with a graceful return to his usual courtesy, "may explain the reason or suggest a substitute."

The broker glanced at the contents of the box with a supercilious smile. "Too old-fashioned, my lord,—long ago played out. Yet," he added, with a gleam of interest, "for a consideration I might offer something—ahem!—that would make a taking substitute for these trifles. Give me," he continued, in a brisk, business-like way, "a slight percentage and a bonus down, and I'm your man."

"Name your terms," said the Devil earnestly.

"My liberty and a percentage on all you take, and the thing's done."

The Devil caressed his tail thoughtfully for a few moments. He was certain of the broker anyway, and the risk was slight. "Done!" he said.

"Stay a moment," said the artful broker. "There are certain contingencies. Give me your fishing-rod and let me apply the bait myself. It requires a skillful hand, my lord: even your well-known experience might fail. Leave me alone for half an hour, and if you have reason to complain of my success I will forfeit my deposit,—I mean my liberty."

The Devil acceded to his request, bowed, and withdrew. Alighting gracefully in Montgomery Street, he dropped into Meade & Co.'s clothing store, where, having completely equipped himself a la mode, he sallied forth intent on his personal enjoyment. Determining to sink his professional character, he mingled with the current of human life, and enjoyed, with that immense capacity for excitement peculiar to his nature, the whirl, hustle, and feverishness of the people, as a purely aesthetic gratification unalloyed by the cares of business. What he did that evening does not belong to our story. We return to the broker, whom we left on the roof.

When he made sure that the Devil had retired, he carefully drew from his pocketbook a slip of paper and affixed it on the hook. The line had scarcely reached the current before he felt a bite. The hook was swallowed. To bring up his victim rapidly, disengage him from the hook, and reset his line, was the work of a moment. Another bite and the same result. Another, and another. In a very few minutes the roof was covered with his panting spoil. The broker could himself distinguish that many of them were personal friends; nay, some of them were familiar frequenters of the building on which they were now miserably stranded. That the broker felt a certain satisfaction in being instrumental in thus misleading his fellow-brokers no one acquainted with human nature will for a moment doubt. But a stronger pull on his line caused him to put forth all his strength and skill. The magic pole bent like a coach-whip. The broker held firm, assisted by the battlements of the church. Again and again it was almost wrested from his hand, and again and again he slowly reeled in a portion of the tightening line. At last, with one mighty effort, he lifted to the level of the roof a struggling object. A howl like Pandemonium rang through the air as the broker successfully landed at his feet—the Devil himself!

The two glared fiercely at each other. The broker, perhaps mindful of his former treatment, evinced no haste to remove the hook from his antagonist's jaw. When it was finally accomplished, he asked quietly if the Devil was satisfied. That gentleman seemed absorbed in the contemplation of the bait which he had just taken from his mouth. "I am," he said finally, "and forgive you; but what do you call this?"

"Bend low," replied the broker, as he buttoned up his coat ready to depart. The Devil inclined his ear. "I call it WILD CAT!"

THE OGRESS OF SILVER LAND

OR

THE DIVERTING HISTORY OF PRINCE BADFELLAH AND PRINCE BULLEBOYE

In the second year of the reign of the renowned Caliph Lo there dwelt in Silver Land, adjoining his territory, a certain terrible Ogress. She lived in the bowels of a dismal mountain, where she was in the habit of confining such unfortunate travelers as ventured within her domain. The country for miles around was sterile and barren. In some places it was covered with a white powder, which was called in the language of the country Al Ka Li, and was supposed to be the pulverized bones of those who had perished miserably in her service.

In spite of this, every year great numbers of young men devoted themselves to the service of the Ogress, hoping to become her godsons, and to enjoy the good fortune which belonged to that privileged class. For these godsons had no work to perform, neither at the mountain nor elsewhere, but roamed about the world with credentials of their relationship in their pockets, which they called stokh, which was stamped with the stamp and sealed with the seal of the Ogress, and which enabled them at the end of each moon to draw large quantities of gold and silver from her treasury. And the wisest and most favored of those godsons were the Princes Badfellah and Bulleboye. They knew all the secrets of the Ogress, and how to wheedle and coax her. They were also the favorites of Soopah Intendent, who was her Lord High Chamberlain and Prime Minister, and who dwelt in Silver Land.

One day, Soopah Intendent said to his servants, "Whan is that which travels the most surely, the most secretly, and the most swiftly?"

And they all answered as one man, "Lightning, my lord, travels the most surely, the most swiftly, and the most secretly!"

Then said Soopah Intendent, "Let Lightning carry this message secretly, swiftly, and surely to my beloved friends the Princes Badfellah and Bulleboye, and tell them that their godmother is dying, and bid them seek some other godmother or sell their stokh ere it becomes *badjee*,—worthless."

"Bekhesm! On our heads be it!" answered the servants; and they ran to Lightning with the message, who flew with it to the City by the Sea, and delivered it, even at that moment, into the hands of the Princes Badfellah and Bulleboye.

Now the Prince Badfellah was a wicked young man; and when he had received this message he tore his beard and rent his garment and reviled his godmother and his friend Soopah Intendent. But presently he arose, and dressed himself in his finest stuffs, and went forth into the bazaars and among the merchants, capering and dancing as he walked, and crying in a loud voice, "Oh, happy day! Oh, day worthy to be marked with a white stone!"

This he said cunningly, thinking the merchants and men of the bazaars would gather about him, which they presently did, and began to question him: "What news, Then O most worthy and serene Highness? Tell us that we may make merry too!"

Then replied the cunning prince, "Good news, O my brothers, for I have heard this day that my godmother in Silver Land is well" The merchants, who were not aware of the substance of the real message, envied him greatly, and said one to another, "Surely our brother the Prince Badfellah is favored by Allah above all men;" and they were about to retire, when the prince checked them, saying, "Tarry for a moment. Here are my credentials or stokh. The same I will sell you for fifty thousand sequins, for I have to give a feast to-day, and need much gold. Who will give fifty thousand?" And he again fell to capering and dancing. But this time the merchants drew a little apart, and some of the oldest and wisest said, "What dirt is this which the prince would have us swallow? If his godmother were well, why should he sell his stokh? Bismillah! The olives are old and the jar is broken!" When Prince Badfellah perceived them whispering, his countenance fell, and his knees smote against each other through fear,—but, dissembling again, he said, "Well, so be it! Lo! I have much more than shall abide with me, for my days are many and my wants are few. Say forty thousand sequins for my stokh and let me depart, in Allah's name. Who will give forty thousand sequins to become the godson of such a healthy mother?" And he again fell to capering and dancing, but not as gayly as before, for his heart was troubled. The merchants, however, only moved farther away. "Thirty thousand sequins," cried Prince Badfellah; but even as he spoke they fled before his face, crying, "His godmother is dead. Lo! the jackals are defiling her grave. Mashallah! he has no godmother." And they sought out Panik, the swift-footed messenger, and bade him shout through the bazaars that the godmother of Prince Badfellah was dead. When he heard this, the prince fell upon his face, and rent his garments, and covered himself with the dust of the marketplace. As he was sitting thus, a porter passed him with jars of wine on his shoulders, and the prince begged him to give him a jar, for he was exceeding thirsty and faint.

But the porter said, "What will my lord give me first?" And the prince, in very bitterness of spirit, said, "Take this," and handed him his stokh, and so exchanged it for a jar of wine.

Now the Prince Bulleboye was of a different disposition. When he received the message of Soopah Intendent he bowed his head, and said, "It is the will of God." Then he rose, and without speaking a word entered the gates of his palace. But his wife, the peerless Maree Jahann, perceiving the gravity of his countenance, said, "Why is my lord cast down and silent? Why are those rare and priceless pearls, his words, shut up so tightly between those gorgeous oyster-shells, his lips?" But to this he made no reply. Thinking further to divert him, she brought her lute into the chamber and stood before him, and sang the song and danced the dance of Ben Kotton, which is called Ibrahim's Daughter, but she could not lift the veil of sadness from his brow.

When she had ceased, the Prince Bulleboye arose and said, "Allah is great, and what am I, his servant, but the dust of the earth! Lo! this day has my godmother sickened unto death, and my stokh become as a withered palm-leaf. Call hither my servants and camel drivers, and the merchants that have furnished me with stuffs, and the beggars who have feasted at my table, and bid them take all that is here, for it is mine no longer!" With these words he buried his face in his mantle and wept aloud.

But Maree Jahann, his wife, plucked him by the sleeve. "Prithee, my lord," said she, "bethink thee of the Brokah or scrivener who besought thee but yesterday to share thy stokh with him and gave thee his bond for fifty thousand sequins." But the noble Prince Bulleboye, raising his head, said, "Shall I sell to him for fifty thousand sequins that which I know is not worth a Soo Markee? For is not all the Brokah's wealth, even his wife and children, pledged on that bond? Shall I ruin him to save myself? Allah forbid! Bather let me eat the salt fish of honest penury than the kabobs of dishonorable affluence; rather let me wallow in the mire of virtuous oblivion than repose on the divan of luxurious wickedness!"

When the prince had given utterance to this beautiful and edifying sentiment, a strain of gentle music was heard, and the rear wall of the apartment, which had been ingeniously constructed like a flat, opened and discovered the Ogress of Silver Land in the glare of blue fire, seated on a triumphal car attached to two ropes which were connected with the flies, in the very act of blessing the unconscious prince. When the walls closed again without attracting his attention, Prince Bulleboye arose, dressed himself in his coarsest and cheapest stuffs, and sprinkled ashes on his head, and in this guise, having embraced his wife, went forth into the bazaars. In this it will be perceived how differently the good Prince Bulleboye acted from the wicked Prince Badfellah, who put on his gayest garments, to simulate and deceive.

Now when Prince Bulleboye entered the chief bazaar, where the merchants of the city were gathered in council, he stood up in his accustomed place, and all that were there held their breath, for the noble Prince Bulleboye was much respected. "Let the Brokah whose bond I hold for fifty thousand sequins stand forth!" said the prince. And the Brokah stood forth from among the merchants. Then said the prince, "Here is thy bond for fifty thousand sequins, for which I was to deliver unto thee one half of my stokh. Know, then, O my brother,—and thou, too, O Aga of the Brokahs,—that this my stokh which I pledged to thee is worthless. For my godmother, the Ogress of silver Land, is dying. Thus do I release thee from thy bond, and from the poverty which might overtake thee, as it has even me, thy brother, the Prince Bulleboye." And with that the noble Prince Bulleboye tore the bond of the Brokah into pieces and scattered it to the four winds.

Now when the Prince tore up the bond there was a great commotion, and some said, "Surely the Prince Bulleboye is drunken with wine;" and others, "He is possessed of an evil spirit;" and his friends expostulated with him, saying, "What thou hast done is not the custom of the bazaars,—behold, it is not Biz!" But to all the prince answered gravely, "It is right; on my own head be it!"

But the oldest and wisest of the merchants, they who had talked with Prince Badfellah the same morning, whispered together, and gathered round the Brokah whose bond the Prince Bulleboye had torn up. "Hark ye," said they, "our brother the Prince Bulleboye is cunning as a jackal. What bosh is this about ruining himself to save thee? Such a thing was never heard before in the bazaars. It is a trick, O thou mooncalf of a Brokah! Dost thou not see that he has heard good news from his godmother, the same that was even now told us by the Prince Badfellah, his confederate, and that he would destroy thy bond for fifty thousand sequins because his stokh is worth a hundred thousand! Be not deceived, O too credulous Brokah! for this that our brother the prince doeth is not in the name of Allah, but of Biz, the only god known in the bazaars of the city."

When the foolish Brokah heard these things he cried, "Justice, Aga of the Brokahs,—justice and the fulfillment of my bond! Let the prince deliver unto me the stokh. Here are my fifty thousand sequins." But the prince said, "Have I not told thee that my godmother is dying, and that my stokh is valueless?" At this the Brokah only clamored the more for justice and the fulfillment of his bond. Then the Aga of the Brokahs said, "Since the bond is destroyed, behold thou hast no claim. Go thy ways!" But the Brokah again cried, "Justice, my lord Aga! Behold, I offer the prince seventy thousand sequins for his stokh!" But the prince said, "It is not worth one sequin!" Then the Aga said, "Bismillah! I cannot understand this. Whether thy godmother be dead, or dying, or immortal, does not seem to signify. Therefore, O prince, by the laws of Biz and Allah, though art released. Give the Brokah thy stokh for seventy thousand sequins, and bid him depart in peace. On his own head be it!" When the prince heard this command, he handed the stokh to the Brokah, who counted out to him seventy thousand sequins. But the heart of the virtuous prince did not rejoice, nor did the Brokah when he found his stokh was valueless; but the merchants lifted their hands in wonder at the sagacity and wisdom of the famous Prince Bulleboye. For none would believe that it was the law of Allah that the prince followed, and not the rules of Biz.

THE CHRISTMAS GIFT THAT CAME TO RUPERT

A STORY FOR LITTLE SOLDIERS

It was the Christmas season in California,—a season of falling rain and springing grasses. There were intervals when, through driving clouds and flying scud, the sun visited the haggard hills with a miracle, and death and resurrection were as one, and out of the very throes of decay a joyous life struggled outward and upward. Even the storms that swept down the dead leaves nurtured the tender buds that took their places. There were no episodes of snowy silence; over the quickening fields the farmer's ploughshare hard followed the furrows left by the latest rains. Perhaps it was for this reason that the Christmas evergreens which decorated the drawing-room took upon themselves a foreign aspect, and offered a weird contrast to the roses, seen dimly through the windows, as the southwest wind beat their soft faces against the panes.

"Now," said the doctor, drawing his chair closer to the fire, and looking mildly but firmly at the semicircle of flaxen heads around him, "I want it distinctly understood before I begin my story, that I am not to be interrupted by any ridiculous questions. At the first one I shall stop. At the second, I shall feel it my duty to administer a dose of castor-oil all round. The boy that moves his legs or arms will be understood to invite amputation. I have brought my instruments with me, and never allow pleasure to interfere with my business. Do you promise?"

"Yes, sir," said six small voices simultaneously. The volley was, however, followed by half a dozen dropping questions.

"Silence! Bob, put your feet down, and stop rattling that sword. Flora shall sit by my side, like a little lady, and be an example to the rest. Fung Tang shall stay, too, if he likes. Now, turn down the gas a little; there, that will do—just enough to make the fire look brighter, and to show off the Christmas candles. Silence, everybody! The boy who cracks an almond, or breathes too loud over his raisins, will be put out of the room."

There was a profound silence. Bob laid his sword tenderly aside and nursed his leg thoughtfully. Flora, after coquettishly adjusting the pockets of her little apron, put her arm upon the doctor's shoulder, and permitted herself to be drawn beside him. Fung Tang, the little heathen page, who was permitted, on this rare occasion, to share the Christmas revels in the drawing-room, surveyed the group with a smile that was at once sweet and philosophical. The light ticking of a French clock on the mantel, supported by a young shepherdess of bronze complexion and great symmetry of limb, was the only sound that disturbed the Christmas-like peace of the apartment,—a peace which held the odors of evergreens, new toys, cedar boxes, glue, and varnish in a harmonious combination that passed all understanding.

"About four years ago at this time," began the doctor, "I attended a course of lectures in a certain city. One of the professors, who was a sociable, kindly man—though somewhat practical and hard-headed— invited me to his house on Christmas night. I was very glad to go, as I was anxious to see one of his sons, who, though only twelve years old, was said to be very clever. I dare not tell you how many Latin verses this little fellow could recite, or how many English ones he had composed. In the first place, you'd want me to repeat them; secondly, I'm not a judge of poetry—Latin or English. But there were judges who said they were wonderful for a boy, and everybody predicted a splendid future for him. Everybody but his father. He shook his head doubtingly whenever it was mentioned, for, as I have told you, he was a practical, matter-of-fact man.

"There was a pleasant party at the professor's that night. All the children of the neighborhood were there, and among them the professor's clever son, Rupert, as they called him—a thin little chap, about as tall as Bobby there, and fair and delicate as Flora by my side. His health was feeble, his father said; he seldom ran about and played with other boys—preferring to stay at home and brood over his books, and compose what he called his verses.

"Well, we had a Christmas-tree just like this, and we had been laughing and talking, calling the names of the children who had presents on the tree, and everybody was very happy and joyous, when one of the children suddenly uttered a cry of mingled surprise and hilarity, and said, 'Here's something for Rupert—and what do you think it is?'

"We all guessed. 'A desk;' 'A copy of Milton;' 'A gold pen;' 'A rhyming dictionary.' 'No? what then?'

"'A drum!'

"'A what?' asked everybody.

"'A drum! with Rupert's name on it.'

"Sure enough, there it was. A good-sized, bright, new, brass-bound drum, with a slip of paper on it, with the inscription, 'For RUPERT.'

"Of course we all laughed, and thought it a good joke. 'You see you're to make a noise in the world, Rupert!' said one. 'Here's parchment for the poet,' said another. 'Rupert's last work in sheepskin covers,' said a third. 'Give us a classical tune, Rupert,' said a fourth, and so on. But Rupert seemed too mortified to speak; he changed color, bit his lips, and finally burst into a passionate fit of crying and left the room. Then those who had joked him felt ashamed, and everybody began to ask who had put the drum there. But no one knew, or, if they did, the unexpected sympathy awakened for the sensitive boy kept them silent. Even the servants were called up and questioned, but no one could give any idea where it came from. And what was still more singular, everybody declared that up to the moment it was produced, no one had seen it hanging on the tree. What do I think? Well, I have my own opinion. But no questions! Enough for you to know that Rupert did not come downstairs again that night, and the party soon after broke up.

"I had almost forgotten those things, for the war of the Rebellion broke out the next spring, and I was appointed surgeon in one of the new regiments, and was on my way to the seat of war. But I had to pass through the city where the professor lived, and there I met him. My first question was about Rupert. The professor shook his head sadly. 'He's not so well' he said; 'he has been declining since last Christmas, when you saw him. A very strange case,' he added, giving it a long Latin name, 'a very singular case. But go and see him yourself' he urged; 'it may distract his mind and do him good.'

"I went accordingly to the professor's house, and found Eupert lying on a sofa propped up with pillows. Around him were scattered his books, and, what seemed in singular contrast, that drum I told you about was hanging on a nail just above his head. His face was thin and wasted; there was a red spot on either cheek, and his eyes were very bright and widely opened. He was glad to see me, and when I told him where I was going, he asked a thousand questions about the war. I thought I had thoroughly diverted his mind from its sick and languid fancies, when he suddenly grasped my hand and drew me towards him.

"'Doctor,' said he, in a low whisper, 'you won't laugh at me if I tell you something?'

"'No, certainly not,' I said.

"'You remember that drum?' he said, pointing to the glittering toy that hung against the wall. 'You know, too, how it came to me. A few weeks after Christmas I was lying half asleep here, and the drum was hanging on the wall, when suddenly I heard it beaten; at first low and slowly, then faster and louder, until its rolling filled the house. In the middle of the night I heard it again. I did not dare to tell anybody about it, but I have heard it every night ever since.'

"He paused and looked anxiously in my face. 'Sometimes,' he continued, 'it is played softly, sometimes loudly, but always quickening to a long roll, so loud and alarming that I have looked to see people coming into my room to ask what was the matter. But I think, doctor—I think,' he repeated slowly, looking up with painful interest into my face, 'that no one hears it but myself.'

"I thought so, too, but I asked him if he had heard it at any other time.

"'Once or twice in the daytime,' he replied, 'when I have been reading or writing; then very loudly, as though it were angry, and tried in that way to attract my attention away from my books.'

"I looked into his face and placed my hand upon his pulse. His eyes were very bright and his pulse a little flurried and quick. I then tried to explain to him that he was very weak, and that his senses were very acute, as most weak people's are; and how that when he read, or grew interested and excited, or when he was tired at night, the throbbing of a big artery made the beating sound he heard. He listened to me with a sad smile of unbelief, but thanked me, and in a little while I went away. But as I was going downstairs I met the professor. I gave him my opinion of the case—well, no matter what it was.

"'He wants fresh air and exercise' said the professor, 'and some practical experience of life, sir.' The professor was not a bad man, but he was a little worried and impatient, and thought—as clever people are apt to think—that things which he didn't understand were either silly or improper.

"I left the city that very day, and in the excitement of battlefields and hospitals I forgot all about little Rupert, nor did I hear of him again, until one day, meeting an old classmate in the army, who had known the professor, he told me that Rupert had become quite insane, and that in one of his paroxysms he had escaped from the house, and as he had never been found, it was feared that he had fallen into the river and was drowned. I was terribly shocked for the moment, as you may imagine; but, dear me, I was living just then among scenes as terrible and shocking, and I had little time to spare to mourn over poor Rupert.

"It was not long after receiving this intelligence that we had a terrible battle, in which a portion of our army was slaughtered. I was detached from my brigade to ride over to the battlefield and assist the surgeons of the beaten division, who had more on their hands than they could attend to. When I reached the barn that served for a temporary hospital, I went at once to work. Ah! Bob," said the doctor thoughtfully, taking the bright sword from the hands of the half-frightened Bob, and holding it gravely before him, "these pretty playthings are symbols of cruel, ugly realities."

"I turned to a tall, stout Vermonter," he continued, very slowly, tracing a pattern on the rug with the point of the scabbard, "who was badly wounded in both thighs, but he held up his hands and begged me to help others first who needed it more than he. I did not at first heed his request, for this kind of unselfishness was very common in the army; but he went on, 'For God's sake, doctor, leave me here; there is a drummer boy of our regiment—a mere child—dying, if he isn't dead now. Go and see him first. He lies over there. He saved more than one life. He was at his post in the panic of this morning, and saved the honor of the regiment.' I was so much more impressed by the man's manner than by the substance of his speech, which was, however, corroborated by the other poor fellows stretched around me, that I passed over to where the drummer lay, with his drum beside him. I gave one glance at his face—and—yes, Bob—yes, my children—it *was* Rupert.

"Well! well! it needed not the chalked cross which my brother surgeons had left upon the rough board whereon he lay to show how urgent was the relief he sought; it needed not the prophetic words of the Vermonter, nor the damp that mingled with the brown curls that clung to his pale forehead, to show how hopeless it was now. I called him by name. He opened his eyes—larger, I thought, in the new vision that was beginning to dawn upon him—and recognized me. He whispered, 'I'm glad you are come, but I don't think you can do me any good.'

"I could not tell him a lie. I could not say anything. I only pressed his hand in mine as he went on.

"'But you will see father, and ask him to forgive me. Nobody is to blame but myself. It was a long time before I understood why the drum came to me that Christmas night, and why it kept calling to me every night, and what it said. I know it now. The work is done, and I am content. Tell father it is better as it is. I should have lived only to worry and perplex him, and something in me tells me this is right.'

"He lay still for a moment, and then grasping my hand, said,—

"'Hark!'

391

"I listened, but heard nothing but the suppressed moans of the wounded men around me. 'The drum' he said faintly; 'don't you hear it?—the drum is calling me.'

"He reached out his arm to where it lay, as though he would embrace it.

"'Listen'—he went on—'it's the reveille. There are the ranks drawn up in review. Don't you see the sunlight flash down the long line of bayonets? Their faces are shining—they present arms—there comes the General—but his face I cannot look at for the glory round his head. He sees me; he smiles, it is '—and with a name upon his lips that he had learned long ago, he stretched himself wearily upon the planks and lay quite still.

"That's all.

"No questions now—never mind what became of the drum.

"Who's that sniveling?

"Bless my soul! where's my pill-box?"

THE END